Love in the Vineyards

Dear Robin,
Bon appétit!! :)
Laura Bradbury

Books by

Laura Bradbury

The Grape Series

My Grape Year: http://mybook.to/MyGrapeYear
My Grape Québec: http://mybook.to/MyGrapeQuebec
My Grape Paris: http://mybook.to/MyGrapeParis
My Grape Wedding: http://mybook.to/MyGrapeWedding
My Grape Escape: http://mybook.to/MyGrapeEscape
My Grape Village: http://mybook.to/MyGrapeVillage
My Grape Cellar: http://mybook.to/MyGrapeCellar

The cookbook based on the Grape Series memoirs that readers have been asking for!

Bisous & Brioche: Classic French Recipes and Family Favorites from a Life in France
by Laura Bradbury and Rebecca Wellman
Bisous & Brioche: mybook.to/bisousandbrioche

The Winemaker's Trilogy

A Vineyard for Two: mybook.to/AVineyardforTwo
Love in the Vineyards: mybook.to/loveinthevineyards

THE WINEMAKERS TRILOGY
BOOK 2

Love in the Vineyards

LAURA BRADBURY

Love in the Vineyards

This is a work of fiction. Names, characters, places, and incidents are the products of the author's imagination or are used fictitiously. Any resemblance to actual events, locales, or persons, living or dead, is entirely coincidental.

ISBN: 978-1-989784-06-8 eBook
ISBN: 978-1-989784-07-5 Paperback

This one is for my amie de coeur Charlotte Buffet. You always make the winemaking life jump alive for me and you have one of the best hearts (and palates!) of anyone I know. Je t'adore.

On a tous besoin d'une personne qui nous rappelle à quel point la vie est belle.

-PROVERBE FRANCAIS

chapter one

SADIE HAD MOSTLY stopped wiping back tears by the time she got to the boarding lounge for her flight to Paris. She wanted to yell at the people casting her curious glances that they weren't sad tears—they were just an outpouring of her frustration at the injustice of life.

Mediocre men with no moral compass got away with far too much. It would be nice to believe karma somehow took care of retribution, but Sadie had learned from growing up with a stunning twin sister that the whole concept of karma was upheld by smart, competent women who were constantly shafted in life and trying not to become bitter shrews because of it. In short, women like herself.

Her eyes burned. Maybe that bitter shrew thing had happened without her noticing. She glanced up at the clock above the boarding desk. Stella, that gorgeous twin sister who had taught Sadie early on that life wasn't fair, was supposed to be in the boarding lounge by now. Their flight was going to board in ten minutes. Stella was always late, but the world forgave her, because winning the genetic lottery meant that all shortfalls in her character (and there were many) were excused. They were even seen as charming.

Sadie tried to unclench her jaw and let herself be comforted by the familiar scent of burnt coffee and potato chips that penetrated the JFK airport. She'd been taking this flight from New York to Paris since she was a child, and it always meant she was going towards her other home in France—the place that was, in so many ways, the home of her heart. She knew that at the other end of her flight, in the Charles de Gaulle arrivals terminal, they would be welcomed by illicit cigarette smoke and the faint scent of urine.... and her best friend Luc, thank God.

Her bones ached with the need to pour out the whole sordid story to him—how she had probably destroyed her hard-won academic career as an archeologist. What would she do without her doctoral program, her thesis and ongoing papers and grants? The terror made her breath come in short, staccato bursts.

When all the stuff with the head of the department was going down, the only person she had wanted to confide in was Luc...and her father of course, but he had been dead for eight months now.

Not many people would understand why she made the decision that essentially put an end to her tenure track at Hudson University, but Luc would. She wasn't sure of much anymore, but she was sure of that. He'd been her best friend since she was seven years old, and nobody knew her like Luc did. She needed to get him to herself, which meant away from Stella for a few hours, to talk it all over with him. Only then would things start to make sense again.

This Christmas vacation to France had been planned several weeks before but, in the end, the timing couldn't have been better. There, at least, she'd had a bit of luck. There was no better place to put some distance between her and this work debacle than Luc's home in the vineyards of Burgundy.

Ah, the crackling announcement that the plane was ready to board. Sadie pulled out her boarding pass and passport from the side pocket of her bag and lined up with the other passengers. God, her hands were *still* shaking.

Where *was* Stella? Hope leapt in Sadie's chest at the idea that perhaps Stella would miss their flight. Maybe Sadie could have Luc all to herself. Sure, it was greedy, but she'd never needed him more. He acted like a different person around Stella—a complete lovestruck idiot. Most straight men did, yet somehow, it only bothered her when Luc was the one under Stella's spell.

As the boarding line crept forward, Sadie felt a familiar tug of regret that she had never—not even for a millisecond—considered confiding her dilemma to Stella. She had always longed for the kind of sisterly relationship some of her friends enjoyed, built on unconditional support and understanding, but she and Stella had always existed on different planets.

There was a tap on her shoulder. She turned to see her sister had appeared beside her like an apparition, tall and stunningly dressed in a chic black outfit with a midriff-baring top. Stella slid off her large black sunglasses, a rather unnecessary accessory for inside an airport terminal in December.

"Sadie!" Stella flashed Sadie a perfect smile. "I was looking all over for you in the First Class Lounge."

Of course. That's where she'd been. "Why on earth would I be in the First Class Lounge, Stella?"

Their vastly different financial situations didn't help the chasm between the sisters. Stella had, effortlessly it seemed, earned money from modeling and TV commercials, and now had segued into a nebulous but apparently lucrative role as an "influencer." Sadie honestly didn't waste much time trying to figure out exactly how Stella earned her money—hers was a career that seemed to morph into something different every week.

Sadie, on the other hand, loved her fascinating but underpaid academic career. Her heart lodged in her throat. *Or had, anyway. Up until I undid it all yesterday.*

Stella sighed. "Of course. Silly me. Here, I wanted to introduce you to Pablo."

Stella pulled an olive-skinned, impeccably dressed man carrying a huge cross-body camera bag out from behind her, like some sort of magic trick. Sadie had never seen him before, but she stuck out her hand. "Hi Pablo. Nice to meet you. Why are you here?"

Stella rolled her huge blue eyes. "Don't be like that Sadie," she hissed, before turning to Pablo. "Don't mind my sister Pablo. She has no social graces, probably because she works mostly with dead people. Sadie, Pablo is my personal photographer. We're working together full-time right now, so of course he has to come to France with me."

The insults weren't worth her time. Stella would never understand her obsession with Gallo-Roman history, still…"But we're staying at Luc's, remember? You can't just foist another guest on Luc's family. Besides, wasn't this supposed to be our Christmas vacation, and to, you know, spread Dad's ashes in Burgundy?"

Sadie, Stella, and their younger brother Max had been shocked when their mother announced that she had made plans to stay with friends in the Bahamas over Christmas because she couldn't bear staying at home in New York without their father. Max was going with her, because the friends had a son his age who he'd always been close to.

Their mother had suggested that Stella and Sadie go to Luc's family in Burgundy and take some of their father's ashes with them. The whole idea of Christmas without their father was disconcerting. Then again, nothing felt right since her father died.

"Well, how long will that take?" Stella shrugged. "It's only *some* of his ashes."

"Just when I think you can't get any worse," Sadie muttered under her breath.

"Yeah, well, unlike you, I was never Dad's favorite," Stella sniffed. "He barely even noticed I existed."

An unpleasant pang of guilt reverberated through her. As close as Sadie and her father had been, he had never been able to relate to

Stella and had given up trying. He viewed Stella as an entertaining anomaly, rather than someone truly worth getting to know. Up until now, Sadie had always wondered if Stella had noticed.

"Besides," Stella continued. "There's no such thing as a vacation from influencing. Just think of all the photo opportunities in France."

"If it was photo ops you wanted, why didn't you go to the Bahamas with Mom and Max?"

"I already have plenty of beach photos," Stella said. "Think of all the different locales I can hit in Europe."

"Europe? But how long are you planning on staying?"

Stella shrugged. "We'll see."

"Don't you think gallivanting all over Europe to get photo ops is a little inappropriate on this trip?"

Stella crossed her arms and raised a perfectly arched, blond brow at Sadie. "So you're not planning on doing a bit of Gallo-Roman research while we're in Burgundy?"

Dammit. Stella had her. Up until a few hours ago, Sadie had been a rising star in the Gallo-Roman academic world. The area right around where Luc and his family lived—and where Stella and Sadie had lived for three years as children while their father was doing research in Burgundy—was ground zero for her work.

Seeing as she was probably no longer on the tenure track at Hudson, she should abstain from research of any kind, but she loved what she did. She wouldn't be able to help herself from poking around a bit, and Stella knew it.

"Stop being so judgy," Stella said. "It pinches up your face. Anyway, Pablo and I will stay at a hotel in Beaune. Probably Le Cep. Besides, I'm sure Luc will be more than happy to welcome me, no matter what."

A lump lodged in Sadie's throat. As much as she hated what Sadie just said, it was true.

"Oh! They're calling First Class passengers!" Stella tossed her curtain of blond hair. “That’s us. Sorry we won’t be able to visit during the flight, Sadie, but I don’t think you’ll be allowed through the curtain.”

Sadie bit the inside of her cheek. She just couldn’t deal with Stella right now…or ever, really. The only thing she could do is maintain her dignity. “I’m planning on sleeping.”

“Beauty sleep? You look dreadful, so that’s probably smart.” She gave a ta-ta finger wiggle and swept off with Pablo, who Sadie realized now, had not said a single word.

Smart? Sadie had just sabotaged her career, and was relying on her best friend for solace, the same best friend who had been in love with her sister since they were all seven years old. Tears pricked her eyes again, and she blinked them furiously away. She was the farthest thing from smart.

Still, at least she wasn’t jealous, as she watched Stella sashay onto the gangway with Pablo in her wake. She held tightly onto that—it felt like the last thread connecting her to any semblance of sanity.

Sure, Stella would be plied with champagne and sleep on a flatbed during their flight, but Sadie had learned the remedy to sisterly jealousy long ago. It was simple. She just never let herself want anything or anyone Stella had.

Luc woke up in yet another strange bed. He cracked an eye. *Ah*. He was in the bed of the wine *négotiante* he’d met the night before. He examined her as the pink sunlight filtered through the gauze curtains into her Montmartre apartment. Her hair was shining and tousled against the white pillow. She was lovely, tall, and blond with blue eyes. Luc definitely had a type, which basically amounted to women who looked like Stella.

Luc lifted the duvet and slid out of bed as stealthily as possible. He strapped his father's watch on his wrist and picked up his discarded clothing as he walked over to the bathroom.

He had other criteria for his frequent one-night stands. No married women. No women who were looking for a relationship. Nobody with children—he never wanted to be the cause of any child's trauma at finding a strange man in their house and then never seeing that man again.

When he emerged shortly after, he was dressed. He cast one final glance at the woman he had slept with last night—Amélie… or was it Aurélie? *Damn.* The heat of shame crept up his neck. What kind of bastard didn't even remember the name of the woman he'd just spent the night with? Especially a woman as stunning and charming as she was. She'd been clear about just wanting a fun, no-strings- attached night together like him. Still, it showed what a cold heart he carried in his chest. That familiar ache returned, his conscience gnawing at him like a sore tooth.

As he gave his final glance at his bedmate, he cursed the damned birthright he didn't want. Thank God Stella was arriving. He was determined to end this curse of serial one-night stands. He'd known since he was seven that Stella was the only woman in the world who could fix him. It was time for Luc to make Stella his, so that he could finally live with himself.

He snuck into the kitchen and after locating a pen and a scrap of paper wrote Aurélie…or maybe Amélie, a sweet note, thanking her for the wonderful night. He rinsed off the dirty wine glasses in her sink and put them upside down to dry on a tea towel he'd neatly folded in half, after sponging off the counter. He might be doomed to be a serial philanderer, but he still had manners.

Luc found a promising café a block from Amélie's—the more he thought about it, the more he was quite sure her name was Amélie. He needed to collect his thoughts before going to the airport and seeing Stella. She was his destiny, so he couldn't afford any mistakes this time.

He ordered an espresso at the zinc bar, looking around and admiring the absolutely ungentrified café and its patrons. Sadie would adore this place. His heart leapt in his chest. He couldn't wait to see her again and share all these places and thoughts only she could appreciate.

Sadie loved Paris in the same way he did. Stella loved the gilded hotels and the Champs-Élysées, but Sadie adored the quirky neighborhood cafés and the hidden vestiges of medieval Paris hidden behind long, winding alleyways.

He was thankful he came several times a year for wine salons or tastings. He appreciated Burgundy more when he could escape it from time to time. Moreover, he rarely slept alone in Paris.

Still, as much as he appreciated women, each one he'd slept with reinforced what his father had revealed so long ago. Luc was cursed with the Ocquidant's legendary wandering eye. Grandfather had broken up a marriage on his deathbed, his father had broken his mother's heart a hundred times over, and Luc, too, was destined to inflict pain. It was in his blood, and Burgundians lived and died by family legacies.

He swallowed hard on the burning black espresso. It always made him slightly nauseous to think too long on the family curse he carried in his blood, but it didn't matter today. Stella—the only woman who could cure him of his infidelity—was arriving at the Charles de Gaulle airport in three hours' time.

He leaned against the zinc counter, as his stomach swooped at the idea of seeing her for the first time in two years. Stella was his last, his only, hope at redemption.

Again, his mind wandered to Sadie, as he stirred the dregs

of his espresso and peered into its depths. Instead of a stomach swoop, the thought of having Sadie in close proximity again kindled inside him like a bonfire, warming him everywhere—even that cold, empty vacuum inside him. Only Sadie could do that.

He tipped the tiny espresso cup to his mouth to finish it, then laid some euros down on the counter. "*Merci,*" he called to the garçon. "*Bonne journée. Au revoir.*"

He strode back out to the chilled street. It was only three days before Christmas and parking his white traffic work van the night before had been a nightmare with all the holiday shoppers jammed into the steep streets around Sacré-Coeur. Its white domes looked like an iced cake in the silvery morning light.

He caught sight of his van and let loose a long, fluid stream of curses. A fistful of pink parking tickets fluttered under the windshield wipers. If he'd just gone back to his hotel for once, he wouldn't have to pay a small fortune in parking fines but, then again, he and Amélie had both had a wonderful time despite how conflicted he always felt the morning after. He *was* a man, after all.

He climbed into his van, his stomach still full of butterflies at the prospect of seeing Stella. So much depended on these next few hours. Maybe it was impossible to ever feel ready for such an encounter. At least Sadie would be there. She would give him strength. That, at least, he could count on.

chapter two

SADIE HAD LOST count of how many times she'd flown in and out of Charles de Gaulle airport, but she was appalled like it was her first time at the rodeo.

The line for non-EU passport checks snaked endlessly in front of her. She could see only one Immigration Officer manning a booth when she peered around the tightly packed mass of humanity ahead of her. Typical. The aggravating thing with Charles de Gaulle was the fixes were obvious—more personnel, more repairs, more functioning toilets—but the pervasive impression was that nobody cared enough to make them.

A beefy man at her back and a short woman in front pressed her like a sardine. How would Stella cope with this? But wait… she wouldn't have to. There was surely an express line for First Class passengers. Stella was probably already hugging Luc and introducing him to Pablo. Sadie suppressed a spurt of resentment, then smiled to herself. Luc was going to be none too pleased about Pablo—at least she would miss that whole bag of weirdness.

She popped in her earphones and hit play on an episode of her favorite archeological podcast and was instantly riveted by Ziegler's theories of rates of fluvial sedimentation and their implications for archaeological variability. She might not have her job when she got back to New York, but nothing could stop her obsession with Gallo-Roman history and archeological digs.

The podcast saw her through the immigration line and the endless wait at the luggage carrousel. Finally, she retrieved her small rolling suitcase, grateful all over again that she traveled light.

Only one thing left—Luc. Beyond those doors.

Her heart leapt into her throat at the idea of seeing him again. *Don't be stupid. Remember how he acts around Stella. He may be your best friend, but when he's around your sister he's just like all the other idiots who are madly in love with her.*

She would have to be patient and wait to get some time alone with him before she could pour out her troubles. Luckily, patience was a skill she'd been forced to develop in her work. Impatience could ruin a dig site within minutes. Impatience about Stella's admirers could turn Sadie into a jealous shrew. She'd learned how to bide her time.

"Sadie!" She heard her name almost as soon as she walked out the sliding doors. She would recognize Luc's voice anywhere. *Please God do not let him be intertwined with Stella.*

She couldn't see him through this maw of people at the Arrivals gate, so she stood on tiptoe. Nope. She still couldn't see him. This was one of those moments when being five foot three felt like an inconvenience. He called out her name again, and then again, so she followed his voice until she saw him. He was waving at her with both arms and jumping up on the balls of his feet.

Her breath left her in a whoosh. It was ridiculous, really, that her best friend had grown up to be so handsome. His build was tall and broad, naturally chiseled by his physical work in the vineyards and around the family winery. It was a miraculous transformation, as Luc had been as scrawny as Sadie when they were little.

She knew for a fact that he would never consider dying his hair himself, as Luc had never been anything but oblivious to his looks, but exposure to the elements had created blond streaks in his tawny hair that would make the highest paid Hollywood colorist jealous.

His eyes were the same startling blue as the ocean in Tahiti, a color that popped up as a complete anomaly amid his brown-eyed family. His skin was olive, so he always looked kissed by the sun, even now, when it was almost Christmas. Physically he was the perfect match for Stella. The thought of how beautiful their children would be pinched at Sadie's heart. Where was Stella anyway?

Sadie rolled her suitcase towards Luc, trying to maintain some self-control, as he ran to her with open arms. She collapsed into them; the whorl of her ear pressed up against his solid chest. So much for restraint. He smelled like Marseille olive oil soap and espresso, and something that she recognized as uniquely Luc. She sighed, as the tension she'd been carrying for the past week drained out of her shoulders.

"How I missed you, my Sadie," Luc murmured, stroking down her red curls that were surely springing madly in all directions after the flight.

A sob lodged in her throat, making it impossible to speak, so she just squeezed Luc tighter. He gathered her even closer against him and began to make that low vibration in his throat, a barely audible hum that could only be heard this close. She loved that sound—he'd been making it as long as she'd known him whenever he drank a particularly spectacular glass of wine, or ate his mother's *boeuf bourgignon*, or they were lying on their backs in a field, contemplating the clouds, the sun shining down on their faces.

After several minutes, Luc pulled back and held Sadie at arm's length. He studied her face. She tried to hide her distress from him, at least until they had some guaranteed time alone. Stella would be arriving any minute.

"What is it Sadie?" He talked to her in French, as they always had.

She blinked. She couldn't start crying again. Not now. She clamped her lips together and shook her head.

"I've never seen you look so tired," he said, his voice low and gentle. "Something's wrong."

It was a statement, not a question. He'd always been able to see through her defenses, which was a terrifying thought.

Sadie waved her hand. "We'll have time to talk later. I'm fine. *Vraiment*."

He frowned down at her. "You're not fine, but I'll wait. Is it the grief for your father?"

Sadie shook her head again. "I'm sad and I miss him, but it's not that."

"Ah, *ma Sadie*, I wanted to come to the funeral but—"

"But we didn't have one." If he started being all understanding and calling her *ma Sadie*—his Sadie—she would be a goner. "You know he was intellectually opposed to all that."

"You must miss talking to him the most. You know, those intellectual discussions I always teased you about."

Luc was right. She hadn't just lost her father, but her intellectual mentor. How was it that Luc saw the truth of it in a way that no-one else did? He *noticed*. That was why, she realized, he was still her best friend, despite his blind spot concerning Stella.

She nodded. "I do. I can't bother my mom with my grief as hers is ten times worse. Since he died, I've just felt so...alone."

Luc tugged her back against him. "You're never alone," he whispered in her ear. "Remember that Sadie. I'm here. Always have been, always will be." For the first time since she had reported her advisor at Hudson University for sexual misconduct, just before heading to the airport, a flare of hope glimmered within her. She could happily stay in Luc's arms forever. Wait. *No.*

"Where's Stella?" Luc asked.

Luc's question splashed over her like the cold bucket of water she needed. Sadie pushed herself away from him.

"She flew First Class, so I assumed she'd have gotten off before me. Maybe I should warn you—"

Too late. Luc's eyes shifted above Sadie's head and his expression changed from his normal warmth to a shocked look, like someone had just stuck his finger in a light socket. He didn't look overjoyed exactly. More like terrified.

"Stella," he said, his voice coming out strangled. Sadie watched as Luc's eyes shifted to Pablo, who was trailing behind Stella, looking miraculously unwrinkled after the seven-hour flight. What sorcery was this?

"Who is *that*?" Luc hissed out of the corner of his mouth.

"Pablo. That's who I was just about to warn you about."

"But who is—"

"Stella introduced him very quickly in the departure terminal of JFK," Sadie muttered under her breath. "He's some sort of photographer for her or something. The details were murky. Also, I wasn't paying much attention."

"Luc!" Stella held her arms open and gave Luc two lingering kisses, one on each cheek. Sadie glanced at Luc's face, which ludicrously transformed to that of a rapt boy, instead of the man he seemed to be a second ago.

"Stella," Luc breathed.

Sadie couldn't deny that Stella had a magnetic effect. People around them were staring, as they always did, many with their mouths open. She radiated brightness in a way that was completely larger than life. Her long fingers rested for a few seconds too long on Luc's chiseled jaw before she swept them away.

"It's so wonderful to see you again, Luc." She flashed her most engaging smile. "You are looking absolutely delicious. I swear I could take a chomp out of you right now." She leaned forward and took a playful, light bite out of Luc's jaw, demonstrating. Sadie didn't know anyone else who dared do such things, not to mention got away with them.

Luc's eyes widened and he flushed pink under his tan. He reached for her hand and said, in French, "I've made so many plans for us, Stella. I booked a canal boat evening cruise, and a beautiful dinner—"

"Luc," Stella interrupted Luc's gushing. "This is Pablo. He's my photographer."

Luc frowned, but stuck out his hand. He'd somehow mastered the ability of being disapproving and civil at the same time. "Pablo," he said curtly. "Should I speak to you in English or French?"

Stella laughed. "English of course Luc," she said in that language. "You should also speak to me in English too. My French is terribly rusty. I didn't inherit the brains of my brilliant twin, you remember." She tilted her head towards Sadie.

It was true that Stella had always chosen the easier courses at school like art and drama and dropped out of French Immersion a year after their family had moved back to New York. She encountered almost no opposition. It had become clear to her parents by then, even to their father who rarely emerged from the Hudson campus or peeked out behind his books, that Stella could easily get by on her looks.

That had never been an option for Sadie. She wasn't ugly, but she was something that sometimes felt even worse. She was average. Far too often people exclaimed that they could scarcely believe Stella and Sadie were sisters, let alone twins. Sadie knew exactly how to take that, and it wasn't flattering.

Watching how Luc, spellbound, gazed into her sister's translucent blue eyes and perfect face, she could see why he attributed all sorts of good qualities to Stella that she didn't possess. Beauty had that treacherous effect on people, and Stella was the epitome of physical perfection.

That was precisely why Sadie could never let herself want someone who loved Stella, especially not Luc. She'd learned that lesson when she was seven, and it wasn't one she was liable to forget.

Luc cast a glance down at all of Stella's luggage. "I thought ahead and brought the work van," he said. "Don't worry, we'll be able to fit all your bags in there, Stella."

Luc's French accent when he spoke English was terrible, but also sort of endearing.

"Don't worry about us." For no reason at all, Stella drew her index finger over Luc's cheekbone. "Pablo arranged for a limo to pick us up and take us down to Burgundy eventually, but we'll be staying here in Paris for a few days first."

"What?" Luc's face fell. "Why? But I've made plans for us Stella."

"To create some content, silly." Stella tousled Luc's blond-streaked hair and he went from looking disappointed to looking confused. "I'm sorry Luc, but I had no idea about your plans. I'll be down in time for Christmas and we can do things then."

Pablo checked his phone. "The limo is here for us Stella."

It was first time Sadie had heard his voice. His English was excellent, although slightly tinged with a Hispanic lilt. He sounded exactly as mysterious and suave as he looked.

Luc was glaring at him with loathing, but Pablo didn't seem to notice. Obliviousness could be a handy thing sometimes.

Stella laughed at Luc's thunderous expression. "Luc, *mon cheri*, you didn't seriously expect me to travel down to Burgundy in a work truck, did you?"

Luc looked down at his feet, his face scarlet. "I guess not… I mean, of course not."

Annoyance and pity pulsed in Sadie. Luc was so deep under Stella's spell, he couldn't even see that she was turning him into a blithering idiot. Why shouldn't Stella ride in a work truck? She wasn't royalty, not yet anyway, although she wouldn't put it past Stella to marry a prince or a duke or someone of that ilk.

"At least let me walk you to the limo," Luc said, his eyes darting back and forth between Stella and Pablo.

"No need," Stella said.

Pablo nodded towards a man dressed in a uniform and pushing a luggage trolley. "There's the bellhop I arranged," he said.

There were bellhops in airports? Trust Stella to scrounge one up.

"Don't look like that Luc." Stella gave Luc's arm a final squeeze good-bye and a quick kiss on his cheek. "I'll see you at Christmas. In the meantime, you take care of Sadie."

"I take care of myself." Sadie hadn't meant for her indignation to come out quite so much, but there was something about the way Luc looked over at her suddenly, when Stella had mentioned her name. He was remembering her presence for the first time since Stella appeared.

His focus on Stella made Sadie feel smaller, lesser. It was a sensation she recognized all too well, and she despised that more than anything. If she let herself care, she would become a pathetic fool.

Luc cleared his throat. "I'll always take care of Sadie."

Stella's eyes flashed at that, and Sadie knew her sister well enough to know that she was recalculating in her mind what she could do to make sure Luc only thought of her, but the bellhop had marched off with her bags and Pablo.

"Like I said, I don't need anyone taking care of me," Sadie said. "Never have." Longing flashed through her for a few undisciplined seconds. What a relief it would be to find the right person, and then they could look after each other.

"I'll make it up to you," Stella said to Luc in a husky voice, before sashaying away.

Luc and Sadie watched her go. People stared at Stella and her entourage as they passed by, whispering to each other.

After Stella and Pablo receded into the distance, Luc turned back to Sadie with the disoriented expression of someone returning to consciousness. The disappointment on his features was ludicrous.

"Oh, my foolish friend." Sadie shook her head. "When will you ever learn?"

Luc looked down at her. "You don't understand. I'm going to make Stella mine this time. I have to—"

"I *do* understand. That's what makes it so hard for me to see you like this. Just like countless other men, you're so spellbound by how Stella looks on the outside that you completely misjudge what she's like inside. Why the hell shouldn't she drive down to Burgundy in your van? I know you Luc. If it were anyone else, you would shred them to tatters for their pretention."

"It's different."

"I don't think it is," Sadie sighed. "And I feel sorry for you."

Luc shoved his hands deep in the pockets of his jeans. "I feel sorry for me too."

Sadie grabbed his arm and tried very hard not to notice the firmness of his bicep against her palm. "At least we agree on something, but let's talk about this over some food. I'm starving. Where can we eat?"

Luc laughed, finally becoming himself again. "When aren't you starving? I know the perfect place."

Finally, she would have Luc to herself. It would be perfect, if only she wasn't acutely aware that she was his second choice.

chapter three

WITHIN AN HOUR, Luc and Sadie were ensconced at a *routier*, one of their favorite type of restaurants in France. *Routiers* were the French equivalent of a truck stop but the homemade food was so, so much better. After demolishing an entrée of *pâté de maison* served with salad and a ceramic jar of house-made *cornichons*, they'd just been served tournedos of beef with a sauce bordelaise and a side of long, crunchy green beans.

It was lunchtime, and the comfortable hum of the truckers and tradesmen eating and chatting around them, as well as the delectable scent of garlic and cooked wine coming from the kitchen, was acting like a band-aid for Sadie's bruised soul. She tried to imagine Stella eating shoulder to shoulder with all these sweaty, dusty men and failed.

"Auberge de la Grenouille," Sadie read the sign above the door to the kitchen out loud. "How on earth did you find this glorious place?"

"I knew I had to bring you here." Luc smiled, then added a little shrug. "You know how it is. *Routiers* seem to find me."

Sadie chuckled. "Kind of like women?"

Luc's mouth twisted in a half smile, half grimace. "I intend to stop that soon."

Sadie rolled her eyes. "Oh really?"

"*Oui*, really."

Even though he had always been enamored with Stella, that had never stopped Luc from having other women on the go.

As an educated feminist, Sadie couldn't entirely make peace with Luc's rakishness. Still, she had somehow managed to reach an uneasy acceptance of reality, thanks to three things. First, if men threw themselves at her the same way women did at Luc, she wasn't entirely sure she would turn them all down. Second, this was France, and French people conducted their love lives on a completely different set of moral principles. Third, Luc filled such a crucial role in her life that she was prepared to live with his more unpalatable habits.

Sadie cocked a brow. "Forgive me if I'm skeptical about you becoming a one-woman man." She took a forkful of the rare beef glazed with the wine and marrow sauce and groaned. She was always amazed anew at how good the humblest food in France could be.

"No, really. I mean it this time. I'm going to settle down."

"How?" The thing was Luc's lovers always seemed to come back for more, even when he'd made it clear he intended to continue playing the field. These were not women who were asking to be saved from Luc's lover-like behavior—quite the contrary, in fact. She could never decide if that was a commentary on the women's appalling lack of self-respect or Luc's prowess.

"By marrying Stella."

Sadie almost choked on her mouthful of beans. "There are so many things wrong with that sentence, I don't even know where to start."

"I've been in love with her since I was seven," Luc reminded Sadie.

"I know that," Sadie said, with more force than necessary. "But still, what makes you think that Stella reciprocates your feelings, or is even interested in anything long-term?"

Luc bit his lip. "I have to believe it."

Sadie had never been able to understand Luc's conviction that he and Stella were destined to be together. It was as mystifying to her now as it had been when she was seven years old. Still, he'd never been in any rush to act on it.

"Why now?" she asked.

Luc bit his lip and the corner of his mouth quirked up. "I guess it started with Clovis."

Sadie thought back to their handsome friend from elementary school in Beaune—now one of the most sought after and wealthy winemakers in Burgundy. He also had a reputation as quite the playboy.

"Ah, Clovis," she mused. "He was the only one who ever gave you a run for your money, as far as female conquests were concerned. What shenanigans is he up to now?"

"The most shocking thing of all. He's madly in love."

"When is Clovis not madly in love?" Sadie chuckled to herself. "He's French, after all."

"No, this is different. He's settled down."

Sadie dropped her fork and it clattered on her plate. "You're not serious."

"I know." Luc grinned at her reaction. "Hard to believe, but it's true. I don't think you've ever met his girlfriend, but she's fantastic. I have this feeling the two of you will get along. Her name is Cerise, and she has two boys."

"Wow." Sadie tried to wrap her mind around the idea of Clovis becoming a family man. It was so preposterous that she started to understand why Luc thought he could do it too.

"And Cerise is pregnant with Clovis's baby."

Sadie clutched her head. "This is too much all at once. My brain is going to explode."

"*And* it turns out Clovis has a daughter in England who is ten or eleven."

"Stop." Sadie held one hand up to Luc as she used her other one to wipe her mouth with her napkin. "Give me a second to digest the idea of someone taming Clovis."

Luc chuckled, his face lighting up in that way she loved when he talked about his closest friends. "I know. When I saw how happy Clovis was, I started thinking that maybe I should think about settling down too. Besides, I'm getting pressure from my parents. I have the Domaine to think about, and they're clamoring for an heir."

Sadie took a thoughtful sip of her wine—a satisfying, heavy-bodied house red. "Heirs and all that already?"

Luc ran his hand through his hair. "You know what a big deal succession is in Burgundy. If I can just manage to get Stella, everything will finally fall into place."

Sadie searched his familiar features, unsure how to respond. How could an otherwise intelligent man be so dense? Why was Luc blind to the fact that Stella had no interest in motherhood? She had little interest in anything beyond herself when it came right down to it.

"That's never going to happen," Sadie said, finally. She wouldn't be doing Luc any favors if she encouraged his delusions. It had nothing to do with the ache behind her breastbone when she thought of losing Luc to her sister.

"Why not?"

Besides the fact they had nothing in common? "First of all, Stella being a mother…well, I doubt that idea has ever crossed her mind. Besides, if Stella ever did settle down it would be with someone flashier than you."

"I can be flashy."

Sadie snorted. "Oh really?" She'd always known Luc to be happiest when he was covered with vineyard mud. "Clovis could be flashy if he wanted. You, not so much."

Luc frowned at first, but then it melted into a wry smile. "I hate that you're right. I'm just not interested in all that stuff. I'm a grape farmer at heart."

"And what's wrong with that?"

"It's wrong if it's not what Stella wants."

"That's ridiculous. Why would you want to change yourself for anyone? My advice would be to pick someone else, maybe a nice local Burgundian girl who brings some vineyards with her in the bargain."

But Luc shook his head. "No. It has to be Stella."

Sadie sighed. "Good God. You're still as stubborn as a mule." They got along about everything else, except her sister. It had always been that way.

Luc reached across the table and gripped her forearms. The warmth of his calloused fingers penetrated her skin. Despite his gilded good looks, Luc fit in with the *routier* crowd. He was jaw-droppingly gorgeous, but he would never be comfortable dressed in designer clothes and carrying a man's handbag like Pablo. His were hands that could prune a pinot noir vine perfectly, fix a tractor, or swirl a glass of wine in its glass and hold it by its stem up to the light.

"Enough about me and my woes," he said. "I've never seen your eyes look so tired, *ma Sadie*. Out with it."

There he went, *noticing* again. How could Luc see her so accurately, yet be so mistaken about Stella?

"I think I just ended my academic career," Sadie said, after a long pause.

"Tell me," Luc said.

That was all it took. The story came out haltingly. A young undergraduate student had come to Sadie after a tutorial, confessing that Sadie's mentor and doctoral advisor, Professor Harris—who also happened to be the head of the Archeology department at Hudson—had slipped his hand up her skirt.

She took the student to the coffee shop and bought her a tea and listened to the whole tearful story. This student wasn't Professor Harris's only victim, as it turned out.

"Her name was Gia," Sadie told Luc, veering back and forth over details of the story, slowly processing it as she talked. "The student who came to me for help. Gia had talked to some friends in the department about what Professor Harris had done, and more stories came out from other girls about the same predatory behavior."

Sadie's stomach had roiled as she listened to Gia's story. How could someone she had looked up to as a mentor and a leader be so evil? But one thing she knew for certain—Gia and her classmates were telling the truth, and they needed her to act on their behalf.

"*Conard*," Luc hissed through clenched teeth. "What did he do to them?"

Sadie rubbed her forehead. "Lingering, inappropriate touches, attempts to lure them into his office and shut the door, inviting them out for drinks, asking them inappropriate questions about their love lives…"

"Did he do it to you?" Sadie looked up from her plate, caught by the edge to Luc's voice. His face was so rigid it looked carved out of stone.

"No," she said. "He didn't. I have no idea why." She hadn't had the time, or the inclination, to ponder such things. She'd headed straight to the administration office after leaving Gia to report Professor Harris. As she filled out the report with her leaky ballpoint pen, she knew she was probably setting fire to her academic career, but she signed her name at the bottom without hesitation.

When she finished, she met Luc's gaze again.

"You did what you had to do," he said. "There is no excuse for any man touching a woman without her consent, ever, but especially not when there are such unequal power dynamics at play."

Relief washed through her limbs at getting the story out of her mind and out to someone who implicitly understood. "I knew you would see it that way, but unless justice is truly real—and I've never seen much evidence of that so far—I don't think I'll have a job to go back to."

"How do you know that?"

"When I signed my report on him, one of the secretaries took me aside and asked me if I was sure I knew what I was doing. She warned me that three other doctoral students of his had lodged complaints, and every single one of them was quickly pushed out of the doctoral program."

"You signed knowing that?"

Sadie nodded. "The secretary also reminded me that Professor Harris has the full, unconditional backing of the Dean of the University, who is his closest friend, as well as many senior members of the faculty. He wields almost unmitigated power. The writing is on the wall for my career, I'm afraid." Even though she managed to say the words, she still couldn't wrap her mind around them.

Luc nodded slowly. His eyes were narrowed, and the tiny muscles around his jaw were clenched. With the glaring exception of Stella, Luc was a pragmatist. "I hate to agree with you," he said. "But he sounds like the sort of guy who will worm his way out of this. He'll need a scapegoat."

Sadie pointed at herself with her fork. "That would be me." She tried to laugh, but instead a sob rose in her throat. She clapped a hand over her mouth. *Shit.* Telling Luc had somehow broken her out of the numb shock that had cloaked her ever since she filed her report at the administration offices.

Luc moved around from his seat to the bench beside her and gathered her in his arms. Sadie tried to reign herself in, but the tears kept coming. The kindly looking proprietress passed by and silently cleared their plates. Sadie didn't want to be weeping in the middle of Auberge de Grenouille and ruining this amazing meal, but that was what Luc did to her. His friendship made her feel more, think more. He never let her hide from herself.

His hand reached up and rubbed soothing circles on her back and that low hum rumbled in his throat again. That sound tapped into Sadie's nervous system like a natural Valium pill. Her body softened. His torso was unyielding against her and his arms provided a shelter that she'd never found anywhere else. She could smell the soap and the vanilla shampoo he must have used that morning in that soft little crook of his neck. That spot was probably part of the reason women kept throwing themselves at him.

She pushed away from him. Thank God she and Luc were only friends because she could see how his arms could be a highly addictive drug. She took a shuddering sigh. "You can go back to your seat now. I think I've made enough of a scene for one day."

Luc gave her a final squeeze, then slid back around the table and into his seat. The proprietress came by with pale yellow slices of lemon tart. "This should cheer you up, *ma belle.* Are you going to be all right?"

Sadie appreciated how the French never ignored emotional outbursts or were at all unnerved by them. "I'll be all right, thank you. Just *un gros chagrin.*" A big sorrow.

The woman's eyes flicked over to Luc in all his golden glory. "A broken heart?" she guessed.

Sadie laughed at this. She knew better than to ever give Luc the power to do that. "No, I think I just lost my job."

The woman waved her hand. "Work? That is nothing. Work is not important. *Love* – now that is what life is all about. And food, *bien sûr.* My *tarte au citron* will put a smile on your pretty face. I guarantee it." She left them with a flick of her dishtowel.

Luc looked down at his plate and then back up to Sadie. "I think she's right, you know. You've always adored a good lemon tart and this one looks spectacular."

Sadie dug in. The shortbread crust melted on her tongue, and the filling was silky and bright with citrus.

"You're smiling!"

Sadie looked up to see Luc pointing his spoon at her and grinning.

"I can't help it," she said, her words garbled through her full mouth. "This tart is just so good."

They ate in contented silence until tiny ceramic cups of espresso were placed in front of them.

"What happened to those girls is terrible," Luc said finally, stirring sugar into his espresso. "Nothing can change that. But you did the right thing Sadie. I'm prouder than ever to call you my best friend."

That thickness in her throat had returned. Sadie swallowed hard. "*Merci* Luc."

"I vow to do everything in my power to support you in getting through this. You know that my house is your house, *n'est-ce pas*? You can stay a year or more if you need it."

Sadie lowered her head and blinked through watery eyes at her espresso cup. *This* was why she put up with all of Luc's ridiculousness about Stella.

chapter four

BACK IN THE van, Sadie gazed out the window as Luc drove, and they talked about everything and nothing. They reminisced about how they used to race down the vineyard slopes and collapse in a pile at the wall of the old stacked stone winemaker's hut—called a *cabotte*—at the bottom. They avoided touching on Stella or on Sadie's current crisis.

When they finally turned into the gravel courtyard of Domaine Ocquidant, Luc's family wine domaine in the picturesque village of Savigny-les-Beaune, Luc's mother, Pauline, and his younger siblings Raphael and Adèle were waiting for them.

"How did they know?" Sadie turned to Luc.

"I called them when we stopped for that last espresso." Luc winked at her. "Be forewarned, you're about to be mauled."

When they caught sight of Sadie in the passenger seat Luc's family began jumping up and down and waving their arms.

Sadie grinned and waved out the window. "I think I can handle it."

How he'd missed that glow in her face that touched a part of him that no-one else had ever reached. "Oh, I know you can."

Luc stood against the side of the van and watched as Sadie tumbled out her side directly into his family's arms. He could feel the smile stretching across his face. His family had always loved Sadie.

It was a shame Stella hadn't driven down with them, but at the same time it was a gift to have Sadie all to himself for a while.

Stella...Stella was different. People tended to be too much in awe of her to really let down their guard. She was much harder to truly know, but Luc was certain Stella was a good person, deep down. She had to be—she was Sadie's twin sister after all, and Sadie was the best person he knew. Stella remained a sublime mystery he longed to discover, as well as the only woman in the world who could heal his current fickle existence.

Stella's natural reserve was surely to protect herself from the world. She was so dazzling, everyone wanted something from her. Luc squirmed with the uncomfortable reminder that he was no different. In a way he was using her too, but at the same time he was determined to do everything in his power to make her happy.

Good God, his family was noisy. He chuckled at the flurry of hugs and exclamations and kisses that surrounded Sadie. Sadie's face was bright with happiness. He hated seeing her like she'd been at lunch, overcome with despair. She was so good; she deserved only the best of life. He'd been aware of an overpowering desire to shelter her from anything that threatened to dim her innate sparkle.

Finally, he entered the fray, conscious of the desire to have Sadie to himself for just a little bit longer. "Why don't you greet me like that?" Luc asked his sister.

"Because you're not Sadie," Adèle said. "There's only one Sadie."

He couldn't argue with that.

Sadie gripped Adèle's hands tight. "How is the oenology degree going? I hear you're completely brilliant, of course."

Adèle blushed. "Who told you that?"

"Your proud big brother, of course, on the way down from Paris. It doesn't surprise me. You've always had the best winetasting palate of anyone I know."

"Hey!" Luc said with mock affront. "I'm the winemaker here, after all."

"Including you." Sadie shrugged without remorse. "And you know it."

"Point taken, but ouch." Luc was smiling again. Sadie was right. Adèle had been a brilliant scholar at school, so many people were shocked, and his parents not particularly happy, when she decided to study winetasting in Beaune instead of going on to a prestigious post-secondary school in Paris. Of course, Adèle was blazing a brilliant trail at the winetasting school.

"And you, Raphael." Sadie grabbed the hands of Luc's quieter younger brother. "How are your illustrations going?"

Luc watched Sadie in admiration. She didn't forget a thing, and he could tell from the way her amber eyes sparkled that her interest was sincere. She was as proud of Adèle and Raphael as if they'd been her siblings. She often referred to the Ocquidants as her French family, and the feeling was entirely mutual.

"*Fantastique*," Raphael said. "I can't wait to show you what I'm preparing for the big Comic Book Conference in Angoulême." He cast an uneasy glance at his mother. "But we'll talk more about that later."

Whereas his parents had been unnerved about Adèle's choice of career, they still hadn't accepted that Raphael wanted nothing to do with wine. His dream was to illustrate comic books.

Pauline, Luc's mother, crossed her arms and frowned at Raphael, but refrained from saying anything.

Sadie went over just then and gave Pauline a massive hug. "I swear, how do French women do it? You get more beautiful every time I see you." Pauline instantly melted under Sadie's contagious warmth.

They all started peppering Sadie with questions about her work, but Luc quickly intervened. Sadie wasn't ready for that yet.

He slid a protective arm around her shoulders. "Sadie has been traveling for I don't know how many hours. I'm going to take her up to her cottage for a rest before dinner."

The rest of his family cried out in protest, but Luc held his ground. Sadie pressed closer to his side. Again, he was aware of an overpowering need to shield her from any awkwardness or pain. He managed to grab her suitcase and her arm and drag her away. Strange. Nobody had commented on Stella's absence.

"Thank you," Sadie whispered when they were out of earshot of his family's protests. "I wasn't ready for the work questions yet. I don't even know what to say to them about my job right now."

"Of course you don't." Luc stroked his thumb down her arm to underline his understanding. Anger flamed in him like it had when she'd first told him about Professor Harris at the *routier*. He hated that she was being punished for doing the right thing. Sadie was the smartest person he knew, and her career was everything to her. The need to help her pulsed through him, but how?

He looked over at the emotion in Sadie's eyes as she stared ahead at the little stone cottage that would be her temporary home with Stella, though *not* that Pablo fellow he hoped.

It was the same cottage where Sadie and her family had lived for three years when her father had taken an extended sabbatical in Burgundy, studying the role of shopfronts in the medieval economy of France. This was the first time Sadie had been back since her father died of lung cancer eight months before.

"Seeing the cottage must be emotional for you." He kept his voice low, as unobtrusive as possible.

"*Oui*," Sadie said. "But not in a bad way, if that makes any sense."

It did. Sadie had always told Luc that those three years in France had been some of the best years of her life.

He nodded. "It makes complete sense." Those years had been three of the best years of his life too— having Sadie as his next-door neighbor and being able to see her every day. And Stella too, of course. Sadie tried to visit them in Burgundy every year or two, as did her parents, and her younger brother Max, before her father had started going downhill. Stella came less frequently.

Luc found it hard to get away from his vineyards and his burgeoning winemaking career and burned with shame that he still hadn't made it to New York.

He leaned down and reached behind the fossilized nautilus his grandfather had found while plowing the vineyards, and which always lived to the right of the painted white wooden door to the cottage. He extracted the long iron key from behind it.

"Still haven't changed the hiding place?" Sadie murmured.

"Never," Luc said. "You know, Burgundians and their traditions."

"You don't know how happy that makes me."

He opened the door for her and pulled her suitcase inside. The cottage gave off a familiar whiff of wood polish and limestone. It was once an outbuilding used to store spare barrels and other winemaking equipment, but Sadie had told him once that it was the kind of place Americans drooled over in decorating magazines. It was simple and unchanging—Luc hoped Sadie would feel protected here.

The piled stone walls were over three feet thick in spots and the ceiling was over fifteen feet high with massive oak beams crisscrossing this way and that. In the summer, a beautiful old orange rose rioted around the long white shutters flanking the windows and the front door.

It was small, only two bedrooms. When they had lived there as a family, Sadie and Stella had shared one and her parents had shared the other with Maximillian, who was lucky enough to be born in France at the end of their first year and was the only one of Sadie's family who had French citizenship as a result.

Inside the hushed space full of memories, Luc rolled Sadie's suitcase into her bedroom as quietly as possible. "My mom made up one bedroom for you and one for Stella," he said in a low voice. "She gave you the one that looks out over the vineyards, of course."

"Did you remind her to do that?" Sadie's bright amber eyes met his.

He knew how much Sadie loved the view out to the rising slope of Ocquidant vineyards beyond. Those slopes had been part of their expansive playground as children. *Bien sûr* he'd reminded his mother. "Got me."

Sadie walked slowly around the main room, letting her fingers graze softly over the back of the overstuffed couch, the wooden *confiturie*r in the corner that had been passed down from one of his great-grandparents, and the neat row of espresso cups hung on a rack beside the coffee maker.

Luc watched her. Why on earth didn't Sadie have a boyfriend? In the van she'd told him there was nobody special, although he knew there'd been the occasional guy in the past—always academic types like her, apparently. In her soft ivory sweater and jeans, he realized with shock that Sadie had become even more captivating in these past two years. Her red curly hair had always been glorious and the scattering of freckles across the bridge of her nose drew him towards her brown eyes, striated with gold. He gave himself a shake. It was Stella that could save him from himself, not Sadie. Besides, he'd never forgive himself if he ever broke Sadie's heart—as if she would let him! She'd never thought of him as more than a friend.

He'd known since first grade that it had to be Stella. By then, he'd already understood that his parents' marriage was complicated. He found out why one day when he was seven and found his beloved father Alphonse having sex up against a tree in the forest with one of his mother's best friends.

It had been Sadie who Luc had run to that day. He didn't know if he could have gotten through it without her support. Later that afternoon, and full of righteous indignation, Luc had confronted his father in the vat room of the winery.

Alphonse hadn't been angry exactly. He rarely got angry with his firstborn and, up until then, Alphonse had seemed almost God-like to Luc with his larger-than-life personality and deep laugh.

Instead, he'd seemed resigned to Luc finding out. He'd sighed. "Yes, it's *plus fort que moi,* son. I can't help it. I assure you I only ever do that with women who are eager and willing, and who understand I will never leave your mother. It's just a bit of fun. You'll understand when you're older."

"No, I won't!" Luc protested. "I'll never understand."

"You will, because it's in our blood, you see. My father and my grandfather were exactly the same. Unless I have the woman that everyone wants, I will never be satisfied. Neither will you."

"But don't you love *maman*?" Luc asked, appalled.

Alphonse put a wide hand on his son's shoulder. "Of course I do, one has nothing to do with the other. That is the way of men in our family line, Luc."

"But—"

"It's in your blood too Luc." Alphonse crouched down to look at Luc in the eye, making certain that Luc understood this point. "You might as well accept it. You will never be satisfied with one woman either."

Luc had stumbled back, horrified. He remembered all the times he'd found his mother crying in the kitchen. The idea that he could cause any other human misery like that was unbearable.

"But what if I can get the woman that everybody wants?" Luc was grasping at straws, his mind frantic to find a loophole in a future that repulsed him. "Can I be different from you then?"

His father cast him an odd look, as though making up his mind about something important. "Who is the girl that all the boys in school are in love with?"

Luc didn't have to think long. "Stella."

His father nodded. "Then if you married Stella, you might be able to break the family curse. That's the only way, I suppose. Now go back inside or your mother will start worrying."

That day marked a Before and After in Luc's life. Up until then girls had only been his friends, like his best friend Sadie. Friends he could do burp competitions with after drinking a bottle of Orangina too fast. Friends he built forts with in the forest. Friends who he cried in front of, if a prickly branch scratched his arm long and deep. But after the day he caught his father with that woman, girls became people he would hurt. There were only two exceptions—Sadie, his best friend, and Stella, his potential salvation.

Luc was startled out of his daydreaming when Sadie came back out from her bedroom and clapped her hands. "*D'accord*. I think I've rested enough. Let's go back to the house so I can visit with everyone."

Luc checked his watch. "When's the last time you slept?"

Sadie's brows pulled together. "I might have dozed somewhere over Greenland."

The trip alone was enough to exhaust her, without even taking into consideration her career anguish. "You sure you don't want to lie down for a bit?"

Sadie shook her head, her red ringlets rioting everywhere. "If I did I wouldn't wake up again until tomorrow morning. That would mean I would miss out on whatever delicious dessert your Mom has made."

"Ah, now I see." She was still his Sadie, despite what she'd been through in the past twenty-four hours. "I know what it is, and I think perhaps you're making the right choice."

She licked her bottom lip and something flipped in Luc's stomach. Maybe he was hungry too.

"What is it?"

"Chocolate mousse. She knows it's your favorite."

Sadie rubbed her hands together. "You see what I mean? It would be a travesty to sleep through that."

He took a few steps towards her, conscious of a need to get closer to her contagious smile. *What would it be like to kiss Sadie?*

He shook his head, shocked at that wayward thought. Sadie was his friend. They had the most platonic relationship imaginable.

He must be more tired than he realized from the drive and the lack of sleep in Paris.

"I'll make sure to tell my meddlesome family not to interrogate you about work right now," he said instead.

Her eyes lost some of their brilliance. "I appreciate it, but what reason will you give them?"

Luc buried his hands deep in the pockets of his jeans so he wouldn't do something stupid like reach out and pull Sadie against him. "I'll think of something."

"Thanks. You're right. I don't feel ready to talk about it yet." She paused and tugged her bottom lip with her thumb and forefinger, deep in thought.

Luc found himself staring again.

"I wonder if I should check my emails?" She said finally. "My laptop is just in my backpack. Is it the same internet password here as two years ago?"

Luc put a hand on each of her shoulders without realizing what he was doing. Her sweater felt soft and warm against his palms. "Sadie, I think that can wait until tomorrow, after you've had a good sleep. Come back to the house with me. Let's have a fabulous dinner and celebrate your arrival properly, then we'll deal with tomorrow, tomorrow. *D'accord?*"

Sadie looked up at him with a grimace. "You're right. It's probably better if I wait. It won't change anything, anyway."

"Exactly. Come on." He pivoted her towards the door outside. "Your chocolate mousse awaits."

Several hours later Luc walked Sadie back up to the cottage after their family's raucous dinner. Sadie had enjoyed every second. Luc's father Alphonse had come back from the vineyards and wrapped Sadie in a joyous bear hug and set a jovial tone, as he always did, for the meal.

She just needed to float into bed without having anything disturb this contented high so she could get a decent sleep. Tomorrow she would cope with the fall-out of reporting Professor Harris. Maybe it was the Savigny-les-Beaune wine from the family Domaine they had with dinner, but tomorrow felt like a far way off.

"Alphonse seems in fine form," Sadie said to Luc. She knew that as much as he loved his father—heck, who didn't love Alphonse?—Luc still struggled with his father's unfaithfulness.

"Always," Luc mused, looking up at the stars.

"Is he still, you know—"

"Cheating on my mother?" Luc supplied.

"Yeah."

Luc took in a noisy lungful of night air. "Unfortunately, yes."

There was not much more to say about that if Sadie wanted to keep her serenity intact. The night was crisp and clear. She craned her head back to look at the stars that winked back at her like old friends. "I always loved the night skies here," she said. "That's one thing I don't like about living in New York, it's almost impossible to see the stars."

Luc followed her gaze upwards. "I would hate that."

"I always try to imagine you in New York," Sadie said. "I wonder what you would think of it all. I can't believe you've never come to visit me there."

Luc opened the cottage door for Sadie. "Trust me, I'm properly ashamed by it, but you know Alphonse. He doesn't like his heir to stray too far from the family vineyards."

"He's probably worried you might not come back."

"Probably," Luc sighed, flipping on the light. "But it's the vineyards that keep me here, not my garrulous father."

"I always understood that," Sadie said.

"I know you did, probably because you feel the same about archeology that I do about winemaking."

With a clench of her heart, she thought of the email that may already be waiting for her on her laptop. Would it be an email that just acknowledged receipt of her report, or would it be an email that effectively ended her career at Hudson, or something in between the two?

Luc seemed to read her mind, because he marched her into her bedroom and spun her around so she faced him. "No emails tonight Sadie. Wait until you've slept at least."

He was right. Sadie eyed the fluffy duvet on her bed. "How did you know I was thinking of checking my computer?"

"Come on Sadie. I know you." He scanned the room. "Have you got everything you need for a good sleep?"

She took in the perfect little bedroom with its antique four poster bed and long sausage pillow called a *traversin* in French. Luc went over to close her shutters against the night, a ritual she always missed when she wasn't in France.

"The room is perfect, as always. I guess all that's left for me to do is take your advice and get into bed."

Luc paused in front of her again and his lips quirked to the side. "Let me just take a moment to enjoy this. It's a rare day that you actually listen to my advice, let alone take it."

She chuckled and pushed him away with an open palm against his chest, but he didn't budge. God his chest was even harder than she'd expected. Solid muscle, from the feel of it. She knew she should drop her hand, but it felt so nice there and she could think about Luc's well-defined chest instead of raging about Professor Harris as she was falling asleep.

Luc reached up and took her hand in his. "*Bonne Nuit ma Sadie.*"

Ma Sadie. At this moment, she did feel like his Sadie.

"*Bonne nuit,*" she murmured, her eyelids heavy. Luc leaned in to give her the customary kiss goodnight on each cheek. His hand rested on her shoulder and her eyelids drifted shut.

She felt Luc's lips brush against her left cheekbone, as soft as butterfly wings. Heat shot down to her toes. Time suspended as she waited for him to kiss her other cheek. There was an odd catch to his breathing as she felt his lips press on her right side, just to the side of her lips. He paused there, with his mouth mere millimeters away from hers.

The ease between them was instantly sucked out of the room. Sadie could almost hear a whoosh as it left and was replaced by a crackling energy between their bodies that had never been there before.

No. Not Luc.

Sadie's eyes flew open and she took a shaky step backwards. Luc stood there in the middle of her room. His eyes held the same bewildered look they did the day she'd hidden his shoes behind the huge statue of the Virgin Mary in Grade One.

"*Bonne nuit,*" Sadie said again, but firmly this time. She turned her back to him. Her hands were trembling as she unzipped her suitcase.

"Sleep well," he said, his voice rough.

"You too. Don't be offended if I don't see you out. I'm dead on my feet. *À demain.*"

"See you tomorrow," he said. She exhaled when she heard the click of the front door behind him and rushed to the bathroom with her toothbrush and toothpaste.

In the yellow light of the bathroom, Sadie stared at herself in the mirror, any chance of a peaceful slumber obliterated.

chapter five

WHEN SHE FINALLY woke up, Sadie had no idea what time it was. The late December mornings were dark and foggy, and she'd drifted in and out of an uneasy doze for the entire night.

She threw off the duvet and shivered. How cozy it had been in the cottage when she'd lived there with her family. During the winter, the fire was always roaring in the stone fireplace by the time she rolled out of bed. That was her Dad's favorite job. Breakfast was hot chocolate in glass bowls with slices of the previous day's toasted baguette smeared with Pauline's homemade jam. Sadie, Luc and Stella always caught the bus together to their school in Beaune, bundled in their winter jackets and scarves, with their school satchels on their backs. In the bus or the car, her and Luc would chatter away while Stella gazed out the window, in her own world.

Luc. Sadie's heart did something funny, as she remembered that strange moment from the night before. She dug her fingers into her tangled curls and tried to force the memory out of her mind.

This was ridiculous. She'd lost count of the number of times Luc had declared his love for Stella. She'd seen the jealousy in Luc's eyes when he'd caught site of Pablo at the airport.

That weird moment when he kissed her *bonne nuit* meant nothing. She'd been exhausted and probably imagined the whole thing. Everything would snap back to normal now that it was daytime again. As her father always told her—don't trust anything that happens after dark.

A grumble in her stomach reminded her it was probably time for breakfast, a delicious *French* breakfast. Sadie checked her phone. Seven thirty. She slipped on a clean pair of jeans and an ivy green cashmere sweater. Her skin still smarted from her blast of a shower the night before. She'd managed to turn her skin lobster red trying to scald away any thought of that odd moment with Luc.

Motivated by the thought of coffee, and maybe even a *pain au chocolat*, Sadie slipped on socks and her favorite pair of Bludstone boots. Wrapping her arms across her chest against the damp December air she crossed the lawn, then the pea gravel courtyard that crunched under her boots, then the back veranda along the side of the three-story main house.

She slipped inside the front door without knocking and shucked off her boots on the front mat. "*Bonjour*!" she called out, as she'd gotten in the habit of doing when she was seven and treated the main house as her own.

Several voices beckoned her from the kitchen. The family was all there, seated around the scratched, round wooden table in the kitchen.

Alphonse leapt up first, drawing her in for an enthusiastic *bises*. He was still a striking man, even in his mid-fifties—as dark and dramatic-looking as Luc was fair.

"*Voyons,* it's Sadie!" he cried. "This day just got brighter!"

He sat back down and patted the chair beside him. "You must come and sit beside me, *ma chère* Sadie. I demand it as the head of the family."

His mouth quirked in good humor and a dimple that had been passed down to both Adèle and Raphael, but not Luc, appeared in his cheek. Alphonse could charm the birds out of the trees. It was a shame he didn't just stick to that, instead of charming all the local women out of their undergarments as well.

Her eyes went to Luc. He smiled at her and her shoulders dropped. Things felt normal between them again. She'd imagined that strange tension in the air when he was wishing her good night. There was no excuse for being so foolish.

Sadie knew it would be unfathomably rude to take her seat before doing the round of giving everyone the customary kiss on each cheek in greeting. She did Luc's quickly, barely touching his face with her own. There. She felt nothing.

When she'd given everyone their kisses, *les bises*, she finally sat down at her place between Luc and Alphonse. Luc's mother poured her a steaming café au lait in one of the glass Duralex bowls the family always used for breakfast.

"Luc went to the boulangerie as soon as it opened and bought you your favorite *pain au chocolate*," Adèle told Sadie, passing her a brown paper *boulangerie* bag that was still warm.

"He did?" Sadie met Luc's blue eyes and raised her brows. "He's probably going to ask for my help with something and he knows I'll be far more amenable if I get my *pain au chocolat*."

Luc's gasped, indignant. "What about the goodness of my heart?"

She took a sip of coffee—so glorious. "C'mon, Luc. What do you need help with?"

Luc let out a long-suffering sigh. "Such a lack of good-faith in your best friend, Sadie. I'm shocked. Maybe I just know by now that you need to be fed at regular intervals, or you become feral."

"Luc!" Pauline's eyes grew wide. "That was ungallant of you. I would never have thought a son of mine would speak to a woman like that."

"It's perfectly true about me becoming feral," Sadie admitted. "Don't worry Pauline. I'm not offended."

"There's no excuse." Pauline adjusted one of the Hermés silk scarves she always wore knotted around her neck.

"Besides *maman*," Luc said. "She's not a woman. She's Sadie."

Sadie jerked back. If she needed further proof the strange moment the night before had been a figment of her imagination, she had it.

"What the difference?" Raphael pushed up the red-framed glasses that were always sliding down the bridge of his nose.

"I can't explain. It's just different," Luc said.

"That makes no sense," Raphael grumbled.

It shouldn't sting, but it did.

"By the way Sadie," Luc said. "When do you think Stella will be coming down from Paris? I've made so many plans for her at Christmas, I hope—"

"I don't know any more than you do," Sadie said. "You heard her. She said she'd be here by Christmas."

"Hmph." Luc crossed his arms. "I hope she leaves that Pablo guy in Paris."

"Don't get your hopes up," Sadie warned, trying to keep the edge out of her voice. "You might be ready for Stella, but that doesn't mean she's ready for you." Luc would never say that Stella wasn't a woman. But what did it matter? Her and Luc were strictly platonic.

To distract herself, Sadie chose a flaky, warm *pain au chocolat* from the bag. "So what is it you want help with Luc? You know that I can be bribed to do pretty much anything with *pain au chocolat*, and these look amazing. Are they from the boulangerie across from the bistro?"

Luc nodded. "*Bien sûr*. I know they're your favorites."

Sadie took a bite and closed her eyes, groaning as the buttery layers and deep chocolate center melted on her tongue. "I'm in heaven."

When she opened her eyes almost everyone was grinning at

her. It was well known that Sadie was a *gourmande* and loved good food. Luc was the only one not smiling. Instead, he had gone completely still and was watching her with an arrested look.

"What?" she asked, rubbing her thumb across her mouth. "Did I smear chocolate on my face again?"

Luc gave himself a shake. "*Non*. Not this time. Sorry, I was daydreaming."

"About Stella?" Raphael guessed.

Luc gave his brother a tight smile. "You got me."

"You still haven't answered me about what you want in exchange for these sublime *pain au chocolats*," Sadie said.

"I was wondering if maybe you wanted to help me with some pruning in the vineyards today?"

Sadie thought about it while she chewed.

"It might be good for you to be outside and busy," he added. "For the jetlag, I mean."

Sadie knew that that Luc was probably more concerned about her job stress than her jetlag, but she appreciated his discretion in front of his family. She knew he was thinking that the physical labor of cutting the unruly shoots off the hundreds of vines might keep her mind off her career.

He wasn't wrong. Besides, she'd always enjoyed getting out and working in the vineyards. It made her feel like she was part of something bigger than herself, which was something that motivated her at her digs as well.

"OK," she said, taking another bite. "The food bribe worked. I'll come pruning with you. Have you got a pair of work gloves I can borrow?"

Adèle snorted. "Only about a hundred pairs in the *cuverie*."

"Not that you or Raphael ever use them," Alphonse said, referring to the career choices of his youngest two. "In my day, a Domaine was a family affair—there is always enough work for everyone."

Adèle and Raphael rolled their eyes in sync, apparently inured to their father's reproaches about their lack of interest in working the vineyards.

Pauline frowned at her husband. "Don't make Sadie uncomfortable."

"I'm not uncomfortable," Sadie said. She was used to the light bickering in Luc's home. Grounded in affection, she'd always found it comforting.

Alphonse brushed the crumbs off his sweater and pushed back his chair. "Must be off. I have an appointment in Beaune. Have a wonderful day everyone. Sadie, it's an absolute delight to have you back. We may never let you leave you know."

Sadie blew him a kiss, incorrigible flirt that he was. She was aware that Alphonse's appointment would likely include a rendezvous with one of his numerous lovers. They all knew it, but they all seemed to accept it without complaint.

Sadie could never figure out if this was one of those stereotypical "French arrangements" she constitutionally couldn't understand as an American, or whether they had so much affection for Alphonse that they chose to ignore his philandering. She was guilty of the same blindness with Luc, yet ironically, Luc was the person who seemed hurt the most by Alphonse's straying.

Luc should do with his father what she did with Stella. If he just walled himself from wanting things to be any different than the way they were with Alphonse, he could protect himself.

Being hurt was a choice, and Sadie had quite simply decided to expect most people would choose Stella over her, if given the choice. From that moment forward, Stella lost the power to hurt her. It had been a turning point in Sadie's life, and she knew she could never let that shield be compromised. With it intact, she was untouchable.

They all lingered at the table after Alphonse left, chatting and laughing. Even if she didn't think she'd ever understand all the intricate Ocquidant family dynamics, Sadie was overcome with a long-lost sensation of having returned home after too long.

Finally, the demands of daily life made everyone reluctantly get up and help clear away the dishes. With that done, Sadie turned to Luc, who was busy snapping a dishtowel at Raphael.

"I'm going to get changed into some work clothes," she said. "Meet you in the *cuverie* in twenty minutes?"

He flicked away a gold strand of hair that had fallen in his eye. "We're going to get dirty," Luc reminded her.

Adèle hooted with laughter. "That makes it sound like you two are going to have sex."

Raphael, Adèle, and Luc's mother exploded with mirth at such a preposterous idea. Sadie tried to join in, but she was aware her laughter sounded hollow.

Just before she left, she glanced at Luc. He wasn't laughing either.

chapter six

LUC LOVED WATCHING Sadie work. She was fast and precise, as well as seemingly tireless. The cold December air cut like a thousand knives but as they knelt in the vineyard dirt cutting off excess canes from each vine, she never complained.

They worked their way up the row, side by side. She didn't need overseeing. Sadie and Luc had started helping Alphonse with pruning when they were seven. She wielded her secateurs with skill and knew how to execute the favored style of "*taille Guyot*" pruning to perfection, judiciously choosing the correct longer and shorter branch to leave on each foot. It would have been more efficient for the two of them to work different rows, but then they wouldn't be close enough to talk.

"I thought tradition said pruning should never start before the Saint Vincent in Burgundy," Sadie said after a while. "What's up with that?"

Luc shook his head. "Things are changing—the weather for starters. The whole winemaking calendar seems to shift earlier every year. If I want to hand-prune all my vines, which I do, January 22nd is far too late to start."

"Did Alphonse give you grief for it?"

Luc snorted. "What do you think?"

"Serious grief."

Luc chuckled. "Yup. I decided to judge by the leaves rather than the calendar. When they've all fallen off the vine, that's when I start pruning."

"Makes sense."

It was easy to talk to Sadie about almost everything, even vine pruning, but he hadn't brought her out here to talk about winemaking. Sadie needed to talk about her academic career and process the possible ramifications of reporting her professor. Luc also wanted to keep her away from her email until she had to time to figure out her way forward.

God knows, they couldn't talk about that moment when he'd almost kissed her the night before, or the fact that when she'd groaned with pleasure over her *pain au chocolat* at breakfast he'd hardened… *everywhere*. He'd lied to Raphael. It hadn't been Stella he'd been daydreaming about.

The sooner Stella arrived from Paris, the better. His signals were somehow getting crossed—he was feeling attracted to the wrong twin.

His body needed to get the message that Sadie was just his friend and Stella was his destiny. It had always been that way.

The less he thought about that, the better. He needed to get Sadie talking about her work. He wouldn't lead into the conversation subtly. He knew Sadie hated being pandered to in any way, shape, or form.

"I'm assuming you haven't checked your email yet." He threw a new bunch of vine cuttings onto the pile they were creating in the dirt between them.

Sadie sighed, long and deep. She'd gathered all her red curls into a haphazard knot on the top of her head, and Luc kept getting distracted by the tendrils of loose hair that had slipped out. He was conscious of a desire to tuck them back up again.

"No," she said.

"I'm surprised. I thought maybe you would when you went back to get changed after breakfast."

"So did I." She grimaced as she snipped off a particularly thick cane. "I guess I'm scared. If I get the email saying I'm fired, it makes it real. I mean…I know it's real, but it means I have to face up to it. No more reprieve."

"Surely they can't fire you without bringing it to a board or something?"

Sadie shook her head, not pausing for a moment in her pruning. "If I was officially a member of the faculty it would go to a board, but I'm not yet. I'm a doctoral student with some teaching privileges, but nothing under contract."

"So they can't really fire you *per se*?" Luc was trying to find solutions in Sadie's words. For the first time in his life he wished he had a firmer grip on ivory tower politics.

"Not technically, but my professor can withdraw his oversight on my doctoral thesis, which in turn obliterates my funding. Because Professor Harries is head of the department and best friends with the Dean, he'll make certain that nobody else at Hudson takes me on. It might not be called firing, but it amounts to the same thing. From what the secretary said, he's pushed out other doctoral students who reported him in the exact same way."

Luc swore under his breath. "That bastard of a professor should be fired, not you."

Sadie rubbed her cheek and left a smear of mud there. "I agree, but you know how it works in sexual assault cases Luc. It's not right, but the victims and the whistle blowers always seem to suffer more than the assailant. I had a day to consider that, before I filed my report, but by the time the secretary tried to talk me out of it, I'd made my decision."

"So you filed the report even though you knew it would most

likely damage your career." There was no question in Luc's words, or reproach.

Sadie threw another cane on the pile. "I figured even if it could tarnish his reputation a bit and maybe give people a bit of doubt… also, I wanted to make sure that those students knew somebody believed them."

"You did the right thing, *bien sûr*," Luc said. "Have you heard from the young woman who came to you? I wonder how she's doing, and the others too."

Sadie shook her head. "I was planning on calling her tomorrow, to check in. She gave me her number."

"I know how much you love your work. It can't have been easy."

Sadie shook her head. "No, but in the end, I asked myself what *you* would do."

Luc's shears suspended mid-air. "What *I* would do? Sadie, you know better than anyone, I'm hardly a paragon of morality."

"Don't worry, I'm aware of that." She didn't look at him but kept snipping the rogue canes. Another burnished curl had escaped her bun. "I would warn any woman off getting involved with you, except maybe Stella. She's so self-absorbed, I don't think it would matter."

"Then why—?"

"Outside the fact that you're an incorrigible rake, you have the surest moral compass of anyone I've met."

Luc snorted. "How do you figure that?"

"Do you remember in Grade One, when that girl Suzette with the lisp and the stutter was being bullied by the Grade Eight girls in the bathroom?"

"Vividly," Luc said. He'd stumbled on the scene by accident but couldn't leave once he saw those Grade Eight girls, who seemed like giants to him at the time, hitting Suzette and pushing her up against the row of sinks.

"Do you remember how you started defending Suzette and drew the Grade Eight girls' attention to you so Suzette could escape?"

Luc fingered the slight bump on the bridge of his nose. "I have this daily reminder that they beat the crap out of me, and then Alphonse yelled at me for two hours when I got home because it was ungentlemanly to get in a fight with a girl, and even worse to *lose* a fight with a girl."

Sadie stopped pruning and peered at his face. "You probably should have had your nose looked at, you know. Do you think those girls broke it?" Sadie's mouth curl in a grin and Luc couldn't help but smile back. "Probably, but Alphonse was disgusted enough with me as it was. I wasn't about to demand to have my nose reset." How the humiliation had rained down on him that day.

"You were tiny back then," Sadie reminded him. "Those girls were Amazons."

"They really, really were."

Sadie chuckled—a particular gurgle of hers that was one of his favorite sounds. "I remember you came back to class with a split lip and two black eyes and your clothes almost ripped to shreds. We were waiting for you because Suzette had run back to tell the teacher what you'd done for her."

Luc snorted. "I remember how that cow of a teacher got mad at *me* for sticking my nose in where it didn't belong."

"I forgot about that part, but incidentally, see what I mean about victim blaming?"

"Point taken."

"I asked you later on that day," Sadie said. "When we were in our *cabotte*, why you'd intervened."

Luc remembered that conversation, but not the details. They had spent so much time in their *cabotte* talking, just the two of them. "I can't remember what I said."

Sadie smiled at him—that smile that made him feel like he'd arrived home. His heart skipped a beat. Probably too much coffee at breakfast.

"You said, 'I had to do it so I could still look myself in the mirror, Sadie'."

"*Vraiment*? Wasn't I the little moralist?"

Sadie laughed. "You were, and even though you would deny it until you're blue in the face, I think secretly you still are."

Luc shook his head. Sadie made him want to be a better person, but he just wasn't. He was his father's son. "I'm not."

"Women aside, you've always just done the right thing, no matter the consequences. That's the standard you hold yourself up to—*you have to be able to look yourself in the mirror*. It's why you're nice to people that are used to cruelty, why you care so much about your father's affairs, why you are unfailingly polite to every single salesperson on the phone."

She went back to pruning, but Luc didn't. Sadie had it wrong. He was *not* a good person. Even though he did his best not to, he'd probably hurt so many women by going from one to the other like a butterfly, trying to fill that hollow space where his heart should be.

"Come on, Sadie. You're making me sound like a saint. I'm far from that, as you well know." Trust Sadie to think the best of him, even when she knew the worst.

"You're not a saint," she insisted. "But you are driven by a moral code that you've had since you were a child. Anyway, it helped me make my decision."

"You would have come to the same answer yourself."

Sadie tilted her head, conceding the point. "Maybe, but at least I knew there was one person in the world who would understand."

She was at least right about that. "The way I see it, you did the only thing you could have done."

"Thank you." Sadie's head dropped down suddenly. "I didn't realize until now how important it was for me to hear you say that."

"Let me say it again then. You did the right thing Sadie. You had no other choice."

"I love my job," Sadie said.

"I know." Luc understood perfectly how that felt.

"I think I'm waiting to figure out a Plan B before I check my emails. I'm…I'm scared." A terrible sound emerged from her, the same sound of choking back tears as at their lunch at L'Auberge de la Grenouille.

Luc was powerless against it. He dropped his cutters on the ground and roughly gathered her against his chest. She needed to cry, but he wouldn't let her cry alone.

"Let's come up with a plan then," he murmured into her curls.

"Ok," Sadie's watery voice emerged.

"And maybe it won't be as bad as you think." Even as the words came out, Luc knew it was probably wishful thinking. Women had to fight so hard for everything in their lives and horrible men still had far too much power.

"He's pushed out several other students," she said in a watery voice against his chest. "Why not me?"

"Because you're brilliant."

"I'm sure the other students were too. If anything, being smart and ambitious is a strike against me. Men tend to see that as a threat, and Professor Harris and I were competing for the same funding for a new project. That'll be twisted to discredit my complaint." She wiped away her tears. "I don't think I stand a chance in Hell Luc."

Luc shook off his heavy work gloves and stroked the exposed back of her neck. All he wanted to do was soothe her. The stray curls brushed against his knuckles, igniting a surge of desire that caught him completely by surprise. Luc felt himself hardening to the point of pain. *Good God, not now.* He gave a silent thanks for his heavy work coat.

This wasn't about his misbehaving body; this was about Sadie. Luc clicked his tongue. "Don't worry, my Sadie. We'll figure out something. I don't know what yet, but that's a promise."

He could feel her melt as the fight drained out of her. She burrowed her face deeper into Luc's winter work jacket. He tightened his arms and dropped a kiss on her hair. It smelled like vanilla and that delicious Sadie warmth. He dropped another kiss, and then another.

No, he had to stop. The bulge in his jeans was not getting the message that he was just comforting a friend.

He pulled away slightly to readjust himself. Sadie didn't need to know about his inconvenient lusts on top of everything else. It wasn't like he would ever do anything about them. Sadie was far, far too important for that.

Besides, there was Stella, he reminded himself. Still, he'd never realized how out of practice he was at having his arms around a beautiful woman like Sadie without having her press her body against his and try to urge things towards a mutual and inevitable physical release. It was also acutely inconvenient that the fact that Sadie was oblivious was turning out to be an incredible turn-on.

Again, his problem, not hers. He could just have to ignore his body's shenanigans.

Sadie sat back and wiped her eyes. It was hard to let go, but he did. When their eyes met, there was a flash of confusion on her features, or had he just imagined it? He went cold. Had she somehow sensed his desire? Part of him wished they could talk about it in the same straightforward way they did everything else, but that was impossible. He couldn't risk his friendship with Sadie. Never. She was far too precious to him.

They got back to pruning after that and worked for several more hours until the light began to fade, chatting about everything under the sun.

Sadie had forgotten the simple pleasure of this—being outside with Luc, working in the vineyards; the scent of burning vines coming from the metal barrels that were staggered every few rows where the other winemakers out working burned their excess canes. Apparently, Luc wasn't the only one who rebelled against the "no pruning before the Saint Vincent" tradition.

"We're going to lose the light," she said, standing up and stretching. Her muscles were punishing her for sitting at desks too much the past few months. She arched backwards with her hands on her lower back, groaning.

"You're going to be sore tomorrow," Luc said, standing up beside her but avoiding her eyes.

She threw her last bunch of pruned canes into their pile. "Very, but it'll a satisfying kind of sore." They both picked up an armful of sticks and walked them over to the fire crackling in the nearest barrel.

"Maybe, but it might also be a can't walk kind of sore," Luc said.

"Very possibly." Sadie took off her gloves and warmed her hands over the lively flame that burst up. "Hmmmmm… that feels good." She glanced around her. The gray light was closing in fast and fog was creeping down the slope. Plumes of smoke dotted the landscape. "Being out here helped. Thank you."

"I thought it might. Thank you for the company, not to mention the free labor."

"I didn't realize we were so close to our *cabotte*," Sadie said, spotting the familiar stone hump in the distance. "Can we go quickly so I can go say *bonjour* to it before it gets too dark?

Luc peered over to the round, stone hut at the foot of the slope they'd been working on. "Sure. Got your secateurs?"

Sadie nodded. "Can we just let this fire burn out?" Sadie pointed at the barrel.

Luc nodded. "*Oui*. It's safe in the barrel. C'mon."

He stuck out his hand for her to grab.

Running hand in hand down this steep slope of vineyards had been one of their favorite games when they were little. Her breath caught on a wave of nostalgia.

She laughed and accepted his outstretched hand. She tried not to pay attention to the warmth of Luc's skin, or the fact that her palm fit perfectly in his. Bare vines flashed past as they ran. The sharp air burned her throat. She could hear Luc's shriek of joy as they gained speed…then came that perfect, suspended moment when it felt as though her feet were no longer touching the ground and she was flying.

That moment never lasted long. The sturdy stone wall of the *cabotte* filled her vision. She slowed herself down, but she still needed to slam her shoulder against the hut to stop. "Ow. Why does that hurt more now?"

Luc just laughed. "I forgot how much fun that was. Hey, you didn't impale yourself on your secateurs, did you?"

Sadie patted her pocket to reassure herself they hadn't moved. "Nope. You?" But Luc was already opening the splintered wooden door. She winced at the creak.

"It needs replacing." Luc lifted his chin at the door. "But somehow I hate to do it."

Sadie went inside and took a lungful of the limestone flavored air. She turned around in slow circles. There was no place like this place. It still felt every bit as magical and yes, even sacred, as when they were children.

"Thank God," she said. "It hasn't changed since I was here two years ago. Except it's much cleaner than I thought it would be." Her eyes began to adjust to the low light let in by the two small openings in the stone that served as windows, and the chinks in the domed ceiling. She toed the fresh pea gravel on the ground. "How did this get here?"

"I brought it in, and keep it weeded." Luc shrugged. "It's better for drainage."

"Drainage? Really Luc?" Sadie turned to him, with her hands on her hips and a grin. Her heart squeezed with affection for him.

He ran a hand through his hair. "You got me. I take care of the *cabotte*. It's on my family's land."

Sadie placed her palm against the wall. The familiar roughness of the stone somehow continued the healing of her aching heart. "That's the only reason?"

Luc dug his hands into his jean pockets. "Also, because it's our special place."

Sadie turned to him and smiled. Aside from the Stella thing, Luc really was an amazing friend. This *cabotte* held so many memories. Some good, like playing they'd been orphans abandoned in the forest, and some bad, like the day Luc had first found his father having sex with his mother's best friend in the forest above the big house.

They'd been playing the orphan game in the *cabotte* when a bossy seven-year-old Sadie had, with her still broken French, dispatched Luc to the woods to get some sticks for their pretend fire.

Five minutes after he left, he came running back, out-of-breath, pale, and shaking. It had taken him a good ten minutes for Sadie to coax words out of him. When he finally talked, and admitted what he'd seen, it had been through tears of shock. Even though she was only a child, Sadie had innately understood that realizing his beloved father was cheating on Pauline ripped Luc's whole world apart

Luc changed that day. Something essential in his soul had broken and grafted a turbulence that had been there ever since.

She looked over at him now, lounging against the door, his hands in his pockets, watching her with a soft curve to his lips in the dim light. How could that skinny, flyaway-haired little boy have turned into this man?

Something in her began to thrum again, filling her ears. Sadie closed her eyes and tried to put Luc back in the mental box of her childhood friend. Somehow her overwhelmed brain had mixed up Luc's category, and she was gripped with an overwhelming need to slot him back in the correct place.

"Please tell me you don't bring your conquests here for illicit rendez-vous." There, that should slice through any awkwardness.

Luc shook his head, his eyes never leaving hers. "Never. This place is ours Sadie."

Every cell in her body urged her to him. She couldn't let him suspect the effect he was having on her. Never. She clapped her hands to clear the air. "Thanks for coming here with me. I'm going to grab a bath before dinner. *On y va*?"

Luc nodded and to Sadie's relief, opened the door and went back outside. Sadie followed and shut the door firmly behind them. Even though it broke her heart, it might be wise to avoid being in the *cabotte* with Luc alone for the next little while.

chapter seven

SADIE SLID INTO a scalding bath back at the cottage, the hot water made her bones feel like they were dissolving. She'd waited long enough—she couldn't put off checking her email any longer. Still, a few more minutes in the bath wouldn't change anything.

Her mind, as well as her limbs, was loosened by the steam rising off the water and it kept circling back to how Luc had pulled her against him in the vineyards when she'd almost started to cry. Even through their layers of coats and sweaters and gloves, his body had felt good wrapped around hers. She'd been overcome with the need to get even closer.

But the only person Luc wanted to get closer to was Stella. That thought was the bucket of freezing water she clearly needed. Trying to think of anything but Luc, Sadie got out of the bath, dried herself off, and pulled on the robe that Pauline had left for her on a hook in the wooden bedroom armoire.

Enough of this ridiculousness, it was time to face reality. She set up her laptop on the simple wooden desk that had probably been in the Ocquidant family for generations.

Fear beat like the wings of a trapped bird in her chest. Who was she without her academic life? She honestly didn't know anymore.

A wild hope that maybe Luc was right, and maybe she wouldn't be punished after all, took hold of her until she spotted the email and began to read.

With each word, her heart sunk lower. It was her worst prediction. A letter from her faculty administrator saying Professor Harris had withdrawn himself as her doctoral advisor, as he felt there was little promise in her research. He was also apparently investigating concerns around her thesis work so far and plagiarism. Plagiarism! At least it was clear. He was bent on destroying her completely.

The letter ended with the standard verbiage about saying she could still apply to other advisors, but even if Professor Harris hadn't been cronies with all of them, he'd made certain with that false charge of plagiarism that she would never be accepted by anyone else.

There were no women advisors in her faculty—a situation she had hoped to rectify before all this by becoming one herself. The Old Boy's Club had struck again, closing ranks to protect each other, not caring if they disposed of her academic career in the process. Her hands hovered over the keyboard, shaking with rage and dread. All those years of work, lost. What was she going to do now?

Sadie remembered to send off a quick email to Gia, checking in with her and letting her know the report had been filed but that she would be in France for the next little while. After all, she had nothing waiting for her in New York anymore. She reiterated to Gia that she had done the right thing and urged her to let her know how she was doing.

Luc. He was the only place left to turn. He couldn't do anything concrete to help her career of course, but he was the only one she wanted to talk to.

Still in a daze, she got dressed and walked over to the main house, where dinner was due to be served. When Sadie arrived, the family were all sitting at the table enjoying a glass of white *aligoté* with some *pâté en croute.*

She needed to get Luc alone. Still, biding her time until then with Luc and his family, was probably preferable to sitting in the cottage alone with her thoughts. Pauline sat Sadie down and put a glass of wine in her hand before setting twelve piping hot *escargots* in front of her. Her stomach growled. She was starving. It was a good thing she wasn't one of those women who lost their appetite when distressed. On the contrary, distress made her ravenous.

Luc was asking Alphonse some questions about bills that had gone unpaid at the Domaine, and Alphonse was making vague promises of looking into it and assuring Luc that it had surely been a misunderstanding.

From the pucker between his brows, Luc didn't seem satisfied, but once everyone had been served and began eating the garlic, buttery *escargots*, Luc nudged Sadie's foot under the table. When Sadie looked up from her plate and her *escargot* tongs, he raised an eyebrow in question. Of course, he saw through her attempts at acting normal. She gave an infinitesimal shake of her head. His lips tightened and he gave her a slight nod which she knew meant *we'll talk later*.

Alphonse was in a particularly garrulous mood, which meant that Sadie could take solace in the perfectly chilled, mineral white wine and the garlic, butter, and parsley-infused snails soaked up with a fresh slice of baguette.

She and Luc would talk it out later. For right now, she would take comfort in the flowing conversation and the delectable food.

After supper, Luc volunteered himself and Sadie to do the dishes.

"But she's supposed to be our guest!" Adèle protested.

"You know that Sadie is never a guest here," Pauline chastised her daughter. "Sadie is one of the family. *Merci* dear," she said, and kissed Sadie on the cheek, leaving a lingering scent of Guerlain perfume. "I've had a busy day."

They vacated the kitchen, leaving Sadie alone with Luc.

He slanted her a glance as he scrubbed out a pot in the sink full of sudsy bubbles. "That's it then? You've been fired, or whatever they call it in academia?"

Sadie twisted the dishcloth in her hands. "*Oui*. Just as I predicted."

Luc let out an impressive stream of French curses.

"Agreed," Sadie nodded.

"What next?"

"That's what's bothering me so much Luc, I don't know," Sadie admitted, as Luc passed her the pot to dry. "I *need* a plan or I'm going to lose my mind."

Luc paused in mid-air as he transferred another dirty pot to the sink. "Could you go back and fight for justice? It's difficult to leave the vineyards for long, but I'd go with you if you needed moral support, or at least just to punch your professor." He smiled to himself. "I'd like that."

"I'd like to punch him too," she said. "But I don't think that's the way forward. I just want to keep doing my research, and that's hard to do from jail."

"Your professor is the one who should be in jail," Luc growled.

"Agreed."

"But if the girls that came to you could—"

She shook her head. "No. They've already said they don't want to testify against him. They don't want to be kicked out of Hudson and given how I've just been disposed of, I can't promise them that wouldn't happen."

Luc passed her the last pot to dry. "But—"

"They're just starting their academic careers. When Gia approached me for help, she told me she just wanted it to stop.

Am I naïve to hope that maybe my complaint might give Professor Harris pause?"

Luc leaned against the counter. "You did everything you could possibly do to make the world a little better. That's not naïve, it's brave." Sadie twisted the dishtowel around her finger. "I can't just give up my research, Luc. It means too much to me. I have no idea what to do next and that scares the crap out of me."

"I know." Luc bit his lip. Why had she never realized how sexy it was when he did that? *No.* She *was* losing her mind. She couldn't think things like that.

"I've just worked too hard for it all to be snatched from me like this."

Luc unclawed Sadie's fingers from around her dishtowel. "I understand. It's like me and winemaking. It would kill me to have my vines taken away." He smoothed out the dishtowel and hung it on the railing of the oven. "We need to brainstorm. One thing is certain—I know you will find a way to continue your archaeology, and probably even a better one than before."

"How can you know that?"

"Because I know you Sadie." He reached out and took one of her curls in his finger and traced its corkscrew spiral. "Better than I know anyone. For example, I'm noticing that your hair is even curlier than usual tonight. Is that due to your righteous indignation?"

Sadie chuckled. "That, and the hot bath."

His fingers paused for a moment, then Luc dropped his hand. "*Voyons*, the way I see it you're still in shock. You don't need to figure it all out tonight. You're also probably exhausted from the jetlag and the work in the vineyards today. How about you relax tonight, and then we'll figure out a plan tomorrow?"

"But tomorrow is Christmas Eve."

Luc shrugged. "Besides going to Clovis and Cerise's house for the Réveillon dinner, we have lots of time to strategize together."

"Maybe you're right, but I don't feel like going to bed yet. I'm too restless. I know I'll just toss and turn—"

"I can help you with that."

Sadie's eyes flew to his clear blue ones. "What?"

"I know exactly what you need tonight."

Sadie couldn't think of anything that would make her feel as good as Luc holding her, like he had in the vineyards, but that was something she could never have, in the same category as getting her position at Hudson back. "What?"

"A Harry Potter marathon with me."

Sadie didn't answer right away. Then slowly she began to smile. It was perfect. A Harry Potter marathon was exactly what she needed. Her and Luc had been obsessed with the movies, and watching them would take her back to a carefree time when she was still in primary school, spending every day with Luc, and living in a world of imagination, nature, and magic instead of injustice and harsh realities.

"That's a perfect idea," Sadie said.

"I know," Luc took her hand and lead her into the living room. "I'm rather proud of myself. I've already got the old DVD player set up in the living room. Come on. Let's go back in time for tonight."

Almost nobody used DVDs anymore, of course, but Luc remembered how excited he and Sadie were when he'd received the Harry Potter DVDs her second Christmas in Burgundy.

They'd been eight then and had spent almost every moment during that school break in a tangle of limbs on the couch watching all the movies, then watching them all over again. Stella wasn't obsessed like Luc and Sadie and complained about feeling left out. She preferred hanging out with her girlfriends and going to her ballet and modern dance classes in Nuits-Saint-Georges.

"I still feel guilty for excluding Stella so often during our Harry Potter phase," Luc said. He hoped bringing Stella up would make his body behave around Sadie when they were on the couch together.

"Yeah, we must have been pretty annoying," Sadie said. She collapsed on the couch and curled her legs underneath her.

"Extremely," Luc said. "But at the same time, those few months remain one of my favorite memories. Also, to be totally honest, I still love Harry Potter."

"Me too." Sadie laughed. "They're my comfort movies. Every winter, when it's miserable outside, I just cozy up under the covers in bed and watch them all back-to-back in one day.

Every cell in Luc's body came alive at the idea of lounging in bed with Sadie while a storm raged outside.

"It's incredible that Stella still talks to us," Luc said. He needed to shift all these obsessive thoughts back to the right sister. She would arrive tomorrow, surely? Please God, let her arrive before Clovis and Cerise's dinner. He'd been planning that event as the perfect way to introduce to Stella the idea of them being a couple.

Sadie didn't respond to that right away. "I guess we did leave Stella out…or she opted out. I was never sure which."

"When she comes back, we need to bring her into the Harry Potter fold," Luc said.

"I thought you had plans for a lot of one-on-one time with her," Sadie said, staring at the blank screen instead of Luc. As much as it pained him to break their connection, it seemed to be working.

"Oh, I do," Luc said. "I've been planning that for months." *There.* That would set his body straight.

Sadie sighed. "I still don't understand Luc. I know you're the heir and you need a wife, blah, blah, blah, but I still don't get it. Why Stella? Why now?"

"Stella has always been my endgame." Luc had never questioned that, ever since that conversation with Alphonse in the *cuverie,* just after discovering his God-like father was irredeemably flawed—a flaw that he'd inherited and which only Stella could fix.

"Fine," Sadie said. "But why *now*?"

Luc tried to find the words to describe the empty space in his heart that kept him going from woman to woman. "I can't go on anymore the way I have been," he admitted. "I just can't bear it."

Their eyes met and slowly, Sadie nodded. "OK," she said. "I don't understand it, but if that's the case, I'll help you."

"I'd appreciate that. I think I'll need all the help I can get." Luc hit play on the remote control. The screen filled up with the familiar theme music. Sadie trembled with anticipation. At least he hoped it was anticipation. This had been a good idea.

"How often do you watch these DVDs?" Sadie asked, just as the theme song was finishing up.

Luc stretched his arm across the back of the couch and settled in. "Not that often anymore. For some reason it just doesn't feel right to watch them without you."

Sadie grabbed one of the many velvet cushions on the deep, soft couch and settled it under her arm. The pillow effectively created a barrier between them—probably not a bad idea. He wanted more than anything for Sadie to feel better, but the same time he didn't trust the crazy spell that came over him now when he was alone with her. He needed to help Sadie while protecting her from himself. Tricky.

"You know what's funny for me?" Sadie said, when Hagrid was busy knocking down the door of the lighthouse.

"What?"

"Whenever I see or hear snippets of the movies with the

original English characters, it sounds all wrong to me, even now. Only the French dubbing sounds right."

Luc chuckled. Quickly, he was swept back into the story and back in time to when he had first watched this with Sadie. Even that vacuum in his heart felt full. Was it the movie or was it being with her?

chapter eight

HE FOUND HIMSELF glancing over often to watch Sadie watch the movie.

His fingers itched with the need to wind one of her tight ringlets around them. His mind kept misbehaving and picturing her lounging in the steamy bathtub. Had she always been this stunning? Her lips moved as she mouthed out some of the lines to herself and reacted to what was playing out on the screen. As for Luc, as much as he loved Harry Potter, he preferred watching it play out on Sadie's face more than on the screen.

The first movie seemed to go by in a flash, and when he got up to change to the second one, Sadie stretched like a cat and made that groaning sound again—that sound that tapped into a lower, less noble part of him.

"Sore from today?" Luc asked, sitting back down on the couch.

She rubbed her shoulder. "I'm ashamed to admit it, but my back is in agony. I used a ton of Epsom salts in the bath, but between the pruning and those airplane seats—"

"I'd be amazed if it wasn't," Luc said, as the theme music started up again. "Also, emotional turmoil always shows up on the body one way or another." That horrible winter after he'd found out about his father, Luc had developed double pneumonia, then nephritis, and ended up in the hospital for two months. Sadie had come to visit him every day.

"That's part of it, I guess," Sadie admitted. "No matter what I do, I can't seem to unwind my body."

Luc had an idea, but could he trust himself? Still, she needed to have a good sleep so they could devise a plan for her in the morning. "Would a little massage help?"

Sadie cocked a brow at him. "Since when do you give massages?"

"Oh…I don't know." There was no good answer to that.

Sadie rolled her eyes. "Dare I probe further?"

"Let's just say I've had a lot of practice. That's a good thing, *n'est-ce pas*? For your back, anyway."

The emotions rippled over her features—she was clearly dying for a massage, but maybe she too had picked up on this new crackle in the air between them.

Still, he could keep it platonic. He was the master of his body, not the other way around. He was gripped by the need to prove this to himself.

"Come on," he urged. "Your back is probably a mess. You'll sleep better if I can unknot some of those muscles. I promise it won't get weird."

Sadie glanced away from the screen to look at him. "Why would it get weird?"

That's right. All of this was playing out in his head, not hers. He was an idiot. "No reason."

She sighed. "All right, but I'm only agreeing because I'm a total massage addict, not because I'm some sort of weakling, understood?"

A flash of heat ripped through Luc at this new piece of knowledge—Sadie loved massages—but he pushed it out of his mind. *Just friends.* "Understood."

She shuffled forward and sat cross-legged on the Turkish carpet overlaying the flagstone floor. She whipped off her heavy sweater and Luc swallowed hard when he saw her bare shoulders covered only by a simple white tank top with spaghetti straps.

He settled himself behind her on the edge of the couch, with one leg on either side of her arms, determined to keep things chummy. *Mind over matter.*

As Sadie watched the first scene, Luc lay his hands on her shoulders. Her skin there was pale and smooth as silk, with delicious clusters of freckles scattered haphazardly, like stars in the night sky. They seemed placed to highlight delectable spots to kiss.

Stella, not Sadie. Sweat broke out at the back of his neck. Why did it feel so hot all of a sudden?

He began to knead his thumbs hard into her shoulder muscles which, as she had said, were like rocks. She groaned again and he realized he too was rock hard. *Merde. That didn't take long.* "Am I hurting you?" he asked, trying to concentrate on the movie instead of Sadie beneath him. Thank God she had no idea.

"No," Sadie gasped, half growl and half plea. "It feels sooooo good. *Harder.*"

He'd never been so confused, but one thing was clear—her wish was his command. He was rewarded as her muscles started to soften beneath his fingers. His head spun with the euphoric delusion that only he could unlock her body. He imagined her murmuring "harder" in an entirely different scenario.

Her soft groans and whimpers guided his hands and made him want to go deeper, bring her closer, feel her disintegrate completely under him. His erection ached against the zipper of his jeans. Was it the fact that he couldn't have her that stoked his desire to such levels?

He had felt connected to Sadie from the moment they first met, when he passed her an Orangina while their parents had a meet-and-greet glass of wine. Even though she didn't speak much French at that point, she'd smiled. The moment he saw that smile, he felt like someone he'd been waiting for had finally arrived. Being with Sadie had always felt as natural as breathing, yet they'd always been strictly friends.

Now he had started wondering about what it would be like to make love to Sadie, he couldn't seem to stop himself. He massaged her warm skin with his right hand and grabbed a stray cushion with his left to cover his groin in case she turned around.

A few minutes of exquisite torture later, she did. Even in the low light, he could see her face was almost as flushed as her flaming hair. "You're making that sound," she said.

"What sound?"

"That hum in your throat, like when you're eating something good. It's like you're purring if you were a cat."

Luc's blood ran cold. "It must have been in the movie."

"No," she insisted. "It's you."

The inconvenient truth was that everything in him hummed with pleasure when Sadie was near. "Maybe," he admitted.

She looked up at him now, her lips slightly open. She studied his face, a question in her eyes.

He was transfixed by her mouth. In which ways could he unlock her from there, make her feel better?

Before a rational thought could intrude, he dipped his head down and touched his lips to hers and gave Sadie the answer. If she had drawn back, he would have done the same, but she didn't.

Any illusion that he had control over his desire for her evaporated. Her mouth was perfection—warm and soft. She tasted like honey and vanilla and so many delicious things he longed to explore. He teased her lips open with his, and her tongue brushed against his. *This was what he'd been searching for all this time.* He had no idea where that thought came from, but electricity flared through his body, every cell jump-starting into something entirely new.

Luc pulled her up into his lap, rough with need. Her clever

hands reached underneath his shirt and splayed along the sides of his torso. Luc couldn't breathe as he felt the delicate exploration of her lips move up the curve of his neck and then the underside of his jaw. He shook with need.

His hand reached under her tank top, and he found what felt like the center of his world—Sadie's heart, pounding as her chest rose and fell quickly. He wanted to soothe her there too, soothe her everywhere. His fingers brushed across her bra and then moved around to her back, fumbling with the clasp. *Mon Dieu*, he'd never fumbled a bra clasp before in his life.

Without warning, Sadie leapt off him and scooted to the opposite side of the coffee table. The movie was still playing. They had missed quite a lot. He just wanted her back.

"What was that Luc?" she demanded, her chest still heaving. She yanked her sweater back on. She put it on backwards, which made Luc want to kiss her all over again, but then he looked into her eyes and saw the wild confusion and hurt there. *Merde.*

He didn't have any answers for her. What *was* that? Even though he'd instigated the kiss, he was every bit as confused as she was. "Sadie...I'm so sorry. I don't know what happened."

"You should know." Her chest was heaving, and he was equal parts aroused and dismayed. "You started it."

"You didn't take much convincing." The words flew out of his mouth before he could take them back. He regretted them immediately.

She gasped with indignation, rightfully so. It was a stupid thing to say. He couldn't act like a guilty seven-year-old with his hand caught in the biscuit jar. No matter how much his body had wanted something to happen between him and Sadie and how good it felt, he could not be with her. The magnitude of his mistake hit him like a slap to the face. He couldn't lose her.

"Please ignore what I just said," he said. "I'm sorry. I don't know what came over me. I shouldn't have kissed you like that.

You're vulnerable after losing your job and I…I was desperate to make you feel better."

Sadie sucked in her breath. "You kissed me out of *pity*?"

"No!"

She waved her hands wildly in the air, a sign he knew meant it was time for him to shut up. "I'm going to bed," she said. "Tomorrow, we are going to forget this ever happened and go back to normal because I need my best friend right now, not another asshole guy in my life. Is that understood?"

"*Oui*," he whispered, not breaking her wild gaze.

"Good, because a friend is what I need, not you seducing me as though I was just another one of your stupid one-night stands."

"It wasn't that Sadie." Luc pleaded, at a loss for the right words to make her understand. "You could never be that."

"Oh, I know," she snapped back. "Don't do this to me Luc. I'm not some sort of fill-in for Stella."

The idea Sadie could even think that filled Luc with repulsion. His desire for her had nothing to do with Stella. "Sadie," he begged. "That wasn't at all— "

But she'd already swung out of the room, and he heard the heavy sixteenth century wooden front door as she slammed it behind her, putting a period on one of the biggest mistakes of his life.

Her feet were clumsy as she tripped over the ground in the dark, running back to the cottage. Her eyes hadn't been working properly ever since Luc had started massaging her. When their lips touched, and he pulled her up in his lap with such urgency—rough and gentle at the same time—she'd felt like she was going to shatter with need.

Goddamnit. He'd made her blind and breathless, and that was *before* she became aware of the bulge in his jeans. Every fiber of her being yearned to lose herself in him, but something about his hand shaking as he fumbled with the clasp of her bra made her think of pragmatic things like bras. This brought other pragmatic thoughts like not making out with your best friend who was in love with your sister, even if felt better than life itself.

She slammed the door of the cottage behind her and locked it. Ridiculous, really. Luc had a key. She threw herself on her bed, wishing there were a way to undo everything that had just happened.

She still didn't understand exactly why he'd kissed her.

She punched the duvet. What was Luc feeling now? She closed her eyes tight at the thought that he'd been using her as a stand-in for Stella, even if he'd denied it.

What a fool she was to expose herself to such humiliation again. Luc had chosen Stella when they were seven, and, until now, Sadie had never given either of them another opportunity to hurt her again.

Her mind went back to that horrific day. It was in January, and as was traditional in France, there were a multitude of occasions where a traditional tarte, called a *galette des roi,* was served to mark Epiphany on the Catholic calendar. Sadie had been instantly seduced by the *galette*—a puff pastry full of almond cream – and the tradition that went with it. Whoever found the tiny ceramic figurine hidden inside the dessert was crowned the king or queen. They, in turn, had to choose another person to be crowned their king or queen.

Stella didn't like *galettes* very much and wasn't enraptured with the tradition like Sadie. Sadie had always been obsessive about things she loved, like Harry Potter, *galette des rois*, the smell of her father's pipe, and the Gallo-Roman walls in the woods above Luc's house.

That day in their Grade One classroom, a *galette des rois* had been served to the class as a treat. Luc had been the lucky one and found in his slice the ceramic figurine, called a *fève*. She'd been happy for him, because he'd just recently found out about Alphonse, and needed cheering up.

Sadie had grinned with anticipation, knowing Luc would choose her as his Queen. She was Luc's best friend, after all. They were so inseparable that people had starting to look surprised when one showed up anywhere without the other. Sadie shuffled her Mary-Janes under her desk, excited to stand up beside Luc with a crown on her head. She caught Luc's eye, but instead of grinning at her, he frowned. His eyes moved over her, as if she was suddenly invisible. His gaze stopped on Stella, sitting serene and exquisite behind her desk. People were already starting to comment on Stella's ethereal beauty.

Luc wasn't the only person in the class that was watching Stella. All the boys in their class had already declared that they were in love with her. It was just expected that if you were a boy, you were *amoureux* of Stella. But Luc...Luc was different. Luc could never be Stella's because Luc was *hers*. Sadie's palms began to sweat. What was Luc doing? Surely...

Luc opened his mouth. "Stella," he called out loud and clear.

Stella glided like a swan up to the front and Sadie had to watch—slouching down in her chair, annihilated with mortification—as Luc placed the crown on her sister's golden hair.

Sadie moved her wild curls like a curtain to cover her face. Her chest ached and she blinked away tears. *She wouldn't cry. She could never let them know.*

"Hey Sadie," an annoying boy named Arthur who was obsessed with Pokémon cards, nudged her. "Did you really think Luc was going to pick you over Stella?" He snorted and that was the moment when Sadie felt something cold and metallic encase her heart. If even her best friend in the world chose Stella over her, maybe she really was invisible.

She surreptitiously dried her tears with a strand of hair and tossed her wild mane of curls. "Of course not," she scoffed. "I don't even want another stupid paper crown anyway. Stella is welcome to it."

Arthur nodded, impressed. That was how she had to be from then on. Always. She would never give Luc and Stella the chance to hurt her.

Every time Luc rhapsodized about Stella, like at the airport, Sadie was grateful for that armor still protecting her heart.

She thought back to the feel of Luc's lips on hers and how they'd fit together like they were made to join. While they were kissing, the protection around her heart disintegrated by the second. He could destroy her so easily if she let him. She clutched her chest now at the thought. She would *not*.

In the past, she could always take refuge in her work when other things like her father's illness and death, her distance with Stella, and now Luc, became overwhelming. Now that she no longer had her job, what on earth was she going to do?

After a few minutes of wracking her brain, she remembered the Gallo-Roman wall that ran above Luc's vineyards. Something about that spot always drew her back, and she'd always had vague dreams of doing a dig there some day. Often, just before falling asleep, she would make plans in her head of how she'd approach it—which section to dig first, how she believed the wall fit into a larger settlement…

The plan had been to get her doctorate first, but what if she didn't need to do things in that order? She was here anyway, and now that she'd lost her job, all that was left for her in New York was her mother, who seemed bent on escaping her grief through travel. Her little brother Max was still happy at boarding school. Maybe this was the perfect time.

She grabbed her laptop from the desk, sat back down on her bed and fired it up. It was time to do some research.

chapter nine

THE NEXT MORNING Sadie woke up to somebody jumping on her bed. She moaned and cracked an eye. *Stella.*

She didn't feel ready to take on her sister…but then again, did she ever? Stella had said she'd be back for Christmas and it was Christmas Eve. Sadie's sleep had been fitful and she'd floated in and out of dreams of kissing Luc.

"You're back." Sadie struggled to get up to a sitting position and rubbed her eyes. Stella always used to wake Sadie up by jumping on her bed when they were little. Despite everything, Sadie felt something soften inside her.

"Bonjour my little sister," Stella sing-songed. "We just arrived. Paris was ah-ma-zing. You should have stayed with me and Pablo instead of coming to boring old Burgundy."

Sadie didn't bother mentioning that Stella had never invited her to do that. Fortunately, staying in Paris with Stella and Pablo was pretty much her idea of a nightmare, so no regrets there. Stella would've probably expected her to hold the reflector lights for her photo shoots or something.

Sadie struggled to get out of bed, not an easy feat as Stella's legs were splayed across hers now. She pushed the memories of the night before aside. It had to be forgotten. "When did you get back?" she asked.

"Late last night. We're staying at Le Cep of course but I thought I'd come and check in on my baby sister to make sure you wouldn't get yourself in any trouble." The mere idea set Stella off into peals of laughter.

If only Stella knew what she and Luc had done last night—and what Sadie had impulsively done on her laptop later at the cottage—but Sadie could never confide in her. "Stop calling me your baby sister," she said instead. "You were born three minutes before me."

"I'll never stop calling you my baby sister."

"Wait, where's Pablo?" Sadie didn't want to waltz out of her bedroom in her pajamas in front of a stranger. "Did you leave him in Beaune?"

"No, he came here with me."

Sadie cast her eyes towards her bedroom door. "Like, in the cottage?"

"No. I dropped him off at the main house before coming out to surprise you. He's having breakfast with Luc's family by now I suppose."

Trust Stella. "Won't that be awkward? Pablo doesn't strike me as a talkative guy."

Stella inspected her nails. "Pablo won't mind."

"But Luc and his family might mind having a stranger foisted on them."

Stella looked at Sadie blankly. "There's always plenty of food."

Sadie leaned back in her bed. There was no point in trying to make Stella see things from anyone else's point of view. Years before, Sadie had reached the conclusion that such a feat was impossible for her sister.

"What is going on between you and Pablo anyway?" Sadie asked. "Are you, you know, *together*, together?"

Stella wasn't the best judge of men as a rule. One day she might get herself in a situation where she would get hurt. Maybe

Stella was born three minutes earlier, but Sadie had always felt like the big sister. Then again, it wasn't like Sadie hadn't just made a massive mistake herself.

Stella shrugged. "Sometimes yes, sometimes no."

Sadie frowned. "What is that supposed to mean? Do you even like him?"

"Let's put it this way—he's useful to me. He's a great photographer. And as a subject, I'm useful to him."

"Really? That's it?" Sadie thought of Luc and wondered how Stella's mercenary approach to relationships would affect him. Then again, maybe his motivations, like having a beautiful wife hanging off his arm, weren't exactly noble either.

"Yeah," Stella cast Sadie a baleful glance. "That's it."

"It sounds kind of thin as far as relationships go."

"So what if it is? Pablo isn't my end-game."

"Who is?"

Stella tossed her golden mane of hair over her shoulder. "I haven't decided yet. Maybe Luc?"

Stella was baiting her, but here was a golden opportunity to prove to Stella and more importantly, to herself, that she didn't care. Sheer willpower had saved her before; there was no reason why it couldn't again.

"Be my guest," Sadie said, tossing off her duvet.

"Really?" Stella asked, her blue eyes wide.

"Sure," Sadie said, pulling on clothes. "Luc really likes you, you know. He always has. Would you ever give him a chance?" She ignored the sharp pain in her heart.

Stella settled her chin on her hands. "He's cute," she said finally. "Who would've thought? He was nothing special when we were kids."

Sadie thought of the contained strength in the lean muscles in Luc's back, and the understanding in his clear blue eyes, and the bump on his nose from when those Grade Eight girls had broken it.

"Luc is more than just cute," she said. "You should really spend some time getting to know him better." Her throat had become so tight she barely got the words out, but she did. She had to.

Stella got a dreamy look in her eyes. "Maybe I will. But Sadie, you and he were always so close. Haven't you ever thought of—"

Sadie let out a poor imitation of a laugh and shook her head. "Luc and I are just friends. That's all we'll ever be." *That's all we can ever be.*

"Hmmmm," Stella said. "Food for thought."

Sadie needed to push Stella towards Luc, even though it felt like slowly driving a steel stake into her own flesh. Pain was the most effective way to stop her heart and her body from being drawn to him. It would feel like an amputation without anesthetic, but based on her past experience, only hurt could heal hurt.

Luc was distracted at breakfast, and not only by the presence of a swarthy, inscrutable stranger at their beaten-up kitchen table. All attempts to get Pablo to talk had failed. He answered their polite questions with one-word answers and seemed completely unaware of the fact that his lack of effort was making everyone uncomfortable.

But Pablo was the least of his concerns. He was consumed by the need to make Sadie understand that no part of their kiss was about Stella. He couldn't bear her thinking that. The feel of Sadie in his arms had reverberated through him all night long.

To distract himself before he did or said something embarrassing, he glanced over at his father. Alphonse had the ability to draw out pretty much anybody, but with Pablo he'd met his match.

Alphonse had stopped eating and was sitting with his arms crossed, staring balefully at their visitor, while Pablo munched elegantly on a croissant, seemingly oblivious to the disbelief aimed at him.

Luc looked over at Raphael and his brother's brown eyes sparkled with mirth. They would have a good laugh about this after. It was a relief for Luc to find something funny, as he could barely sit still in his chair as he waited to see Sadie again.

Of course, the kiss had meant nothing. It *had* to mean nothing. Stella was the only woman who could stop Luc from becoming like his father and all the men in his family line. He was determined to make things better with Sadie. He hadn't quite figured out exactly how he was going to do that but held on to a wild hope that he would figure out a way when he saw her.

The problem was that their kiss felt like it meant something. More like everything if he was honest.

Sadie walked in then, looking every bit as perfectly herself as the night before. The memory of holding her ran through every muscle. He raked his hand through his hair. *Arrêt Luc. Arrêt, arrêt, arrêt.*

He tried to cudgel it into his brain that Sadie was off-limits and would forever remain that way.

It was only Stella who he couldn't hurt, so he needed to turn all this hunger back on her.

There she was, beside Sadie. How long had Stella been standing there for? Luc waited to feel something—he would be satisfied with even a fraction of the pull he felt with Sadie.

Sadie's twin was as beautiful as ever, blond hair in loose waves on her shoulders, huge turquoise eyes, full lips…she was every man's dream. He tried to imagine kissing her. Of course, it would be incredible.

Stella bestowed a dazzling smile on them. "Have you been behaving yourself Pablo?" she asked, laughter in her voice.

Pablo merely looked up at Stella and frowned. Luc stifled a

laugh, and Stella moved her gaze over to him, and gave him a complicitous wink.

"I know Pablo is not the most talkative of guests," Stella said. "But he's a brilliant photographer."

His family made reluctant noises of assent.

Luc flashed her a smile back. He *could* make this work. The most definitive way to make Sadie safe was to forge his relationship with Stella, as he'd been planning since he was seven. If only his body would obey his mind.

Sadie and Stella had to, of course, go around the table and with polite *bises* wish everyone at the table good morning.

Luc lost track of where Stella was as she went around the table, but his eyes never strayed far from Sadie. Her freckles stood out on her paler-than-usual face. The crease between her eyebrows hadn't been there the day before. As she neared him, Luc's ribs felt too small to contain his galloping heart.

Sadie leaned down and gave him a kiss in the air, not even touching his face with hers. A stray ringlet disobeyed, however, and fell forward to brush his jawbone. He caught a glimpse of her eyes just before she pulled away. *Zut.* He'd hurt her already. A frantic need to undo the pain he'd caused took hold of him. God, he was a complete mess.

Stella was right behind Sadie and her *bisous* were far more enthusiastic. Her skin smelled like expensive perfume. Still, her proximity didn't make his heart clench.

The only empty chairs were on either side of Luc. He turned to Sadie first as Pauline filled up the sisters' coffee bowls, but she was already deep in conversation with Raphael about the portfolio he was creating for the Angoulême comic book festival.

He turned to Stella as a default, his stomach sinking. It was torture to have Sadie beside him and not be able to talk to her, but he had to concentrate on Stella. "It's wonderful to have you back," he said to her. "Can you come with me to the Réveillon dinner at Cerise and Clovis's house tonight?"

Stella blinked. "Just you and me?"

"Well…no. There will be quite a few people, and Sadie of course."

"Oh." Stella's smile vanished. "I thought you'd promised me some time alone with you."

It was exactly what Luc had planned, so where had his enthusiasm gone? "I was hoping for that too," Luc said. "That's why I'm so thrilled you're back. It might not be tonight, but I'll make it happen, I promise you."

Stella smiled—objectively, a truly glorious sight. A man would be a fool to lack enthusiasm for such a woman. "I'd like that Luc."

"*Parfait*. How was Paris?"

"Fabulous!" Stella said. "I don't think I've ever drank so much Dom Perignon in my life. Pablo got some truly wonderful photos and, as you know, photos are the lifeblood of my brand."

He *didn't* know that, or maybe just hadn't bothered to think about it before. "How could anyone take a bad photo of you?" Luc said, trying to flick his flirting switch on. "I think that's impossible."

"That's true," she said, with no false modesty. "But I put a lot of thought into what I do. I'm running my own small business. Nobody really sees that part of it, behind the scenes."

"I'm looking forward to hearing more about that," Luc said. Usually he flirted on automatic pilot, but he was scrambling for things to say and his own voice sounded rusty and awkward.

"Really?" Stella narrowed her eyes at him. "Most men don't. Sadie has always been the clever one in the family. Everybody thought I was stupid."

Luc frowned at her. "I never thought you were stupid."

"Really?" She still looked skeptical.

"Of course not."

"But I'm still not as smart as Sadie."

Luc laughed. "That's not fair," he protested. "I don't know anyone as smart as Sadie."

"Hmmmm," Stella said, brushing her fingers up Luc's thigh. "Maybe I will prove you wrong. I'm talented in many other areas. Brilliant, some say."

Luc was acutely aware that Sadie and Raphael had taken a brief pause in their conversation, and that Sadie would hear what he said next.

"Ah," he said, trying to stay as evasive as possible. He felt Sadie flinch beside him.

His shoulders dropped. What an utter failure. He hadn't managed to take any of the hurt away from Sadie, and when Stella dragged her fingers up his leg, it left him absolutely cold.

He had to try harder.

chapter ten

AFTER BREAKFAST, STELLA and Pablo went back down to Beaune to take some more photos at Hotel Le Cep, the chicest address in an already chic town. Stella had obviously decided not to stay at the cottage in the room Pauline had so kindly readied for her. She hadn't informed anyone, in typical Stella style.

Sadie, though, was grateful to be alone as she flopped onto her bed, her heart still in her throat. She'd overheard enough of Luc and Stella flirting to know that Luc was well on his way to charming Stella as he'd always planned.

She should be happy about that, or at least relieved. She'd been far too hurt in her life to let herself care for a man who flitted from woman to woman. She needed someone dependable she could trust with her heart. Luc could never be that person, so why was a weight pressing down on her soul?

Enough of this moping around. She didn't even want Luc as more than a friend, so it was stupid to obsess over one mistaken kiss. She grabbed her laptop and opened her email. Her listlessness changed to shock as she read the top message—so much so that she forgot to breathe for a few seconds.

Without pausing to think of all the ramifications, she typed off a quick and definitive reply. Here was the rope she needed.

Excitement vibrating up her spine, she pushed her computer aside, and hurried out the door of the cottage and up to the forest behind the big house.

When she reached the remains of the Gallo-Roman wall that had first sparked her obsession with archeology, Sadie breathed in the familiar scent of the overhanging hazelnut trees. Their bendy branches had been perfect for making forts with Luc when they were little. She shivered—it probably would've been a good idea to grab a jacket before running up here, but she'd been too excited to think of that.

The rocks in the low wall were covered in moss. This was built so, so long ago to mark the old Roman road. Adrenaline whooshed through her limbs. The thrill of being able to touch something that had seen so many centuries and people go by never got old. Sadie dropped on all fours and began to crawl across the ground, carefully clearing away leaves and undergrowth with her bare hands as she went. Gloves might have been handy, too, come to think of it. The damp of the forest floor soaked into the knees of her jeans, but she didn't stop.

She cleared away a wet clump of leaves and her fingers hit something unyielding. She dug down a little further, dirt wedging deep under her fingernails. There it was, the top of a stone that poked through the dirt, then another beside it. She frantically dug some more. Another. It looked like a line of stones. She hungered to know what they were and how far down they went. She'd always had a hunch there was more to this area than just the wall, but she'd never had the means or the time to find out.

Now she did.

There was something to discover here. She was sure of it. Something that could be crucial to the understanding of Gallo-Roman civilization. Her pulse sped up. Finally, she had something to do, not to mention a possible way out of academic purgatory.

It was inconvenient that the dig site was on Luc's land, but there was no way around that. Besides, it gave her the opportunity to prove to both of them that they could go back to being friends despite that stupid mistake.

Of course, this site could be an illusion, just like her kiss with Luc the night before. *But no.* This was different. She splayed her fingers over the ground and smiled. This, at least, was solid ground she could depend on.

A rustle of leaves made her snap around. Luc appeared, stalking through the trees. He caught sight of her and froze, his face a picture of indecision.

Just friends. Sadie cleared her throat. "Based on your expression, I'm not going to accuse you of following me here."

Luc shook his head. He was bundled up in his heavy work coat and a scarf was wrapped several times around his neck. Sadie was struck by the memory of the warm, inviting scent of his throat. She bowed her head, staring at the rocks poking up from the ground, banishing this useless piece of knowledge.

"I had no idea you were up here," Luc said. "I'm sorry. I just needed to think away from the house. I received a worrisome call from the bank and Alphonse won't—". He waved his hand to dismiss that. "Often, I come here to be alone, or go to the *cabotte*."

"No need to apologize," Sadie said, leaning back on her haunches. "I'm trespassing on your property, not the other way around."

"You could never be a trespasser here." His eyes narrowed as he noticed that Sadie was sitting on the ground. "What are you doing down there?" His eyes roved over her. "Are you hurt?"

"No, *bétion,* I'm looking at this Gallo-Roman wall." It felt good to call him an idiot in the familiar Burgundy slang from their youth. Words like that between them created a safe distance.

"Of course." He didn't sound at all surprised. He knew her well enough not to be. "Look, about last night— "

Sadie held up her hand, palm out. "I don't think it would do any good to talk about it." She stood up and tried to brush the dirt and leaves off her jeans. "It happened. I was in a bad place. It was a mistake and that's that."

Luc's steady blue gaze searched her face for long enough to make her look down and pretend to be engrossed in rubbing the dirt off her hands. It didn't help when he looked at her like that.

"Right," he said, at last.

She couldn't let him see how that kiss still reverberated in her. "In fact, I did you a little favor this morning to show you there are no hard feelings." Her stomach filled with bitterness, but she couldn't quail.

"You did?"

"Yes. That's what friends do, right? I started to talk you up to Stella, and she sounded receptive." *There.* She straightened her spine.

Luc didn't respond right away, but when he did, he said, "You're a good friend."

Good. He believed her. She'd kept her dignity. She'd never be tempted to lose herself with Luc again. "I have a favor to ask in exchange."

Luc's face softened in a way that Sadie had to resist. "I would do anything for you Sadie. There's no need for an exchange."

She shook her head. "Humor me."

Luc frowned. "What's the favor?"

"Can I start a proper dig here?" Sadie pointed to the mossy ground. "I've always suspected this might be some sort of important halt on the old Roman road. Now is the perfect time for me, not to mention my career, to find out. It will all be done responsibly, of course," she added hastily. "I'll work alongside the museum in Nuits-Saint-Georges, but this is your family's property, so—"

"Of course you can."

Sadie laughed, shocked at the ease of his acceptance. "You can take a moment to think it over."

"I don't need a moment."

"But this land doesn't truly belong to you yet, does it? Alphonse is one of the most generous people I've ever met, but need I point out that he's a Burgundian, through and through? You know how you Burgundians are about your land."

In Burgundy, land was sacred. Alphonse was a typical Burgundian in that he would never consider selling or leasing the Domaine's land, and would be quick to take his shotgun off the rack from above the fireplace to defend it.

Once when she was nine Sadie had gone out rabbit hunting in the vineyards with Luc and Alphonse. Alphonse had spotted someone hunting in his vines and had begun to take potshots at him when the man refused to leave. Luc's father had seen it as an entirely legitimate way to defend his land and nobody in the family or the village had disapproved in the slightest. How was Luc going to convince him?

"I'll handle Alphonse," Luc scuffed the toe of his work boot in the dirt. "Don't worry about him. But isn't this a huge undertaking on your own? Digs usually involve a whole team of people, don't they?"

Sadie considered this. "Well, for one thing this is a relatively small-scale dig. Secondly, when I got back to the cottage last night after—". She swallowed.

Luc lifted an eyebrow. "You can mention it, you know. As I said, we should probably talk about—"

"Not necessary." She waved her hands. "A dumb mistake. I've already forgotten it." She'd never be ready to talk about that with Luc. "Anyway, when I got back to the cottage, I applied for a research grant offered by Cambridge University on a desperate whim. They emailed me back this morning to say I've been awarded the grant. I couldn't believe it. Things like that usually takes months, but this one is funded by an individual benefactor."

"Really? Who?"

"They've chosen to remain anonymous."

"That's wonderful. I'm happy for you Sadie. I knew you'd figure out a plan. You always do."

"I see it more as life throwing me a rope. Cambridge is sending the head of the grant program to do the dig with me, he's a professor of archeology there."

"That's *incroyable.*"

Sadie nodded. It truly was such incredible luck. "This may be my way back into doing a doctorate. I'm already fantasizing about the day I can throw my discoveries back in Professor Harris's face."

"That's an entirely laudable goal," Luc said, with that quirk to his mouth.

Luc wouldn't judge her appetite for revenge. Sadie wanted nothing better than to become successful enough that she could ruin Professor Harris, once and for all, and put a stop to his abuse. Only then would Gia and her friends get the justice they deserved.

"So an English guy will be coming over here?" Luc interrupted.

Sadie shook herself out of her revenge fantasies. "Yes. He has a ridiculously British name that made me laugh…what was it? Oh yeah. Frederick Fothergill. Have you ever heard anything so absurdly British?"

"I suppose he's ancient," Luc said. A strange observation, but most likely an accurate one.

"I'm sure he is. I tried to find a photo of him on the faculty website, but the buildings aren't the only thing that's ancient at Cambridge, apparently. Their website is atrocious. Anyway, most professors in archeology are well on their way to becoming fossils themselves. He would rent a place in Beaune, of course, and maybe I should stay in Beaune as well."

"Please stay here," Luc said, his features urgent. "Please stay in the cottage. That's what you would normally do without even thinking about it if it wasn't for—"

Sadie held up her hand again to stop him. "Like I said,

forgotten." She doubted she would ever forget their kiss, but she would rather die than let Luc know that.

Luc grimaced. "If you stay in the cottage, you would be close to the dig."

Proximity was a massive advantage. Digs needed protecting from many things—storms, wild boars, looters, partying teenagers—if she was close by, she could react quickly.

"All right," Sadie conceded. "If you're sure you don't mind me camping out in the cottage for a few months."

"I always love having you around Sadie," Luc said quietly. "You know that." He opened his mouth, then closed it again. "My whole family does. That thing 'you've already forgotten' doesn't change that."

The idea it hadn't changed anything between them was both a relief and a torture.

"Can you still come to the Réveillon dinner at Clovis and Cerise's tonight?" Luc asked.

The pity in his voice irked her. She wasn't nursing a broken heart. It was easier to be indignant than vulnerable, and she grabbed on to that gratefully.

"Why wouldn't I be? I need to witness this transformation in Clovis that you talked about."

Luc's shoulders dropped. "It'll be worth the price of admission, I promise you."

Sadie was only half listening to him, as she frowned down at the wall. "I'm still not convinced that Alphonse will agree to this easily. I applied for the dig grant on an impulse. I should have asked Alphonse myself. I apologize for that, but I was desperate."

Luc reached out as if to soothe away her worries but let his hand drop at the last moment. "Please don't worry about that Sadie. It will be fine. I'm just so glad that I can help in some way."

Ugh. Was that pity again? "I still think Alphonse won't like it."

"I'll go and talk to my father right now," said Luc. "But consider it done."

"I don't envy you that task. I would go and ask him myself to spare you."

Luc shook his head. "Let me do this for you Sadie. *S'il te plait.*"

Luc left Sadie in the forest, determined to bring Alphonse onside for the dig, no matter what it took. The spark in Sadie's eyes was back. He was prepared to do anything to ensure it stayed there.

Still, Sadie was right. Alphonse was not going to like it.

Sadie had seen only a glimpse of Alphonse's obsession with land. Luc often wondered if vineyard acquisition was the true motivation behind his parents' marriage. Many of the vineyards now owned by the family Domaine had been brought by Luc's mother into the marriage. Of course, in the traditional Burgundian way, they'd been signed over to Alphonse the day the wedding vows had been exchanged. Land consolidation was always the ultimate goal in wine country.

Was that why Pauline never dreamed of leaving Alphonse, despite his serial infidelity? He'd never been able to understand the dynamic between his parents, and never would. The world became a bewildering place that day he'd found out that his father wasn't the perfect God-like creature he'd believed him to be. Nothing had really made sense since then.

For a few years now, Luc had been trying to convince Alphonse to pass the reigns of the vineyards over to him. It's what Luc had been bred and trained for, after all.

Alphonse, however, was still reluctant to give up control. Luc was beginning to worry that it went beyond the normal resistance most of his fellow winemaking friends found when trying to wrest control from their parents.

His gut told him, as well as that call from the banker, that something was wrong with the Domaine finances, and that Alphonse was covering it up. Until Alphonse gave him control, Luc couldn't even look into it for himself to see where things stood.

He found Alphonse, as expected, deep in the Domaine's wine cellar, barrel tasting the previous year's vintage with a long glass tube called a *pipette.*

"Papa, I need to talk to you about something."

It was a good thing that Sadie had no idea what she was asking of Luc. It had never crossed his mind to refuse her, no matter what the cost. This dig was exactly what she needed. From the moment she asked, he knew he would move heaven and earth and, yes, even his truculent father, to make it possible for her.

Maybe he couldn't kiss her again, but he could do this.

"What do you want *mon fils*?" Alphonse grinned. "Trouble with the ladies? If so, you've come to the right person."

Mon Dieu, he was shameless. Like Luc, women threw themselves at Alphonse. With his reputation as a formidable lover well-established in the region, blatant invitations from lonely or frustrated women were never lacking. Alphonse was always ready to oblige.

"No," Luc said, curt.

"It was a silly question. You have my blood, so of course you don't have any such troubles with the fairer sex."

Alphonse was aware of Luc's conquests. Everyone was. He was clearly in a playful mood. Luc couldn't decide if this was good or bad.

"You're not going to like it," Luc warned him.

"Now, how can you assume that, son?"

Even though Alphonse was generally supportive and loving,

somehow everything that Luc needed for the Domaine—a modernized grape press, a new tractor, a labeling machine that actually worked—was a battle with his father. In the most charming way possible, Alphonse made simple things difficult.

Luc had even threatened to quit over it in the past. Somehow, and he was never quite certain how, Alphonse had always managed to guilt and jolly him into changing his mind. Lucky for Alphonse, Luc had a well-developed sense of duty to all his family members, and as the future head of the Domaine, they all depended on him. Alphonse knew this, and never failed to use Luc's own conscience as a weapon against him.

Luc squared his shoulders. "Sadie is going to conduct an archeological dig at the Gallo-Roman ruins up in the forest. You know, up by the old wall."

"She will do no such thing." Alphonse shook his head in disbelief. "I adore Sadie, of course. Who doesn't? She's a dear girl, but as for ripping up my forest and bringing strangers on our land? *Non*!" He dropped the glass pipette back in the barrel—not a good sign.

"She will," Luc said. "I gave her the right to do so."

"That was not your right to give." Alphonse's face hardened.

"It will be next year," Luc said. "Unless you're not a man of your word, and I know you are, *papa*. We made a deal for the Domaine to come under my control then, remember?"

Alphonse broke Luc's gaze. Had Alphonse forgotten, or did he have no intention of following through on that promise in the first place? Words were easy for Alphonse, but the follow through was often touch and go.

"That is still an ongoing discussion," he said. "Nothing definite has been decided."

"Yes, it has." As much as Luc loved Alphonse, lately Luc had been feeling more aggravation than affection for his father. "We agreed. We shook hands and everything."

"But Luc," Alphonse turned cajoling. "I don't want anyone to butcher the Domaine's land, even our lovely Sadie."

"She's not going to butcher it. She's an expert at her job. Also, just think—what if she discovers something of historical importance?"

Alphonse blanched.

Merde. He immediately realized his mistake. He'd said the worst possible thing.

"That's the last thing the Domaine needs!" Alphonse cried. "Strangers tramping all over our land to see some old Gallo-Roman ruins, and then the government deciding that the site is of such cultural value that they need to expropriate it from us." Alphonse shook his finger. "Remember what happened to my father!"

"How could I forget?" Luc and his siblings had grown up with the tale of how the village of Savigny had expropriated most of his grandfather's vineyards for a pittance to build a bunch of new houses for the village. It *had* been a terrible injustice—the value of the vineyards lost was mind-boggling now. It was a legitimate grievance that constantly gnawed on Alphonse's mind.

"Well!" Alphonse blew out a breath of disbelief. "Then I cannot even conceive how you would consider this folly."

"Sadie needs it," Luc said, bluntly. "And I need to give this to Sadie. What can I offer you in exchange?" He'd hoped it wouldn't come to this, but here they were.

Alphonse pursed his lips and didn't answer right away. "I want more time," he said, finally.

"More time for what?"

"I want more time to be in control of the Domaine, enough time for me to settle some things so everything is in excellent shape to pass on to you."

"What nonsense is this? What things? I'm here to help you with bank accounts and all that. You should never feel you need to work out problems without my help."

"I want three more years."

Luc took a step back. This was far worse than he'd imagined. "You mean I wouldn't get control for *four* more years?"

The extra years spooled out unbearably in Luc's mind. Worrying about his father's secrets with the Domaine finances was becoming tortuous, but what else could he do? He had to carry on for the family as well as his love of the land and his vineyards.

"Yes," Alphonse said. "And that would mean leaving me in peace to deal with the financial side of things the way I see fit."

"But Papa— "

"I mean it Luc. Do we have a deal? If you agree, I won't say a word about Sadie doing her dig. You can manage that directly with her."

"But—

"I feel it is more than a fair exchange."

"Can we compromise?"

"No. You know I can stop her dig with the snap of my fingers if I choose, Luc. I wouldn't even have to do it myself. I could call the necessary people to get her permanently tied up in paperwork and authorizations. Three years, or I do just that."

Blood pounded in his ears. His father had him over a barrel. Four more years of this same stagnation…but weighed against that was the sparkle in Sadie's eyes when she was crouched down beside that stone wall.

"Fine," he agreed. "But I never want Sadie to know anything about this agreement."

Alphonse made a theatrical gesture of zipping up his lips. "What agreement?" he said with a grin that made Luc feel he had borne more than enough for one day.

Luc would never tell Sadie, of course. The last thing he wanted or needed from Sadie was a sense of obligation. She deserved this chance, plain and simple. If fate wasn't going to reward her for all the good she put into the world, he would. It's what any good friend would do.

chapter eleven

IN HIS BEDROOM in a separate, distant wing of the house with its own entrance, which Luc had claimed as his own when he turned eighteen, he pulled out his gray chinos and blue button-down shirt from a huge wooden armoire that had been passed down in his mother's family for generations. Moving out of the main part of the house was part of the deal struck with his father when Luc agreed to stay on and eventually take over the Domaine.

Luc put on his shirt. It was one of those slim-cut styles. A past girlfriend had bought it for him as a gift because she said it matched his eyes.

He supposed he should be glad that Sadie had already forgotten about their kiss. He had to be.

She'd looked like some sort of forest creature crouched on the mossy earth beside the wall, yet another of their secret places as children. He'd had to fight the urge to join her on the ground with every fiber of his being.

Non! He raked a hand through his hair. He had to stop. His fingers were fumbling as he tried to button up the wrists of his shirt. He needed to be fantasizing about Stella, not Sadie. He and Sadie could never be. He and Stella *had* to be.

He sat down on the side of his bed, grabbed his phone, and went to Stella's Instagram account. There she was in Paris, dressed in a sumptuous ball gown with layer upon layer of pale pink chiffon, posing in front of the Eiffel Tower like something out of a fairy tale. A man would be crazy not to want such a divine creature as his own. She still epitomized the woman that every man wanted, which made her the only woman he knew that would prevent him from straying like his father.

Then why was he still so attracted to Sadie?

He dropped his head in his hands and groaned, his pants still lying on the duvet beside him. He had never wanted a woman on such a visceral level, especially not the woman that he could absolutely not, under any circumstances, have. Why Sadie? Why now?

He pulled his pants on and yanked a grey cashmere sweater over his head

He tried to push Sadie out of his mind by replacing her image with Stella. He checked Stella's Instagram again. That photo of her in Paris had hundreds of thousands of likes and countless gushing comments. Here was proof that she was the woman everyone wanted, a million times more than when he'd focused his future plans on her when he was seven.

It had to be Stella for him. He'd been planning this evening for ages. He'd already asked Clovis and Cerise to sit Stella beside him at their dinner, and he needed to use his time to show her what kind of life he could offer her—a beautiful home, financial security, emotional support and above all, fidelity. That was something he could *only* offer to Stella, according to Alphonse. So far, Luc had never had any reason not to believe his father.

He was fully aware that Stella might not want to be with him. She had her own life, after all, and she might not see his offer as enticing in the slightest. He had to try though. If she accepted him, he would spend his life trying to make her happy that she made that choice. She would be his savior—the only way for him to escape his own destructive tendencies—and in return he was determined to be hers as well.

Resolute about following through with his plans for Stella, Luc gave himself a last check in the mirror and walked through the house to the front hall. He took out his wool pea coat from the armoire and put it on.

He traced the seams of the old flagstones on the floor with his foot as he waited for Sadie. Sadie and Pablo were two obstacles he hadn't anticipated. So be it. He could manage them.

Surely his attraction to Stella would grow with time. She was beautiful, desired, and she was, after all, Sadie's twin. There had to be *something* there.

His parents were invited to another Réveillon dinner at their neighbor's house, and Raphael and Adèle had plans with friends. Tomorrow, of course, they would all spend Christmas day together.

He tried to drum up excitement about seeing Stella. They had planned to pick her and Pablo up at Hotel Le Cep in Beaune before heading back up to the Hautes-Côtes to Cerise's house.

When Clovis had moved from his prestigious Domaine in Morey-Saint-Denis to Cerise's home in les Haute-Côtes, everybody questioned his decision, but Clovis could be as unbiddable as he was rich and handsome. It was better for the children, he said, and he hadn't hesitated for a second.

Luc chuckled to himself, amused that his suave friend had become such a father hen. He'd never seen Clovis so contented. There was something tortured in Clovis that Luc innately recognized, but since Clovis moved in with Cerise, that tortured part of Clovis was just…gone. What a relief that would be.

Luc wanted that same transformation for himself. It was what he'd always expected to happen when he finally had Stella. That restless itch he and his father had, and apparently his grandfather and even his great-grandfather had, could only be cured by Stella. Clovis had managed it, so surely Luc could too?

The front door swung open and Luc looked up from the flagstones.

Sadie carried her jacket over her shoulder and was wearing a black wrap dress shot through with the occasional gold thread. The V of the wrapped material highlighted her creamy décolletage and stopped just under the knee in a swingy skirt. She'd paired it with tall black suede boots that looked as soft as butter. His mouth went as parched as the Sahara. *The things he wanted to do to her.*

He pulled the sides of his pea coat over his middle and buttoned it up to hide the evidence of his reaction to her. He desperately tried to conjure up mildew on vineyard leaves and his grandmother's chin whiskers.

It was no use.

Black washed most people out, but on Sadie it seemed like the most daring choice of all. It's very lack of color highlighted her pale, freckled skin and fiery hair, which hung down in lose curls. His fingers itched to bury themselves deep in those ringlets, then move down and feel every nuance of how the fabric hugged her curves. How could he have been so *blind* all these years?

"You're staring," Sadie said. "Is something wrong? Do I have a toothpaste on the side of my mouth?" She scrubbed the side of her mouth with her finger.

He swallowed. "No. You just look so beautiful." The words went from his heart to the air without Luc being able to stop them. *Wrong sister, Luc.*

Sadie's amber eyes flew to his and widened. She shook her head slightly—to herself or at him—he wasn't sure, but he received the message, loud and clear.

He couldn't go back down that road with Sadie. *Stella*, he tried to pound into his brain. *Stella, Stella, Stella.*

"Do these boots look OK?" She peered down at them. "I'm worried they're a bit too dominatrix."

He was blindsided by a vision of Sadie in only those boots,

or maybe those boots and the black coat she had slung over her shoulder with only her delicious freckled skin underneath. The air in the front hall thinned, as if all the oxygen were being pressed out of it. He was in dire need of a cold shower.

"Just the right amount of dominatrix," Luc somehow managed to say.

"Oh...well, good. I guess that's good?" Sadie's forehead puckered. "You haven't said anything about Alphonse and the dig yet. Is it bad news? If it is, just tell me. I can handle it."

The truth was Luc had completely forgotten about that. Sadie seemed to push everything else out of his mind. "Sorry! That should have been the first thing I said. It's fine. Alphonse has agreed and he charged me to oversee any property issues concerning your dig. You're free to start whenever."

A slow, beautiful smile grew on Sadie's face. It felt worth every second of those extra three years of indentured service he'd exchanged for her happiness. "Words feel completely insufficient, but I hope you know that you just saved me."

Luc shook his head. "You saved yourself."

Sadie looked like she wanted to say something else, but hesitated. Finally, she clicked her tongue. "We should go. We have to pick Stella and Pablo up. You know how she hates being kept waiting."

Luc grinned. "I wonder if Pablo will talk tonight."

"That *would* be a Christmas miracle."

Besides the lust, he just liked her so Goddamn much. He wished he were a different kind of man, one that deserved her.

For the first time ever, he wondered if the restlessness in him could be held at bay if he was with Sadie. Clovis had found contentment with Cerise, after all, and Cerise was not a Stella sort of woman. Still, Clovis did not have Luc's cursed blood running through his veins.

Even if Luc managed to stay faithful to Sadie, she would sense his underlying emptiness. It would break her heart. He felt like everything he'd always accepted as certain was crumbling under his feet. The only safe thing was to concentrate on practicalities.

He reached past Sadie and opened the front door. "It's cold outside," he said. "Why aren't you wearing your coat?"

"I was preoccupied with my whole boot situation."

"No need. Your boot situation is an unmitigated success." That was the understatement of the century. Luc made the mistake at glancing down at them again, and his mind filled with even more things he would like to do to Sadie with the boots still on. Getting out of the front hall, which seemed to have shrunk tenfold in size, would be a wise course of action. "Can I help you put your coat on?"

As soon as he asked it, he knew it was a dangerous idea—any proximity was. Still, he couldn't undo an upbringing that had emphasized good manners.

"Sure." Sadie passed Luc her coat. "It's heavy. Used to be my mother's, but it's the warmest thing I own, even if it probably smells like mothballs." She turned around so her back was facing him. Luc was grateful for the icy December air that rushed in the front door.

He closed the distance between them, holding the coat in front of him like a shield. He was so close to her that he could make out the hundreds of different shades of gold, russet, and auburn that made up her curls under the hall light. He couldn't resist inhaling, hoping that maybe with the coat on Sadie *would* smell like mothballs. That would certainly make his life easier. He breathed in her scent of vanilla and ink and moss after the rain. *Bordel.*

"You're doing that humming thing again," Sadie said.

He swallowed. He never realized when he was doing that around her. He had to stop. It was a dead giveaway.

"Right arm." He wanted to lift that heavy cascade of curls and kiss the nape of her delicate neck. Jealousy roared in his chest. He hated anyone who would have the privilege of doing that.

"Left arm," he said. Perspiration sprung out behind his ears. "There you go." He stepped back and fumbled in his coat pocket for the keys to the front door.

"Do you really need to lock it?" Sadie asked. "Your parents and Raphael and Adèle haven't left yet, have they?"

"Ah…no…you're right." He shook his head, hoping she didn't notice the flush of arousal he could feel under his skin. "*Stupide*."

Sadie chuckled as he ushered her out onto the porch. "And to think you haven't even drunk one of Clovis's deadly *apéritifs* yet."

He tried to laugh, but it sounded hollow. Tonight was supposed to be all about Stella, yet Sadie had so far occupied almost every thought. There was nothing amusing about the situation he was finding himself in.

In Luc's little black Renault he used when he wasn't working, Sadie felt desperate to shatter the tension between them. There were flashes of their familiar friendship, but they kept being interrupted by this new…whatever it was.

It didn't help that Luc looked so damn attractive dressed nicely. He was acting strangely preoccupied. Sadie hated the idea that it was probably because he was already strategizing how to win Stella over at the Réveillon dinner. She crossed her arms over her torso. She needed to get Luc out of her system.

As they drove through the winding streets of Savigny-les-Beaune and past the castle at the entrance to the village that sat like something sprouted straight out of a Grimm's Fairy tale, Sadie turned to Luc, trying not to be overwhelmed by the sheer perfection of his profile in the yellow light of the street lamps. "So, who exactly is going to be there?"

Luc touched the bump on his nose, something he did when he was thinking. Why had she never realized how endearing that was? "Well, you know the gorgeous Clovis, *bien sûr*."

Cerise heaved a sigh. "He's a hard one for any woman to forget."

A muscle jumped in Luc's jaw.

"Then there's Cerise, the new love of his life. She's a brilliant winemaker."

"She didn't go to Saint-Coeur, did she?"

Luc shook his head. "No, otherwise you would have known her."

"Okay, who else?"

"She has two sons from her first marriage, Marc and Yves. There will also be Clovis's daughter Emily, who lives in Britain with her mother."

"Right. Hard to believe all of this, but you told me about her. It sounds like a complicated family situation." The lights of Beaune lit up the sky in the distance.

"It is, yet somehow it works beautifully. I guess that's what happens when you meet your soul mate."

"You believe in soul mates?" Sadie turned in her seat to watch Luc. She'd never heard him talk about relationships in such terms.

Luc's mouth twisted into a bitter grimace. "For other people, *oui*."

There it was, the truth, reverberating like a blow to the gut. Luc was a man who was damaged goods, commitment-wise. Finding out about his father's extracurricular activities had broken him.

Sadie cleared her throat. "Who else?"

"Hmmm...Gaspard and Amandine, *bien sûr*."

"And they'll end up fighting at some point." Sadie always enjoyed those two, but could never figure out, ever since they'd all been in elementary school together, whether they were in fact mortal enemies or kindred spirits.

"Always. Did you know they were actually engaged last year?"

"No!" Sadie gasped. "Why is this the first I'm hearing of this?"

Luc grinned at her shock. "It lasted about a millisecond, so I guess I forgot to tell you. They had a huge blow up and called it off. Neither Clovis nor I have been able to weasel the details out of them."

Sadie sat back in her seat, her mind spinning. *Engaged? Those two?*

"And Jean will be there," Luc added.

Sadie smiled at the thought of the manager of Clovis's Domaine du Valois, called the "*régisseur*" in Burgundy. Her father and Jean had become fast friends during their three years in Burgundy. She'd always felt a connection with Jean, almost as if he was another father figure. His kindness was extraordinary, as well as his patience with an overeager, inquisitive red-headed girl.

"It's going to be strange seeing him for the first time since my father died."

Luc reached over and squeezed her knee. She knew it was meant to be a comforting gesture, but somehow, sparks jettisoned up and down her entire body. "That won't be easy for you."

Sadie swallowed the lump in her throat. After she collected herself, she said, "So, that's all? Anyone else?"

"I imagine Cerise's aunt Geneviève and her uncle will be there too," Luc said. "Geneviève is a character. She never leaves anyone lukewarm. You'll either love her or hate her."

They drove around the Place Carnot in Beaune, just around the corner from Stella's hotel, Le Cep.

"I've been told I have that effect on people," Sadie said. "At work I can be 'demanding and perfectionist' according to some student reviews. I hope the person they send over from Cambridge for the dig doesn't feel the same way."

Luc sent Sadie a speculative look that sent waves of warmth up her spine. “I don’t believe it,” he said. “How could anyone not love you?”

chapter twelve

AT THE HOTEL, they waited for Stella and Pablo to emerge from the elevator doors. Her sister was late, as usual.

Luc tapped his foot on the marble floor of the reception lounge. Sadie could feel the nervous energy radiating off him in waves. He was no doubt stressed about winning over Stella. Sadie's heart in her chest felt like it was made of lead.

As for Sadie, she expected Stella's tardiness in the same way she expected guy friends, work colleagues, and pretty much every person Stella crossed paths with to fall instantly under Stella's spell.

Years before, ever since that day with the *galette*, Sadie had adjusted her expectations to avoid being hurt. Disappointment lived in that gap between expectations and reality. Here was a perfect example. She didn't expect Stella to be on time, so she wasn't particularly upset by her lateness now. Yet again, no expectations meant no pain.

When the elevator doors finally opened and Stella emerged, Sadie watched as Luc stared at her sister. She had the odd impression that it was like someone had a hand on the back of Luc's head and was forcing him to stare…but then again who didn't stare at Stella? Sadie's nails dug into her palms. She needed to do a better job of lowering her expectations about Luc. They clearly were not low enough.

Surely seeing Luc and Stella together was what she needed to cure her of that kiss. It was the type of cure that might almost kill her, but so be it. One side benefit of being Stella's twin was that she'd been training in emotional toughness her whole life.

The couple in the wingchairs near the crackling fire and the man behind the reception desk, as well as the bellhop, stopped what they were doing and stared at Stella. As usual, she was dressed to encourage attention.

She wore a short slinky sequined dress in a wash of rainbow colors paired with vertiginous stilettos. Stella's makeup was air-brushed to perfection with a delicate sparkle on her eyelids. Her hair fell in cascading waves.

Sadie had to admire her sister's skill with things like makeup and hair—she knew better than anyone that as much as her hair was curly, Stella's was naturally straight. That took some skill.

All Sadie did before she left the house was swipe on a coat of mascara from a tube that had probably expired two years before.

Pablo was dressed in a suit that was so slim cut Sadie wondered how he was going to sit at the dinner table without his pants splitting. Hopefully the shiny material contained some spandex. He was surrounded by a cloud of musky cologne and his hair looked wet with some gel-like substance. He didn't smile at them or say bonjour. He just stood beside Stella, his features utterly impassive. Maybe he'd recently overdone it with the Botox?

"What, no camera?" Sadie asked him, seeing if she could get him to move his face. Stella certainly looked ready for a photo shoot, but then again, when didn't she?

Stella answered for Pablo, in English. "Not tonight. I doubt everyone at the dinner is looking photo ready. She looked pointedly at Sadie when she said that. Sadie sighed. She'd thought she'd washed up fairly well before she'd seen Stella.

"Are we ready to go?" Luc said, opening the hotel door to

the rue Maufoux. Thanks to Stella and Pablo, they were already running late.

Stella climbed into the front seat of Luc's car without asking if anyone else wanted it. She giggled. "My legs are twice the length of Sadie's, so I always get the front."

Luc held the back door open for Sadie and she slid in the backseat beside Pablo. Good. She wasn't really in the mood for chitchat.

Luc settled in behind the steering wheel. He cleared his throat and turned to Stella. "You look beautiful," he said to her.

Stella winked back at him. "I know." She flipped her hair. "I made a special effort for you."

"It was worth it."

Sadie's chest felt heavier. This dinner couldn't be over soon enough. She wanted to be digging in the dirt under the trees in the forest. She wanted to be anywhere but watching Luc and Stella flirt in the front seat of the car. Sadie stared out the window, the distance between her and Luc growing by the second. Why did something so necessary feel so wretched?

They pulled up inside the gravel courtyard of Domaine du Cerisier in the Hautes Côtes—a beautiful rolling area above the prestigious Côte de Nuits and Côte de Beaune. The wine from these hills was traditionally less prestigious and less costly, but according to Luc, Cerise was making something extraordinary with it.

Sadie wouldn't quite believe Clovis had settled down until she saw it with her own eyes. It was easier to think about that than Stella and Luc in the front seat and silent Pablo beside her.

Even as a young child, Clovis had been so beautiful it was almost ludicrous—he was insanely wealthy too. He'd always kept mostly to himself. Sadie had always sensed a core of sadness in him, something akin to what she felt in Luc since he'd discovered his father's infidelity.

People had always wanted to be Clovis's friend or, later on, more than that, but Sadie knew that Clovis only kept a core group of people around him—Luc, Gaspard, Amandine, and of course Jean. That was it. The idea that he would let in a new person, let alone a new person and their children, in any permanent way was astounding.

She couldn't get out of Luc's car fast enough. Her boots crunched on the pea gravel as she crossed the courtyard. Welcoming light spilled out the windows of the big house. Even from the outside, the place gave off a feeling of being a home.

Stella and Luc walked in front of her, Stella holding on to his arm as she teetered like a fawn with her high heels in the gravel. They giggled as she struggled and finally Luc scooped her up and carried her. Stella threw her head back and shrieked with laughter. She'd always been full of light-hearted fun in a way that Sadie, obsessed with "old stones and dead people" as Stella phrased it, could never be. Sadie couldn't seem to catch her breath in the frigid air.

She just had to survive the dinner. The only way to the other side was through—a side where the sight of Luc and Stella together left her unruffled.

The front door opened and Luc, despite Stella's playful protests, set her down on the front porch. First, Sadie just saw empty space beyond Stella and Luc, then she looked down and was rewarded with the impish face of a little boy dressed in a suit and a red bow tie. His rich brown eyes were full of excitement.

"*Bonsoir*," he said, with considerable ceremony. "*Bienvenue au Domaine du Cerisier*"

Stella giggled again, which made the little boy frown at her, his dignity patently offended.

Luc stuck out his hand. "Bonsoir Yves. *Joyeux Réveillon*. You look very smart this evening."

Yves accepted Luc's hand and shook it manfully. "Clovis put me in charge of the door because I'm charming."

They crowded into the front hall. Yves shut the door behind them.

"I'm not about to argue with that," Luc said. "Yves, I'd like to introduce you to Stella, Sadie, and Pablo."

"Welcome to our home." Yves lifted his chin. "May I take your coats?" Luc looked down skeptically. Sadie knew exactly what he was thinking. Yves was small and the winter coats were heavy. "I'm going to keep mine for a while," Luc said. "Caught a chill on the way here."

Stella, on the other hand, plopped her faux fur coat in Yves's outstretched arms, as did Pablo.

"I'm going to keep mine too," Sadie said, enchanted by Yves. "Cold out there."

"Suit yourself," Yves said and trotted off, his small frame almost submerged with coats.

Luckily, there was a coat rack just to the right of the entrance. Luc tugged on the back of Sadie's coat and she let him slip it off. He hung their coats up on the rack and gave her a wink.

She didn't have time to respond, because Stella linked her arm around Luc's and dragged him forward over the beautiful flagstones and past the staircase decorated with fresh holly and twinkling lights.

"Now," Stella said, stroking Luc's forearm. "Let's make our grand entrance."

Sadie, along with the impassive Pablo, followed Luc and Stella into the living room which was full of books and huge, slouchy couches covered in linen slipcovers. It was decorated to the nines with a Christmas tree in the corner full of children's crafts and a hodgepodge of ornaments. It was the kind of completely uncoordinated Christmas tree that Sadie had always loved, one that spoke of family history and love. It was not the style of Christmas tree she ever would have associated with Clovis, but she was starting to wonder if maybe she'd never truly known him.

The room was empty of people, but there was a rumble of voices coming from further back in the house.

"Ah." Luc lifted an index finger. "They're all in the kitchen."

Stella nestled closer to Luc and Sadie felt a punch of pain, as though her heart was being ripped out of her chest. Pablo, in his usual anti-social manner, sat down on one of the couches, picked up a heavy picture book about Burgundy, and began leafing through it.

Sadie opened her mouth to say something, but Pablo was Stella's responsibility, not hers. She left him there and trailed after Stella and Luc, the golden couple. They wound through the dining room that boasted a beautifully set and decorated table full of children's crafts, like a lopsided, wax-dipped pinecone that served as a candle in the middle.

Finally, they arrived in the kitchen. It was hot and full of steam, people, and the delicious smell of brioche and chestnuts—an excellent distraction from the sight of Stella glued to Luc's side.

"Is that my Sadie?" A shout came from her left. Sadie turned to see a familiar figure coming towards her with his arms outstretched. She could never mistake those bright blue eyes.

"Jean!" she cried and fell into his arms. Normally she should give him the *bises* as a greeting, but she desperately needed one of his hugs. He hugged her back as she clung on to him like a buoy in an ocean storm.

After a while, she forced herself to ease her grip. Jean held her at arm's length, studying her face, the same way Luc had at the airport. "What's wrong Sadie?"

She shook her head. "I'm fine."

Jean narrowed his eyes. "You're not, but perhaps tonight isn't the time or the place to delve into that. Will you come and visit me at the Domaine du Valois? I'd love a good chat and a catch up. You know I'm always here for you, *n'est-ce pas*? Especially now that your father has left us."

Sadie nodded, blinking away the tears that had gathered in her eyes. "*Merci*. I know Jean. I'll definitely come and visit you."

"*Fantastique ma belle*." He smiled into her face, and something in his azure gaze steadied her.

"Can I drive the tractor when I come visit?" Sadie asked, grinning at him.

"You don't even need to ask." Jean pinched Sadie's chin. "Best tractor driver I ever trained."

Jean looked over at Luc, who had miraculously detached himself from Stella, and was making his way through the chaos and steam of the kitchen towards them.

"Luc!" Jean said, with genuine affection in his eyes.

Luc put out his hand and then, surprising Sadie, leaned over and placed an enthusiastic kiss on each of Jean's ruddy cheeks. "It's Christmas, after all," Luc said with a grin.

Jean's face was infused with pleasure, making his white head of hair look even more striking. "That it is, my boy, that it is."

"Luc!" Sadie stood on her tiptoes to see who was calling and saw Clovis waving Luc over with a wooden spoon. "Is that Sadie you've got there?" Clovis was stationed in front of a gorgeous pale blue Lacanche stove.

"Go say bonjour to your host." Jean winked at them, then gave them a nudge in Clovis's direction.

As they got closer, Sadie saw that Clovis was wearing an apron that had "*Crème de la Crème*" written in sequined cursive on the front. Luc was right—Clovis was clearly a changed man. The was no way he'd have been caught dead in that apron before. He wore oven mitts emblazoned with tiny red Christmas trees and had a baster in his hand. "You made it!"

He was still every bit as gorgeous, even more so. The alienating perfection of his face and body looked somehow more worn in, softened. His hair was a bit shaggy, there were laugh lines in the corner of his eyes that hadn't been there before, and his face was not only flushed from the heat but suffused with a contagious sort of joy. He kissed them both and gave them an awkward group hug, while trying not to let the turkey juice drip on them.

Envy for what Clovis had so clearly found struck her like a fist in the gut. Luc had been right. Clovis had changed. She understood a little better why Luc had been struck with the urgent need to settle down as well.

"I'm sorry we're late," Luc began. "We had to…ah Cerise!"

A petite, raven haired woman with brilliant dark eyes and a pudding spoon in her hand came up behind Clovis. "No apologies needed between friends," she said. "Besides, we're running late… like one hour, would you say?" she asked, looking up into Clovis face and smiling. Something passed between them in a private, unspoken language which ignited a wave of longing in Sadie. She just knew that the two of them must share private jokes, long kisses and their worries.

Clovis shrugged. "Maybe two? Honestly, who's counting? He leaned down and gave her a kiss.

After, Luc gave Cerise *les bises*. Before he could make the introduction between Cerise and Sadie, Stella materialized and grabbed Luc's arm again. Sadie was overcome with the need to escape somewhere else, but it would be rude not to stay and be introduced at least.

"Cerise," Luc said. "I'd like you to meet Stella and Sadie."

Stella was still holding tight to his arm, but she looked a bit dazed, as though she might actually need it for support. Everyone was speaking in rapid-fire French, and Stella had perhaps not been lying about hers being rusty. Sadie always chalked that up to laziness, but the truth was that Stella had always struggled at school, both at home in New York and in France. Maybe she truly *was* feeling lost?

But then Clovis and Cerise exchanged a loaded, knowing look, one that swept away any sympathy Sadie was feeling for Stella. She knew with certainty from that look that Luc had already confided to his friends his plans to make Stella his.

"Pleased to meet you, Stella," Cerise moved forward to give both of them *les bises*. "And you, Sadie." She leaned back against Clovis.

He slung a still oven-mitted arm over her shoulders. "So, you finally decided to grace us with your presence, Stella," he said.

Stella fluttered her eyelashes at him. "Yes, I thought it was about time."

Clovis's eyes shifted between Luc and Stella. "Ah," he said. "I see."

"I heard you domesticated the formidable Clovis." Sadie smiled at Cerise. "I could scarcely believe it when Luc told me."

"Or he domesticated me," Cerise said. "It went both ways."

"Believe it." Clovis must have overheard and gazed down at Cerise. "I've never been happier. Turns out all I needed was my soulmate and a passel of children."

"And that apron," Cerise laughed, looking pointedly at the *Crème de la Crème* sequins reflecting the ceiling lights.

"Well, of course my happiness would not be complete without this apron Yves chose for me."

"You wear it well," Sadie grinned. She wanted what they had, so badly that she ached with it.

Cerise smiled back at Sadie. Sadie felt an instant connection with her.

"Thank you, Sadie," Clovis said. "I rather do, if I say so myself."

"It's an absolute delight to meet you, Cerise, and I'm assuming that proficient little welcoming committee was Yves?" Sadie said, as Stella hung back close to Luc.

Cerise grinned. "Yes. He adores getting dressed up and hosting."

"He did an excellent job."

"I'll pass that on. Come with me." Cerise grabbed her arm and steered her to the other clusters of people in the kitchen. "I'll introduce you to everyone else, while Clovis deals with his turkey."

And leave Luc alone with Stella.

chapter thirteen

MORE THAN TWO hours and several traditional Burgundian kir served with bubbly *crémant* later, everyone finally sat down at the long monastery table.

Cerise had taken Sadie over to reunite and catch up with Gaspard and Amandine, connected by their mutual antagonism as always, then introduced her to her aunt and uncle, Clovis's daughter Emily, and her older son Marc. Sadie's head was spinning and not only from the heady effects of the potent cocktails.

Clovis, assisted by Marc and Emily, distributed the first course plates—*foie gras* along with toasted triangles of brioche and a dab of fig jam. Cerise tried to help him but her four-month pregnant belly was beginning to show and Clovis guilted her into sitting down and letting herself be served.

Emily, Clovis's daughter, was a quirky little thing with flyaway pigtails and Clovis's stunning eyes. Marc was the most serious of the three children, and he and Sadie had enjoyed a fascinating conversation about the various Gallo-Roman sites in the immediate vicinity. That boy knew his history.

The food in front of her was mouth-watering, and she was sitting beside Cerise, Amandine and Gaspard, who were all excellent company. Thank God, because Sadie needed a distraction from the sight of Luc and Stella seated side by side near the middle of the table. Clovis and Cerise, seemingly well-informed of Luc's plans for Stella, had engineered the seating plan accordingly.

Pablo had been put on the other side of Stella, but he apparently had no need for conversation as he delicately consumed his food and wine. Poor Jean was on the other side of Pablo. Luckily, Cerise's Aunt Geneviève was livening things up on the other side of Jean.

Cerise leaned towards Sadie and said in a low voice. "Tell me about Pablo."

"Yes, do." Amandine leaned forward. "Handsome, but a man of few words, I see. Still, I wouldn't kick him out of bed."

Gaspard glowered at Amandine, but Amandine ignored him.

"I wish I could, but I can't," Sadie admitted. "I've barely said two words to the guy. I have no idea why Stella thinks it's fine to drag him along everywhere, but often Stella...well, she's never been very good at reading a room. Let's put it that way."

Cerise peeked around Sadie to get a better look at the trifecta of Luc, Stella, and Pablo. "I imagine Stella gets away with a lot of things." She clapped her hand over her mouth. "*Merde.* I'm sorry I said that. For a second there I forget she was your sister. I'm an only child, you know, so—"

Sadie laughed, her mood buoyed by the silky texture of the foie gras melting on her tongue. "Don't worry about it. Lots of people forget we're sisters. We're nothing alike, even beyond the obvious differences. As for Pablo, he's ostensibly traveling with Stella as her photographer, but he's the most anti-social person I've ever met, and I work in academia.

"Maybe he's cultivating the '*artiste*' image?" Cerise speared a slice of foie gras with her fork.

Sadie shrugged. "If so, it's comes across as pretentious rather than impressive. I feel bad for Luc and his family, and now you and Clovis, that Stella has foisted Pablo on you."

Stella and Luc had their heads together, chuckling about something.

"I'll say this for them," Amandine said finally. "They make a beautiful couple."

"I think they're all wrong," Gaspard said. "It will never work."

Sadie was quickly reminded that despite his loyalty and good heart, Gaspard had always been blunt, to put it mildly.

"That's because you don't have a romantic bone in your body." Amandine rolled her eyes.

Gaspard responded with an eminently French shrug.

How could these two have been engaged for any amount of time, no matter how short? Talk about a disastrous pairing.

"Luc told us about Stella a while ago," Cerise admitted as Clovis filled each of their white wine glasses up with a honey-toned Sauternes to go with the *foie gras*. He kissed Cerise's head in passing, and Sadie felt that tug of envy again.

"Did he?" Sadie tried to sound detached.

"*Oui*." A line appeared between Cerise's finely etched brows.

"Oh my God, did he ever," Amandine added. "He became extremely boring about it. All he ever wanted to do was talk to us about Stella and show us photos of her stupid Instagram account."

That's right. Amandine was blunt, too.

"He seems hell-bent on marrying her," she continued. "As if she was the only woman in the world for him. I didn't get it then, and I don't now. I mean, your sister is clearly stunning, but—"

"Like I said," Gaspard interrupted. "It will never work, no matter how badly Luc wants it to."

"I don't know about that," Cerise said, thoughtfully. "We can never truly understand what goes on in someone else's heart."

Luc had a heart, but did Stella?

"You really believe they're a good match?" Gaspard demanded, with something close to a sneer.

"I have no idea," Cerise said. "But I have to admit that I

thought maybe I'd understand Luc's fixation when I met your sister in person, Sadie, but I still don't. He certainly looks under her spell, though."

Stella and Luc still hadn't looked up from each other to talk to anyone else. Ugh. Sadie hated that she noticed.

Fixation. Sadie took a moment to let that word sink into her heart. *Use that pain. It will rebuild your armor.*

Her throat scratched and she cleared it. "Luc's always been in love with her, ever since we were seven."

"Maybe," Cerise said. "But from what I know of Luc, it doesn't seem as though they have much in common. Luc is just so inherently kind. He's one of the main reasons that Clovis and I ended up together, you know."

Luc was kind, but he was also weird about women. "That doesn't surprise me, but he's always been screwed up about his own relationships. Also, Stella isn't a bad person."

Cerise, Amandine, and Gaspard wore matching skeptical expressions. Gaspard pursed his lips. "Maybe not bad, but I get the impression she's a very *selfish* person."

"Gaspard!" Amandine slapped his hand. "That's like the pot calling the kettle black, besides being an incredibly rude thing to say."

Gaspard blinked at Sadie. "You know me, Sadie. I can't *not* tell the truth. Do you hate me, too?"

Sadie couldn't help but smile. Gaspard's honesty wasn't always easy to hear, but it never failed to add an interesting astringency to conversations. "No, and you're not completely wrong. Stella can be a bit self-centered, but she's had people catering to her smallest wishes her entire life. To be fair, how could she have turned out otherwise?"

Cerise nodded. "Good point."

"Besides, she's full of charisma and fun and adventure. It's not as if she has nothing to offer Luc, besides her looks."

Amandine and Cerise exchanged a look. "*On verra*," they both said at almost the same time. *We'll see.*

Sadie had talked about Stella and Luc quite enough for one night. A change of subject was well overdue. She clinked her wineglass against Cerise's. "Clovis is so content. I'm thrilled for both of you. Congratulations on the baby, by the way."

Cerise slid her hand protectively over her rounded stomach. "Thank you. We're both so excited and don't even get me started on Marc and Yves and Emily—they're beside themselves. This true love thing." She looked back speculatively at Stella teasing Luc. "It's terrifying, but it's worth it, you know."

Sadie shrugged. "I've been preoccupied with my academic work, so I haven't had much time for that."

Clovis joined them for a few minutes to finish his plate, and Sadie took the break in conversation to savor the amazing combination of the silky, *foie gras*, the sweet fig jam, and the crunchy, yet soft, bite of the toasted brioche, washed down by mouthfuls of a honeyed Sauternes wine. No one could knock Réveillon dinner out of the park like the French.

"Luc told us how smart you were," Cerise said, after Clovis hopped up to offer seconds to everyone. "You make him very, very proud."

Sadie felt heat rushing up her face—completely inappropriate when discussing a mere friend.

They began talking about Sadie's work, and she found herself confiding in Cerise about her career suicide. She didn't usually open up to people this quickly, especially not about so painful a topic, but something told her Cerise would understand without plunging into pity. She struck Sadie as a highly pragmatic person.

The courses kept rolling out of the kitchen. A turkey with chestnut stuffing and delicious sauce, a gargantuan cheese platter, three different flavors of *bûche de noel*, then finally, espresso and chocolate.

"I have to get you to talk to my boys," Cerise said. "Especially Marc. He is obsessed with history and archeology.

"Oh, we've already had a chat." Sadie smiled. "Earlier, in the kitchen. He blew my mind with what he knows already."

Cerise's face flushed with pride. "Marc is a thinker. I worry sometimes that he's too clever for his own good."

Luc must have finally emerged from his Stella spell, because he called down the table. "Sadie was just like that! She was always first in the class at Saint-Coeur, even in her second language, and she was one of the youngest students to ever get into a doctoral program in her field and— "

"What about my followers?" Stella interrupted. "Why don't you ever boast about me?" She poked his side, a little too hard for it to be just playful.

"Um…well Sadie and I talk a lot about her work," Luc said. "We don't talk about your job very much."

Stella pouted. "We should."

Luc smiled at her. "You're right, of course." He turned back to Stella and said something to her in a lower voice.

Cerise looked at Sadie, her brows raised at Stella's behavior. Sadie flushed with embarrassment that Stella surely didn't feel. Stella was seemingly born without a filter between her thoughts and her words. Sadie never knew if it was some sort of social blind spot or just plain narcissism, but she wasn't going to make excuses for her twin.

Before she could think of a way to change the topic of conversation, the wax covered pinecone candle that was lit in the middle of the table exploded with a loud pop. Everyone yelped. Glowing cinders floated in the air for a moment, then fell down on the people closest, including Stella.

"It's singeing my dress!" She screamed and hopped up from the table, trying to tap it out with her hands.

"Are you hurt?" Luc hopped up and swatted the glowing embers with his napkin.

"Stop! That's not helping!" Stella shrieked. "This dress is couture! It's ruined!"

"Maybe we can fix it," Luc said, taking her arm. "As long as you're not burned."

"Didn't you hear what I said?" Stella yelled. "This dress is from the Fall Chanel line. It's irreplaceable."

Emily was standing across the table from Stella, staring at her with huge eyes and trembling from head to toe.

Luc exchanged a glance with Sadie. He'd seen Emily too. Sadie was certain Emily had made the pinecone candle. Luc had to get Stella out of the room.

"Why would someone put such an ugly thing like that hideous, lumpy wax pinecone on a beautiful Christmas table anyway?" Stella cried. *Too late.*

Emily looked down at the floor. "I made it at school," she said, in a quiet, clear voice. "I brought it from England for Papa and Cerise."

Stella narrowed her eyes at the little girl, tossed her head, and stormed out of the room. After hesitating for a few seconds, Luc followed her.

Sadie reached behind her and took Emily's hand. "I loved it, Emily," she said. "Don't mind my sister. She'll be sorry for her tantrum, I'm sure of it."

"I didn't know it was going to explode," Emily said, her voice watery.

"Of course, you didn't," Sadie said. "That was just bad luck. It *was* pretty awesome though—better than fireworks."

A dimple flashed in Emily's cheek. "Fireworks," she whispered to herself in a low voice.

"It was glorious," Sadie whispered back. "And don't worry about Stella's dress. She has hundreds of other ones."

"Are you sure?" Emily said.

"Positive. Let me tell you the story about my mother trying to bake a Christmas turkey in a brown paper bag."

Emily perched on Cerise's lap while she listened intently to the story, laughing until Luc and Stella returned to the room. Stella didn't exactly look happy, but her pouting expression indicated she was slightly chastened. What had Luc said to her?

Luc nudged her. "I'm sorry I yelled," Stella said. "I was surprised." But she didn't sound sorry. She sounded petulant.

Luc patted her back. "*Merci*," he mouthed to her. Sadie blinked. He forgave her so much. Didn't he realize he was condemning himself to a lifetime of making excuses for her?

"But this dress *is* couture," Stella mumbled under her breath, but loud enough that everyone heard.

Sadie was mute with shame for her sister, but she was even more embarrassed on behalf of Luc for pinning his future and his hopes on such a woman.

chapter fourteen

LUC WOKE UP the next morning with dread weighing him down like a lead blanket. Christmas morning, and nothing was working out the way he'd planned.

His family, contrary to many of their countrymen, had the tradition of opening their presents on Christmas morning rather than on Christmas Eve.

After dropping off Pablo and Stella at Le Cep on the way home from dinner, Sadie had barely said a word to him in the car. She said she was tired, but Luc knew that she had been holding herself a million miles away from him. He hated it, but he could hardly blame her. Kissing her and then making a fool of himself over her sister, who had acted appallingly towards Clovis, Cerise, and worst of all, *la pétite* Emily.

Or maybe just making a fool of himself, period. The evening hadn't gone at all as he had planned. Stella and he were very much treated as a couple, and Stella seemed, for once, interested in playing her part. But there was the problem—that was exactly what it had felt like for him—like he'd been play-acting his interest in her.

He kept waiting for the spark he'd felt with Sadie. Perhaps he expected it would come with someone so objectively beautiful and coveted, but it just…hadn't. And when she'd screamed about the candle and made Emily feel badly, well, enough was enough.

He'd taken Stella into the living room and told her, rather crossly if truth be told, that it was an accident, and that she owed Emily an apology. No matter what Stella was or wasn't to him, he was not going to let her get away with upsetting a child.

He had to face the facts. The more time he spent with Stella, the more the shine came off his "dream woman". His stomach churned with confusion. Where was the Stella of his daydreams and future plans? He'd begun to wonder if she'd been a figment of his imagination all along.

Today, they would all be together. He needed to get Stella alone, to see for sure whether her behavior and his lack of interest at the Réveillon had been a fluke. Stella had been the dream of his boyhood. His life plan made sense with her as a solution to his infidelity problems. If he let go of that, what was he to become?

When he arrived in the living room, showered and dressed, the family was already assembled on the couches and chairs around the Christmas tree. The air was perfumed with the scent of thin orange slices decorating the tree boughs. Tiny lit candles shimmered in there as well, yet all of he could think about was that unforgettable kiss he'd shared on the couch with Sadie.

He wished everyone a *Joyeux Noel* and did the round of *bisous*. Blessedly, Pablo seemed to have opted out of the Ocquidant family Christmas, unless he was lurking somewhere in the kitchen or behind the tree, or God forbid in their cellars, but Luc didn't really care enough to find out. Sadie didn't meet his eyes and gave him the briefest of pecks. He deserved that.

Stella lost no time in commanding the attention of the room, declaring in a penetrating voice that she had brought everyone gifts from Paris. She stood up and with some blatant grandstanding distributed the fancily wrapped packages. Stella hadn't been this hungry for attention when she was a child—what happened to make her this way? Luc couldn't believe it was innate.

Everyone began to unwrap their packages, and shortly after the air was filled with ooohs and aaahs.

She'd bought Pauline and Adèle lovey silk Hermès scarves, a silk pocket handkerchief set from Louis Vuitton for Alphonse, which pleased him greatly, and one for Raphael, which didn't please him at all. Still, nobody could fault Stella for a lack of generosity. Surely that was an attractive feature in a woman?

Sadie opened her shiny box and took out a slinky Versace evening dress that consisted more of fabric cut-outs than actual fabric. Luc watched Sadie trying to school her expression into something grateful with a sinking heart. He was trying so hard to give Stella the benefit of the doubt, but there was no excuse for misjudging her sister so badly.

Sadie would have loved a fossil or a new history book or a warm cashmere scarf, but not a slinky evening dress. Not that Sadie wouldn't look phenomenal in it. She absolutely would, but she would also be uncomfortable. One of the things he loved best about Sadie is that she'd always been so resolutely herself.

Anyway, she didn't need a brand name dress to look sexy. As far as he was concerned, Sadie looked sexy all the time.

Jesus. *What*? He had to get his head screwed on right.

Sadie's face flushed. "Thank you, but I'm not you Stella. I don't really have many occasions to wear this type of dress. How about I give it back to you?"

Stella stared at Sadie, blinking. "How can you not like it? I've been lusting after it for a month. I got you the best present of *all* Sadie."

Sadie looked down at the meager scraps of fabric that made up the dress in her lap. "I don't doubt that your intention was sincere," she said. "But if you love it, it would make me happy if you took it and wore it."

"But—"

"And when you do, you can think of your twin sister, happy in her mud and work boots."

Stella reached out and snatched away the dress, muttering something indecipherable under her breath. "That means I don't have anything for you."

"That's okay," Sadie said softly. "We're here together. Isn't that enough?"

Stella sniffed. "Luc! You haven't opened your present yet!"

Luc tried to muster up some enthusiasm. He opened the rectangular, ornately wrapped package.

He slid out a Louis Vuitton man purse, complete with a strap. It had that ubiquitous and, as far as Luc was concerned, vulgar, LV logo splashed all over the leather. Pablo would love this. Maybe Stella had mixed up her presents? Now it was Luc's turn to school his face. It was not exactly the sort of thing that he could easily wear to the wine co-op amongst the other winemakers, just like Sadie couldn't wear her couture dress on an archeological dig. He caught Sadie's eye, and she clapped a hand over her mouth to stifle a laugh.

"Don't you love it?" Stella asked, as Luc saw Adèle and Raphael collapsing in mirth behind her at the sight of Luc holding his very own designer purse. So…no mix-up with Pablo's present then.

"*Oui, bien sûr.*" It must have cost a fortune.

"Don't talk French to me Luc." Stella shook a finger at him, playful. "We talked about this, remember? Do you already have one?"

"A purse?" Luc asked, watching Adèle and Raphael clutch each other's arms in silent convulsions. "No. I don't happen to have one." He was amazed he managed to answer that with a straight face.

Stella clapped her hands together. "Wonderful! You'll see how handy it is. I don't know what I'd do without a purse. Besides, in France it's fine for men to wear them too. I've seen that myself."

Luc caught Sadie's eyes again. She rolled them towards the ceiling.

The rest of the presents felt a bit anticlimactic after that, but Sadie was thrilled with the sharp set of trowels and brushes Luc had collected for her dig. They were all tools used in the vineyards, but it had occurred to him that they were different sizes and shapes than she might find elsewhere and might come in handy for her imminent dig.

He loved the wool scarf she'd bought him in New York. It would be perfect for pruning in the frigid winter weather. Stella might not know him…yet, but Sadie always had.

Stella liked the Chanel perfume he had bought her, but he could see a little pout when she opened it. It was probably a very small present compared to the ones she'd bought everyone. The thing is his family had never gone into grandiose gifts—the focal point of Christmas had always been the shared meal.

Their spheres were so different. Why had that never occurred to him until now? He needed to get her alone to see if he could muster up that passion he should be feeling for her—to see if they could ever work. He couldn't continue this charade any longer. The make-or-break moment with Stella had arrived. He sensed that with every cell in his body. But if it turned out they weren't compatible, what would his life look like then?

Was he doomed to be like his father, hurting his future wife with his constant straying? He had to give this thing with Stella one last try. He couldn't let Sadie get into his head. He could never have her, no matter what happened with Stella, so he just needed to forget about how it felt to have her in his arms.

Seeing as Pablo wasn't lurking around for once, he had a brief window of opportunity. No time like the present, as Jean always quipped when faced with an unenviable task.

Luc knew his moment had come when Stella started to

complain of being cold—not surprising, as she was wearing a short, silky dress—not exactly cozy Christmas attire.

"Stella." He stood up and beckoned her. "Come with me. You can borrow one of my sweaters. I even have some cashmere ones."

"You mean to your bedroom?" She smiled.

"Yes." He couldn't bear to look at Sadie.

"It won't go with my outfit!" Stella said, but she tapped his hand playfully.

"You're among family now," he smiled, again feeling like he was a bad actor in an even worse play. "Nobody minds."

"I mind," She said archly.

"At least you won't be cold. Come." Luc took Stella's hand, and she followed him with a backward glance at Sadie. Sadie was busy examining her new tools—she didn't look up at them, not once.

Stella followed him silently through the hallways and the stairs, until they reached his wing of the house. He opened the door to his room and shut it behind her.

Her blue eyes opened wide. "Why are you shutting the door Luc?" Something in her voice gave him a hunch that she was acting too.

He waited for that sense of urgency he felt with Sadie, that magnetic pull so strong that resisting it made him ache. *This* was the moment he'd been fantasizing about for the majority of his life—the moment when he and Stella would finally get together, and the moment she would fix the thing he hated most about himself.

Suddenly, it dawned on him that perhaps it was not a particularly wise thing to let his life be driven by an idea forged when he was seven years old. It was now or never. He took a step closer and Stella giggled. That was a bit off-putting to say the least, but he would not be deterred. He needed to know.

He wrapped his arms around her, and it was…awkward. He'd

never been unsure about how his body should fit with another woman's, but of course he was nervous. This was Stella, after all.

As he drew her closer and she went loose to allow him, none of the angles felt right. She wrapped her arms around his neck, but her elbow jutted into his collarbone, and he couldn't figure out how to tilt his mouth to fit hers. The rhythm of his heart was completely, disappointingly regular.

He somehow managed to touch her lips with his and waited for that spark. One second. Two. Three. She moved her lips over his, but his overpowering reaction was a strong desire to stop kissing her. There was nothing there.

He stepped back. Now his heart was beating fast, but for all the wrong reasons. If Stella couldn't fix him, then could anything, or was he condemned to choose between a life without marriage or children or a lifetime of following in his father's footsteps?

"What?" Stella lifted up her hands. "Why did you stop?"

He dug his hands in his pockets, not sure how to articulate what he was feeling without offending her. Surely, though, it hadn't been good for her either. "Ah…how did that feel for you?"

Stella pursed her lips. "I don't know…fine. I've had worse kisses, trust me."

"But it wasn't great," Luc said, trying to fill in the blanks she left.

"If it wasn't great, it certainly wasn't *my* fault!" She tapped her chest with her palm.

Luc shook his head. "Of course it wasn't. It was me…" Sadie had ruined him with that kiss. He thought of telling Stella about Sadie, and how his heart felt like it was going to explode whenever he was near her, but no. No good could come from that. "I'm in a strange place."

That was a lame excuse, but it was also completely accurate.

Stella narrowed her eyes. "There can't be another woman,

because—" She waved her hand up and down her body, encompassing her appearance. "*C'mon.*"

Luc just chuckled. If Stella knew who the other woman was, she probably wouldn't believe him. How could he have harbored such a deluded fantasy for so many years? He finally understood why Sadie called him an idiot for loving Stella. It was completely nonsensical—why had he never seen that clearly until now? How could he still be holding on to some idiotic thing his father had told him when he was seven?

He didn't know the exact answer to that, but it likely had something to do with how deeply traumatized he'd been at the time.

"We should get back to the party," Luc said, going to his armoire, unlocking it, and passing a black cashmere sweater over to Stella. "Here you go, as promised. I can't let my guests come down with pneumonia."

Stella's shoulders dropped. "I'm confused." She took the sweater.

"So am I," Luc said. "So that makes two of us. Let's go back to the others."

Later that night, Sadie sat on the couch with her laptop on her lap, ostensibly doing research for the dig. She'd still been unable to find out much information about Dr. Frederick Fothergill, who would be arriving the next day to begin the dig with her. All her searches had resulted in the same basic information about his academic career. No photos. No details about age or anything else.

She couldn't just blame it on the terrible website at Cambridge. Dr. Fothergill seemed to be almost as mysterious as Batman.

Wondering about that helped her mind push aside the torture of being in the same room with Luc and Stella all day.

Her fingers shook with anger still. She couldn't seem to turn off her mind that kept circling back to the feel of his mouth against hers, to that electrifying connection between them. *Damn him.* Then there was the matter of what had happened when Luc had taken Stella to his bedroom…

The mere idea he could be comparing her and Stella made bile rise in her throat. It was her own damn fault for being weak. She had learned to stay away from Stella's suitors, and now she was getting payback for breaking her self-imposed rule.

Stella banged in the door.

Sadie opened it and frowned at her. "I thought Luc had driven you to Beaune already. Poor Pablo must be lonely."

"Pablo is fine on his own."

"Really? He doesn't strike me as very entertaining company."

Stella shook her head, and from the way she flounced over beside where Sadie was "working," Sadie could tell she was in a troublesome mood.

She leaned forward towards Sadie. "Actually," she said in a breathy voice. "I'm going to leave with Pablo early tomorrow morning to get content in other parts of Europe."

"You're not staying longer here? But I thought—"

Stella pouted. "I just can't stay Sadie. After what happened in the bedroom with Luc and me."

Sadie knew Stella was dying for her to beg for the details, but she would never.

"He's just too in love with me Sadie." Stella pouted. "He came on so strong. I have to give myself some time to think. Distance would be good."

So Luc did go through with it. Sadie hadn't realized until that moment that she'd been entertaining the hope that he wouldn't. "You're not going back to New York?"

Stella flipped up her hand. "Pablo and I figured while we're here, we might as well get as much content as we can. Besides, the world is my home. You know that Sadie."

She was still reeling at the fact that Luc had thrown himself at Stella. A sharp point of pain pierced her breastbone. "Yeah. OK. Right."

"The thing is I lost my bank card in Paris and I was wondering if you could loan me some cash. You know, just until I get a new card reissued."

Sadie looked at her sister, wondering. "What about Pablo? Doesn't he have money?"

"Well, if you're going to be like that after the dress I bought you—". Stella stood up and let out a beleaguered sigh.

Should she be worried about Stella? She'd never asked Sadie for money before.

Stella began to tap her foot. "Fine," Sadie said. "I guess that's what sisters do, but I only have three hundred Euros in cash, and I was planning on using that for equipment."

"Perfect!" Stella said, and as soon as Sadie gave her the money, she wrapped her arms around Sadie and clung on for an unusually long time.

What was going on?

"Stella," Sadie said. "Are you sure you're all right? I'm here for you, you know."

"What are you talking about?" Stella shook her head. "I'm amazing, as always. Try to comfort Luc for me, will you? He's going to be devastated I'm gone."

chapter fifteen

LUC WALKED INTO the kitchen in the morning, relieved that Stella had left.

He woke up to an echoing void where his future mapped-out life used to be, but it was better than trying to force himself to love someone who was wrong for him in every way. He tried to comprehend how he'd hung on to his fixation with Stella since he was seven. It was probably due to the fact that he'd barely seen her, and when he did, only in passing or on the carefully curated squares of her Instagram account.

In any case, grief at the wretched, desperate boy he'd been when he found out about Alphonse tugged at his heart. Now that he saw that trauma clearly, perhaps he could make better sense of it with adult eyes.

He wasn't expecting to find anyone up this early in the morning, but his heart sunk when he caught the familiar sight of his mother facing the sink, rigid as a statue. Luc knew that stance far too well. Damn Alphonse.

"*Maman.*" He rushed over to put his arms around her. "Is it *Papa* again?"

She turned an ashen face to him. "It's not his fault, Luc, but it's the *boulangère* that I have to see every day when I pick up the baguettes."

Luc held her tighter. "Look, I'll talk to him."

Pauline looked up then, startled. "No Luc, under no circumstances should you mention this to him. I forbid it."

"But *Maman*."

"*Non*! This conquest is particularly embarrassing, but what I'm mainly upset about is that your father acts like this because he's in terrible pain."

"What?" Luc had heard this before, but his mother's excuses for his father were incomprehensible. "That's ridiculous. You have to stop justifying his behavior."

"Luc, this is between your father and me. You have no idea what's really going on."

Luc sucked in a breath of disbelief. "Yes, I do! Everyone in the region sees exactly what's going on. How you put up with it—"

"Luc!" His mother said, her voice sharp. "Let me handle your father, *s'il te plait*." She dried her hands, straightened her shoulders, and gave him a peck on the cheek. "There's coffee ready for you."

She left, and Luc stood staring out the window to the vat room beyond. No matter what happened with Sadie, he couldn't risk truly being together with her. He couldn't imagine wanting any other woman, but could he be sure about that, carrying Alphonse's blood as he did? Sadie deserved a man who never wanted to be with anyone but her.

Sadie crept towards the kitchen as quietly as she could. She had to be up early to pick up Dr. Fothergill from the train station and she needed to borrow a car, but she still didn't want to wake the whole family who were probably sleeping in after Christmas.

She stopped at the open door to the kitchen and shrunk back when she saw Luc comforting his mother, who was bracing herself in front of the kitchen sink.

"But *Maman*...," she heard Luc plead. Pain pulled on Luc's features, still desperate to fix an unfixable situation, as he'd been since he'd found out about Alphonse.

It must have been horrendous for Luc to see his mother humiliated like this since he was seven, yet powerless to do anything about it.

Sadie took a silent step back and then another, until she found a hiding place in a bend to the hall where she waited until she heard Pauline leave.

Only then did she swing into the kitchen.

"*Bonjour*," she said to Luc and grabbed a Duralex bowl of coffee from the coffee maker. She sipped it, eyeing Luc over the brim. He turned, his eyes stormy with confusion and hurt. Even if he was madly in love with her sister, her heart reached out to him.

"Did you just come in now?" he asked.

"Yup." She stepped forward and gave him the customary peck on each cheek. She wanted more than anything to wrap her arms around him, but the idea that he'd had his arms around Stella the day before was enough to dampen that urge. *No.*

He cleared his throat and gave her a long look. "Where are you going?"

Sadie was nicely dressed in another knit dress, this time forest green, with those suede boots. She was aiming for a combination of elegant and approachable.

"I'm going to pick up Dr. Fothergill at the train station." She grimaced as she remembered she needed another favor. "Any chance I can borrow your car?"

"He's arriving already?" Luc asked. "Today?"

Sadie nodded. "No time to lose with things that have been buried in the ground for centuries." She grinned, but Luc either didn't get the joke, or was still too preoccupied with his parents, or maybe upset that Stella had left. The last one was probably it. Stella had warned her he'd be devastated.

"What time?"

Sadie checked her thin, silver wristwatch. "His train from Lille arrives in about forty-five minutes, but you know me and driving a stick-shift. I should probably give myself plenty of time."

"Are you going to burn out my clutch again?" There it was, the glimmer of a smile. Luc rinsed his coffee bowl in the sink and put it on the drying rack. "I'll drive you."

"Now that's unfair. I never *completely* burned it out. I just finished the job."

"And the scratches?"

That was more like it. They were acting like friends again. "I only scratched it once." In fact, she'd rear-ended a parking pole.

He laughed. Now there was a welcome sound. "If I remember correctly, I had to replace the left rear light, the entire bumper, as well as get a brand-new clutch."

She clicked her tongue. "I've never known you to hold a grudge Luc."

"Maybe not," he said. "But I'm also not known for making the same mistake twice."

"I don't want to take up your time. In my experience, trains in France are late, even when they're not on strike. Who knows when you'll be able to get back out to the vineyards?"

"It would be my pleasure to drive you Sadie," he said with mock grandeur. "Besides, your professor is most likely one hundred years old and shouldn't really be carrying luggage. We don't want him expiring of a heart attack on the train platform, before we can even get him up here to the dig site, now, do we?"

"I guess you're right," she said. "How could Dr. Fothergill not be one hundred with a name like Dr. Fothergill?"

Luc tilted his head. "Goes without saying."

Sadie sighed as she rinsed out her bowl. "*D'accord.* If you don't mind coming, I'd appreciate the help." She pushed herself off the counter and executed a self-deprecating spin. "Am I making a good first impression, or do I look like a woman who torpedoed her academic career back in New York?"

Luc blinked. "You look like you Sadie."

Sometimes, it was like Luc spoke in riddles. "What is that supposed to mean?"

"It means you look perfect."

Sadie stuck out her tongue at him. "Only Stella looks perfect. The rest of us mere mortals have to satisfy ourselves with passable. *On y va*?" she said, tilting her head towards the door. "Can't be late. Dr. Fothergill administers my grant. I have to make a good first impression."

"You will," Luc said. "Like I said, perfect." He grabbed his keys from the shelf near the back door.

If she was so perfect, why was he still so stuck on her twin?

They arrived at the train station a few minutes early and stood on the platform, waiting to catch their first glimpse of Dr. Fothergill. Sadie shifted from foot to foot, trying to keep from shivering. Even her mother's wool coat was not warm enough in the biting cold of late December in Burgundy.

"Take my coat," Luc said, and already had it half off.

Sadie pushed it back on him again. "Thanks, but it would completely ruin my outfit. Remember, first impressions?"

Sadie shook her hand after touching him. That damned bolt

of warmth, despite whatever happened between him and Stella. She was pathetic.

"So, you've never seen a photo of this guy?" Luc asked. "How is that even possible in this day and age?"

"I'll be asking him that," she said.

"How will you know who to look for?"

Sadie should be troubled by that, but she wasn't. She was far more troubled by Luc standing beside her on the platform, his hair glinting in the late December sun, his long, firm body like the proverbial tall, cool drink of water she hadn't stopped thirsting for, despite her best efforts.

She'd been trying so hard to turn off that switch that Luc's kiss had flipped on in her brain. She yearned for things to go back to that easy friendship they had had between them. Still, something fundamental had changed—a piece between them that she couldn't slot back, no matter how hard she tried.

"He's a Cambridge professor," she said to Luc. "No doubt he'll be wearing a dusty tweed jacket with suede patches on the elbows and walking with some sort of cane. He'll stick out like a sore thumb."

Luc chuckled low in his throat, a sound so enticing that Sadie wanted to move closer to feel it against her ear, or better yet, her lips.

"How excited are you about this dig?" Luc asked. "On a scale of one to ten?"

"About one thousand." She looked up at Luc. "I still can't believe your father agreed to it." Something about the apparent ease of that still nagged at her. "I need to know how you convinced him," she said. "You know, so I can sleep at night."

"It was nothing." Luc winked at her, but a muscle twitched in his jaw. It hadn't been nothing. "I have my ways of getting around my father."

Sadie knew all about Luc's well-concealed stubborn streak. She wouldn't get anything out of him. Not right now anyway. Fine. She could bide her time. He may be stubborn, but she was tenacious.

"I know I've said it already but thank you. If this site yields what I think it will, not only will it contribute to historical knowledge of Gallo-Roman civilization, but it will be preserved—"

Luc stopped her by reaching out and touching her hand, his fingers lingering on hers. "You sound like a talking brochure, *ma Sadie*. I hope you don't think I need convincing."

She swayed at the electric current of his touch. "It's just weird being so much in your debt."

"You're not in my debt. I didn't do it for the value of the historical research or cultural preservation, although those are nice benefits." The corner of his mouth quirked, but his eyes were calm and serious. "I did it for you."

Her throat thickened with emotion. His fingers were still touching her hand. All she could do without losing herself to this tumult of sensations was nod and whisper, "*Merci.* You don't know how much this means to me."

Luc smiled down at her, a smile full of tenderness, and something else she couldn't put her finger on. "I have a good idea. That's why I did it. Don't you worry for a second more about Alphonse."

The tracks started to vibrate. Luc's fingers dropped from hers. It was a good thing because she needed to focus. It was imperative that Dr. Fothergill took her seriously as an academic.

Luc squinted into the distance. "Where did Dr. Fothergill have to change trains, again?"

"Lille and Dijon. He's obviously been to France before, because it sounded from his emails like he was familiar with the available train connections."

"At his age, one would hope he's been able to see a bit of the world."

As the train pulled into the station with a rumble, it became far too noisy to talk. They waited as the TGV pulled to a complete stop with a metallic screech that made Sadie wince. The doors depressurized with a puff, then slid open. She didn't know which train car Dr. Fothergill was in, so all they could do was wait on the platform.

"How much do you want to bet he smokes a pipe?" Luc rubbed his hands together.

"I'm sure not going to bet that he doesn't."

"Spoilsport."

"More like too smart to let myself be fleeced." Passengers streamed out of the train doors, but so far, there were no wizened professor-types amongst them.

Sadie started to look back and forth on both sides of the platform. "I don't know where he—" she began but was stopped short by a tap on her shoulder.

She whipped around to see one of the handsomest men she'd ever been privileged to share air with—he was right up there with Luc and Clovis. He wore a tweed jacket, but that was the only thing she and Luc had gotten right. The tweed was paired with perfectly worn blue jeans and leather work boots and an untucked white shirt. Sadie never dreamed a tweed jacket could look so *hot.*

"*Merde.* How could I forget about Indiana Jones?" she heard Luc whisper under his breath in French.

Dr. Fothergill's glossy dark brown hair curled over his collar in the back. Sadie's senses were full of this, his weathered olive complexion, and his coal black eyes.

"Dr. Fothergill?" Sadie asked, still not believing this specimen of perfection had such a fuddy-duddy name.

He stuck out his hand to Sadie. "Yes, but please call me Frederick. Fothergill is such a mouthful."

Sadie laughed and shook it. His grip was firm and pleasant. "How did you know it was me?"

"Yes," Luc said, his eyes narrowing at Dr. Fothergill... Frederick. "How did you know Sadie?"

Luc's English sounded even more stilted than usual.

Frederick's beautifully sculpted lips twisted in a rueful smile. "I suppose I should confess to a little bit of internet research. I'm sorry, Ms. Coleman, but you are quite simply unmissable. I've been following your career closely ever since reading your brilliant paper on Gallo-Roman sanctuaries and the dearth of spiritual artifacts."

"Really?" Sadie, not surprisingly, found her voice coming out quite breathlessly. "Please, call me Sadie."

"Your argument, that the syncretism of pre-Christian Roman Gaul beliefs was not lesser because of the lack of relics found was daring, not to mention convincing."

He'd read her papers?

Out of the corner of her eye, Sadie saw Luc's hands clench into fists, then unclench again, something he'd done since he was a boy to calm himself down.

Sadie turned back to Frederick. Luc had had no compunction about turning to Stella, after all. "Why couldn't I find any photos of you on the internet? It was the strangest thing."

"I work hard to stay anonymous."

That didn't satisfy her. Why did he want to be anonymous, in contrast with almost every other professor she knew who was constantly seeking notoriety that would bring in grant money? She'd have to delve into that later. "You're not *at all* what I expected," Sadie said, instead.

Frederick laughed. "Dare I ask what you *did* expect?"

Sadie found herself sharing his smile. It was impossible to resist Frederick's charm, so why bother? After all, they would be working together for the next few months, and he could be the perfect person to cure her of her inconvenient feelings for Luc. "Definitely more Albert Einstein than Indiana Jones. Oh, this is my friend Luc Ocquidant," she said. "He's a wonderful winemaker and the dig site is on his family's property."

Frederick smiled and stuck out his hand. Luc hesitated a few seconds longer than was polite enough to shake it.

"*Bonjour*," Frederick said.

Luc merely nodded. His lips stayed in a firm, straight line.

Sadie stared at her friend. Where were his manners? He was acting jealous, but how could he be? He loved Stella. They'd gone into his bedroom, and he'd made such an overpowering declaration of his love.

"I cannot thank you enough for this opportunity," Frederick said, transferring his smile back to Sadie. "Your email fell like a gift from the sky. Sadie, I've been following your work, ever since I read your paper on the terra-cotta lamps found in Eastern Gaulle. What a privilege to be able to do a dig here in this area of the Côte D'Or." He looked back and forth between Luc and Sadie. "How do you two know each other, again?"

Sadie looked up at Luc. "Oh, Luc and I go way back. We're childhood friends. More like brother and sister, actually."

Luc flinched. *What was going on with him?* He couldn't have it both ways.

"How charming," Frederick said in the plumiest of British accents.

Luc dug his hands deep in the pockets of his jeans. "Let's head back up," he said, his usually clear brow stormy. "I need to get back out to the vineyards. Sadie can show you around, Frederick. By the way, where are you staying?"

"Hotel Le Cep," Frederick answered, "I've stayed there a few times in the past."

Luckily, Stella had already checked out. Still, how could an academic afford to stay in the most expensive hotel in town? Professors, even gorgeous ones, were not known for their flush bank accounts.

"Is it all right if I call you Sadie?" Frederick asked her, as they moved slowly towards the stairs taking them back to the main terminal.

Luc started stalking ahead, and Sadie and Frederick were falling farther and farther behind him.

"Yes, as I said, I prefer it." She smiled at him. She noted Frederick was doing a fine job carrying his own medium-sized leather suitcase. "We're going to become familiar, working with each other day in and day out in the mud. I just hope it doesn't snow."

"Me too. Where will you be staying, Sadie?"

Luc had paused for a second for them to catch up, just in time to hear Frederick's question.

"Sadie is staying with me," Luc snapped. "At my Domaine, like she always does when she's in Burgundy."

"Ah," Frederick said, unperturbed by Luc's boorish behavior. "Perfect. How wonderful that one of us will be so close to the site."

Luc took off again down the stairs.

"Sorry for his mood," Sadie whispered to Frederick. "You wouldn't know it from today, but he's usually quite charming."

"He strikes me as very...er...possessive of you."

"Maybe, but just as friends." Sadie felt a spurt of anger. "He's been in love with my twin sister since we were all seven."

"Really?" Frederick regarded Sadie with a speculative glance.

"Yes. We'll drop you off at the hotel and then perhaps I can pick you up after lunch to take you up to the Domaine?"

Frederick waved a hand, adorned with a heavy gold signet ring. "I've arranged for a car rental with the hotel. It will be waiting there for me. I can drive up. Say, two o'clock?"

"Perfect," Sadie said. "I thought professors were supposed to be absent-minded?"

Frederick chuckled. "Are you?"

"No, but I'm not a fully-fledged professor yet. Not quite, anyway." Sadie wondered how much, if anything, Frederick knew about what had gone down at Hudson.

"That will happen sooner rather than later, I'm sure. Anyway, being absent-minded is terribly selfish don't you think? It would mean forcing the people around me to pick up the slack, and one thing I cannot abide is rude people."

Then what must he be thinking of Luc? She didn't even know what to think herself.

chapter sixteen

AFTER DROPPING FREDERICK off at the Hotel Le Cep, Sadie and Luc drove back to Savigny. Luc could tell from the way she twisted her curls around her finger and gritted her teeth that she was furious with him. He didn't know where this seething jealousy had come from, but it still hadn't left.

When Sadie climbed out of the car at the Domaine, she went over to him and caught his arm. She clearly had no intention of letting him off the hook.

"Frederick wasn't what we suspected, so what? That's no excuse for your behavior."

Well, she wasn't the only one who was simmering with anger. He knew it was completely unreasonable, but he couldn't seem to help himself. How dare that man be allowed to spend whole days with Sadie on the dig? How dare he be so young, and with a profile like a Grecian God? Luc felt duped, but at least had the sense to realize that he needed to be alone until his common sense returned. Until he did that, he didn't even trust himself to open his mouth.

"Say something and stop acting like a Gallic rooster." Sadie stood in front of him, her eyes sparking and her fists clenched at her sides. God, how he wanted to gather her up in his arms and kidnap her so he didn't have to share her with Frederick.

"What's the big deal?" she continued. "There's a handsome guy on your turf, but I never took you for such a caveman. Are you worried Stella will come back and fall in love with him?"

Did Stella not tell Sadie what had happened in his bedroom, how the kiss had closed the door on any possibility of a future together?

He couldn't let Sadie think that, even if he hadn't calmed down. "No! I know I can be a short-sighted idiot, but you've got it all wrong." He searched for the right words. "I'm *not* a caveman," He said desperately, but realized how lame it sounded after it had escaped his lips.

"Well, you're acting like one! If it's not jealousy about Stella, who's not even *here*, why are you acting like such a jerk?"

Because I'm in love with you. Luc shook his head. He couldn't tell her that. At first glance he'd immediately identified Frederick as a threat, someone who could take Sadie away from him, but wasn't that what he wanted for her happiness in his more noble moments? He tried but couldn't seem to summon even a scrap of nobility when it came to Sadie anymore. It was drowned in his desire for her. His mind spun with contradictions.

"I don't trust him, Sadie." Even he could hear how ridiculous he sounded.

Sadie burst into laughter, but it had a sharp edge. "*Mon dieu,* Luc. Sure, maybe there's his weird thing about privacy, but if I think he's legit, who are you to judge?"

"No photos on the internet, Sadie. It's suspicious."

Sadie crossed her arms in front of her torso and narrowed her eyes. "Good God, you're ridiculous. This is what gets you into trouble with women. You have to have every woman adore you, all the time. You're no better than your father."

Luc gasped. That was the lowest blow—she knew it tapped into his deepest fear. He and Sadie never fought like this. He could tell from the way that she wasn't blinking, and how her freckles stood out starkly on her skin, that she'd never been this angry with him. Maybe it was happening because they'd never been able to finish what they'd started with that kiss. Maybe they should. He reached for her, then was stopped by the sight of Sadie's bottom lip trembling.

Just like that, she broke through all his fury.

How could he have acted in such a way that he could have potentially jeopardized Sadie's career, after all she'd been through? A wave of guilt crashed over him. He'd pushed her to the breaking point and he'd never forgive himself.

"Jesus, I'm so sorry Sadie." Luc crushed her against him. "I'm acting like an idiot. I didn't mean to embarrass you."

At first Sadie remained stiff as a board, then Luc's breath caught as he felt all the fight go out of her muscles. She melted against him, and it felt astonishingly good—warm and soft and perfect. Thank God she could still draw comfort from his presence and not just aggravation.

Luc smoothed down her hair and whispered a stream of apologies in the shell of her ear. What he couldn't tell her is that she didn't understand, she didn't understand at all.

His reaction had nothing to do with ego, and everything to do with how his feelings for his best friend had changed completely. He was so bewildered to be burning with jealousy over Sadie. He didn't understand himself, so how could he possibly hope to explain himself to her?

He took her face in his hands. "Am I forgiven?" The tracks of tears on her face squeezed his heart. He was a monster for making her cry. His thumbs awkwardly tried to brush her tears away. That overpowering need to comfort her gripped him.

"No Sadie," he said. "Sadie, *mon amour*, don't cry because of me. Please. I never wanted to hurt you." Words didn't feel like enough, even though he'd just called her 'my love', so he leaned forward and tried to communicate what was in his heart with light kisses landing on her soft lips like butterflies. Her fingers dug into his back, and their tongues touched. After that, he was lost.

He spun her around and backed her against the side of his Renault, worshiping her precious face with his lips, his hands traveling up and down her body, relentlessly trying to communicate how much he cherished her. Need for Sadie pulsed in every cell. That magical connection they'd always had expanded to contain both of them and everything around them—the metal of his car door, the roar of a tractor driving up to the vineyards, the silver sky above—everything about this moment was as it should be. He wanted to inhabit this sense of rightness as deeply and completely as possible and exist there forever.

"Luc!" his father's voice boomed out from the vat room.

Luc swore, and jumped back.

Sadie remained against the car, flushed, rumpled, and so desirable. He couldn't stay one second more and not surrender to it. If he surrendered, would he hurt her and end up ruining everything?

"Go," she said.

"But— "

"I mean it. Go. That was stupid. I was overwrought. You were being weird. Another mistake. The last one."

"No Sadie, it wasn't—"

"It was. You love my sister. I'm not some sort of replacement while she's making up her mind about you."

"Sadie, that's not the way things are."

But Sadie was shaking her head, her eyes bright with tears. "I don't even know what's happening to you Luc, but you need to straighten yourself out. You're dangerous right now and I don't want any part in it."

He opened his mouth to tell her the truth about Stella, but before he could, she ducked under his arms and hurried away. Sadie was right. He was a hazard to himself and her.

Sadie was still breathing hard when she slammed the cottage door behind her, just like after the first kiss. *This had to stop*. How could she have gone from being so furious with Luc to melting into him? It's just that his mouth on hers felt so…there were no words for it really, except that it made her want more. It made her want *everything*.

She could still feel his hands on the side of her face, his thumbs brushing away her tears. How could something so wrong feel so right?

It could never happen, so logically that kiss should have never happened. Luc was upset about having to wait for Stella, and macho about Frederick invading his territory. It had to be that.

Sadie got changed in a hurry and went up to the dig to begin to prepare for Frederick's arrival. She had to act professional.

The sooner she could throw herself into the dig with him, the easier it would be to avoid Luc. She tried to burn off her self-recriminations and anger at Luc by hauling up to the dig site the equipment she'd been able to buy before Stella took the rest of her money. When that was done, all there was left to do was get working.

The afternoon weather was cold—her breath condensed into puffs in front of her face—but there was no rain in the forecast. Perfect.

Her phone chimed with a text from Frederick. He was only five minutes away, so Sadie ventured back down to the courtyard to wait for him.

As painstaking and sometimes frustrating as they could be,

digs were the favorite part of her job. She was, as her father had always observed, a treasure hunter at heart. As she waited, her pulse quickened at the thought of all the miracles they might unearth. It was good to be reminded there were things besides Luc that got her blood rushing.

Mon amour. That's what Luc had called her. Why? He didn't love her, he loved Stella. Why did he keep torturing her with this… this *thing* between them? It could destroy her if she let it, but she wouldn't allow that to happen. Maybe she hadn't been able to completely eradicate her attraction to him, but surely hard work and Frederick were the solutions.

Frederick drove into the courtyard in a shiny black Mercedes sedan. It was an odd choice of vehicle for a professor, but that was none of her business. Luc's suspicions made Sadie want to trust Frederick. Sadie directed him to where he should park his car behind the vat room. Luckily, Luc was nowhere to be seen.

Frederick was just as attractive as she remembered in his worn jeans and a black wool sweater now, perfect for a dig. A pair of work gloves dangled from his back pocket.

"Sadie," he nodded at her and smiled. Good God, the man even had dimples. "My excitement is almost embarrassing. I feel like a child on Christmas morning."

A kindred spirit then. "Don't be embarrassed." She laughed. "I'm the same. As she led him up to the dig site in the forest behind the Domaine, he showed her the paperwork that he'd stopped by to pick up at the Gallo-Roman center in the Nuits-Saint-Georges museum. So that's why he'd been a little later than expected, but he'd saved Sadie another trip when she really preferred to spend time on the site. He was thoughtful too? She could scarcely believe her luck.

Sadie gave him a quick overview of the site and pleasure flickered in her chest as Frederick's black eyes mirrored her own anticipation.

"Amazing," he murmured under his breath. "How did you find this place?"

She let out a breath she hadn't realized she'd been holding. Frederick seemed to understand that this place was special, maybe even sacred. "Luc and I used to play in this forest when we were little. It may sound far-fetched, but this particular spot always felt unique to me. I sensed there was something more." Sadie touched the wall gently with the toe of her boot. "I can't shake this hunch that this wall we can see is only the tip of the iceberg."

Frederick pursed his lips, taking it all in. "What exactly are you hoping we might find?"

Sadie crossed her arms over her chest and frowned at the wall. "When you consider that creek running behind the site, I feel this area could have been a key stopping point on the Gallo-Roman road."

Frederick cocked his exceptionally well-formed ear to the faint burble in the distance. "Accommodations?" he guessed. "Agricultural storage?"

He was quick on the uptake. Perfect. Sadie nodded. "Maybe."

Frederick's eyes gleamed like obsidian. "Correct me if I'm wrong Sadie, but I had a feeling you didn't include your wildest dreams for this site in your grant application." His beautifully formed mouth quirked to the side.

She couldn't help but smile. Luc wouldn't agree of course, but she just knew in her gut she could trust Frederick. "A temple," Sadie admitted. "With maybe some relics?"

Frederick grinned and it was like the sun coming out from behind a cloud. Sadie couldn't believe her luck—he was perfect. "Wouldn't that be incredible? It would revolutionize—"

"Don't jinx us!" She held up her hand. "First, let's decide how to section it off, so we can stake and cordon off parcels."

Frederick laughed, an open, bright laugh. "I can't help it. I find it easy to get carried away by your enthusiasm."

There seemed to be nothing tortured about him at all, none of that anguish that resided deep in Luc's soul.

Sadie clapped her hands together. "All right, I don't know about you, but I'm ready to get this rodeo started."

"That's a charmingly American thing to say," he chuckled, then went and grabbed a handful of stakes.

Hours later, they were both grimy and cold as they'd been crawling around on their hands and knees plotting sections. They'd only stopped for a brief four o'clock snack of *jambon beurre* on baguettes that Frederick had asked the hotel staff at Le Cep to prepare for them. He was an utter dream of a dig partner. Scratch that. He was a dream, period.

Their conversation was effortless and centered mainly around their work. Several times she'd been tempted to confide in him about the circumstances of her banishment from Hudson but lost her nerve.

The dark fell fast when it came. Frederick sat back on his haunches after pounding a final stake into the ground. He rubbed his lower back, even though he looked to be in incredible shape. "I can't believe we have the opportunity to do a dig on private property like this."

Sadie pointed her stake up beyond the creek. "A few feet past the creek is village land, but this has always been part of the Ocquidant Domaine. I still can't figure out exactly how Luc convinced his father, Alphonse, to let us do the dig. Burgundians are extremely territorial."

"More than the British?

"I'm not sure. By the way, if you see a large, usually charming, dark-haired man stalking around the Domaine, that's Alphonse. Best to be polite, but otherwise avoid him."

Frederick tossed his head to get the hair out of his eyes. Even dirty from the mud, he looked like something out of a magazine ad.

"Can I ask you a personal question?" he said, out of the blue.

Sadie hesitated a moment. It had to be about what had happened at Hudson University before she left. Academic circles were pitifully small. However, with the hours they would be spending together, it was probably better to get things out of the way immediately. "Sure."

"Luc seems possessive when it comes to you."

She jerked back in surprise. Not the question she'd been anticipating, but a valid one all the same. She shook her head, annoyed to feel heat race up her spine at the memory of how he'd pressed her against the car, and how her blood had secretly thrilled at being caught.

"He's just ridiculous like that." She shrugged. "French men can be macho. It's annoying, but don't worry, I can handle Luc."

"I have no doubt of that, but it was just…odd." Frederick mused, shooting her a speculative look.

Sadie shook her head. "I know what you're thinking, but you've got it wrong. Like I said earlier, Luc has always been madly in love with my twin sister Stella."

Frederick frowned. "Yet that's not how he was acting."

Sadie hated that she had to talk to Frederick about Stella so soon and ruin the spell of the dig, but at the same time she was eager to get it over with. Stella's existence always made Sadie less somehow, even with her new dig partner.

"You'll understand when you meet Stella," she said. "She looks nothing like me. She's stunning—she's been a model and everything. Men always become obsessed with her once they meet her. It's been happening my whole life. I just accept it now; in the same way I accept that the sun will rise every morning." She was glad she had the grounding, reassuring scent of the forest around her to prevent her from getting too emotional.

Frederick sat back on his heels. "I have a hard time believing that."

"Believe it," Sadie said. "She'll probably turn up here over the next couple of weeks. You'll see for yourself."

Frederick frowned again. "I'm still skeptical."

Why was he laboring this point? "I guarantee when you see Stella, you'll understand why Luc and I have always been strictly platonic. We're truly more like siblings than anything else." Well, except for those kisses... Why was Luc torturing her like this? More importantly, why did she respond to it so viscerally?

Frederick raised his dark brows. "Take it from a man. He wasn't looking at you like you were his sister. I'm just hoping it doesn't cause issues with the dig, given that it's on his family's land."

"It won't," she assured him. "I won't let it."

"If you say so," Frederick said, but it was clear from his tone that he harbored reservations, regardless of her assurances.

"How about you?" Sadie asked. If he could ask, so could she. "Wife? Girlfriend? Boyfriend?"

Frederick shook his head. "None of the above. I got out of a long-term relationship with a woman about a year ago. Since then I've been concentrating on my research."

"What was she like?" Sadie blurted out the question before she could stop herself. Frederick intrigued her. With his looks, she imagined him going out with super-model types, yet at the same time he was down-to-earth and cerebral in a way she related to. Then there was his complete lack of presence on the internet. "Sorry," she apologized before he could answer. "That is probably too personal."

"It's fine," Frederick said. "We're going to be spending a lot of time together, after all."

He was right. Honesty was the best policy. "True."

"Besides, I have this instinct that I can trust you. I can't explain it."

There was something reassuring about Frederick. It was a

welcome break from the cocktail of pain, pleasure, and confusion she'd felt around Luc lately.

"I'm basically a human vault." She laughed.

"Her name was Alexandra. Lady Alexandra."

"An aristocrat?"

"Yes, but one of those new generation aristocrats. She tried desperately to be creative—painting, fashion design, weaving, to name a few, but she was never able to shake the burden of being so privileged."

"Some people wouldn't consider that a burden," Sadie pointed out. Her life had been full of travel and interesting encounters due to her parents' academic careers, but they'd lived a modest life besides that.

"I suppose not, but Alexandra experienced it that way. She'd never worked a day in her life, and unfortunately, it showed."

"Oh dear."

"We weren't very compatible intellectually. She thought my fascination with archaeology was tedious. I suppose it is to most people."

"I guess." Sadie stood up with a groan. "But to me, it's the most fascinating thing in the world. I'm obsessed. I have been ever since stumbling on this site when I lived here with my parents. Luc explained to me that it was an old Gallo-Roman road, or at least that's what his grandparents and elders from the village had always told him. That's what sparked it off. From that point on, I was a lost cause. I suppose we do have to accept that most people aren't obsessed like us, though."

Frederick sighed and stood up, too. "You're right, but it's still incomprehensible to me."

"Me too."

"We're well-suited then." He gave her a wink and bent to collect the remaining tools on the ground.

Something still niggled at Sadie. "So that's what broke you and your girlfriend up? Archaeology?"

Frederick paused in his clean-up and frowned. "It was more than that. Alexandra was a lost soul. She leaned on me too much for too long. I decided the best thing I could do for her was to set her free so she could stand on her own two feet."

Sadie took this in. "And has she?"

Frederick smiled. "Yes. She's actually started taking a degree in art history. She's got an excellent eye. I'm proud of her and we've remained friendly. That's a good thing because our families are close, and we run in the same circles. I'm even friends with her new boyfriend, who is much better for her than me."

That was hard to imagine. "That's nice. It's rare when break-ups end up working out well for everyone concerned."

"What about you?" Frederick asked. "Anyone special?"

Besides my best friend who kisses me but loves my twin sister? Sadie shook her head. "I'm usually too wrapped up in my work. Men get fed up with always coming in second place."

"Maybe you just haven't met the right person." Frederick was brushing the dirt off his trowel and didn't meet her eyes.

"Maybe," Sadie agreed, but before she could stop them, her thoughts flew mutinously back to Luc.

chapter seventeen

TEN DAYS LATER, Luc recognized Gaspard's beat up Citroen as it pulled over beside the rows of vineyards where Luc was working like a demon, trying to exhaust himself so he wouldn't feel the frustration of knowing that Sadie was spending her days on the dig with Frederick.

He'd barely seen her in passing since he'd held her in his arms against the car. She'd thrown herself into the dig with the same ferocity he'd applied to his vineyards. She told his family that she was so tired after her day's work that she didn't even have the energy most nights to join them for dinner. Pauline always put together a tray for her, but he was aware, thanks to Adèle, that Sadie had dined more than a few times in Beaune with Frederick.

Luc missed her, and his jealousy over her handsome dig partner threatened to hollow him out from the inside. His longing for her wasn't easing like it was supposed to; it was getting worse.

Add the fact that he'd received two more deeply worrisome phone calls. One was from the bank asking about the non-payment of a line of credit, a line of credit that Luc knew nothing about and could find nowhere on the Domaine's records. The other was their label supplier saying that they refused to send them any more labels until their last two overdue bills were paid in full.

Luc had confronted his father, of course, but Alphonse waved it away and laughed at Luc's concerns, protesting that he'd forgotten and that the line of credit had been to repair the bottling machine before Luc had begun working at the Domaine in earnest.

Luc could not get a word of truth out of his father, or even something as simple as the amount of the outstanding line of credit. As long as Alphonse remained in control of the Domaine and its bank accounts, Luc's hands were tied. The situation was becoming more unbearable by the day.

Alphonse never missed an opportunity to tease him that the finances weren't in Luc's hands yet because of their deal to allow Sadie to conduct her dig—the dig with the dashing colleague.

Gaspard got out of his car and strolled over to Luc with his hands in his pockets. Luc was thinning his vines like he was possessed by the devil—fast, brutal, and unrelenting.

Gaspard rubbed his nose, tilting his head to better scrutinize Luc's pruning technique. Finally, he stuck out his hand and Luc gave it a curt shake.

"You're going to have a heart attack like my father if you keep going at this pace." Gaspard fingered the vine closest to him. "You're overthinning."

Luc was not in the mood to put up with Gaspard's criticisms. "I'm fully capable of looking after my family's vineyards, *merci.*"

Gaspard raised his hands in front of him. "I don't know what's got you so defensive. I'm just telling you the truth, but that's not why I'm here. Clovis and I wanted to take you out for a drink after work today. We're worried."

"I'm fine." Luc threw a bunch of pruned branches on the ground with unnecessary violence.

Gaspard jumped out of the way just in time. "You look like an angry bear."

"So what? You look like an angry bear all the time."

"But you don't. It's very uncharacteristic of you."

Luc glowered at his friend. Between Alphonse, Sadie, and Frederick, Luc's life had become a living hell that would put an archangel in a foul temper, and he was no archangel.

Gaspard whistled long and low. "It's worse than I thought. Is it Stella? Are you upset that she's gone away with that Pablo person?"

Stella? He hadn't thought about her for days, but Luc hesitated. As far as Clovis and Gaspard knew, he was still yearning for her. Maybe it would be easier to just continue on that tack. His mind was too snarled to begin to explain what had happened with Stella, even to his good friends.

"That's it," Luc grumbled.

Gaspard squinted at him. "I've never known you to get upset over a woman before. Will you meet us at the bar?"

Luc knew which bar Gaspard was referring to. It was the one on Savigny's main square, next to the chateau and across from the stone fountain. The same one they'd been meeting at for years.

"Can Amandine come?" Luc said. He hadn't seen her since Réveillon, and she was an equal member of their friend quartet. Besides, a female opinion could come in handy, even though Amandine's opinions tended to be of the ruthless variety.

"Probably." Gaspard tapped his thigh with his index finger. "But she won't."

Luc sighed and his secateurs stilled at last. "What did you do Gaspard?"

"I offered her financial help to start her own small Domaine to get out from under that dreadful brother of hers."

Luc rolled his eyes. "Don't you ever learn? You know she'll never accept your help."

"Why not?"

"Because Amandine is as independent and pig-headed as you are."

Gaspard's tapping picked up pace. "She's doing all the work

and gets none of the credit. How can she just accept that? It drives me crazy."

Luc studied the harsh lines of his friend's face. "Are you sure it's got nothing to do with the fact that the two of you were engaged not that long ago?"

Gaspard's eyes shifted away from Luc's. "Absolutely not."

"Yet, you've never tried to interfere with Clovis or me like that," Luc reminded him. "And my father is being a complete pain-in-the-ass at the moment. You haven't even asked how things are going with Alphonse."

"She should let me help her," Gaspard said, undeterred. "I would help you or Clovis if you needed it. Amandine is no different."

Luc grimaced. Gaspard *would* help any of his friends, but the one he was obsessed about helping was Amandine.

Luc bit his lip.

"What?" Gaspard demanded, his dark eyes narrowing over his hawk-like nose.

"Do you always have to be so overbearing with Amandine? Will you never learn?" It felt good to see a situation clearly for once and dole out unsolicited advice. He would resent it if he was in Gaspard's shoes, of course, but it made him feel better than he'd felt in days.

Gaspard made an exasperated sound. "*Ta gueule* Luc. It's in my nature to be autocratic. You know that. My father is exactly the same. We can't change our genes, even if we wanted to."

Luc's heart sunk again. "You're right there." Without knowing it, Gaspard had pretty much nailed Luc's problem on the head. He couldn't act on his feelings for Sadie because he couldn't be sure he wouldn't end up hurting the person he cared about most in the world.

"Meet you there at six thirty?" Gaspard said, giving Luc a parting pat on his shoulder.

"*Bien sûr.*" Luc called out over his shoulder as Gaspard walked back to his car. "But you're buying the first round."

The bar was the place where all the local winemakers and wine industry people went to exchange gossip and information. There was always a wine *négotiant* or exporter who was eager to make a useful connection with one of Burgundy's young up-and-coming winemakers. It was no surprise that this is where Luc had met many of his former conquests. It was a transactional place, and everybody there understood the nature of a no-strings fling implicitly.

When Luc walked in, showered and freshly dressed after his day of punishing work in the vines, Clovis and Gaspard were already there, saving a spot for him at their table.

They thought he needed to talk his feelings out, but Luc had no intention of satisfying them. That hollow chasm in his soul was roaring tonight.

Clovis saw him first and waved him over. They shook hands and Luc sat down, positioning his back against the wall so he had the best possible view of the bar. He was quickly enveloped in the hubbub and the familiar scent of spilled Chablis and the stale smell of tobacco that impregnated the walls from the years before smoking inside was banned.

"Bonjour, stranger," Clovis grinned at him, looking annoyingly contented. "We were getting worried about you. It's like you've dropped off the face of the earth."

"I'm been thinning the vines," Luc said.

"*Over*thinning." Gaspard added.

"*Ta gueule*," Luc snapped back. "I know how to prune."

Both Gaspard and Clovis frowned at him. They knew, as well as anyone, that January was the only time of year where the vineyard work slowed down to a far more leisurely pace while the vines enjoyed their winter sleep. Luc had no real winemaking reason to be working so frantically.

"You've been avoiding everyone," Gaspard said, trenchant as usual.

Luc's eye landed on a vivacious redhead talking to another woman at the bar. "Who is that redhead?" Luc asked. "Do either of you know her?"

Maybe that's what he needed—a distraction. Why hadn't he thought of that until now?

Clovis and Gaspard looked over their shoulders. "That's Celeste," Clovis said. "She just started working for Patriarche in Asian Exports. She's from Chorey. Why?"

"I'm feeling restless tonight," Luc said, but when he looked closer, he saw that her red hair was stick-straight, and he couldn't see so much of a hint of a freckle. Nah. He'd keep looking.

"That's not what we're here for tonight," Clovis said, his voice stern. "We're here to talk."

"About what?" Luc turned to them, widening his eyes in mock surprise.

"Don't Luc," Gaspard said. "We've known you too long."

Luc sighed. They were right about that.

"Is it about Stella?" Clovis asked. "Did something go wrong? Cerise and I did everything we could at Christmas—"

"It's never going to happen with Stella." Luc cracked the knuckle of his index finger.

Gaspard guffawed. "That's no surprise. A more ill-suited pair I've never—"

"Not now Gaspard." Luc glowered at his friend.

"What happened?" Clovis asked.

Luc rolled his eyes. "Do we really have to do this?"

"We do." Clovis crossed his arms on the tabletop, settling in for the duration. Good God, he could be stubborn. "And we're not leaving here until you tell us what's really going on."

"Stella and I kissed and there was…well, nothing. I'd built her up to be this goddess and in the end, there was just zero connection between us." He let out a puff of air. "Nada."

Clovis sat back. "She's been your end-game since you were seven."

"I know."

Clovis clicked his tongue. "No wonder you feel lost."

"I, for one, am not surprised," Gaspard said. "Stella and Luc never made sense. Sadie, on the other hand—"

"Don't gossip about Sadie," Luc warned.

"Ho!" Gaspard laughed. "I hit a sore spot I see. Now that *does* make sense. It always did, if you ask me."

"I didn't ask you, but that has never shut your mouth before, *n'est-ce pas*?" Gaspard was getting too close, and a wave of panic rose in Luc. They couldn't find out. "Back me up here, Clovis."

Clovis pinched his nose in thought, then finally he said, "I would, but I happen to agree with Gaspard. I think Sadie is wonderful. I always have."

Luc swore softly. "I'm going to get myself a drink." The waiting staff was so busy nobody had come to the table yet, and Luc needed a break from the unrelenting interrogation. He went up to the bar and, while he waited, took a closer look at the woman the redhead was talking to. She had black hair and green eyes. He nudged a little closer to her. She might be perfect.

"Bonjour," he smiled down at her. She turned around and her face lit up as she saw who was talking to her. "Can I buy you a drink?" he asked.

She tilted her head, coy. "But I don't even know your name."

He stuck out his hand. "Luc. Luc Ocquidant. I have a family Domaine here in Savigny."

The girl's beautiful eyes went wide, and she laughed. She really was lovely. "I've heard of your Domaine…and you…" she fluttered her eyelashes. "You have a bit of a reputation."

"Is that so?" Luc smiled. In a way it was a relief she'd heard of him. It was always a good litmus test to help find the women who understood the limits of what he could offer them. "Does that scare you off?"

She shrugged. "I'm not easily scared."

He nodded, slowly. "I'm so glad. What's your name?"

"Lucie. I work for Louis Jadot. North American exports."

"It's an absolute pleasure to meet you, Lucie." He *was* just like his father—the lines, the seduction—it all came flowing back so naturally and it always worked. It was only with Sadie that he felt like he had no idea what he was doing. It was only with Sadie that he'd ever lost control.

"What can I buy you for a drink, Lucie?" he asked.

"A glass of Puligny," she said.

"Excellent choice." Still, white wine in the evening? Luc had never been a fan and was always suspicious of people who were, but he needed to persist, if he was ever going to rid Sadie from his body and mind.

Just as he'd planned, Lucie snuggled closer to Luc as he waited to order for her, but like Stella, she felt all wrong pushed up against his side. Her hipbone poked into his thigh and her shoulder jammed into his ribs.

The bartender came to them then. He and Luc knew each other well, so after Luc had chided him good-naturedly about the wait that evening and they exchanged a few friendly insults, he ordered his own glass of Clovis's Morey-Saint-Denis and Lucie's glass of white. He turned to her when the waiter was pouring them. He leaned down to whisper in her ear about meeting later on that evening when he got rid of his friends, but when he got closer, he recoiled. She smelled all wrong—like expensive perfume instead of like vanilla and sap and coffee.

"What?" Her big eyes blinked up at him. "What were you going to say?"

Luckily the bartender came just then and slid their drinks towards them across the bar. "Nothing," Luc said. "Just that you're lovely and please enjoy your drink."

"But-!" she said.

"I'm sorry, but my friends will be angry if I don't go and talk to them. It was lovely meeting you, Lucie. *Bonsoir.*"

He left her then, probably confused, but at least with a free drink. Since when had he turned away a beautiful woman because she didn't smell like Sadie? This was going to be much harder than he'd initially thought.

Clovis narrowed his eyes at him when he sat back down again. "What was that all about? You're not going to get up to your old tricks just to avoid talking about Sadie, are you?"

Luc grimaced. That's exactly what he'd been trying, and failing, to do. He sighed, giving in to the inevitable. "We kissed," Luc confessed. "Twice."

Both Gaspard and Clovis gasped, like a pair of gossipy old ladies.

"How…what was it like?" Clovis asked.

"What kind of question is that?" Gaspard demanded.

"I mean, did it feel *right*?"

Luc thought about this. It had felt terrifying and joyous and astonishing and so hot he was surprised he hadn't burst into flames on the spot—was that what right felt like? "I don't know about right," Luc said. "But it's all I've been able to think about since."

"Uh oh," Gaspard said. "I know that feeling."

He did? With Amandine? "I'll be grilling you more on that later." Luc tapped the back of Gaspard's hand but then turned to Clovis.

"How did you know with Cerise that she was the one?" he asked him.

Clovis smiled to himself. "Cerise felt like home," he said, then lay his hand on his chest. "For my heart. No-one else ever came close to reverberating in my soul on that level, and I don't believe anyone ever could."

This struck them all to silence for a long time.

"The thing is, I don't know if my heart deserves a home," Luc said. "I'm just like my father—I've inherited that family gene for infidelity and destruction."

Clovis made a noise of disbelief. "I know you've always believed that Luc, but I've always thought it was ridiculous. Remember what a wastrel my father was? I'm nothing like him. It's a choice, you know. You don't have to be like Alphonse either."

"Clovis is right." Gaspard nodded.

Luc shook his head. "It's different with you Clovis. Your father was an anomaly. Your grandfather, Maxime, was wonderful. For me, my father, my great grandfather, even my great-great grandfather were famous for their philandering. With me, it's in the blood."

Gaspard shook his head. "That's a load of crap."

Luc bit his lip. How he would love to be free of that curse, but the sight of his mother standing rigid by the sink, like the day after Christmas, drove it home every time, as well as the ease he would have had at seducing Lucie into his bed. No, he couldn't deny it.

"I have to protect Sadie from myself," Luc said. "Don't you see? I care about her too much to risk hurting her."

"I'm convinced you're wrong Luc," Clovis said. "I always have been. Even if you believe there is such a thing as a family curse, can't you be the anomaly?"

Luc shook his head. "I've already proven I'm not."

Gaspard sighed. "He's not budging, Clovis. I think we may have to take up this fight again another time."

Clovis nodded slowly. "Fine, but do you at least admit that you are in love with Sadie?"

His heart expanded three times its size at the mere sound of her name. *Oh no.* All he wanted to do was go home to her. He dropped his head in his hands. "*Mon dieu,*" he groaned. "I think I am."

chapter eighteen

FREDERICK HAD BEEN silent for a while. Sadie glanced over from her plot and saw he was digging with even more intensity than usual. She caught a gleam in his dark eyes.

"What is it?" she asked, crawling over to him.

"There's a wall here, I think. It feels curved."

"No way," Sadie breathed. He looked at her and they both shared a wide-eyed look of barely contained glee.

They started digging like mad. Neither wanted to stop, but finally dusk fell and Frederick reached over and put his hand on Sadie's forearm. His touch was warm and comfortable.

"We have to stop," he said. "It's getting dark. Trust me, I don't want to either."

Sadie laughed at herself. "There's not one of us to hold the other back, is there?"

"No," Frederick agreed. "I've never had so much fun in my life."

Sadie grinned at him. She was covered head to toe in dirt and mud, but she didn't care. "Me neither. Let's start early tomorrow, OK?"

Frederick got up, too. "Deal."

He looked down at the hollow they'd begun to empty out which now clearly had stone walls curving downwards beneath the earth they had yet to uncover. "What do you think it is?" he mused.

Sadie considered it. "A drinking basin, perhaps?"

"Maybe," Frederick agreed. "In any case, I think it's a solid indication that your hunch was right. There's something here."

"If it is in fact a basin, do you think it's for people or livestock?"

"Both, perhaps? Maybe split somewhere down there?"

Sadie adored how they talked in their own sort of shorthand. Being with Frederick was so effortless. "I'd bet we'll find it runs off the creek."

"Or where the creek was then. I wonder about the sedimentation —"

"I have the *best* podcast about that. I'll bring my phone with me tomorrow so we can listen to it tomorrow while we dig."

"I could talk for *hours* about sedimentation theories," Frederick said.

"Do you realize we are two of a very small group of people in existence who can say that with a completely straight face?"

He burst out laughing. "You're absolutely right."

Oh, it felt good to laugh with him. She couldn't have asked for a better dig partner and she couldn't help but wonder what it would be like to be more than that with Frederick.

By the time they'd covered up the dig and Sadie walked Frederick down to his car the light in the sky had turned a grainy grey.

Again, there was no sign of Luc, which left Sadie with an odd combination of relief and sadness. She missed her friend. He'd been avoiding her, and it had been easy for her to do the same as she spent most of her time either working or sleeping.

Even after the day on the dig site was finished, she needed to record all her notes and then type them out into some sort of order. It was a grind, but she loved working this hard again.

Frederick's stopped by his Mercedes and pulled the keys out of his jean's pocket. "That was a fantastic day Sadie." He rested his hand on her shoulder. "One of the best I've ever had. I was looking forward to this dig, but I had no idea—"

She tilted her head up to him. It was a nice sight. "Had no idea about what?"

His put his other hand on her other shoulder. This felt like something more than friendly camaraderie, but could she be sure?

"Just how much I would enjoy working with you," he said, his voice low and sincere. "And, more importantly, spending every day with you."

Sadie smiled. What would her life be like with Frederick? Fairly wonderful, she imagined. "We make a good team." Still, she gritted her teeth against at an uncomfortable sense of *déjà vu.* This whole scenario was too much like Luc and her by the car less than two weeks before. She couldn't stop remembering how Luc was shaking with urgency when he leaned against her and how her blood had raced in response.

Now, Frederick was moving closer to her and was angling his head just so. Was Frederick, who was pretty much every woman's dream, leaning in to kiss her too? She sensed none of that zinging energy in him that she'd felt in Luc. Her mind flailed. If he did kiss her, could she prevent herself from comparing it to her kiss with Luc?

"Sadie!" A shout came from around the house. Relief filled her, which was ridiculous. She would be crazy not to welcome interest from someone so compatible and perfect.

Adèle was walking briskly across the pea gravel, holding a bottle of wine. "You have to taste this!" she cried.

Sadie moved slightly as Adèle drew close. Adèle stopped in her tracks and grasped convulsively onto the neck of the bottle she was carrying when she realized Sadie wasn't been alone.

"*Eh merde*," Adèle said. "Did I interrupt something?"

Frederick dropped his hands and pulled open the car door which acted like a barrier between him and Sadie. "Not at all," he said smoothly. "We were just going over our day."

Adèle approached, but more cautiously now, her gaze flicking between Frederick and Sadie.

Frederick winked at Sadie. "I'm going to go back to the hotel to take a long, hot shower so I can still walk tomorrow. Will you come to Beaune to have dinner with me tonight?" he asked, "I can come and pick you up. I'll book somewhere good."

Sadie was tempted, but that confusion when she thought he was going to kiss her made her hesitate. She needed some time to set herself straight.

"I'm exhausted," she said. "My plan for tonight is a hot bath and then bed. We'll be starting early tomorrow. Rain check?" She was crazy to be turning him down.

Frederick smiled at her. "Rain check. And don't forget to bring the podcast tomorrow. I can't wait to hear it." He climbed into the car, shut the door, and rumbled out of the courtyard.

Sadie waved at him as he left.

"Phroar!" Adèle said, with all her heart when he'd spun out of the courtyard, all shiny black car and well-bred testosterone. "Podcast? I hope it's about something sexy."

Sadie turned to Adèle. "It's about sedimentation rates."

"Are you certifiably crazy Sadie?"

"*Quoi*?" Sadie was distracted, still trying to make sense of why she'd turned him down.

"Any sane woman would have taken him up on dinner, and dessert back in his hotel room afterwards, not to mention the hot shower." Adèle sighed with her whole body. "Can you even *imagine*? Why aren't you jumping his bones? He's divine *and* nice. Frederick is the whole glorious package."

She took a deep gulp of air. "He's a work colleague Adèle. I have to tread carefully."

Adèle snorted. "Don't give me that."

Sadie pointed at the bottle of wine in Adèle's hands, opting for diversionary tactics. "What is this wine that I have to taste?"

"I thought all you wanted was a hot bath?" Adèle chided.

Sadie slung her arm around Adèle's shoulders. She'd always felt that Adèle was the little sister she'd never had. "Shut up *petite pestouille*," she said, reaching up to mess up Adèle's hair.

Adèle grinned back. "I still think you're an idiot."

Sadie sighed. "I happen to agree with you."

"Let's go to the cellar and find a corkscrew."

"Now you're talking."

Sadie loved the scent of the Ocquidant cellar even more than the many other cellars she'd done tastings in.

When she and Luc were younger, the Ocquidant cellar was a mysterious place full of mold and dark, dusty corners. Alphonse always said he liked it that way, but over the years Sadie realized this had just been laziness.

Luc had transformed it completely. It was now clean and well-organized, as well as artistically lit. His touch was everywhere. It honored the past, but in a modern way, and now smelled the way a cellar should, with the familiar scent of limestone and damp earth. What was Alphonse waiting for to give Luc control?

Her stomach dropped when she thought of the easy camaraderie between her and Luc that seemed to have vanished.

She'd thought they were getting it back, but then Frederick had arrived, and Luc had acted so churlishly. Then they'd kissed again—she was an idiot to have let that happen—and now they were avoiding each other like the plague. Even though Frederick was quickly becoming a fixture in her life, what she felt with him was different from that invisible bond she'd always shared with Luc, from the moment they met.

Adèle took two tasting glasses out of a wicker winemaking basket and grabbed the traditional Burgundian corkscrew made from an old chunk of gnarled grape vine.

"It's Cerise's wine from last year. Luc told me about what a brilliant winemaker she is, but I didn't have the opportunity to taste any of it until now. Her wine is flying off the shelves. Actually, it barely makes it to the shelves. I've heard she has waiting lists going into the next decade."

"Good for her." Cerise deserved the acclaim. She was someone Sadie wanted to get to know better.

Adèle nodded as she twisted the corkscrew down into the cork with a practiced hand. "I've heard she's great. What were your first impressions?"

Sadie thought back to Christmas Eve dinner. "I liked her a lot. I think she's someone I could become friends with."

Adèle uncorked the bottle with a satisfying pop and poured some of the garnet liquid into Sadie's glass. "That's good to hear. Clovis was always Luc's friend, of course, but he was always kind to me. I would hate him to end up with a shrew."

Cerise laughed. "She's definitely not that. They're blindingly happy together."

"Good." Adèle nodded. "Frederick is amazingly gorgeous." She passed Sadie her glass. "You do realize he's into you, don't you?"

"*N'importe quoi*," Sadie scoffed.

"Don't 'whatever' me," Adèle said. "I know the signs, and he's smitten."

There were times when Sadie herself wondered, but she couldn't quite let herself believe it. Besides, she couldn't count on anything until Frederick had met Stella. Chances were good he'd forget all about her when he did.

Sadie still didn't answer, but instead swirled the wine in her glass, holding it up to the light and admiring its rich palette of ruby tones.

Her father had always encouraged Sadie to educate her palette in wine. She remembered when she was about fifteen years old, and one night her father had taken her to their favorite restaurant for dinner. The restaurant had a superb wine list and the waiters never seemed to mind if Sadie's father poured her a little bit to taste in her glass, despite the fact that she was underage.

Sadie was looking forward to time just for the two of them, without Stella or their little brother Max around. She always had wonderful conversations with her father, who recognized in her an intellectual equal and never failed to spark a thousand new ideas and interests.

Their favorite restaurant also happened to be a popular gathering place amongst the Hudson professors of her father's generation. Several of them were confirmed bachelors and were in the habit of gathering at the restaurant bar for long evenings of alcohol-soaked debate.

When Sadie and her father walked in the door, it was clear from the way his colleagues hailed her father—calling out his name in slurred syllables—that they were already sloshed. Sadie, for her part, was preoccupied with deciding whether she would order the tortellini or the *caccio e pepe.*

Sadie's father greeted them politely but reservedly as they waited to be seated. Lolling around drunk in a local restaurant with his academic colleagues had never been his style.

"Where's that daughter of yours!" one of them—a gangly man that Sadie thought might be a professor of medieval history, shouted.

"I'm here with my daughter Sadie for dinner," her father said proudly, bless him. Sadie leaned against him, taking in his familiar scent of old books and pipe smoke.

"I don't mean that one!" the medieval professor slurred. "I meant the other one—the gorgeous one, not that plain one. Nobody has any use for her."

Sadie's veins filled with ice. She'd realized by then how differently the world viewed her and Stella, but it had never slapped her in the face in such a way before.

The hostess began leading them to their table in a far corner on the opposite side of the restaurant.

"Don't pay any attention to that," Sadie's father said, with a squeeze of his arm around Sadie's shoulders. "He's sauced. He won't even remember he was here tomorrow morning."

But Sadie's enjoyment of their meal was ruined. The tortellini tasted like ash in her mouth, and for once her father's conversation fell flat in her mind. She knew what her father didn't say. The drunk professor had merely spoken the truth while his barriers were down. Because of some genetic lottery, Stella would always be considered more worthy, lovable, and interesting than Sadie, no matter what either of them did.

That night had lacerated her heart and deepened the wound in her soul. Luc had made the first strike by choosing Stella over her when they were seven, but the professor's drunken truth opened it up all over again.

She learned to move slowly when a man seemed interested in her. She always bid her time, waiting until the potential suitor met Stella. Luc had failed that test miserably. Why would Frederick be any different?

"You're not answering me," Adèle chastised, and took her first sip of wine, rolling it around on her tongue like the expert she was. "I don't think I've ever seen such an attractive man before. If he was giving me the signals he's giving you, he would already be in my bed."

Sadie shrugged. Adèle didn't have a sister like Stella; she couldn't understand how hard she'd had to fight to hold onto a sense of her own self-worth, and how impossible it felt to trust anyone with her heart.

"Seriously Sadie, what are you waiting for?" Adèle asked, her voice curious.

Sadie sighed. "I'm waiting for him to meet Stella."

Adèle let out a surprised puff of air, then her eyes grew wide with sympathy—a reaction Sadie hated above all else. Anything but pity.

"You don't need to compare yourself to her," Adèle said.

"Yes, I do, because that's what everyone else does."

Adèle was opening her mouth to argue when the door to the cellar opened, and Luc's feet appeared on the top of the steep stone staircase.

When he got far enough down to see his sister and Sadie standing in front of the wine barrel with a full glass each, his eyes darted around them. "Where's Frederick?"

Luc still couldn't pronounce the name properly, but he nevertheless managed to imbue it with a good dose of animosity.

"He's gone back to Beaune," Sadie said. "We're done for the day—a *great* day—I may add, and you can stop acting like an alpha wolf around him. There's absolutely no need."

"I still don't like him."

Adèle's mouth dropped open. "What's got into you Luc?"

Even in the dim light of the cellar, Sadie could make out the flush on Luc's face.

Luc joined them at the barrel. "I don't think Frederick is what he seems."

"I think he's *exactly* what he seems," said Adèle, her chin firm. "Gorgeous. Smart. Nice…not to mention enamored with Sadie."

"*Quoi*?" Luc's head snapped over to Sadie. "Is that true?"

"If it was, it would be none of your business Luc," Sadie said, willing herself to stay calm. She wasn't going to pay attention to his absurdity, and she had to forget the glorious fit of his body pressed against hers. "How about we taste some of Cerise's wine?"

"Good idea." Adèle uncorked the bottle again and poured Luc a glass.

Luc's shoulders fell and after a moment of hesitation, he nodded. "What is it?" He turned the bottle and looked himself. "Ah, the precursor to Cerasus. I've tasted this before at their house, it's delicious. Cerise is brilliant."

Sadie watched as Luc caught up to them, holding the glass up to the ceiling light as he swirled it expertly in his glass. From the looseness across his shoulders it appeared as though he'd settled down. On closer inspection though, there was a new tightness in his usually smiling mouth and dark circles under his eyes. He was taking his time.

"Can we get to the tasting?" Adèle said. "You've been peering through your glass forever Luc. I don't know what you're thinking about, but I've never seen you this distracted at a tasting before."

He nodded with a slight grimace, and they tasted.

The rich taste of cherry was the first thing Sadie noticed, but it was so beautifully balanced with just the right amount of tannins and the deeper notes of pepper and undergrowth. She rolled it around on her tongue. The savors just kept coming and coming. "This is sublime."

"I told you, she's a genius," Luc said, his face softening. Truly fine wine always had a mellowing effect. "She's like you are with your archeology, but with wine. Ever since I met Cerise, I've thought you two have similar minds."

"How's that?" Adèle asked.

"Rigorous. Creative. Intuitive."

Was that a peace offering? "Merci," said Sadie. "That's kind."

"It's true." Luc gave her a tentative smile. "Speaking of Clovis and Cerise, I bumped into Jean this morning at the Wine

Co-op. He wants me to bring you over to Clovis's Domaine for a winetasting."

"That's right! I promised him I would and then I got so preoccupied with the dig. I'd love that. Maybe I should ask Frederick too. I'm sure he'd love to join."

"Jean didn't mention Frederick."

Adèle snorted. "When has Jean ever objected to having extra people at a winetasting? Never, that's when."

Luc looked down at his glass and bit his lip. He said, in a gentler voice. "Is it true what Adèle said, is there something going on between you and Frederick?"

Sadie looked steadily into the depths of Luc's blue eyes. Goosebumps prickled down her arms, but she ignored them. "Anything between Frederick and me is my business."

"But we're best friends," Luc said.

That was low.

"It sounds like you haven't been acting like a friend to Sadie, more like an annoying over-protective brother," Adèle pointed out. "Yet, I'm your actual sister and you've never acted like this around any of my boyfriends and, God knows, there were some duds."

Luc's mouth quirked over to the side. "There certainly were."

Sadie took a deep breath. "Sorry Luc, you're just acting too weird about Frederick. It's making me uncomfortable to talk to you about him, so let's just make him off-limits between us."

Luc didn't say anything but started rolling the wine in his mouth again. Adèle caught Sadie's eye and rose her eyes to the vaulted ceiling of the cellar in exasperation.

Luckily, they got on the topic of the wine, then Sadie started telling them about the discovery of the basin at the dig. As they chatted, Luc seemed to settle into his old self once again.

Sadie lost all sense of time, something she tended to do below the ground in the magical environment of a wine cellar.

Finally, Adèle happened to look at her watch. "Oh my God,

I'm already twenty minutes late for meeting my friends at Le Parallèle for drinks.

She shrugged on her coat and dashed off. Sadie smiled after her. She always loved spending time with Adèle.

The back of her neck prickled with a new awareness as she turned back to Luc. It dawned on her, too late, that the two of them were now alone in the cellar.

chapter nineteen

LUC HADN'T PLANNED this in any way, shape or form, especially not after the revelation Gaspard and Clovis had coaxed out of him at the bar a few days before. He still hadn't digested this new, unworkable truth that he was madly in love with Sadie, not Stella.

Since then, his mind went back and forth in a never-ending debate. Should he tell Sadie or keep his change of heart a secret?

He couldn't imagine ever wanting to stray if he was lucky enough for Sadie to love him back. On the other hand, why would she after he'd made such a fool of himself over Stella? Also, a flicker of doubt remained that stopped him from confessing everything to Sadie—he couldn't stomach the idea of being Alphonse to Sadie's Pauline. How could he be absolutely sure that would never happen?

It was torture having her so close and at the same time off-limits. Knowing she was *not* off-limits to Frederick filled him with a roar of jealousy in his chest. He tried—he truly did—to remember his better self and fight against it, but he wasn't having much success.

He was ashamed of the way he'd been acting, like a crazed, jealous devil. He'd always been the most easygoing boyfriend and lover, so this tumult of longing and jealousy was a novel experience. For Sadie's sake, his conscience told him he had to do better.

She was so close now, just on the opposite side of the barrel. There was a smear of dried mud on the side of her nose, and more in her hairline. She was wearing her work jeans and a pilled wool sweater with fraying wrists. His need for a woman had never vibrated through every atom of his being like this—never even close.

Should he tell her?

Sadie was watching him with a wariness that made him wince.

"I'm sorry Sadie," he said, trying to keep his voice steady, despite the longing that was zinging through him. "I haven't been fair to you."

Sadie's amber eyes glowed in the dim yellow light of the cellar. She waited, silent. God, she was hypnotizing, like the flame of a candle.

"I will do better," he said. She deserved that and so, so much more.

"Thank you," she said, finally. "Why has all this strangeness happened between us?" She gripped the edge of the overturned barrel with her free hand and leaned against it. "I hate it, Luc. I need my friend back."

"I know." Maybe if he told her, she might understand better, but it could make everything more difficult too.

"It was the kissing, wasn't it?" she asked, pulling distractedly on a stray curl. His fingers twitched to do the same.

Luc drank her in, remembering that feeling of her opening up to him, and how they fit together like their individual bodies had been forged from a whole. "I think so," he admitted, at last.

Sadie took a deep breath and fiddled with the stem of her wine glass. "What I can't figure out is why you care so much about Frederick being around."

"What do you mean?" Couldn't she see he cared so much it was pulling him apart?

"Well…you've always been in love with Stella."

"No." Luc said, watching her. He hadn't decided on the rest, but he couldn't let her believe that for one second longer.

"What do you mean?" The freckles over her nose stood out in a face which had gone terribly pale.

"I…I stupidly convinced myself long ago that I was in love with Stella, but now I realize I never was."

"What are you talking about?" A crease appeared between Sadie's brows.

"I'm not in love with your sister, Sadie. The truth is, I never have been."

The past few days he'd ruminated over his past. For most of his life, his true feelings for Sadie had been like vineyards hidden by a heavy fog. He thought the fog was reality, but when his growing understanding lifted it, he saw the vineyards for what they really were, and what they'd always been. His beliefs about Stella had obscured the truth, but those were banished once and for all. The truth was, he'd always loved Sadie.

"But you *are* Luc," Sadie insisted. "Ever since we were seven, remember?" The wine glass in Sadie's hand began to shake and she put it down quickly on the barrel.

He shook his head wordlessly, never breaking their gaze.

"It's not true." Sadie took a step back. Then she turned and hurried up the stairs and out of the cellar.

He swore softly, then turned off the lights and locked the door and ran after her. Luckily, it was almost a full moon, so he could see the shape of her hurrying away from him.

"Stop following me!" Sadie yelled over her shoulder. "I can hear you."

"No," Luc said.

"Stop it. Leave me alone."

"I can't, not until we— "

"We have nothing left to talk about, you and I."

She disappeared into the trees at the beginning of the forest, above the courtyard. "Where the hell are you going, Sadie?" he yelled. "It's dark!"

"Go away!"

"I'm not going away," he said. "We need to finish this conversation." The sharp scratches of tree branches against his face and hands didn't even make him pause. Luckily, he knew the way through these woods, even in the pitch dark.

Finally, he got to the opening where Sadie and Frederick were doing their dig. Sadie was there, alone in the moonlight, sitting on the Gallo-Roman wall, scowling at Luc as he broke through the trees.

"I told you to go away. I need to be alone. That is *a lot.* My whole life, you've loved Stella. Even when we kissed, I thought you loved Stella."

Luc kneeled in front of her and took her hands in his. He shook his head. "The two times we kissed…if I'd loved Stella, it wouldn't have been as extraordinary as it was. I know that now."

Her eyes were huge, but he needed her closer. With the blood rushing in his ears, he cupped the side of her face. "If I loved Stella, it wouldn't feel like I'm holding my own heart when I take your face in my hands."

"Luc," she pleaded.

"Noone has ever had this effect on me, Sadie."

"It's not true." She shook her head but didn't move away. Neither did he, even though the cold and the mud were seeping through the knees of his jeans. His thrumming heart was keeping him plenty warm.

"You've been with countless other woman," she said, sounding bewildered.

Their mouths were very close, and Luc's breathing matched Sadie's ragged staccato.

"Maybe, but it's never felt—". He was overcome with a desperate need to make Sadie understand that when they'd kissed, he'd been consumed with her, and nothing but her.

"Like what?" Sadie breathed.

The only way was to show her. He lowered his mouth onto hers and immediately, she filled every one of his senses. Desire and belonging roared through his body. He'd finally arrived home.

It was so dark, but the warmth and delicate curve of her lips undid any rational thought in his brain. If she didn't believe she was completely different from any other woman he'd ever kissed, he had to show her.

"No," she murmured underneath him.

He pulled away so he could look her in the eye.

"Do you want me to stop?"

"No," she whispered. A gust of wind made the tree branches rattle overhead. "Wait. Yes. Stop. I have to protect myself Luc."

He let go of her immediately, but added, "I would never hurt you." In that second, he was certain of it.

She shook her head wildly and pushed herself away from him, then hopped up. "No Luc. I can't do this with you. I have to be smart."

Luc rocked back on his heels. It killed him, but he also understood. "Is there anything I can do to make you trust me?"

"Just be my friend. Please."

He'd blown it, but if that was all she wanted, then that was what he would give her. His heart was erratic with despair. "Yes," he said. "I will."

That night, alone in bed, Sadie's mind wouldn't settle.

Not love Stella? Ever since she was seven, Luc loving Stella was an immutable reality of her life—like the whoosh of the subway doors in New York.

It was also, strangely, a cornerstone of her friendship with Luc. Because he loved Stella, it freed them, or until this trip anyway, to be the most uncomplicated type of friends. Something about that relationship reassured her as much as it had always left her wanting.

Sadie didn't have to look far for the reason for that. Her mind flew back to Thomas, the boy who she'd lost her virginity to when she was seventeen. He was brainy and slightly nerdy like Sadie, and they'd bonded over their joint project on the differences between Lava Dome and Composite volcanos in their Earth Sciences class.

Sure, she'd caught him looking at Stella on several occasions—but all boys did that. Besides, she was determined to lose her virginity and Thomas seemed to genuinely enjoy talking to her about school. Theirs was like a pale imitation of the connection she shared with Luc. Being an ocean away from Luc and only able to communicate via their phones and computers, she missed him desperately—somehow, she always caught herself looking for people to fill that void.

She'd decided to sleep with Thomas, and they did it two nights later. Unfortunately, it was awkward, mechanic, and had none of the romance that Sadie's secret self had hoped for. Sure, first times had a reputation of being bad, but this was truly doing the union minimum just to get the job done.

Afterwards, they'd both pulled their clothes on quickly, embarrassed about what they'd just done.

"What did you think?" Sadie asked Thomas, almost as though conducting a scientific survey to cover up her disappointment.

"Strange," he'd said. "Not bad exactly, but not what I'd expected."

Sadie died inside then. She'd always harbored a romantic side she kept strictly to herself. What was the point of even having a romantic side when she had a twin like Stella, who inspired love poems, songs, and declarations on a daily basis?

"Oh," she said. "Well, we got it done at least."

"I almost didn't, but when I found my interest waning," Thomas said, more than happy to discuss their sex in the most pedantic way imaginable. "I just imagined you were your sister, and that helped."

Mortification washed over her, freezing her to the marrow. She began to shake. Thomas hadn't chosen to have sex with her, really. He'd been using her as a method of having sex with Stella.

"I have to go." She jumped off the mattress and tugged on her shoes.

"Yes," Thomas said. "That's probably for the best. I'm feeling tired now."

Sadie fled, desperate to be alone so she could try to piece herself back together again, but deep down she knew that she could never erase the knowledge that her first sexual partner had been using her as a stand-in for her sister.

That's what nobody seemed to understand. Being Stella's sister was like dying of a thousand tiny cuts until there was nothing left of her. It was a lifelong battle to try and keep something for herself.

Luc had been her friend. Now he was something else, but he could never be anything more than a friend because he had loved her sister first. When exactly had he transferred his affections? Was it before or after he'd confessed his love to Stella in his bedroom on Christmas night?

Thinking of Thomas, Sadie knew that whatever way she sliced this thing with Luc, he would end up hurting her too. She let the tears fall, finally. She wished he hadn't told her that their kisses had meant so much to him too. Ever since that first night in the living room, Sadie had a hunch, just like she did about the Gallo-Roman wall, that maybe Luc was the person who could make all those silly romantic dreams of her youth come true.

But she was no longer a child, and she had learned how to protect herself. She'd never allow another Thomas situation to happen again. She had to do the smart thing, which was clearly to pursue her relationship with Frederick.

And there would be hell to pay if Luc ruined that.

chapter twenty

THE NEXT MORNING, Luc was moving barrels in the far depths of the cellar, recriminating himself for botching things so badly with Sadie. He hadn't even told her explicitly how much he loved her, and already he'd scared her off.

He'd jumped the gun, not fully taking into account how Sadie must have been affected by his misguided obsession with Stella. Of course she had no reason to trust him with her heart.

As much as the mere idea made his chest burn and his fists clench, Frederick probably would make a good boyfriend for Sadie. They had so much in common, damn the posh bastard.

But Luc was certain of one thing—Frederick could never, ever love Sadie like he did. If she wanted him to just be her friend, that's what he would do. It would be torment, but that was nobody's fault but his own.

In the distance, the cellar door opened with a creak. His heart leapt. *Maybe it was her.*

"Luc!" Alphonse's familiar voice put an end to that.

Probably for the best. He needed to talk to his father anyway.

"Did you get Les Talmettes pruned?" Alphonse asked, giving his son a buffet on the back. "Look at how strapping you are.

Thank God, because I don't think I have the strength to haul barrels around like that anymore."

Luc looked at his father's ruddy complexion and burly shoulders. Even though he was past fifty, Alphonse still radiated strength and vitality.

"Don't talk like you're some decrepit old man Papa," Luc said. "When we both know you're far from it."

Luc had found his father's phone in the cellar three days before, and there were text messages from three different women who were not his mother on the screen. Alphonse continued to demonstrate in spades that he was plenty spry enough to complicate Luc's life.

"Papa, I need to ask you about that line of credit again," he said. "I received another vague email from the bank about it. They wouldn't tell me anything—"

"Because it's not in your name, it's in mine," Alphonse grinned when he said this, damn him.

"*Exactement.* But I got the distinct impression they were warning me that something had to be done about it. Tell me Papa. I'm sure I can help, but you have to be honest with me about what is truly going on."

"You don't need to worry your head about that." Alphonse patted Luc on the back. "I have everything under control son, I promise. Don't you trust your papa?"

Luc bit his lip. He adored his father, but trust him? No, he didn't, and that hurt.

"Besides, we made a deal. You would not meddle for three more years so that Sadie can do her dig. I brought you up to be a man of your word. Are you not?"

Luc could never figure out why Alphonse thought that wedding vows were somehow exempt from this philosophy, but besides that, Alphonse had instilled honor into Luc's brain.

Part of his anguish in regard to his father's behavior with his mother was the fact that he just couldn't understand it. In every other way, Alphonse was a model husband and father. The few times Luc had ventured to ask his mother about this, she merely told him that people didn't make sense, and that his life would be far smoother if he would stop being so idealistic and accept this fact.

"Of course I am." Luc said. He was yet again at a dead end. His father was blackmailing him—charmingly, as Alphonse did everything, but it was blackmail all the same.

Still, Luc would do whatever it took to protect Sadie and her dig. It was crucial for her happiness. As much as jealousy poisoned him from the inside every time he thought of her working with Frederick, he got the distinct impression that the Brit had the necessary connections to reinvigorate Sadie's academic career.

"If there are any problems," Luc tried one last time. "I could help solve them. You need to give me access to the finances."

"I need do no such thing," his father said, jovial as ever. "I know you're stubborn Luc but remember that particular trait came from me."

Luc made an effort to straighten out his hand, which he'd balled into a fist.

The worry that his father was hiding something, and something big, was growing by the day. However, pushing further might compromise Sadie's dig. He would never risk that.

He would just have to shoulder the worry for a while longer.

A week later, Sadie and Frederick rolled up in front of Clovis's stunning Domaine in the village in Morey-Saint-Denis. They'd come directly from Nuits-Saint-Georges museum to give them an update on the dig. The staff there were fantastic to work with, interested and a constant source of ideas and advice.

Luc hadn't looked happy, but he hadn't balked either, when she confirmed she'd be bringing Frederick to the winetasting with Jean. She got the sense it had cost him, but he was making good on his promise to just be her friend. There were no renewed conversations about Stella or anything else awkward, and he continued to give Sadie and Frederick wide berth to do their work.

Still, she missed him.

But things with Frederick were progressing nicely. They had hugged a few times—namely when they'd found a secondary basin and what was looking like a large food preparation area—and Frederick had clung on for longer than was polite. His lusts didn't seem to drive him as Luc's did, but surely that was an excellent thing.

Luc had sent her a text to tell her that he had business in Beaune and was going to meet her and Frederick at Clovis's after he was done.

She led Frederick into the majestic courtyard of Domaine de Valois. He'd reached out and taken her hand when he'd helped her out of the passenger side of his Mercedes, and he didn't let go.

Her stomach fluttered when she tried to predict Luc's reaction to seeing her and Frederick together, but he would have to get used to it. She'd made the right choice. Frederick's hand wrapped around hers, grounding her. She was certain she would stop yearning for that uncontrollable desire she'd felt with Luc…eventually.

The one person she could barely wait to see was Jean. He somehow always made everything lighter and less confusing.

They found him in the *cuverie*. Jean paused for a moment as his blue eyes locked onto where Sadie's fingers were intertwined with Frederick's, but then he gathered his wits and welcomed her with open arms, crushing her in his embrace. Frederick had no choice but to let go. As she leaned into his hug, tears pricked at the corner of her eyes. Frederick stood politely by.

Her father and Jean had struck up a friendship while her family had spent their three years in Burgundy and maintained it during their visits in the years after. Jean's hug felt like a father's hug should.

Jean had always been so incredibly kind to her. Even when she was seven years old, he had talked to her like an adult and considered her opinions with respect and thought. He'd also let her drive the tractor whenever she asked, with him sitting right beside her, of course, making sure she was safe and didn't run over any of the world's most expensive vines.

She also suspected he had a soft spot for her which he didn't have for Stella, even though he was always equally kind to her twin. Still, the fact that Jean had singled her out as a favorite…it meant more to Sadie than he could ever know.

When Sadie finally let Jean go, he shook hands politely with Frederick. Frederick was perfectly charming in thanking Jean for setting up the tasting—he was truly a man who could fit in anywhere—but Jean remained a bit more reserved than usual with him. Surely, Jean couldn't have found anything to dislike in Frederick. That was impossible. "You're the first ones here," Jean said. His blue eyes twinkled down at her. "How is the dig going?"

"Amazing," Sadie said, walking towards the stairs down to the cellar with Jean's arm slung over her shoulder. "I was right—it's shaping up to be a good-sized halt on the Gallo-Roman road. We've uncovered a basin, and it is far larger than we initially thought, which has given us some crazy hopes for what else we'll uncover."

"Wonderful, *ma belle.*"

"I couldn't have done any of that without Frederick," Sadie said, pointedly. "We work beautifully together."

"Is that so?" Jean said, non-committal.

"Yes, Sadie is an absolute genius." Frederick smiled at her. "As well as one of the hardest workers I've ever met."

Jean glanced over his shoulder at Frederick. "We've always known that here in Burgundy." His tone was sharp.

Sadie couldn't believe it. Jean was almost acting uncivil. In fact, his attitude was giving her déjà vu of Luc's possessiveness. Just like with Luc, it was completely out of character.

Jean should be thrilled to see her with such a lovely man. Working with Frederick was a dream. For the first time in her life, Sadie didn't feel as though she needed to fight to be respected. Frederick listened to what she said and praised her for her insights and instinct. It was a novel experience, and she was relishing every minute. The only frustrating thing was she couldn't exactly tell where the distinction between liking Frederick as a dig partner and liking him as a man began and ended. Did it matter, though, in the end?

"What does Luc think about all this?" Jean demanded as they stopped and waited by the stairs for Luc.

"About what? The dig?"

Jean's eyes flicked to Frederick. "Amongst other things."

Sadie lowered her brows at Jean. "He's happy to leave us alone to do our work."

"Hmph," Jean said. "I'm sure he has…thoughts."

Sadie blew out her breath in frustration, but before she could riposte, Jean asked, "is Stella back yet from her photo tour?"

Finally, neutral ground, Sadie just wished it wasn't about Stella. "No. She'll just appear one day out of the ether, but I have no idea when. I never do."

A whistle from the gate at the courtyard made them all turn. It was Luc, walking towards them, he raised his hand in greeting. He was a striking sight as usual, lean and golden, even bundled up in his winter sweater and coat. Sadie quickly glanced between Frederick, who had taken her hand again, and Luc. These two were complete opposites in almost every way.

As he drew closer, Luc looked pointedly down at their clasped hands, reminding her uncannily of Jean's expression. From the clenching and unclenching of Luc's right fist, Sadie knew that it was taking him a heroic effort to reign himself in.

"*Bonjou*r," he greeted Jean and then looked down at Frederick's hand, which was the one he would normally shake in greeting. A muscle in his jaw clenched. "Shall we go down?" he said.

At least in the cellar they'd have something to keep them distracted. Jean led them down the narrow stone stairs into the vast cellars of Domaine de Valois. Sadie had been down there a few times with Jean or Luc when she was younger. Domaine Ocquidant's cellars were already impressive, but Clovis's were probably three or four times that size.

They arrived in the smaller tasting room where an upturned barrel sat in the middle, surrounded by wine racks. It felt like a place suspended out of time. Jean busied himself over at the racks, debating *sotto voce* to himself which ones to choose.

This left Luc on one side of the tasting barrel, and Frederick and Sadie on the other. Frederick held her hand still—he was really making a point of it and she couldn't decide if she liked that or resented it. In any case, he was making his intentions crystal clear.

Luc, on the other side, bit his lip and touched the bump on the side of his nose.

"Has Sadie been keeping you apprised of the news from our dig?" Frederick asked. He was being a gentleman in trying to find a polite topic of conversation, but he had emphasized the word 'our' too.

"Not really." Luc gave Sadie a piercing look. "I haven't seen Sadie much in the past week. However, I'm glad to hear it's going so well."

"It is!" Frederick said, patently relieved at the thaw in the air. Luc was at least doing as Sadie had asked him—being her friend, though it was obvious from his clenched fists on the barrel top, and the tension around his eyes that it was costing him dearly. "We've found two basins already and have begun to uncover a sort of communal house, we think. Sadie's instincts were brilliant."

"They always have been," said Luc.

"Yes, I'm just discovering that for myself. I feel so privileged to work with Sadie and get to know her better.

Sadie frowned. "Why are the two of your talking about me like I'm not standing right here?"

"Sorry," Luc said, and gave her a smile—that old smile she loved and missed so much. "Do you think your findings will move your career forward?"

"It will transform both of our careers if it continues as it's been going," Frederick supplied.

Why was Frederick answering for her?

Luc opened his mouth then shut it again. He'd been about to tell Frederick off—Sadie was sure of it. "Wonderful," Luc said, dryly.

Sadie tugged one of her loose curls, landing on something to continue pushing this conversational boulder up the hill. "How are things in the vineyards?"

Luc turned his calloused hands over to show how hard he'd been working. "Good. Lots of pruning, but I'm ahead of the work this year, which is unusual at this stage. Gaspard accused me of overthinning. Can you believe his gall?"

"You've lost weight," Sadie said. He'd taken off his jacket and she couldn't help but notice changes in him. He didn't seem skinny so much as leaner. There was barely anything left on his body but pure muscle, so much so that his jeans were hanging lower on his waist and his cheekbones jutted out. He could get a job modeling on high-fashion runways with his current look. Sadie smiled to herself. That would be the last thing that Luc would ever want to do.

He looked down, where the washboard abs that Sadie had

felt when her fingers had inched up his torso were underneath his sweater. A telltale heat rose in her face. She couldn't blush now, not when Frederick was here beside her.

"I guess I have," he said. "I've been forgetting to eat. You have too," he observed. Of course he would notice—he always did.

"I think Sadie looks beautiful," said Frederick, mistakenly defensive. Sadie was touched, but Frederick had completely missed the subtext of her exchange with Luc. They were checking in on each other. For a second, Sadie felt herself wishing Frederick hadn't come. But no, that was stupid. Frederick was giving her the kind of devoted attention Sadie had craved her entire life. What was wrong with her?

Luc's eyes narrowed at Frederick. "I'm not going to argue with that."

"I guess I have." Sadie continued as if Frederick hadn't spoken. "You know how I get obsessed and forget to eat."

"Oh, I know." Luc met her eyes then, and his gaze warmed her everywhere, even some places that she didn't want him to warm. "Are you enjoying it as much as you thought you would?"

"Even more," she said. "You saved me, by letting me do it on your land."

Luc's eyes flared then, like the flash of blue at the hottest part of a flame. Sadie's breath caught in her throat.

"Yes, truly," Frederick chimed in. "I can't tell you how grateful we are."

"Ah! You guys are going to enjoy this!" Jean came back with five bottles in his hands, thank heavens.

"I'm sure we will." Frederick cleared his throat. "I can't wait."

Luc and Sadie exchanged a glance that made Sadie feel guilty for the rest of the tasting.

chapter twenty-one

AFTER SADIE AND Frederick left, Luc lingered, ostensibly to continue his debate with Jean about whether moon cycles affected the vinification and bottling of wine, as per the old traditions; but it really was because he was hurting, and it was a relief to chat with Jean for a bit longer, before going home to sit with his own thoughts.

His body was still pulsating with possessiveness. Seeing Frederick holding Sadie's hand, and acting as though Sadie was *his* made fire roar through his veins.

He knew theoretically he should be encouraging Sadie's relationship with her colleague, but the idea of her with Frederick—with anyone besides himself, to be entirely truthful—lacerated his soul.

He had never felt possessive of any other woman in his life, however, and was baffled as to how to stop it. What would happen to his wandering lusts if a miracle happened and Sadie would have him? He was beginning to entertain serious doubts that he would ever want anyone else.

"So, those are my reasons for abandoning the idea of waiting to bottle until the moon is in the right cycle," Jean said, breaking into Luc's thoughts. "I've never seen, or more importantly, tasted, any proof that it makes any difference, and it doesn't take into account the hundred other things that determine the optimum bottling time for a wine."

Luc argued for moon cycles on automatic pilot. It would be deeply insulting to Jean if Luc suddenly agreed with him. Debates were one of life's greatest pleasures, after all. Being with Jean had just always been easy. When he was younger, and even now, he felt the occasional flash of envy that Clovis always had Jean nearby for daily advice, support, or just chats. Alphonse was a good father in many ways but working with him had always been an emotional minefield.

"Café?" Jean asked, nodding over to the corner of the *cuverie* where an old couch and table had been parked by a fancy, gleaming espresso maker that didn't look Jean's speed at all.

"*Oui, merci*," agreed Luc. "Let me guess, Clovis bought that espresso maker for the *cuverie*?"

Jean sighed, his hands on his hips, looking mournfully at the expensive-looking contraption. "How did you guess? It took me over a week just to figure out how to use it. I would have refused, but it seemed to make Clovis so darn happy."

Luc chuckled.

"He and Cerise bought one and loved it, so he insisted on buying one for the workers in here."

"It wouldn't be a bad thing if some of Clovis and Cerise's happiness rubbed off on the rest of us." Luc mused as he settled on the couch while Jean busied himself with the beautiful, but complicated-looking contraption.

"Isn't that the truth," Jean let out a happy sigh. "It does good for this old heart of mine to see. Both of them had their fair share of heartache, but now—"

"*Oui*," Luc sighed.

Jean shot Luc a sharp, questioning glance over his shoulder, and then turned to busy himself at the espresso maker again. Luc remembered the feel of Sadie's lips against his, and her silky skin against his palms. "I'm split between being happy for them and being eaten alive with jealousy."

"Who isn't?" Jean turned and leaned against the counter while the machine rattled and whistled as it made the espressos. "How are things at home?"

Luc's father's reputation was widely known, as was the general knowledge that his father's carousing made his parents' marriage a complicated one.

Luc had never been able to figure out why his mother stayed with his father despite constant betrayals, but they seemed determined, for whatever mysterious reason, to stick it out. Luc raked his hand through his hair. "The same."

Jean looked down at his feet. "Your mother?" His voice was gentle.

"Still makes excuses for him."

Jean's lips pressed together, but he said nothing.

"My father will never change," Luc said.

"No," Jean agreed. "Knowing him as long as I have, I don't think he ever will. Have you and your father talked succession planning at all? Do you know when you'll be assuming control over the Domaine?"

The power struggle between the younger generation of winemakers and their parents was a familiar one in the Côte and repeated, ironically, generation after generation. Luc's stomach dropped when he remembered he was now committed to three extra years of being in the dark about the true nature of the Domaine's finances.

Every second during the past few weeks that he hadn't been out working in the vineyards, he'd been trying to get to the bottom of the convoluted trail of accounts and loans that Alphonse had set up over the years. It bore a suspicious pattern of someone trying to cover their tracks.

Luc sighed. "It was supposed to be this summer, but it's been delayed."

Jean narrowed his eyes at Luc. "Why?"

Luc debated whether or not to tell Jean, but if there was one person he could trust, it was this man in front of him. Besides, he could never talk to Sadie about this. She'd be mortified to learn the cost of her doing her dig. He never wanted her to think, not even for a second, that she owed him anything.

"Sadie was desperate to do the dig on our property," Luc said. "She'd just lost her job for reasons…well, for reasons that were not her fault, and would disgust any decent person. The dig on our land was a lifeline for her. I knew I had to make it work, so I brought it to my father, and he demanded—."

"How much time did he blackmail you into giving him?"

Luc bit the inside of his cheek. "Three years."

"Good God, son." Jean set down a little espresso cup on the table in front of Luc and then sat down in the bashed-up armchair directly across with his espresso cup cradled in his large, capable hands. "I'm so sorry."

Luc unwrapped a sugar cube and dropped it into his cup. "Alphonse is affable enough, but I'm at an age where I want to have more control over my own destiny. More importantly, I'm worried about some financial inconsistencies I've noticed."

"But he won't let you see the accounts," Jean guessed.

Luc grimaced and nodded.

Jean leaned back in his chair and swore softly.

Luc looked at Jean steadily. "I don't regret what I did. Especially when I see Sadie so happy. This dig can get her career back on track. She shouldn't be punished for doing the right thing. I saw an opportunity to make things right for her—"

"So you took it, and it didn't matter that you had to pay the price." Jean didn't sound surprised so much as resigned.

"You can't tell her," Luc said. "She can't know."

Jean shook his head. "I would never do that."

Luc waved his hand dismissively. "Sorry. I know you wouldn't.

I just had a moment of panic there - it would ruin everything if she found out. She's just so full of joy with this dig, like a light has been turned on inside her. When she got here, she was just so heartbroken—I couldn't bear seeing her like that. I would make the same deal with Alphonse over again a hundred times."

"When did you realize you loved her?" Jean said, softly.

Luc looked up into bright blue eyes that would see through any lies. "How—?"

"What you just said. That's love Luc."

"But—"

"I've been around you two. I can see it." Jean smiled.

"See what exactly?" Luc had never felt so exposed, but at the same time Jean was just so inherently kind, he made it…not easy exactly, but easier. It was such a relief to talk to someone completely removed from his dilemma.

"The same thing I see with Clovis and Cerise."

Before Luc's mind could get into gear, his heart leapt with hope. "I just realized on this trip. Yes, I'm in love with her." Then he remembered his family legacy, and his chin dropped to his chest. "Unfortunately."

Jean frowned. "Why 'unfortunately?' I always thought you two would make a good match of it."

Luc groaned. "Where should I start?"

"Pick one reason," Jean said. "Start there."

"First of all, since I was seven, I believed I was in love with Stella, and was very vocal about that fact with Sadie. With everyone actually." He cursed his former self for his naivety and blindness.

Jean pursed his lips. "Not ideal."

Luc let out a strangled sound between a laugh and a groan. "That's putting it kindly."

"When did that change?""

Luc thought back to that first kiss with Sadie, and that pulse of joy that had raced through him. Not only did he want to gather her as close to him as humanly possible, and count every freckle sprinkled like fairy dust on her face and body, but he'd been overwhelmed with a sensation of wholeness that he'd never experienced before. It had been such a novel experience that he was only making sense of it now.

"The day after she arrived," he said. "We kissed. That was it for me. It took me a while to admit it, but from that moment I knew I'd been in love with her all along."

Jean gnawed at his lip. "Difficult, but not impossible," he muttered more to himself than to Luc.

But Luc shook his head. "It is impossible. Sadie has always made it clear she would never consider being with a man who had any interest in Stella, ever. It's one of her unbreakable rules, more like a vow she's sworn to herself. I can't blame her. She's been hurt too many times, and it kills me to think I added to that hurt. Still, I wish she knew that—"

"She's worth a thousand of Stella?" Jean said.

"*Oui*." Jean had read his thoughts.

"It sounds like you've only realized that yourself pretty recently. It might take some convincing for her to believe it too, even though it's obvious to so many of us."

Luc nodded, mentally flagellating himself for his countless mistakes. "I was such an idiot. I thought I should love Stella if that makes any sense."

Jean shook his head. "Honestly, not really."

"It has to do with my father."

"Ah." Jean said darkly and wouldn't meet Luc's eyes. "What did Alphonse do this time?"

"When I was in Grade One, shortly after I realized he was cheating on *maman*, he told me that he would stop having affairs and hurting my mother if he was able to get the one girl that all the other men wanted."

"I still don't understand." Jean's forehead puckered.

"He told me I was cursed to be like him and of course I was desperate not to be. In Grade One, Stella was the girl all the boys were in love with, so I asked my Dad if I had a chance of not being like him if I married the girl everyone wanted when I grew up."

Jean's blue eyes were incredulous. "And he said yes?"

"Yes." Luc grimaced, disgusted with the convoluted logic that had brought him to this point. "I believed him. I was so distraught after learning about my father. My seven-year old mind latched onto that as my only possible salvation. What can I say? I have clung to that idea for so long that I hardly know who I am without it. I just knew I didn't want to be like him.

Jean whistled long and low.

"It's ridiculous now that I look back on it, as I never had more than the mildest affection for Stella. It was always Sadie I wanted to spend time with, it was her I wanted to talk to. My eyes have been opened, but far too late."

"It's not too late Luc. You can explain all that to her, surely?"

Luc twisted his hands in front of him. "It's impossible. Besides the whole Stella thing, I think Sadie's falling in love with Frederick."

Jean rubbed his chin, deep in thought. "That *is* a problem. What do you think of him?"

"I hate him, *bien sûr*, especially because he's perfect for her. He shares her passion for archaeology, he respects her, and he seems to absolutely adore her in the way she deserves to be adored. It's a living nightmare."

Jean bit his lip as he mulled this over. "I still think you might have a chance," he said finally. "If you told Sadie how you felt."

Luc shook his head, vehement. "That can never happen."

"Why not?"

"Because even though I was wrong about Stella, what if I *am* like my father?" Luc was embarrassed that his words came out on something that almost sounded like a sob.

"That's ridiculous."

Luc shook his head. "I've been with many women and I've had that same emptiness he has in him when it comes to relationships—that need to rove on always to the next woman, the next thing...I share his blood, Jean. I'm his son."

"But Luc—" Jean's face was ashen.

Luc held up his hand. "If I ever convinced Sadie to be with me, how could I be certain that I wouldn't hurt her the way my father has hurt my mother? Sadie is better off with Frederick. As her friend, I know that."

Jean didn't say anything for a long while. "But you love her?"

"I love her so much it's killing me."

chapter twenty-two

SADIE ACCEPTED FREDERICK'S invitation to dinner at Le Petit Paradis in Beaune. Adèle had been right, she was stupid to keep turning down his invitations. Even though she couldn't count on anything until Frederick had met Stella, what was the harm in spending time with him outside of their dig?

Ensconced within the whitewashed walls of Le Petit Paradis, one of Sadie's favorite restaurants in Beaune, Frederick sat across a small round table for two, gazing at Sadie over the flame of the candle that sat between them. The air was filled with the delicious scent of wine and garlic, and the atmosphere couldn't be more intimate.

Sadie fidgeted. She couldn't find a comfortable position for her legs under the table without playing footsie with Frederick. She didn't want to be *that* kind of woman.

"I'm so glad you agreed to have dinner with me," Frederick said, his eyes glowing.

"Me too," Sadie said. "I love this place. We deserve a reward after all our hard work."

"We do," Frederick said, running his hand through those shiny, dark locks of his. A few women at the other tables were openly gawking at him, and a guilty satisfaction filled Sadie's chest.

She was the one who Frederick seemed to want. Wasn't *that* a turn of events?

"I so enjoy spending time with you, you know." The words weren't easy to say, but after they were out, Sadie was relieved.

Frederick reached across the table and took her hand in his. It was warm and elegant despite his being a hard worker. His fingers were long and tapered and his nails were impeccably clean and trimmed. He was zealous about always wearing gloves on the dig.

Sadie would often forget about gloves when her enthusiasm got the better of her, which was often. Her nails were rough and ripped, and dirt was ground into the lines of her palms.

"I just have to ask," he said. "Am I making my intentions clear enough? I'm interested in you as more than just a work colleague Sadie. Sometimes I'm not sure you understand that."

She had to believe him. It would be crazy not to. He was perfect for her. "I was starting to wonder…." She looked up at him shyly.

"Wonder!" Frederick laughed. It was an altogether wonderful sound. "How could you have ever doubted it Sadie?"

"It's just…you're so…"

Frederick picked up her hand and kissed it softly. It felt nice. Secure. "You are extraordinary," Frederick murmured. "And the fact you don't see it makes you even more so."

Their first course of saffron risotto wrapped in circles of prosciutto and zucchini arrived. It was delicious, but not as delicious as the fact that, throughout their meal, all the women in the restaurant openly admired Frederick, but he had eyes only for her.

They held hands in Frederick's car on the way back up to Savigny. Sadie had wondered if Frederick was going to invite her back to his hotel room, but instead he'd told her that this felt too important to take too fast. She squashed down the insecurities that bubbled to the surface, and decided he was just acting like the quintessential gentleman he was.

When he parked in the courtyard of Domaine Ocquidant, he walked around and opened Sadie's car door for her.

"You don't need to walk me up to the cottage," she said. "I know the way."

"Please," he said. "Let me or risk lacerating my feelings."

Sadie smiled. "Well, we wouldn't want that."

They walked part of the way hand in hand until they got to the path to the cottage. Suddenly, Frederick stopped.

"What?" Sadie turned to him in the dark.

"There's been something I've been wanting to do since I first saw you on that train platform." He leaned in and with two fingers under her chin to tilt her face up to his, he kissed her long and slow.

His lips were soft and warm and extremely competent, but why was she still able to have thoughts when this incredible man was kissing her?

She kissed him back. It was lovely. Anyway, that blinding passion like she'd had with Luc, that total loss of herself, was a dangerous thing. This was much better. They broke apart. Her heart started beating fast. What did Frederick think?

"That was perfect Sadie," he said. She breathed a sigh of relief.

Of course it was, because Frederick was the perfect man for her. This could really work.

He looped her arm in his and began to walk her back to the cottage. She had no idea if he'd accept, but she decided to invite him in for a coffee, and whatever else might happen. It was time to take her future into her own hands. A few feet away from the front door, however, Sadie saw a slumped shape in the dim light.

Fear prickled behind her neck.

"Is that a person?" Frederick asked, but she was already hurrying forward.

Sadie recognized Stella's suitcase and was already kneeling beside her sister's inert form.

"Frederick, call an ambulance." She didn't recognize her own voice.

"On it." He was already dialing.

She felt for a pulse. No matter how impossible Stella was, Sadie couldn't lose her twin. There is was—a steady beat on the side of Stella's neck. Relief crashed over her.

"She's breathing," Sadie said, and rested back on her heels. "Thank God."

Déjà vu flooded all her senses. Stella used to faint like this when they were in high school. Was this the same thing?

Stella's eyelids opened then. "Sadie?" she asked in a thin voice.

"Yes, I'm here."

"Should we carry her inside?" Frederick asked, leaning down to get a better look at Stella.

Sadie's heart dropped to her knees. It was starting already. Frederick would no longer be hers to discover. He would fall in love with Stella's ethereal beauty, especially given she was the archetypal damsel in distress which men could never resist at the best of times. He would be just like the other men. It wouldn't take long to transfer his affection to her twin—it never did. She felt that familiar shrinking sensation to a paler, lesser, version of herself.

"I think so," Sadie said, hating herself for her petty jealousy.

Frederick reached down and scooped Stella up with ease. Stella's eyes fluttered open.

Carrying her over the threshold? That clinched it. Frederick was as good as lost to her forever.

By the time Frederick and Sadie settled Stella down on the bed in her bedroom, the whoop-whoop of the ambulance—an entirely different sound than the ambulances in New York—could be heard in the courtyard.

"You stay," Frederick said. "I'll run down and meet them."

"Thank you," Sadie whispered. He was so good, but now his heart was Stella's.

Stella's eyes had closed again, and Sadie slid her hand under the duvet and placed it on top of Stella's chest.

She was breathing evenly, asleep rather than unconscious. Stella's normally ivory complexion was much paler than usual, and there were little beads of sweat at her hairline. She was still stunning, of course, but this was no act. She was glad Frederick had called the ambulance.

Stella's eyelids fluttered again.

"Hey Stella," Sadie kept her voice soft. "How are you feeling?"

"Terrible," Stella groaned.

When they'd been sixteen, Stella had looked exactly like this and had started passing out. "When was the last time you ate anything?"

Stella's fingers emerged from the duvet. "Can't remember. "

It wouldn't be the first time that Stella had starved herself. Sadie thought her sister's eating disorder was no longer an issue. She should have been paying more attention.

The paramedics rushed into the cottage, followed by Frederick and, not surprisingly, Luc. Of course, he'd heard the sirens.

Stella seemed quite awake now, and the paramedics were asking her a bunch of questions. Sadie had to translate as Stella's French was not great at the best of times, and certainly not under these circumstances. Sadie filled them in on Stella's history with anorexia and the fact that Stella couldn't remember the last time she ate.

They checked a bunch of things—blood pressure, dehydration, a blood sample, heart, lungs, reflexes, but in the end they just turned to Sadie and whispered to her that if she could get her to eat, then they didn't feel there was any need to take her into the hospital.

"*Merci*," Sadie said, and Frederick walked back down with them to the ambulance.

Luc stepped forward. "What can I do?

"A tray of food and drinks, probably something with some sugar."

"Done," he said. He reached out and gave her hand a squeeze before he left.

Stella was watching them all. Why had Stella stopped eating again, and where was Pablo?

"What can I do?" Frederick asked, arriving back in the bedroom, out of breath.

"Could you stay here with her while I go help Luc with the food tray? I know what she needs."

"Of course," Frederick said, and drew the old wooden chair from the corner of the room to beside the bed.

Of course, he would. Not only was it the gentlemanly thing to do, but he was as good as in love with Stella already. There were not many men who could resist such a damsel in distress set-up. Sadie tried to resign herself to that reality as she jogged over to the house. Frederick was the perfect knight in shining armor, and Stella was the princess that all knights dreamed of.

chapter twenty-three

SADIE RAN INTO the kitchen where Luc was putting the finishing touches on a tray piled high with food.

"What happened with Stella?" he asked.

"Frederick and I found her unconscious in front of the cottage."

"What were you and Frederick—" Luc began, but then he shook his head. "Never mind."

"What did you grab?" Sadie asked, glad that Luc had stopped himself before she had to.

"*Pétit beurre*," Luc waved his hand over the tray. "Orangina, Danette. Look, I have to go and reassure my parents, but I'll be along in a second. I'll bring the right things, trust me."

Sadie knew she could. He'd always been gifted at taking care of people. "Merci Luc," she said. She hoped he realized how much she meant it.

She was almost out the door of the kitchen when he called her name.

She turned around. "What?"

The line of his throat convulsed as he swallowed. "When I heard the ambulance, I was so terrified it was you…that something happened to you. I need you to know something."

Stella's breath caught as his eyes, intent and blazing, met hers.

"I love you Sadie," he said, his voice cracking on her name. "I know it probably doesn't make any difference to you, but I just need you to know."

Sadie's head spun. When had Luc realized this? It had to have been after Christmas, at least. Was he doing this because Stella wouldn't have him? Nothing made any sense.

He waved his hand. "I've been an unforgiveable fool. I realize now that I've always loved you. Only you. You don't have to say anything. Stella needs you. Go back to your sister."

Sadie nodded curtly. Even if she could form a coherent sentence, which was doubtful, she didn't have any idea what to say. The truth hit her like a mallet over the head—she'd been waiting her whole life to hear Luc say he loved her, but now it was too late. Sadie sped back, her mind in a knot.

She went into the bedroom just in time to see Frederick tucking the duvet around Stella's arms. That rich dinner sat like a lead weight in her stomach.

Stella reached out to Sadie, "Sadie! Thank God you're here." Yet, just after saying that, Stella cast a winsome glance up at Frederick.

Sadie went to her and squeezed her hand. "Luc's getting you some food. Am I right that you haven't been eating?" There was no point in beating around the bush.

Stella gave a tiny shrug of her shoulder. "Maybe."

"We're going to talk about that, but not now."

"But Sadie—"

"Not now." Sadie squeezed her hand again. "Where's Pablo?" Sadie wouldn't put it past Stella's mysterious companion to be lurking behind an armoire or something.

"He's gone."

"Oh." She had no idea if this was a good thing or a bad thing.

"Sadie," Stella said, plaintive. "Frederick, he's a—"

"He's my dig partner," Sadie explained patiently, exchanging glances with Frederick. His dark brows were drawn together, and he cleared his throat. It dawned on Sadie that something was making him acutely uncomfortable. She could practically read his mind. He was in love with Stella and didn't know how to break it to Sadie. Well, she'd make that easy for him.

"But he's—" Stella tried again.

"You should really try to close your eyes, at least until the food arrives." Sadie let go of Stella's hand and placed it back under the duvet. "You're probably dizzy from low blood sugar."

Stella shook her head wildly. "No Sadie, you don't understand. Frederick is a Lord! He's one of the richest men in England. Lord Fothergill."

Sadie's eyes raised to meet Frederick's sheepish ones. "What?" she asked him, rather than Stella. "Is she hallucinating?"

It didn't make much of a difference to Sadie, aside from the fact that he'd lied to her, but she knew it *would* make a difference to Stella. Stella would be after Frederick, Lord Fothergill, like a cheetah after a gazelle.

He dug his hands deep in his pockets. "I'm afraid not."

"I met him at a party last year," Stella said. "He's famous. He's heir to the— "

"I think that's enough for now," Frederick said to Stella. "Sadie, can we have a quick word in the living room?"

Sadie nodded, then got up and left the room with Frederick. Why had he been keeping that secret from her? Then again, she was hardly in a position to judge. She hadn't told him about the weirdness with Luc, or her expulsion from Hudson.

Frederick began to pace around the main room, rubbing his chin.

"Why didn't you say anything?" Sadie asked, more out of curiosity than hurt.

"When I arrived, I figured you already knew."

"I'm not going to lie. I tried to research you, but I could

hardly find anything about you on the internet. How is that even possible?"

Frederick shrugged. "I make it my business not to connect my academic life and my...well, my other life."

"How can one man influence the internet? It sounds ludicrous."

He nodded, his face a picture of exhaustion all of a sudden. "It's not easy and it's a constant battle to maintain a low profile. Knowing some very powerful people helps."

"Ah." The penny dropped. Frederick must be vey powerful indeed in his world.

"Precisely. Anyway, it dawned on me after we started working together that you didn't know and, more importantly, that you probably didn't care. You can't know how refreshing that was."

"I imagine." So, she'd just kissed one of the most eligible Bachelors in Britain?

"I didn't want you to find out this way." He took two strides towards her and took her hands in his. "I know I should have told you, but it was such a delight to spend time with you without all that baggage, for once."

"Wait." Sadie's mind was spinning. "You're really a professor, aren't you?"

"Of course I am." Frederick squeezed her hands for emphasis. "Being a Lord is my birthright, but being a professor is my passion."

"So you and Stella...you've already met like she said?" Sadie braced herself to accept the inevitable transfer of affections. A familiar nausea roiled in her stomach.

"Apparently. She seems to remember me, but I have no memory of her."

Sadie laughed and it came out sounding far more bitter than she'd intended. "I've certainly never heard that before."

Frederick dropped her hands and stared at her. "What do you mean?"

Sadie sighed, full of grim resignation. It would be better to set things straight sooner rather than later. "I mean that every man I know falls in love with Stella. It's just how things are."

Frederick shook his head side to side, never taking his eyes from her face. "Not me."

Sadie's disbelief must have shown.

"Truly, Sadie." Frederick stepped forward, closing the distance between them and he took her hand, then placed his hands on her shoulders and pulled her closer. He smelled completely different from Luc—like expensive cologne. "I have no interest whatsoever in Stella. From the little I've seen of her, she reminds me of my ex-girlfriend, Alexandra."

"What do you mean?" she said against his chest.

"They both seem lost somehow." His arms slipped around her. "Lost souls."

He wasn't interested in Stella? This was an entirely new experience, and Sadie had no idea how to react.

She'd never thought of Stella as being lost at all. Stella was the one who got everything handed to her. She needed to think more about Frederick's observation, but he nudged her chin up again with his forefinger.

"Besides Sadie," he added. "Who could be interested in Stella when you're around?"

Her jaw went slack.

Frederick leaned forward and brushed his lips against her bottom one. It was as much a question as a kiss. She kissed him back with gratitude. *Finally, someone chose her*. She'd been waiting for this her entire life.

They were interrupted when Luc clattered through cottage door. She jumped back from Frederick, but not quick enough. Luc's eyes flashed like a lightning strike. With his two hands he was carrying a tray full of food and glasses. Thank God, because if his hands were free, he looked as though he might have punched Frederick.

Luc said he loved her. Frederick wanted her. Sadie couldn't make sense of these new pieces of information.

She straightened her spine and met Luc's blazing gaze. "Stella's in her bedroom," Sadie said, trying so hard to control her voice that it came out sounding imperious. "Frederick and I will be there in a moment."

Frederick cleared his throat. Is that something he did every time he was uncomfortable?

Luc didn't move. That little muscle in his jaw was twitching again.

Frederick cleared his throat more meaningfully this time. "Do you need me anymore, Sadie? If you do, I'll stay, of course."

Sadie smiled up at him. "No, but thank you for everything. Go back to Beaune. You've been a life saver. Truly. I can't thank you enough."

Frederick took Sadie's hand in his. His touch thankfully didn't emit its own electric charge like Luc's. "It was my pleasure, Sadie. I'll see you tomorrow morning. Please call me if you need absolutely anything."

"She won't need anything," Luc growled. "I'm here."

Sadie glanced over at Luc. "Stella needs that food sooner, rather than later."

He didn't budge. Fine then, she would just ignore him. She squeezed Frederick's hand before letting it go. "I'll see you tomorrow morning."

Frederick glanced up at Luc's stormy face and raised a questioning brow at Sadie. "You sure you'll be all right?"

"I'm sure of it. I'll call you later. Good night."

Frederick nodded and sidled out the door, giving Luc a wide berth. Luc's fierce eyes followed Frederick's every move until the door closed, then they snapped back to Sadie.

"You can stop looking at me like some sort of angry wolf." Sadie didn't give him a chance to speak first. "You expect me to fall all over you because you decided you love me now? Given your past, how am I to know that won't change tomorrow?"

"It won't."

"You can't be certain."

"I am. I'm more certain of it than I've ever been of anything,"

Sadie shook her head. "This is getting us nowhere. Stella needs food. Come on." She walked to Stella's bedroom, and could hear Luc following her after a few seconds. She would *not* look around.

Sadie sat down on the bed beside Stella and motioned for Luc to put the tray on the bedside table. The tray Luc had prepared was absolutely loaded with all of their childhood favorites – *pétits beurres*, a glass of grenadine syrup mixed with water and a swizzle stick, Danette pudding cups, and a six pack of Pétit Gervais flavored *fromage blanc*. Her heart contracted. He was impossible, but he was also so thoughtful.

Luc knelt on the floor beside Stella. The anger had drained from his face, replaced by drawn brows and his front teeth gripping his bottom lip. For someone who didn't love Stella anymore, he looked plenty concerned.

"Not eating, Stella?" he chided her in the old way they used to as children. "What's this all about? I remember how much you loved *les petits beurre*."

"Not hungry," Stella's voice came from the duvet half covering her face, muffled.

"Too bad," Sadie sat on the bed beside her, holding up the glass of grenadine. "Luc's made you a glass of grenadine. Remember how we used to pretend it was wine?"

Stella made a half-hearted sound of protest. Sadie had no choice but to resort to harsher tactics. "Stella, if you don't drink this and eat at least four *pétits beurres* and a *pétit gervais,* I'll have no choice but to take you to the hospital. The paramedics said so."

"I can't," Stella's voice was thin and pitiful.

"You know I make good on my threats," Sadie said calmly.

She had no reason to raise her voice. Stella knew she meant it. She prided herself on never going back on her word, even if it broke her heart.

Stella cast her a baleful look and dragged herself up to sitting. She took a *petit beurre* from the plate.

"Luc," Stella said, out of the blue, "Did you know about Frederick—"

"Stella, why haven't you been eating?" Sadie interrupted her.

Stella just shrugged.

"What about Frederick?" Luc said, a crease between his brows.

"He's a Lord and crazy rich." Stella lifted her eyebrows, looking much improved.

Sadie ignored both of them. "Stella, is it because of what happened with Pablo?"

"That charlatan?" Stella made a sound of disgust. "I would never lose sleep over *him*."

"Then what?" Sadie pressed.

Luc passed Stella a second *petit beurre* and she took it, but Stella still didn't answer the question.

Sadie gave Luc a meaningful look. "Luc, maybe you could give Stella and I a chance to talk? *Merci* for the tray. It's perfect."

"Luc doesn't have to leave!" Stella protested.

"That's fine," Luc said, but with a pointed glance at Sadie that promised he wasn't done with her yet. "I hope you feel better, Stella." His eyes shifted to Sadie again. "You know where to find me."

"Yup," she said casually, but she was not about to go looking for him in the cellar or the *cabotte*, or anywhere else for that matter. Frederick had chosen her over Stella. That mattered far more than the fact he was a Lord and had a ton of money. A few seconds later, Sadie heard the front door slam shut.

Now she could properly deal with Stella. "You have to tell me what this is all about, Stella," Sadie urged. "If you don't, I can't help."

Stella snorted. "You'd like that, wouldn't you?"

Something thudded in Sadie's chest. "What do you mean?"

"Well, you have it all now, don't you? A brainy career, a catch like Frederick...you've been waiting your whole life to rub it in my face."

Sadie's face burned with shame. Stella was not entirely wrong. "Stella, what are you talking about?"

"Pablo cheated me. Are you happy now?"

Sadie covered Stella's trembling hand with hers. "You mean he cheated *on* you?"

"No! He cheated me. He made me sign this contract before we started working together. I thought it was just a standard thing, and I never read things like that in any detail, but it turned out it meant he owned all of the photos he took of me, and can use them however he wants."

Sadie sucked in her breath. *How dare he?* "But, how could he? Didn't you read the contract at all?"

"Shut up Sadie." Stella crossed her arms across her chest.

Sadie nudged her with the Pétit Gervais and a spoon. Stella took this with a roll of her eyes.

"Did you?" Sadie wasn't exactly sure why she was probing this point, but instincts were screaming at her that there was something important behind it.

"No."

"Why?"

"Because I'm not smart like you, okay? I can't just understand everything so easily."

"It's just reading," said Sadie. "It's so important to *read* contracts, especially when they concern your livelihood."

"Stop it!" Stella pressed her palms against her ears. "Just stop harassing me! I told you I'm not smart like you. I never have been. I've been able to get along just fine without reading contracts until now, it's just that he was a lying, cheating bastard."

A horrible thought dawned on Sadie. "Stella," she said, her voice gentle. "You *can* read, can't you?"

Stella crossed her arms in front of her and stared at Sadie. She was breathing so fast she was almost panting.

"Stella?" Sadie prompted.

"I can't talk about this with you." Her eyes darted everywhere except Sadie's face.

"Why not? Surely, we can talk about this, can't we? I mean, you graduated high school, so you must know how to read." There was no way Stella could have passed grade after grade if she wasn't fully literate.

"Well, I can't!" Stella burst out. "At least not very well. It takes me forever to understand the letters and put them together and half the time I can't at all. I dictate the captions on my Instagram and my assistant adds them. There! Are you satisfied now? Your stupid twin sister never learned how to read properly."

Sadie sucked in a breath. "What? But Stella, how can this be? How could teachers have passed you?"

Stella snorted. "That's the thing with looking like me, I could always find a way to make people do what I wanted."

Shame crept up Sadie's spine. She should have paid more attention. They had always been in the same grade, after all, even if they weren't in the same classes. "But how did none of us notice?"

Stella's eyes were watery. "Our parents paid no attention to me Sadie. They had you as their brilliant protégée, and then Max. I've always been the one who doesn't fit. They never knew what to do with me, so they didn't even try."

As she sat there at Stella's bedside, holding her twin's cool, delicate hand, the past rearranged itself into a new pattern. Maybe instead of aloof, Stella was resentful and hurt. Still, she couldn't go as far as saying she hadn't been loved.

"They loved you," Sadie said.

Stella shrugged, blinking away tears. "Maybe, but they never felt I was worthy of their attention."

Stella always got so much attention from the world because of her looks. That always seemed to be enough. "Do you think perhaps they thought you didn't need them?"

Stella sat up straighter under the duvet, her face flushed. "What child doesn't need their parents? Especially a child who never learned how to read properly?"

She was right. Sadie couldn't imagine a worse hell. She'd always taken it for granted that their family had been a bunch of academics, except Stella. Her father was a brilliant, beloved professor. Her mother was a revered mathematician. Even their younger brother Max, although he was rugby crazy, somehow managed to pull off effortless A's at his elite boarding school. For the very first time, she realized how alone Stella must have felt within their family.

"I'm so sorry," Sadie said, and her heart wrenched within her torso. She'd always thought their bad relationship was Stella's fault, but now those waters weren't so clear.

Stella sniffed. "They never cared about me, because all they cared about was you."

Sadie's world suspended in that instant. This was exactly what Sadie believed about everyone in her life, *except* her parents. Her heart softened towards her twin.

"Do you have an idea of why reading is difficult for you?" Sadie asked.

Stella traced the faded flowers on her duvet. "Besides the fact that I'm stupid?"

"You're not stupid Stella," Sadie said, but even as she said the words, guilt squeezed in her chest. She too was guilty of assuming beauty and intelligence was on a proportionate scale, and that because Stella got so much beauty, her intelligence didn't need to be high. Stella had probably struggled against this prejudice her whole life. Again, the order of the world shifted on its axis, reordering everything she had previously accepted as the truth.

Stella was looking down at the duvet she was twisting in her hands. "I've often thought maybe I have that thing where all the letters and symbols are in the wrong place, scattered around and upside down," she said, finally.

"Dyslexia?"

Stella nodded.

Finally, something concrete she could fix. "I can get you help with that Stella. Also, learning differences have nothing to do with intelligence."

Stella nibbled a final biscuit. "I'm tired Sadie. I need to sleep."

Sadie's eyes shifted to the platter. Stella had eaten enough for tonight. She eased Stella back in bed and tucked her in as if she was a child. She leaned forward and kissed her sister's forehead, feeling an unfamiliar tug of compassion in her heart for Stella.

"I love you, sister," she said, words that had not passed her lips in years.

"I love you, too," Stella whispered, as Sadie turned off the lamp beside the bed.

Everyone paid attention to Stella, so it had always seemed like there was never anything left for Sadie. Could it be possible that Stella suffered from a different version of the same pain?

chapter twenty-four

THE NEXT MORNING, Sadie made her way up to the dig, eager to throw herself into the backbreaking physical labor of her work.

There were so many things she needed to think through—Frederick's kisses, Luc's confession, Stella's perspective on their childhood which completely reframed most of her memories—and she could never think as clearly as when she was working with her hands and her knees in the dirt.

Frederick was probably already waiting up there for her and it would be so effortless to rely on him. Besides, he'd met Stella and he'd preferred Sadie over her twin. When he'd said that, he'd gone a far distance in spreading a balm on a lifetime of pain. That had to be the key to her heart she'd searched for all these years.

She hadn't completely exorcised Luc from her system yet, but it was just a matter of time. His change of heart had come too late—years too late. He'd just hurt her too much with his obsession with Stella. Frederick, on the other hand, had proven she could trust him.

Stella had seemed a bit better that morning and, much to Sadie's relief, had joined her for a breakfast of toasted tartines and wild strawberry jam made by Pauline.

Stella had resisted any of Sadie's rather blunt attempts to discuss the possibility of dyslexia over breakfast, and said airily that she was going to spend the morning resting and phoning a few people to see if there was anything she could do to get the rights to her photos back from Pablo. Sadie had warned Stella that she wasn't letting the dyslexia thing drop.

As Sadie skirted the edge of the courtyard, she caught sight of the familiar figure of Jean emerging from his battered blue Citroen 2CV. She called his name and headed down to him.

Jean turned his head suddenly. He didn't have his usual grin for her and he just gave her a weak wave back. Something was off. Sadie hurried down to him. He didn't walk to meet her, but instead waited by his car, wringing his blue beret in his weathered hands.

Alarm grew in her chest. What had happened? Her mind immediately flew to Luc.

"Jean," she said, when she reached him. His normally bright blue eyes were dim with worry. "What is it?"

Jean opened his mouth and closed it again. He shook his head. "I can't tell you yet. We can talk about it after, but not yet.

Sadie frowned at him. "After what? You're scaring me Jean."

Jean shook his head. "There will be fallout, but it is a fallout I have been wanting to face for years now."

She couldn't make heads or tails of his words, but it seemed like Jean was talking more to himself than to her. She'd never seen him this preoccupied. Sadie's face must have held the question in her mind.

"I know you're worried," Jean said. "But I must go and do something. Can I ask you a favor?"

"Anything," Sadie said, without hesitation.

Jean gnawed his lip.

"Whatever it is, let me help." She hated seeing Jean like this.

He nodded once. "Luc is going to need a friend in about an hour. Can you make sure you're around?"

Need a friend? What did that mean? At least it meant he was physically safe.

"I can't explain more right now," Jean said. "I will later, but not yet."

Sadie could tell from Jean's energy that he needed to leave her and do this thing that was eating at him – whatever it was.

"Where will I find him? Luc, I mean."

Jean frowned. "I hadn't thought of that. Wherever he goes when he needs to be alone to think. I'm sure that's probably not much help."

But it was. "I know where to go. You can count on me."

Jean reached out and squeezed her hand, as though he was trying to absorb some courage from her. "I know I can," he said. "I've always known I can count on you. So can Luc." She watched him walk towards the door of the house.

The dig would have to wait. She thought of going to tell Frederick, but he wouldn't worry if she was late. He would just assume she was spending time with Stella. Sadie changed her direction and headed straight for the *cabotte*.

Luc was finally getting into a rhythm of plowing the vineyards with fresh rich dirt in *les serpentières* parcel when Jean's Citroen chugged up the hill. Despite feeling he was going to leap out of his own skin ever since seeing Frederick and Sadie kiss, he sighed in relief. If anything could settle him, it was talking to Jean. It would be a welcome relief because Jean already knew the truth in his heart.

As the Citroen came closer, Luc squinted. Was that his mother in the front seat? What was she doing with Jean?

His mind immediately leapt to Alphonse. Had something happened to him? A heart attack? Murdered by a jealous husband? He dropped the plow and strode over to where they were getting out of the car. "What happened to Papa?" he demanded.

His mother shook her head, her features tight and her face pale. "Your father is fine."

She and Jean exchanged a look that he couldn't decipher.

"Maybe not fine," Pauline rectified. "But healthy." Her hands were shaking, and Jean lay his fingers on her back, lightly. He'd never seen Jean and his mother interact much before, but in that small, seemingly unconscious gesture of Jean's, there was a wealth of unspoken intimacy. What the hell was going on?

"What is this?" Luc's voice came out as impatient as he felt. They couldn't leave him confused and worried like this. Something was very wrong. He knew his mother and Jean were friends since they were small, but Luc only saw Jean at Clovis's or in Beaune. He never came to Domaine Ocquidant.

Again, a charged look between Jean and his mother.

"Luc," Pauline began, her voice unsteady, her eyes darting between him and Jean. "There is something you need to know."

"And it has to do with Jean?"

"Yes." She looked over at Jean and he nodded, encouraging her to continue.

The vineyards tilted sickeningly. He reached behind him and grabbed onto a wine picket. He would give anything to have Sadie beside him. Luckily, he was becoming well-practiced in conjuring her up in his mind, like he'd done thousands of times since that first, incendiary kiss.

"Well…," his mother began.

"Go on," Luc said, tightening his hold on the wooden picket.

Pauline's hands fluttered in front of her. "Before I met your father, Jean and I used to date—"

"Just tell him and then we can work backwards," Jean

murmured to her in a low voice. "Put the poor boy out of his misery."

"Jean's your father," she blurted out.

Luc went cold all over. He was sure if he looked down, he would see the blood rushing out of his veins and soaking into the dirt at his feet. *His father?*

He'd always felt *something* with Jean, a deep, unspoken connection that wasn't there with Alphonse, no matter how much Luc adored him. He'd never thought anything of it—after all, Clovis and Jean had a very father-son relationship and they weren't related. He needed to sit down, but there was nowhere to do that except the ground.

"Say something son," Jean said, his beret crumpled between his hands. His blue eyes were clouded with tension. *Son.* How many times had Jean called him that in the past, and he'd thought nothing of it, when actually it meant something? It meant *everything.*

His mind spun. Did they look alike? People had always commented on how Luc was the only blue-eyed member of his brown-eyed family.

"Does Papa know?" Luc asked. Luc's ribs felt too small for his pounding heart. Whatever way, poor Alphonse...

"Yes," said Jean. "He's always known."

"Does he know I know?" Luc asked.

"Yes," Pauline said in a small voice. "We told him that we needed to tell you. He was against it, *bien sûr.* Broken-hearted, actually. But Alphonse has been broken-hearted forever. He married me and claimed you as his, knowing that I loved Jean and could never love him in the same way. Please, be gentle with him."

So that's why Pauline refused to blame Alphonse for his adultery. She had betrayed him first by marrying him when she loved Jean. If his father had been feeling even a fraction of the shock Luc felt reverberating through his cells, he had nothing but compassion for him. Luc made an incoherent sound of disbelief.

"Everything Alphonse does with other women," his mother said. "He does from a place of pain."

How he wished he'd truly understood the context of this all along. Then there wouldn't have been his fixation on Stella, or his doubts about his own ability to be in a monogamous relationship.

"Why didn't you ever tell me?" It was a miracle his voice sounded calm because anger, confusion, and grief roared through him.

"To protect Alphonse," his mother said. "And you."

Luc snorted in disbelief at this. How spectacularly it had backfired. "Why tell me now?"

Again, they exchanged a look. Pauline gave Jean a little nod. Since when had they developed this shorthand communication between them? Luc shook his head. Everything was out of place. He'd not only been blind to Sadie. He'd been blind to so many things.

Jean cleared his throat. "It was because of what you said to me after the winetasting."

Luc wracked his brain. "What did I say?"

"That you couldn't ever be with a woman—with Sadie—without hurting her because you shared your father's curse of an unfaithful heart. Your mother and I…we couldn't live with ourselves knowing that you were deprived of happiness because you didn't know the truth."

You are not Alphonse's son Luc," Pauline said. "You're nothing like him. However, you are very much like Jean."

Luc raked his hand through his hair, trying to make sense of all this.

"I've never loved another woman besides your mother Luc," Jean said. "I have a faithful heart, and I wouldn't be surprised if you're the same. You just needed to settle on the right woman. From what you said to me, you've found her."

He had, but Jean and his mother had left it too long to tell him the truth. Years too long. Long enough for Luc to be convinced he too was doomed to unfaithfulness, and to convince himself that Stella was the solution. Long enough to have hurt Sadie so deeply that she would never be with him. Long enough to ruin any chance of his happiness. The damage was irreparable.

"Why aren't you two together then?" Luc demanded them. He turned on Pauline. "Why on earth did you marry Alphonse and not Jean?"

"I was under immense pressure from my family, who threatened to cut me off if I didn't marry Alphonse, because of the vines."

"Still—"

"I felt I was below your mother," Jean supplied. "At that time, things like social status counted. Hell, they still do. I didn't have any vineyards and came from a family of laborers. I believed I had nothing to offer her."

"It's no way to live Luc," his mother said. "Trust us."

Luc swore under his breath and began to pace back and forth up and down the row of vines. "I can't believe this. I cannot believe you kept this from me. This is my *life* you were both playing with. If you only understood what you've done."

"We will never stop being sorry," Jean said. "But Alphonse begged us to keep it a secret and your future is so bright."

His spinning mind finally clicked, like landing on the right combination of a lock. The vineyards. If he wasn't Alphonse's son, Domaine Ocquidant wasn't his to inherit. He'd never had any claim over them.

His life fractured in two with a splintering sound in his ears. He could not absorb one more piece of information without going mad.

He needed to be alone. No, he needed to see Sadie, but no-one else.

His mind quickly formulated a plan. He would go to the *cabotte* and phone her from there to tell her to meet him. Please God, let his cell phone get reception, for once.

He couldn't bear one more revelation until he'd seen her. He would go to Alphonse, but there was no use trying to help Alphonse with his pain before first facing his own. For that, he needed Sadie.

"I need to go," Luc said, and stalked off towards the *cabotte*.

"Wait!" his mother called behind him, but then he heard Jean's voice. "Let him go. He needs time."

His lips curled. Jean, or rather his real father, still gave good counsel.

chapter twenty-five

SADIE WAITED INSIDE the *cabotte*, sitting on the ground against the stone wall with her legs tucked up and her head resting on her knees. Her mind kept circling back to her last kiss with Luc, against the car, and how different it had been from her kiss with Frederick. That heart-swooping connection when Luc had kissed her wasn't there with Frederick—with him she'd been filled more with gratitude and a feeling of safety. Surely that was more important than the whole swooping thing,

She should have been fretting about why Jean thought Luc would need a friend, but she couldn't even begin to speculate. Jean's behavior had just been so out-of-character. She had no idea what to do with it. Instead, she kept coming back to Luc's hurried confession in the kitchen. He *loved* her? Why now? He'd been pale and shaky when he told her, but she still couldn't help but wonder if Frederick's presence accounted for that. It was just so hard to trust that Luc wouldn't change his mind.

Sadie softly banged the back of her head against the stone wall, grateful for the painful solidity of it. *Solidity.* That's what she needed in her life. Not doubt and risk.

Had she guessed right about Luc coming to the *cabotte*? Maybe he wouldn't need a friend after all, and maybe even if he did, he wouldn't choose her. He might go to Clovis or Gaspard or even Amandine. Jean might have been wrong. Luc might not need her in particular.

Yet an unruly part of her hoped he did.

She was so deep in thought that when Luc burst through the door, she jerked back so fast she banged her head on the rock behind her, swore, and clutched her head as she stood up.

"You're here?" Luc stared at her, his eyes wild. "Did you know? How did—?"

He was making no sense, but distress was radiating off him in waves. That déjà vu again. It was just like the time they were seven, and Luc had run up to the *cabotte* to tell her when he'd discovered Alphonse having sex with his mother's friend in the forest.

Now, just like then, he was breathing fast. Luc was freaking out; she knew that look. He raked his hands through his gold-streaked hair. Maybe he should sit down, but no. He clearly had a lot of adrenaline racing through him. Sadie suspected he would burst if he didn't keep moving.

"I don't know what happened Luc." Sadie kept her voice calm. "But I bumped into Jean earlier, and he told me you might need a friend. He wouldn't tell me anything else. I came here because this is...well, I guessed you might come here."

He just stared at her, vibrating with emotion.

Fear clamped over her heart. "What is it?"

"Jean is my father," Luc said, the last word coming out like a gunshot.

Sadie rocked backwards on her heels. Of all the things she had imagined, it wasn't this. She didn't ask him if it was true. Those extraordinary blue eyes of Luc's—why had she never realized they were almost identical to Jean's? And the way they both bit their lip when they were deciding something...

"My God," she murmured, her mind reeling with the implications.

"Right?" Luc said, his eyes wide and wild.

She wanted to pepper him with questions, of course. She wanted to know how this had possibly happened, and why he hadn't been told before now, but she knew Luc needed to talk first.

"They came up to the vineyards to tell me," he said, his chest still heaving. "Jean and my mother. Can you believe that? Apparently, all these years I've been thinking my father was at fault for cheating on my mom, and she was the one who'd been in love with another man all along.

"Holy," Sadie breathed.

"Did you guess Sadie? You have to tell me. Even Alphonse knew. Am I the only one who is completely blind about... about *everything*?"

"No." Sadie shook her head. "I never would have guessed Luc, not in a million years. You're taller and leaner than Jean, and you have your mother's beautiful cheekbones. I can honestly say it never crossed my mind—not for a second." Luc's parents had always felt like an immovable fact, despite their troubles.

Luc made a strangled sound, half groan and half sob. He covered his mouth with his arm. Sadie didn't stop to think, she went to him and wrapped her arms around him. She squeezed tight, just like the time before when he'd come to her in the *cabotte* this distraught. She couldn't see him in this much pain without wanting to take the burden from him and shoulder it instead.

"I'm here," she said. It didn't feel like enough, but at least he wouldn't have to process this alone. When she'd arrived at his home so bruised from New York, he'd been there for her, even though they'd quickly messed things up.

They stayed like that for a long time, anchored to each other. Her left ear pressed against his solid chest, just over his heart. She listened to it gallop, then trot, and then eventually slow to an almost normal rhythm. Maybe she should get him to sit down. Now that the adrenaline was subsiding, he'd be exhausted. She pulled him down to the ground, sitting with their backs against the wall like she'd been doing for who knows how long before he arrived.

He flexed and unflexed his hands, then finally made a sound of exasperation and pulled her on his lap. He slid his arms around her again, as if it was the most natural thing in the world.

"I just need to hold on to you," he murmured in her curls. "I'm sorry, but I feel like I'm going to drown in it, if I don't."

Sadie stroked his soft, messy locks of hair. It felt far better than it should. "I'm here. You don't have to explain."

She wrapped her arms around him. It felt so natural that their breathing fell into the same, slow rhythm.

After a long time, Sadie asked, "Luc, what can I do to help?"

His head stayed pressed against her for a while.

"Luc?" She couldn't even imagine what he must be thinking. His whole life—his very identity—had just been turned inside out. "Tell me."

Instead of answering her, he looked up and their eyes met. He was fiercely gripping his bottom lip in his teeth, and she was worried he was going to make himself bleed. The need to soothe him, to take on some of the agony she saw in his face seized her heart.

She lowered her mouth to his and gave him a desperate, searing kiss. She poured all of her frustrated need for him into it.

He reacted immediately, taking her face in his hands and saying her name on a sigh. His wildness rose to meet her own.

"Luc," she gasped after several frenzied minutes, during which every one of her senses was filled with him. "We can't do this."

He pulled back. "You're right," he mumbled. "I promised you."

He tried to just hold her, but he was having a hard time catching his ragged breath, as was she. Sadie's heart was softened by his attempts to restrain himself. The fact that it was so clearly difficult for him...well, that was the sexiest thing she'd ever experienced. Hell, she would always wonder what it would be like to make love to Luc. This circumstance would never come again. Maybe if they made love, they would both be able to move on. At least then, she wouldn't spend her life wondering.

Besides, every inch of her wanted to discover how they would fit together.

She reached over and cupped his chin and moved his face towards her. She leaned forward and pressed her lips against his.

"But Sadie," he gasped. "You said—"

"This is different," she said. "I changed my mind,"

Luc needed no further prompting. "Sadie," he groaned, and showed her with his mouth and his fingers the rightness of this, how perfectly their bodies fit together.

They swept each other along on the same wave. With Frederick she'd felt special, but with Luc she wasn't even herself anymore. Somehow, they merged together to create something far more powerful and elemental than their separate selves. His fierce need for her found its echo in the deepest, most secret part of her soul. It called to her, and with that part of herself that was beyond words, she couldn't help but answer.

He tugged his jacket off and lay it down on the earth, then lowered her gently on top, as if she was some sort of sacred thing.

"Before we…," Luc said, his voice rough. "I need you to know. There may have been others, but you're the only one who's ever had my heart."

The enormity of what they were about to do stole her breath away. It was chilly, hard packed earth beneath her back, but somehow this spot was perfect. This was the place where only the truth was allowed between them. She couldn't lie to Luc here and deny the need for him that thrummed in her blood.

He stretched out beside her, gloriously tall and firm. Their limbs quickly tangled together, side by side on the ground which smelled of limestone and grass and comfort.

"Sadie," Luc murmured, his voice full of the longing that overwhelmed her.

She couldn't explain this feeling—as though all the experiences in her life had been leading her back here to their spot, with Luc, like this. She couldn't stop herself from murmuring his name.

She wanted him closer. Her hands slipped underneath his waffle weave top and skimmed over the smooth, golden flanks of his torso. Her fingers traced his spine and fanned over his shoulder blades, memorizing every dip and curve. He shook beneath her, and she thrilled to feel his firm length against her thigh.

Luc yanked her sweater off over her head, leaving Sadie in just her bra.

She gasped as the cold ground seeped through Luc's jacket. Luc pressed urgent kisses against her mouth and gathered her up in his arms so none of her bare skin touched the ground.

All these years, she'd daydreamed of what it would be like to have sex with Luc. She'd always forced those visions out of her mind as soon as she was conscious of them, but still...she'd imagined.

And here she'd gotten it all wrong. She'd expected Luc to be smooth and polished in lovemaking—not this shuddering, passionate man who held her in his arms like she was the only thing he had ever wanted or would ever want.

"*Je t'aime*," he murmured in soft French in her ear, his voice raw with need. "I hope you know that *ma Sadie*."

He flipped her on top of him, clumsy with lust. Luc's lack of elegance was exactly what she wanted. She realized now what had been missing with her past lovers—this inexorable pull towards each other, like gravity—part of the earth beneath them and the ancient stones arching above.

To answer, she undid the button to his worn jeans and her fingers brushed the stiff shape of him. Part of her reeled that she was doing this with *Luc*, but as he pulled her even tighter to him, that was drowned in the visceral *rightness* of it.

"I don't know if I can wait much longer." Luc's voice was shaky with laughter and disbelief. "I need you now."

"Let's not wait then." She kicked off her boots, then felt the warmth of Luc's calloused fingers sliding into the waistband of her jeans and opening them, then pulling them down and off.

She did the same with his.

Finally, the only thing left separating them was the thin silky layer of Sadie's underwear.

"I'm scared," Sadie confessed, feeling his hardness against her. There was no going back from this.

"You?" he kissed her tenderly. "Nothing scares you."

"This does," Sadie said. This was the truth place after all. But still, need overpowered her fear, and she arched her hips against him. Luc cried out something unintelligible.

"Here." She felt Luc's hand join hers, and their fingers intertwined like magic. "Hold my hand, like when we ran down the vineyards when we were little. He pushed down the final barrier between the two of them.

With Luc as her mooring, she moved slightly—a move that made all the difference.

"You are perfect," Luc breathed as he slid into her.

Sadie gasped at the feel of Luc inside of her, filling her everywhere. He began to move inside her, so incredibly lovingly that tears were pricking her eyes. *This*. This was what she'd yearned for her entire life. He hummed low in his throat, every stroke an expression of joy and connection.

Sadie's heart pounded with the rightness of them. He shifted so she straddled him and took her other hand in his.

"Know this Sadie," he gasped, a while later, as he increased the pace, driving them both to the edge. "You'll always be mine and I'll always be yours."

Sadie flew beside Luc as she had when they were children, racing beside each other until the air seemed to lift them both. Then, as now, everything else fell away, leaving only exhilaration and each other. She flew higher than she ever had before, linked with him.

chapter twenty-six

AFTERWARDS, LUC COLLAPSED beside Sadie on his jacket, but didn't relinquish his hold on her.

He didn't want this moment to end—this perfect, crystalline moment when Sadie was his.

He finally gathered the courage to release Sadie just enough to look down at her. She met his eyes, a question in hers.

"What?" he asked, brushing a strand of hair out of her eyes.

"Do you regret it already?"

"How could you ask that?" He shook his head at her. "Never. What we just had together, *that* was the truth."

Most woman would ask what it had all meant, but not Sadie. She just dropped her head against his chest, flattening her ear to where his heart beat strong and steady.

Luc knew, without Sadie saying anything, that she was as stunned as he was. The explosive feelings between the two of them were amplifying rather than fading away.

Even though he felt wrung out, and more deeply satisfied than he'd ever been, he couldn't stop himself from running his hands over Sadie's body—so familiar and yet so unfamiliar at the same time. He knew already that far from sating any hunger he had for her, making love to her had stoked it a hundredfold.

To Luc, it felt like their lovemaking soldered their two souls together for good.

Besides…he wasn't Alphonse's son anymore. He never had been. That new piece of knowledge changed so much, even though it hadn't completely sunk in. Those terrible predictions Alphonse had made to him as he grew up were lies—Luc would have been furious, but right now he felt too good to be angry at anyone.

Sadie began to reach for her underwear and jeans, and Luc helped her. Her face was still flushed. *Bon Dieu,* she was beautiful.

She pulled her jeans up her legs and her lips quirked up to the side.

"What?" he murmured, brushing a curl out of her eyes.

"That was *not* how I saw this playing out."

Luc grinned. He just couldn't help himself. "Me neither, but I'm not sorry. You have to know Sadie, that was—"

She nodded with her lovely mouth curved in that smile that made even the worst day better. "I was there, too."

Luc chuckled. "It would be nice if next time we can actually make it to a bed, or at least a couch."

Sadie looked away, ostensibly to find her boots. With her back to him, she said, "I'm not planning on there being a next time. You know that, right?"

Luc went cold all over. How could she think that? He sat up and began to pull on his clothes too. It couldn't end like this. "It was more than that, Sadie. For me, it was everything."

She bowed her head and tugged on her boots.

"What was this for you, Sadie?"

"Two months ago, you were crazy in love with Stella," she said. "You were ready to go all in with her."

"But back then I thought that Alphonse was my father and— "

She turned quickly and covered his lips with her finger. "I realize that changes things…for you. The thing it doesn't change is that you chose my sister over me for most of our lives."

"But—"

"Even if it was for the wrong reasons."

"But Sadie—"

"Don't you see Luc? I'll always wonder why you were so blind to me for so long. I'll always have doubts. I don't think I can live like that Luc. It's not a stable basis to build a relationship."

"But this isn't just any relationship Sadie, we're soul mates." Sadie's words were destroying him. He realized that his obsession with Stella must have destroyed Sadie a thousand times, exactly like this, in the past.

"I know we are," Sadie said. "But being Stella's sister almost destroyed me several times over. I'm starting to get a different perspective on the past, but it doesn't change the fact I can't make such an illogical choice for my future."

"Sadie." Luc groaned. "I've been so stupid, I know. But please, give me chance to prove to you that I can be everything you need."

Sadie turned her shoulder away from him. "I know you're sorry, and would take it back if you could, but I'm just too scared Luc. I would never stop being scared if I was with you. What we just did—it was the most amazing experience of my life so far—you need to know that. I have no regrets, but I can't build my life with someone who spent most of theirs in love with my sister, even you."

Luc arched his head back and covered his face with his hands. *This wasn't happening.*

"I'll always be your friend Luc."

That was the worst of all. He wanted all of Sadie now, not just her friendship, and he knew there was no forgetting or going back on what just happened. He wanted to marry her, for them to live on the Domaine while she did her incredible research work, to have children, to—

Then he remembered. He couldn't stay on the Domaine. It was never his to begin with. He'd lost his soulmate, best friend, his vocation, and his home in one day.

"I need to go and talk to my family," he said, standing up, and swallowing down bile. "I don't know if you put two and two together yet, but I have no right on the Domaine now that I'm not Alphonse's son."

Sadie clapped her hand against her mouth. "Luc…I never even thought."

"No," Luc said, his voice coming out bitter. "I hardly gave you time for that."

"Talk to me," Sadie urged. "As your friend." He could never think of her as just a friend, not after what they'd just done, but he couldn't keep it inside him either. "The vines—I have no right to them. I never did."

"I didn't realize," Sadie said. "Oh Luc…I'm so sorry."

She was horrified for Luc but above all she was paralyzed with fear. Making love with Luc made her realize that if she went with her heart rather than her brain, that armor that had protected her all these years would be ripped away forever. Even after half an hour with him, it was gravely in need of repair. She could so easily fall for Luc with her entire body and soul. If he hurt her she honestly didn't think she would survive. It was impossible to live in such a state of vulnerability.

Luc couldn't know. Besides, right now he was preoccupied with the vineyards and rightly so. As horrible as the situation was for Luc, the distraction gave her time to gather her wits about her. "You said your father knew, and yet he has always expected you to take over. Maybe he doesn't intend for that to change. He's always acknowledged you as his son."

There, she sounded somewhat rational despite the yearning to wrap her arms around Luc again.

Luc shook his head. "I have no idea what's going through Alphonse's head right now, or ever for that matter, but regardless of what he thinks or wants, I can't take the Domaine when it is legitimately Adèle and Raphael's inheritance."

The full ramifications of Jean's revelation began to sink in. "*Oh, my God*," Sadie whispered. How she wanted to hold him and kiss him and soothe him again.

Luc had been born to be a winemaker. Whether from Jean or Alphonse or his own inclinations, it was in his blood. Sadie knew that, like her, Luc questioned many things, but never his life's work and how much he adored it. All he had ever wanted was to make wonderful wine and have the Domaine flourish so he could look after his family.

Why would Pauline and Jean work so hard to keep Luc's paternity a secret for so long, and then tell the truth? "Why now?" she asked him. "Why did Jean and your mother tell you now?"

"You," he said, his blue eyes full of torment.

"What?" Her heart skipped a beat.

Luc dropped his head to his knees, then lifted it after what felt like a long time. "After the winetasting, Jean guessed how I felt about you. I told him we couldn't be together because I was too much like Alphonse and was doomed to hurt you in the end, and that I couldn't live with that. I think he's always been rooting for us to end up together, so he decided it was time to tell me the truth."

A rush of doubt broke through all the vows Sadie had made to herself. Maybe Luc really had changed, and maybe, just maybe, his choice of Stella was born from the mind of a seven-year-old who was suffering and grasping for help.

Then why did she feel like a trapped animal who was trembling with the need to flee? She remembered Thomas, and that horrible moment when he'd confessed he'd been imagining Stella to keep himself aroused during Sadie's horrible first attempt at sex.

If she'd been devastated then, it would be nothing compared to how Luc could hurt her. Her spine stiffened. Maybe Jean's revelation had cleared the way for Luc, but it hadn't for her.

She remembered the *galette*, and that wave of grief when he'd chosen Stella over her in front of all their friends. And then he'd done it again, and again, and again throughout the years, always choosing Stella. If she gave Luc her heart, which would be so effortless, she would also be giving him the power to destroy her completely.

"I'm confused about pretty much everything Sadie," Luc said, running his index finger down from her temple to her jaw. "But not how I feel about you."

But that was the problem, wasn't it? Luc had come to her with his sudden change of heart in weakness—at his most vulnerable moment—not in strength. Who was to say he wouldn't change his mind once these storms had passed? All Sadie had ever dreamed of was to be wanted for herself, like Frederick seemed to want her.

She wanted to reach out and touch Luc's golden skin, kiss the creases on his brow away, feel the hard warmth of his body against hers, but that was just lust, surely. A chemical reaction. That was not enough to base a life on. Frederick's clear words and actions were. She was going to have to tell him that she'd slept with Luc. Keeping it a secret from him had never crossed her mind. She wouldn't blame him if he lost interest in her completely.

Sadie scooted back on her knees. "Your whole life has changed in an instant Luc. You shouldn't even be thinking of relationships right now. There is too much for you to figure out first. I'll be here for you to vent to and support you and anything else you need, but you should know that as for us…for me, anyway, this"—she nodded to the earth where they had just made love—"doesn't change anything."

Who was she kidding? It had changed everything, and she'd never forget it.

"Please—"

She shook her head. "I'm the least of your worries right now Luc."

"I love you Sadie, and it's not going to stop."

She pressed her lips together to make sure she didn't reciprocate. It would be so easy, and so glorious, to just give in and be with Luc, but it would also be far too dangerous. "When are you going to talk to Raphael and Adèle? I can come with you for that."

He shook his head. "I need to talk with my father first and I need to do that alone."

If Luc was hers she could soothe him in a million different ways, but the fact he turned to her in a moment of weakness didn't predict what he would do when he inevitably found his strength again.

"You can come and get me whenever you need me."

Luc lifted his left brow.

"I mean, as a friend."

He reached out and crushed her against him, his lips meeting hers.

There it was again—the physical pull she didn't understand and that obliterated all logic—binding them together like magnets. Her fingers caught in his soft hair and stroked that tender skin on the back of his neck, wanting him inside her again.

Frederick's kisses were questions; Luc's were answers. Sadie was overwhelmed with the need to know all the answers.

His fingers slipped up under her sweater as she shivered in pleasure underneath him. Then the rumble of a vineyard tractor outside brought her back to her senses, and Sadie pushed away from him and stood up, breathing hard.

"No," she said. "We can't Luc." She paused at the door of the *cabotte*. "I'm here for you if you need me as a friend, but no more."

She had to leave him then, completely battered, even though it tore out her heart. She knew with visceral certainty that if she stayed one minute longer, her self-denial would be no match for the pull of him. They would end up making love again. It would be spectacular and wild, and after that she would be beyond saving herself.

chapter twenty-seven

LUC WALKED DIRECTLY from the *cabotte* to the Domaine's cellars after taking a moment to wallow in the wreckage of what used to be a fairly good life. He may have even shed a few tears, grieving for what had been taken from him, and what he had screwed up all on his own.

Now that he'd felt his own pain, even though he was far away from reconciling himself to any of it, Luc needed to find his father, although strictly speaking Alphonse wasn't Luc's father anymore.

Alphonse would be hiding in the cellars just like Luc went, without thinking, to his and Sadie's *cabotte*. No matter what Sadie said, he would always know the rightness of how it felt to be with her so completely.

Normally, he would be dreading this conversation with his father, but after Sadie's rejection of him, nothing much seemed to matter anymore. He'd lost his most solid foothold in life and everything else—even the fact that Alphonse wasn't his real father—felt immaterial.

How had he been so stupid to think Sadie was ready to jump into a life with him just because his paternity had changed and he confessed his love for her? He realized now that none of that, or their heart-stopping lovemaking, could make up for the hurt he'd caused her in the past.

In the end, he was doomed to repeat the dismal example of his true biological father, Jean, yearning for a lifetime after a woman he couldn't have.

Sadie was right about one thing. After Jean's revelation, Luc felt like he barely knew himself anymore. Who in their right mind would want to be with anyone in his current state? Then there was the material side of things. He couldn't support a wife and a family as a winemaker with no vineyards.

He descended the cellar stairs into that hushed, timeless place. Alphonse must be hurting too. If all Luc could accomplish in this rubble of a day was take away even a fraction of his father's hurt, then that would be something.

As expected, Alphonse was there in the tasting room, leaning heavily against a barrel, an open bottle of wine on the barrel and a half-drained glass in his hand. From his defeated posture and the smell of freshly spilled wine, Luc knew he was already drunk.

"Papa," Luc said, to get his attention. It seemed so strange that this overwhelming, overbearing figure who had formed Luc's view of the world and himself was, in fact, not related to him at all. Luc didn't belong to Alphonse, as he'd always believed.

If he didn't belong to Sadie either, did he truly belong to anyone?

His father raised bleary eyes to Luc's face. "I'm not your Papa," he choked out. "But you know that by now."

"Why?" Luc put his hand on Alphonse's burly forearm. That one word summarized so many questions. Why had his father decided to bring him up as his? Why had this been such a secret? Was this why his father wouldn't give him control of the Domaine?

Instead of answering, his father covered his eyes with his big, meaty hand and crumpled into a chair nearby. He bowed his head and a wail of pain, like something coming from an injured animal, filled the room.

Luc pulled a chair beside him and sat down. He took his father's hand in his and squeezed tight. Alphonse gripped Luc's hand so hard that the bones in his fingers felt like they were about to shatter. It reminded Luc of how he had held on to Sadie in the *cabotte* as though his life depended on it. In all the ways that counted, it did.

"She never loved me," Alphonse gasped after a while. "I've always loved your mother, but her heart was already taken. I was a fool. I thought I could make her love me."

An understanding began to dawn on Luc. "Is that what all the other women were about?"

His father knuckled tears from his eyes. "I was trying to make her jealous. Trying to get her to show something for me besides duty. But it never worked. Never."

"I'm sorry Papa," Luc said. He truly was. He was sorry for all of them. His mother had been correct. All of Alphonse's womanizing came from a place of deep suffering. It hadn't been a wise course of action, but it was a profoundly human one, just as Luc's fixation on Stella had been.

The backstory of his life—that his father constantly betrayed his mother, was only a fraction of the truth. His mother had betrayed too—marrying Alphonse when she knew she could never love him.

"Was she pregnant with me when you married her?" Luc asked, his voice quiet.

Alphonse nodded again, still not raising his head.

"And you knew?"

Alphonse squeezed Luc's hand in confirmation.

"You knew I wasn't your child, but you married *maman* anyway?"

"Of course." His father finally raised his head and met Luc's eyes. "I would do it again. I've always wanted you to be my son and it killed me you weren't. You couldn't be his either, when I was the one who fed you and taught you how to harvest the grapes and…I tried everything, but it still didn't make you mine."

In a way it would be easier if his real father was someone evil and neglectful, but Jean was neither of those things. Luc adored Jean, so he couldn't promise to reject him to make Alphonse feel better. Still, he could reassure Alphonse on one point. "Jean may be my biological father," Luc said. "But you will always be my *Papa*."

Luc's father raised teary eyes to him. "You mean that?"

"Yes."

"Can you keep this a secret?"

Luc hesitated. He wanted to take away his father's pain, but he couldn't make that promise yet. He couldn't go back to not knowing or keeping the lie alive now that he knew.

"I can't promise that Papa," Luc said, as gently as he could. "But know that I will always be your son, no matter what." He squeezed his father's hands tightly to underline this point. "You're not going to lose me that easily."

Alphonse sniffed. "It breaks my heart to think that you're not mine."

Luc didn't know what to say to this. As he was quickly learning, there were some regrets that could not be fixed, just carried.

"What we must talk about sooner rather than later is this Domaine," Luc said. He hated to hurt his father further, but he had no choice. What was wrong needed to be put right. He stood up and began to pace back and forth. "I have no legal right to it."

Alphonse looked up at him, his eyes sharp now, despite all the wine he must have consumed. "On your birth certificate I'm listed as your father. As far as I'm concerned, this changes nothing. I groomed you to take over the Domaine, Luc, knowing all along that you were Jean's child."

"Is that why you've been so reluctant to turn the reins over to me?"

Alphonse heaved himself up and walked over to the barrel. "*Non*! I know damn well you'll do a better job than I ever did." He shoved his hands deep in the pockets of his jeans.

"Then why, Papa?"

"Tell me this Luc," Alphonse poured himself another glass of wine. "What will I be left with when I stop working? Retirement with a wife who has never loved me?"

Luc stopped pacing and leaned against the other side of the barrel. "I never thought of that. Is that the only reason you haven't wanted to pass on the Domaine to me, to keep busy? Is that why you blackmailed me for three extra years so Sadie could do her dig?"

Alphonse scrubbed one of his hands over his face. His shoulders dropped. "The truth is—I might as well get it all off my chest—I've been hiding some things from you financially-speaking, and if I gave you control you would find out."

Luc's heart sunk. He didn't think his terrible day could get worse, but here they were, with his worst suspicions about the finances of the Domaine about to be confirmed. "How bad?" he asked.

"Bad," Alphonse said.

Luc emerged from the cellar even more stunned than when he'd gone in. His father had opted to stay down there, too ashamed to confront his wife and other children yet.

The extent of Alphonse's poor financial decisions and bad debts was nothing short of catastrophic. Only an hour before, Luc had been convinced that by taking over the Domaine he would be usurping a role that was no longer rightfully his. Now, after hearing his father's confession, he was inclined to think that giving his siblings the Domaine as the rightful heirs might, in fact, be cursing them with a poisoned gift.

The financial situation of the Domaine was as bad as it could be without actually declaring bankruptcy—yet. If all the different banks knew the myriad of loans Alphonse had taken out, and under different names, no less, they would foreclose within hours.

Everything hinged on the year's harvest. If it was a great year, meaning both exceptional yields and quality of the grapes, they had a slim chance at squeaking by with the advice and knowledge of his friends like Clovis, Gaspard, and Amandine.

Alphonse had been masterful at hiding his squandering of the Domaine's funds on all sorts of bad investments and straight-out gambling. Luc suspected they were desperate attempts to strike it rich and finally win over his children's love and his wife's adoration.

In the past, Luc would have felt contempt at such reckless behavior, but since wanting Sadie…he felt only sympathy for Alphonse. What lengths would he go to in order to capture Sadie's heart? He wasn't sure there were limits for him anymore either.

He opened the door to the main house and was struck by the unusual hush. Knowing his mother, she'd surely told Adèle and Raphael already to soften the blow for Luc. How exactly they found out didn't much matter. What mattered was in its current state the Domaine was a nearly impossible situation to just hand over to his sister and brother, and then duck out. He couldn't abandon them like that, even though it was their Domaine now.

Sure, Alphonse might say it was still Luc's, because his name was on Luc's birth certificate, but there was the practical side of things and then the moral side.

He couldn't take what was rightly his siblings' and look at himself in the mirror ever again. He rubbed the bump on the side of his nose. It was the same as defending Suzette against those Grade Eight girls when he was little, and Sadie reporting on Professor Harris. There was just a right thing to do. Period.

Again, the need to have Sadie by his side left him hollow. He couldn't ask that of her, not after the way she'd left him, resolute and untouchable. She'd been right that he'd come to her in crisis. He knew he would need her just as much, if not more, in better times, but of course she didn't believe that. Why would she after he'd been preoccupied with Stella for years? He could only blame himself for Sadie's conclusion.

However, when Luc entered the kitchen, he found Sadie there, sitting at the kitchen table beside Adèle and Raphael. The silence filled the air more than any chatter ever could. They'd been waiting for him.

"You didn't need to come," Luc said to Sadie, but the easing of his heart told him something very different.

"Do you not want me to be here?" Sadie asked, her golden eyes meeting his, direct as usual.

"Actually…I do," Luc said. "Very much."

Sadie gave a short, quick nod. "I figured you'd come here next and I also knew you'd need a friend."

Her words were a punch in the gut. Every inch of his skin remembered the feel of being inside her. *Friend.* No. It could never be enough.

But that wasn't why he was here. It was clear from Adèle and Raphael's pale, tight faces that they knew.

"Where are *Maman* and Jean?" Luc asked as he came in, pulled out one of the empty kitchen chairs, and sat down.

"They left a while ago," Raphael said. "After telling us."

Luc couldn't even imagine where they had gone.

"How are you?" Adèle asked, sliding her hand across the table and squeezing Luc's forearm. "I just want to make one thing clear—for Raphael and me, this changes nothing. You've always been one hundred per cent our brother and you always will be."

Sadie smiled at Luc, as if to say *you see?* Luc remembered the hitch in Sadie's breath when they joined.

"*Merci* Adèle," he turned to his sister. "It doesn't change anything in my heart for you two either."

"Good," said Raphael, sighing. "So, this means you'll still be just as annoying?"

"You can count on that."

Raphael rolled his eyes, but then moved over to his brother, and clasped him in a firm hug, before sitting down again. Luc bit his lip. His siblings were at various stages of failing at holding back tears, but Luc had already shed his—although truth be told there had been more tears over Sadie than his parentage—alone in the *cabotte*. Luc kept one of each of their hands firmly in his.

"However, this does change some practical things," Luc said, squeezing their hands. He looked up at Sadie, and she nodded. "Because I'm not Alphonse's biological child, I have no right to this Domaine, this house, or any of it. It should all rightfully be yours."

Adèle's and Raphael's eyes went wide.

"I don't want it," said Adèle, shaking her head wildly.

"Good God, neither do I." Raphael waved his hands in front of him. "That would ruin *everything* for me."

"Same for me," Adèle said.

He was bereft of words. How could anyone not want to be a winemaker? It was inconceivable.

"Luc, you must understand," Adèle continued. "Both of us purposely chose other careers, despite pressure to go into winemaking. We are happy doing what we do, and neither of us wants to change. Isn't that right, Raphael?"

He nodded vigorously. "*Absolument*."

They weren't seeing the whole picture. "The thing that troubles me is, if you'd known that the Domaine would come to you instead of me, would you have made those same choices in the first place?"

Both of them nodded so vigorously that Sadie chuckled. She and Luc exchanged glances and Sadie flashed him a wry smile. Luc remembered the feel of her skin under him.

"Please, Luc," Raphael said. "You cannot know what a relief

it is to us that you take the Domaine off our shoulders. Take our shares. Take it all. The Domaine is a burden to us, not a gift."

They had no idea just how true that statement was. Luc had planned on telling his siblings about the dire straits of the Domaine, but now…it would just create extra stress for them, and what was the point of that if he could manage to pull them all out of this financial abyss? As the older brother he had always tried to protect them from such things, and the habit was hard to break.

Also, Alphonse was already crumbling under the revelations of the day. It might destroy him for his other children to know of how his actions had placed the entire family in jeopardy.

All that was left for Luc to do was fix what his father had done.

"*D'accord*," Luc said. "But if I do continue, I want to make both of you equal shareholders and trust me that, as of next year, I'll make everything completely transparent so you can check in on the finances or anything else at any time."

"But we don't need that Luc," Adèle said. "We trust you."

"It's not just for you," Luc said. "It's also for me."

chapter twenty-eight

SADIE DIDN'T GET back to the dig, or to Frederick, until the next day. She'd gone straight from the *cabotte* to the house to be there when Luc told his siblings.

She'd sent Frederick a quick text to say because of personal matters she wouldn't be back on the dig until the next morning. That was the honest truth of it, yet she still felt as though she was lying to him by not telling him the whole story.

She would, though. She was going to tell him the truth about what had happened with Luc. If she was going to aim for a normal, healthy relationship, it couldn't be based on an omission.

Besides, they were starting to dig a new section of the site and they needed to log a solid workday if they were going to move forward. Sadie knew if she didn't get things out in the open, she wouldn't be able to concentrate. She needed all her focus, because this next patch of the dig felt—she couldn't explain it—like it held something extraordinary.

If only she could get the memory of Luc's expression of reverence when they were making love out of her mind, it would be easier to concentrate on what she needed to do.

At least she didn't need to worry about Stella in all this uproar. She'd accepted the news that Jean was Luc's real father with little more than a shrug, and had been busy doing an internet search on Frederick when Sadie had finally returned to the cottage. Seeing as he worked so hard to stay anonymous, that could keep her busy all day.

Stella still refused to talk any further about her possible Dyslexia with Sadie. Maybe she should have pushed harder, but she comforted herself with the observation that Stella was eating again.

The cold morning air, and her conscience, nipped at Sadie as she arrived on the dig. How should she broach the topic of her and Luc, and the fact they'd made wild, passionate love in the *cabotte*, with Frederick?

She paced back and forth on the edge of the new section of the dig, peering at the subtle undulations of the ground, her unruly mind wandering back incessantly to the euphoria of Luc caressing her, whispering his love for her in the whorl of her ear, telling her, showing her in a million different ways… *No. Stop.* She couldn't ruin the sense of herself she'd struggled her whole life to build.

Making love to Luc had felt like she was leaping off a cliff—that same breathlessness, that fleeting, euphoric sensation of being caught by the universe, then the inevitable crash when it was over.

Why did it have to be so completely unlike anything she'd ever experienced before? The fierce hunger in his blue eyes, the sheen of sweat on his muscled forearms, his hands shaking with need. She cursed the trees around her—why did she have to feel that connection she'd yearned for her entire life with Luc? She could never let herself have him, so what was the point to it all?

She wanted to feel angry with Luc—it would make this tumult of emotions easier to sort through—but being mad at Luc, particularly after they had made love, was like being mad at a part of herself. Sadie had made love to him just as much as he'd made love to her. In the deepest intimacy they'd been as they'd always been, equals, running side by side. But so what if they had an overpowering physical connection? That didn't mean that all of a sudden just because he'd changed his mind she could trust him with her heart.

Given the nature of her relationship with Frederick, Sadie was aware her confession might seem bizarre, even if it was the right thing to do. They had kissed, and it had been lovely, but that was all so far.

Rationally, Sadie knew that Frederick could be the perfect person for her. He had been upfront and unequivocal about his interest in her. That was a welcome change. Frederick had never hurt her like Luc had, and signs were he never would. However, chances were Frederick wouldn't be interested in her anymore after he learned what she'd just done with Luc. Why would he?

Sadie shook her head. She'd almost certainly sabotaged any future of working with Frederick on this dig too. She'd been so foolish. Still, she couldn't quite regret making love with Luc.

Now she knew just how good it felt to be with him, and how completely he could destroy her. She had to make her decisions accordingly.

"Sadie," Frederick appeared through the trees. "What happened yesterday? I was so worried. Was it Stella?"

"I have to tell you something," she said. "I don't think you're going to like hearing it."

Frederick stood beside her, dark and dashing and intellectual, not to mention a Lord if Stella was right, not that Sadie cared much about that part. He was everything she ever searched for in a man.

"Is it to do with Luc?" Frederick's dark eyes met hers.

Sadie nodded. She had no idea how he'd guessed, but she was glad that he had.

Frederick cleared his throat. "Did you sleep with him?"

Her eyes leapt to his. "How did you know?"

He turned so his back was to her and put his hands on his hips, as though he was trying to collect himself. After what felt like a long time, he turned back and faced her again. "There was something palpable between the two of you, something unresolved. It didn't take a genius to—"

"It was a mistake," Sadie said, yet something about saying that felt wrong. Surely it couldn't be a betrayal towards Luc if she'd told him straight up the same thing.

"Are you two together now?" Frederick asked, his vowels clipped and precise.

"No. Like you said, it was just something we had to get out of our systems, but I made it clear it won't happen again. It's finished now. I swear." Her mind meant every word, even if her heart hadn't quite caught up.

"So, you don't want it to happen again?" Frederick asked. He remained completely rigid and still, a slight frown on his lips.

"Never." The word pierced her heart like a blade. *Never.* She would never experience that sense of ecstatic belonging again. Or maybe she could, with Frederick. She owed it to herself to try.

Silence descended between them, but not the familiar, comfortable silence of them working side by side. Finally, Frederick said. "Then it doesn't matter."

"What?" Sadie didn't trust her ears.

"What happened yesterday with you and Luc. Let's forget it."

"Could you really do that?" Even though it was more than Sadie had ever hoped for, somehow it felt rather...bloodless... especially compared to Luc's unbridled, illogical emotions. But surely, Frederick's way was better. It was a good thing to have a man that was ruled by his head rather than his heart.

Frederick tilted his head. "I'm obviously upset about it and I wish it hadn't happened, but at the same time part of me feels like it was inevitable. Does this mean we can put Luc behind us?"

"Yes." Sadie's voice broke in the middle of that simple word.

"Then this clears the way for us."

Sadie was so shocked at Frederick's phlegmatic approach; she honestly didn't know how to react. "Ah...yes. If you're...I mean—"

"I'm still interested, if that's what you're getting at." Frederick gave her a crooked smile. "You're exactly the woman I've been searching for."

"Really?"

"Yes."

"And you are not in danger of falling in love with Stella?"

Frederick chuckled. "Absolutely no risk of that. Like I told you, my ex-girlfriend was very similar to Stella in many ways. Never again."

"And you have no problems working with me, now that I've told you that?"

Frederick shook his head. "Of course not. If I did, I'd inform you."

His straightforwardness was exactly what she needed in her life. Frederick would never break her heart, leave her guessing how he felt, or get carried away by desire.

Still, Sadie was bothered by something. Was it his calm or his ruthless logic? Maybe it was because she was used to Luc, or because Frederick was British, and an aristocrat no less. They were known for being detached, weren't they? She would be self-sabotaging if she didn't grasp at this unexpected chance.

"I'm interested," she said, looking at him in the eye. "And the thing with Luc is over."

"Let's just soldier on, then," he said, nodding briskly.

Let's just soldier on? "But surely you must be upset." Sadie flung her arms out to encompass not only their dig but their whole relationship she had just stomped all over.

"I am," he said, his dark eyes meeting hers. "But I have been brought up to govern my emotions, rather than let them govern me."

Sadie swallowed. "I suppose that's an excellent thing, although I don't feel as though I deserve such forbearance."

Frederick took two steps until he was close to her. So close, she saw the trouble in his eyes. It was costing him to be this rational.

"Like I've said before Sadie," he said. "You're special. I wouldn't be this forgiving if I didn't think you were worth it, and then some."

Frederick leaned forward and pressed a light kiss against her mouth, then another, then another. They didn't set fire to her soul like Luc's kisses, but that was for the best. Surely a courteous partner with incredible patience and understanding and shared interests was a good thing?

He held her lightly. "How about we get to work?" he said, dropping his hand from her neck. "I think some physical exertion and distraction would do us both some good."

"Wonderful idea," she said, and dropped to her knees in the dirt. Relief warred with confusion under her breastbone.

They worked like demons, both possessed to pour their pent-up emotions into the soil they dug up. Early in the afternoon, Sadie had felt her spade hit something hard, and when she took her finer instruments to dust it off, she saw it was a bronze bell. Then she found another one, then another, then another, each bigger than the next.

She called for Frederick, and he ran over. They hugged and kissed and laughed with delight over their find. They debated whether the bells were used for agricultural or worship as Sadie theorized (and hoped) or something else entirely.

At the end of the day they were dirty, drained, and elated, and there seemed to be a new understanding forged between them. The basis of something good and real. How wonderful to be with a partner in work and life who shared her obsession with archaeology. So what if they didn't have the crazy passion together she had with Luc? They had other shared passions that could prove just as powerful.

Frederick kissed Sadie—long and full of promises—before he left.

She grabbed his sleeve as he was about to walk away. He turned to her with a wide smile.

"How are things going to be when you see Luc?" She hated to ask the question, but she had to.

"I can't speak for him, but I can keep a civil tongue in my head. I'm in this for the long game," Frederick said.

"Thank you," Sadie squeezed his arm, feeling truly grateful for his steady good sense.

chapter twenty-nine

LUC AND ALPHONSE were at the Notary's office. It was the culmination of two weeks of solid meetings with bankers, suppliers, and straight up lowlifes who loaned out money at extortionate rates.

He'd barely seen Sadie and his soul felt like it was splintering off bit by bit. It was probably for the best—if he was to have even the slimmest chance of pulling his family and the Domaine out of this abyss, he could not be distracted. If only his mind and body listened to logic—which they did not. She somehow infused every thought and every thud of his heart.

The Notary moaned, which jerked Luc to attention. "*C'est un disastre,*" he sighed.

Of course it was a disaster. There was no point in moaning. Luc wanted to fix the problem, not waste time lamenting it unlike Alphonse and almost everyone they'd met with (except the loan sharks, who'd been downright threatening and difficult to appease).

"But with the way I've organized things now, if we have a good harvest, maybe we could—" Luc began.

"*If* we have a good harvest," Alphonse said, imbuing his first word with doom. "There could be mold, or hail, or a late frost."

"Yes, yes, I'm aware of all that," Luc said, struggling to rein in his temper. "But our only other option is declaring bankruptcy now and losing the Domaine. I refuse to do that without a fight."

"It will be all but impossible," intoned the Notary.

Luc bit his lip to stop himself from being rude to the Notary who had been serving the family since Luc was a child.

"Well," Luc slapped his knees, trying to infuse a more energetic, less fatalistic mood to the proceedings. "I have a Domaine to save. We're done here, are we not?"

The Notary squinted at him over his half-moon spectacles. Full of his own consequence, he'd never been a man who liked to be rushed. "You've always been impetuous, haven't you?" he said to Luc.

"I'm not so sure about that," Luc said. "But one thing I've never been is defeatist."

They said their good-byes and Luc herded a teary Alphonse out the office door as quickly as he could. Luc didn't have time to sort out his emotions, but between Sadie, Jean being his father, and the fact that he actually shared no blood with Alphonse at all, he knew that he had a lot of work ahead of him to know his own mind. However, he had to save the Domaine first. Only then could sort out the tatters of his life.

Alphonse leaned on him heavily as they made their way across the parking lot on an unseasonably warm March day. The vines were already showing signs of flowering, which was the most dangerous time of all for late frosts. Luc never trusted it when the early Spring was warm, especially now when everything rode on this harvest.

Alphonse was still blinking away tears. He'd seemed to age ten years in the past two weeks and was acting helpless in a way that filled Luc's chest with a confusing mix of compassion and anger.

If only Alphonse had let him see the bank accounts earlier, if only he'd let Luc in…but then again, who was Luc to blame his father for making mistakes? God knows, he'd made more than his fair share.

If only he could talk to Sadie, this whole mess would be so much lighter to bear. He heard through his family that Stella was getting healthier, and that Sadie and Frederick were making incredible discoveries. Not only did he not have the time to go and see what all the fuss was about, but he knew he couldn't bear seeing Sadie and Frederick together as a couple. Frederick probably was better for her, but Luc knew one thing for certain—no one could ever love Sadie like he did.

Sadie was enjoying a celebratory glass of Vosne-Romanée with Frederick and Stella after yet another successful day on the dig. She was getting along with Stella better than she ever had in the past, with the exception of Stella stonewalling her whenever she tried to bring up getting testing and help for her likely Dyslexia.

Stella's presence was convenient in a way—Sadie and Frederick had continued to kiss and make out, but Stella's presence in the cottage meant that so far they hadn't progressed beyond that. Sadie's mind still felt too full of Luc to feel right about getting intimate with Frederick. He was being remarkably patient.

Sadie sensed, and believed Frederick did too, that Stella's progress with her eating properly might be setback if she realized that Frederick and Sadie were a couple. She was still vulnerable, so Sadie and Frederick acted with a circumspection that suited Sadie well. He was lovely, there was no doubt about that. Being with him also felt so very safe.

Sadie just had to be patient. Surely it was just a matter of time to get Luc out of her system.

Frederick was telling Stella the tale of how Sadie had dug up three statues out of the area of the dig they were now convinced was a sanctuary—a place of prayer and worship—something that historians knew very little about in Gallo-Roman culture. Their findings had already made this dig historically significant.

"Sadie has the most remarkable instincts of any archeologist I've ever worked with," Frederick said to Stella, his gorgeous face glowing from exposure to the warm Spring air and the jubilation of how this dig was going to change the face of Gallo-Roman history forever. "She is brilliant…just brilliant."

Stella usually had a rapt expression on her face when she listened to Frederick talk, but now her lips were pressed in a straight line. "Yes, Sadie has never let me forget her brilliance for one second. It's made me feel even more stupid than I already am."

Sadie made an incoherent sound of protest. "That's not fair Stella. I never flouted my grades in front of you."

Stella narrowed her eyes. "How do you think I felt when you came home with all your A+'s when I had D's?" Stella's eyes darted to Frederick and she forced a smile. "Of course, with our parents being academics, you can imagine how much importance they put on school."

Sadie was still reeling with indignation. *She* had been the one who was overshadowed her whole life by Stella's beauty. Sure, maybe her parents cared about school over looks, but they were in the vast minority.

But Frederick reached out and took Stella's hand across the table.

"You poor girl," he said. "I cannot even imagine the suffering you experienced your whole life. I can't believe your parents, especially being academics, didn't think to look into your learning differences and help you."

Stella's shoulders straightened and her face took on a new glow. Sadie wondered, not for the first time, if Stella was not half in love with Frederick. A burst of jealousy flared in her chest, and she tried to douse it with the memory of Frederick telling her he would never be interested in Stella.

"They just ignored me." The shine of tears in Stella's eyes was real. "They had two other smart children, so I guess they just figured 'why bother with the stupid one?'"

Sadie opened her mouth to defend her parents then shut it again. As difficult as it was to admit it, Stella had a point. Her parents shouldn't have just let Stella accumulate D's without looking into it. Maybe they had been embarrassed to seek help for their daughter, which was a horrible thought.

"I'll tell you what," Frederick said, still squeezing Stella's hand. "One of my closest friends back at Cambridge is one of the world's preeminent Dyslexia researchers. If you come to England with Sadie and me in the future, I will set you up with him."

Stella leaned forward, blinking. "You would do that for me?" she asked breathlessly.

"Of course," Frederick said, squeezing Stella's hand one last time before letting go. "It would be an honor to help Sadie's sister."

There was bitterness in the look Stella sent Sadie, but she turned a bright smile on Frederick. "That would be wonderful, when do you think we can go?"

Frederick took a deep breath and looked over at Sadie with a complicit grin. "I've been meaning to talk to you about this anyway Sadie," he said. "I think perhaps we should take a break and head to England over the next few days to report into the University. They've been nagging me for an update but I've been putting them off as I wanted to, of course, talk to them with you by my side. I cannot wait to see their reaction. I think this may be an opportunity to scale up our funding and our publications, but Cambridge is sticklerish about face-to-face meetings."

"What about the dig?" she asked. It felt like her baby. She didn't want to leave it, even for forty-eight hours.

"We'll cover it up and protect it. Besides, Luc's family are right here on site. I'm sure it will be fine."

Maybe it would be a good thing to put some physical distance between her and Luc. It would be the exact thing she and Frederick needed to give their relationship a fresh start.

Sadie smiled back at Frederick. "That's a wonderful idea. I'd love to."

Luc walked into Clovis's courtyard, dread curdling his stomach. Not only would he have to see Jean and confront the emotional mess of his parentage, but he was coming to pick up spare bottles from Domaine du Valois to reuse in bottling wine.

Even though Clovis would never make him feel badly about the dramatic fall of his fortunes, awareness that he had hit a low point—to be begging bottles off his friends—pulsed through every part of him.

Clovis was waiting in the courtyard, the bottles already boxed up and secured to pallets. Of course, his friend would want to shorten this humiliation for Luc as much as possible and not draw out the transfer process. Luc blinked back tears at Clovis's kindness. It was amazing how small gestures meant even more than big ones, especially at rock bottom.

Luc walked over, his head as high as he could make it, and shook Clovis's hand. "Thank you for preparing the bottles."

Clovis cut him off with a dismissive wave of his hand. "*De rien.*" Yet it wasn't nothing. At that moment, it was everything. "I have the small forklift ready in the hanger so the workers can lift them into the back of your van."

Luc nodded. "*Merci*." Jean would be in the hanger too. He was sure of it.

Clovis draped his arm over Luc's shoulder and walked with him to the *cuverie* that way, neither of them needing to say anything. Luc was suffering, and Clovis knew it.

Jean was there, leaning against the forklift. Usually they shook hands, but Luc had a sudden moment of doubt. A father was meant to be kissed with the traditional *bisous*, but what was Jean to him exactly?

Jean smiled at Luc and stuck out his hand, putting Luc out of his misery. Despite everything, something in Luc's chest eased at seeing him, just like it always had.

"Bonjour, *fiston*," Jean said with a twinkle in his eye. *Fiston* was the informal way of saying son but could refer to any young male held in affection. Relief filled Luc that Jean had a sense of humor about the situation and was not going to enact an emotional scene. Luc didn't think he could bear any more emotions at that moment.

"I cannot even imagine how strange this must all still be for you," Jean continued. "Rest assured, I don't expect anything from you. I'm just glad you know."

His chest unknotted a little more.

"Café?" Clovis asked him, tilting his head towards the fancy espresso maker.

Jean chuckled. "You just want to show off with the fancy espresso maker, Clovis."

"I sure do," Clovis said.

"I hate to steal your thunder, but I've already made Luc a coffee with it." Jean shrugged.

"Mine will be better." Clovis grinned.

Luc was summarily pushed down on one of the chairs and Jean sat across from him on the tattered old couch while Clovis busied himself with his beloved espresso machine.

Jean studied Luc's face. "You've had a rough time of it my boy. I'm sorry for any part I had in that. Truly I am."

Luc waved his hand. "It's always better to know the truth. It's strange, definitely, but it's actually the least of my worries at the moment."

"You mean the financial mess Alphonse has left you with the Domaine?"

"Yes." And Sadie, but what was the point of talking about that again?

Jean bit his lip. Good God, had Luc gotten that habit from him? "Is Domaine Ocquidant really that close to bankruptcy?"

Luc sighed. "Teetering on the edge. It was only through meeting at least twenty different people that I managed to cobble things together enough to keep going until the harvest. It had better be a good one though—a *perfect* one—if I'm going to have any hope of saving the place."

Clovis brought them their espressos and sat on the couch beside Jean. "You know I would lend you the money to tide you over so that you can keep the Domaine."

He appreciated Clovis's offer so much, but he held up his hand to stop his friend before he got carried away. "*Merci*. You're a good friend, but you know I could never accept that."

Clovis, however, got that mulish look in his face that Luc knew well. "But—"

"I still haven't decided what I'm going to do if I'm able to save it. It doesn't belong to me anymore, you realize, seeing as I'm not Alphonse's son."

Jean groaned and leaned back on the couch. "I was worried about that, but I never thought Alphonse would disown you. He loves you so much."

"He hasn't. He wants me to stay on. They all do, but I'll have to figure out a way of distributing the shares three ways, I guess."

"You'll make it work," Clovis said. "Those vineyards have made you theirs. They won't let you go as easily as that."

"What about Sadie?" Jean asked, abruptly.

What about Sadie? He loved her and would always love her, but she wanted nothing to do with him. Frederick probably was the better man for her.

"Luc?" Clovis prompted.

"I love her," Luc said. "I realize now that I've never been in love with anyone before her."

"Not Stella?" Clovis asked.

"Definitely not Stella."

"So what have you done about it?" Jean asked, sitting up straighter.

Luc took a deep breath. The hurt made the words hard to let out. "I told her how I felt, but she said she could never love me."

Jean and Clovis thought on this for a moment, then Jean blew out a puff of air. "I don't buy it. I've seen the two of you together since you were children."

Was Jean really going to make him dive back into this pain?

"She loves you too," Jean said.

Yes, he was. Luc sat back in the couch. "She told me she could never be with me because I thought I was in love with Stella for so long. She's been hurt too much in the past Jean, especially by me, to be willing to take that risk. I hate it, but I understand it."

"So…*quoi alors*?" Jean lifted his chin, pugnacious. "You're just going to give up?"

It wasn't like he hadn't tortured himself over this. "She's with Frederick now. She says he's much better for her. I have to stop standing in her way if I want the best for her."

Clovis was slowly shaking his head side to side, a bemused quirk to his lips.

"What?" Luc demanded him. "What else can I do?"

"You can fight for her," Jean said, his eyes at their most piercing.

"But she said—"

"You'll never be able to live with yourself if you let her go, take it from me. What do you think the best way is to convince her that you have changed and that she can trust you?"

"I'm guessing it's not giving up on us," Luc said.

"You're damn sure it's not," said Jean. "You have to fight for her, and love her, and keep loving her, until she feels safe with you. You hear me?"

Luc did. Like trying to save the Domaine, convincing Sadie she was safe with him was almost certainly doomed to failure, but also like the Domaine, he would never be able to live with himself if he didn't try.

"Luc," Clovis said. "There's no room for error here. This is probably the most important thing you'll ever do in your life."

That's right. Clovis had almost lost Cerise too. That was almost impossible to imagine now, when he saw them together, but there was a time when it seemed like Cerise would never accept Clovis.

Hope flared in his chest. "OK," he said. "I'll fight."

"Good," Jean leaned forward to slap Luc's knee. "Now you can drink your café."

chapter thirty

TWO DAYS LATER, Sadie woke up with dread curdling her stomach. Frederick had asked if he could visit the nearby Chateau de la Rochepot and he'd invited Stella.

Stella had mentioned it to Luc, so now Sadie had to spend the day as part of the most ill-suited quartet of people ever to gather together. She would never comprehend how *she* had ended up in the middle of a love triangle.

Luc had all of a sudden started trying to get Sadie alone over the past two days and it was taking every last bit of her wits to outsmart him. What could he possibly want to say to her anyway? Whatever it was, it was too risky. Her thoughts and memories circled back to him constantly. Part of her hated him for showing her the full extent of what she could never have.

By the time she was showered and dressed and waiting with Stella for Frederick, her mood hadn't improved one bit. Stella was in full sparkle mode with fresh makeup and hair done. She looked healthy again—radiant actually—and she was definitely showing all the signs of a crush on Frederick. Ugh. That old jealousy hovered, waiting to burst into flame.

Sadie yanked her wayward curls up in a messy bun. Today was merely about enduring, and she certainly wasn't about to dress up fancy for that.

"Frederick was telling me all about his house in London, where we'll stay when we go over there. It's in Belgravia."

"Oh. Nice." Sadie couldn't really care less where Frederick lived, as long as it was close to a good library.

Stella rolled her eyes, clearly disappointed with Sadie's lack of reaction. "Of course, you wouldn't know. Belgravia is *the* chicest part of London."

She just didn't care as much as Stella did about such things. It wasn't her world. The only thing that excited her about Frederick having money and connections is that it could mean more interesting and larger-scale archaeological digs.

Frederick walked in the door just then, a huge smile on his face.

Stella was struck mute for once, and Sadie noticed a blush rising up her neck. She had it bad.

Frederick came over right away, took Sadie in his arms, and planted a hearty kiss on her mouth. It was so wonderful how he never let her doubt his feelings for a second.

"What?" Sadie asked Frederick, noting the gleam in his eye. He looked incredibly dashing in his worn jeans, white button-down shirt open at the neck, and a khaki blazer. He stepped forward and took Sadie's hands in his. "Guess what I've arranged?"

Sadie shook her head, a little irked that he had the nerve to arrange anything without talking to her. "What?"

"I got you an interview at my college in Cambridge for a fellowship."

She'd never thought of studying in England, and she wasn't entirely sure how she felt about it, but a fellowship at Cambridge would secure her academic future, as well as being a massive middle finger to Hudson and Professor Harris. "That's amazing," she breathed.

"I'm thrilled," he said. "I've been trying to get this for you for the past month, but I wanted to make it a surprise."

Despite her gratitude, Sadie wondered why Frederick would try to plan her academic career for her without discussing it with her first. Still, it was an incredible gesture with mind-boggling possibilities. She would go to the interview, of course. She would be a fool to say no to such an opportunity, or to Frederick for that matter.

"We need to leave for England tomorrow," he said, and then turned to Stella. "I'm sorry this is so last-minute, but Cambridge is not exactly understanding when it comes to rescheduling. I've also arranged an afternoon for you with my friend that I talked to you about who specialized in Dyslexia. Will you come too Stella?"

Stella's face was beet red—that was a first. Sadie had never seen Stella be so affected by a man before. "Yes," she stammered. "I would love that. So thoughtful—"

Frederick waved it away. "I would be honored to escort you two wonderful women to my fair country."

A niggle of unease wormed through Sadie's mind. Frederick treated Stella, and everyone else, so gallantly. Somehow it made his attention to her feel less special.

Stop being ridiculous. Frederick was a perfect gentleman—exactly what she needed.

The castle was fascinating as usual with its ramparts and brightly tiled roof and turrets, but Sadie couldn't shake a pervasive sense of dissatisfaction with everything.

It made no sense. Luc was behaving himself and while Stella was doing her best to monopolize Frederick's attention, he never missed an opportunity to touch Sadie or hold her hand or give her pecks on the cheek.

It was still the shoulder season for tourism, so the castle was extremely thin of visitors, which should theoretically make her happy, as Sadie hated crowds.

The thing was, a wild part of her craved more than Frederick's manners and decorum. She wondered if making love to Frederick could be anywhere near as fierce as it was with Luc, then tried to banish that thought from her mind.

Luc was looking thin and pale, but that didn't make the memory of their connection any less immediate. A Cambridge fellowship. Her career. A man she never needed to doubt. She reminded herself of all these things. She had to use her brain.

Stella managed to urge Frederick up to the roof of the castle to see the view from the battlements, leaving Sadie alone with Luc in the round bedroom in the turret below.

Luc kneeled down on the terra cotta *tomettes* on the ground. "Remember the paw print?" he asked, catching her eyes with his. They were so unfathomably blue.

Sadie ventured over, despite the volatile rhythm of her heart at being alone with Luc again.

"Of course," she murmured, kneeling down to inspect the paw print that must have been made by some anonymous medieval cat in the *tomette* Luc was crouched beside on the floor. Whenever they were on field trips together in Elementary School, they would always race up to this bedroom to be the first one to find it. She was hit by a wave of sadness. If only Luc hadn't stuck to that whole business with Stella for so many years, things could have been different.

Luc got up and began wandering around the edge of the room. When Sadie looked up from inspecting the paw print, he had disappeared. Had he gone up to the ramparts too? Sadie was at the edge of the rock wall of the bedroom, wondering how he could have vanished.

Suddenly, Luc's arm flew out from behind the massive tapestry hanging on the wall and caught hers. He dragged her behind it with him. They had done this too on every single field trip, giggling when they could hear their classmates wondering out loud where they had gone to. Hiding behind there with him, hand in hand still, Sadie knew she should step out, but something wistful and nostalgic in her heart stopped her.

This imminent trip to England could mean the symbolic end of a life intertwined with Luc's and the beginning of her life with Frederick. She turned to tell Luc, but before she could, he pivoted and laid his palms flat on either side of her against the massive stone wall.

"Got you," he whispered. "It hasn't been easy."

"You don't have me," she said, keeping her voice low. "Not really." His mouth was just an inch away from hers and she could feel that charge in the air between them, setting everything in her alive.

Before Luc could answer, they both heard the unmistakable sound of Stella shrieking.

They reacted in unison, scrambling out from behind the tapestry and dashing up the spiral, crooked turret stairs out onto the battlements.

Luc burst out on the roof before Sadie and held his hand back to stop her momentum. She stifled a gasp when she saw why.

There was a little blond boy on the wrong side of the squared off, low walls of the medieval ramparts. He was teetering on a narrow ledge on the exterior edge of the chateau. In front of him was empty air. A fall from such a height would be instant death.

Nausea rose in Sadie's throat, and she swallowed it back down. *No time for that.* They were so high up, the houses of the village below seemed to be made of miniatures.

Frederick was bellowing commands like a British Army officer for the boy to come back over the battlements where it was safe, but the boy was not moving. Of course he wasn't. He was paralyzed with fear and Frederick was making the problem worse, not better.

Stella opened her mouth to yell again. Sadie moved quickly and put her hand over her twin's mouth.

"Stop yelling," Sadie hissed at her. "You'll scare him." She turned to Frederick. "You too," she said, in a sharper tone than she'd ever used with him before.

Tears began to trickle from Stella's eyes, but Frederick nodded at Sadie, then turned and moved Stella away against the wall of the chateau.

With them out of the way, Sadie turned to Luc. His face reflected the shock that was ricocheting inside her. "How are we going to do this?" she whispered.

"I'll climb out and get him back." Sadie's heart dropped, but there was no other option.

"Or I can," Sadie said, her stomach lurching, but both she and Luc had always been equally good at climbing trees.

Luc leaned down and picked up a heavy linked chain that was bolted in the ground, who knew what for. "I need you to stay here and be ready to pull this chain in, and most importantly keep talking to the boy. If I try to do both, I'll fall."

Sadie nodded. Her blood turned to ice at the thought of her world without Luc, no matter how complicated their relationship was. "Yes."

Frederick called over to them. "You can't Luc. It's too dangerous."

"*Tais-toi,*" Luc snapped, in French. "Not now."

The little boy started to shake. They didn't have long before his grip would start to weaken.

Sadie stood, her heart in her throat, while Luc climbed gingerly over the parapet. She needed to start talking to the boy.

"My name's Sadie," she said in the calmest voice she could

muster. "My friend is coming to get you. You don't need to do anything at all, just stay where you are. What's your name?"

"Guillaume," came a small, shaky voice. "You have a funny accent," the little boy added.

"Yes, I'm American." Her breath caught as her eyes shifted from the boy to Luc. Luc was halfway there. If he fell...no, he *couldn't* fall.

"Where in America?" came the thin reedy voice.

New York. Have you ever travelled to New York?" She needed to keep him talking, so Luc could secure him before the boy moved a muscle. There was so little margin for error and a mistake would be unequivocally fatal.

"No. Have you seen the Statue of Liberty?"

"Definitely. I see the Statue of Liberty at least once a week or so." Luc was getting close. The rusty weight of the chain in her hand felt slippery in her sweaty palms. She tightened her grip. "My friend Luc will be touching you soon. You don't need to look. Just keep staring straight ahead, but you will feel him touch you. He's very good at climbing. You don't need to do anything."

Sadie's heart seemed to fill her whole body with its dreadful thudding. She didn't know what she'd do without Luc as her touchstone in life. She knew she couldn't cope with the mere idea of him betraying her with another woman, but she'd never even considered he could be taken from her by death.

The boy had begun to fidget. She had to keep talking. "Even though I live in New York now," she said. "I went to school here in France for three years when I was about your age. I came here to Chateau de la Rochepot on school trips. I always loved old things, and now that's what I do for a job—I get to dig up old artifacts."

"Like a treasure hunter?" the little boy asked.

"Just like that. I have quite a few Roman coins I've dug up, and if you let my friend Luc help you and do just as he says, I'll give one to you."

"I'm scared," came Guillaume's tiny thread of a voice.

"It's OK to be scared," Sadie said. "I used to think grown-ups didn't get scared, but now that I'm a grown-up, I can tell you that they do. The thing is though, I've learned I can do pretty much anything, even when I'm scared." *Except trust Luc with my heart.*

Luc was reaching out to Guillaume. "That's it, take Luc's hand, Guillaume. You can trust him. I would trust him with anything." *Almost anything.*

Luc looped the chain around Guillaume's slender torso, then under his arms and pulled it tight. Guillaume, bless him, did not move an inch. Sadie's heart felt like it had stopped altogether, but she knew she needed to keep up her flow of chatter.

"Luc and I used to love our field trips here when we were in school. Have you seen the cat's paw print on the terra cotta tile in the bedroom downstairs? Keep holding onto Luc, and I'll take you down and show you after this."

This, as if it was some sort of mundane activity.

Luc hung on to the boy, teetering slightly, and they were almost back to her. Sadie couldn't remember when she'd breathed last.

After what felt like far too long, Luc handed Guillaume over to Sadie, who hauled him over the ramparts. The boy weighed almost nothing, or maybe she was just so full of adrenaline that she was stronger than usual. Pinning him against the parapet with her body, she pivoted and grabbed Luc's arm and pulled him in as well.

Luc made it back over. *Safe. He was safe.* Sadie dropped to her knees. Guillaume gave a funny little yelp and collapsed into her arms. Luc and Sadie's eyes connected over the little boy's blond head, transmitting fear and relief.

"Thank God," Sadie mouthed to Luc. Luc shakily lowered himself to his haunches and rested his head on his knees.

Sadie glanced quickly over at Stella and Frederick, still huddled together, staring at her and Luc with eyes like saucers.

Sadie held Guillaume tight. He was shaking all over. After a while, she shifted one of her hands to Luc's knee and whispered to him. "He's OK. You're OK. It's all going to be OK, Luc."

Luc gave her an attempt at a smile. "It must just be the adrenaline."

She knew what he meant. Her heart was still galloping like a racehorse and she felt like her legs might not support her. After a long while, she stood up again. Her legs shook but she needed to get Guillaume back to whoever he came to the chateau with. She could do this. She didn't relinquish Guillaume's hand. "Who did you come here with?" Sadie asked the boy.

"My teacher."

"She's probably looking for you. Out of curiosity, what made you climb over the parapet, Guillaume?"

"I saw a cat and I wanted to pet it."

"Ah." There had always been cats who made the chateau their home and slinked around the most treacherous roof angles with ease. "The thing to always remember about cats is that they have nine lives, but us humans don't. I'm going to take you back to your teacher, *d'accord*?"

"Will you show me the cat's pawprint in the tile on the way down?" Guillaume asked.

"Promise," she said. Without a doubt, children were more resilient than adults.

"What school do you go to?" Sadie asked.

"Saint-Coeur," he said.

"No way," she said. "That's where Luc and I went to school as well."

Guillaume seemed unimpressed, but Sadie made a note to tell this to Luc when he'd recovered a bit. She hoped Frederick and Stella would give him some space and just let him be.

Luc had never even questioned whether or not he would risk his life to save Guillaume. He just had.

Sadie and Guillaume admired the paw print in the turret

bedroom and then found Guillaume's teacher and his fellow students in the armory downstairs, admiring massive broadswords and metal helmets.

Sadie considered the teacher—she was on the older side and something about the resigned, yet kind air told Sadie she had probably seen a thing or two in her teaching career. Perfect. An unflappable teacher was exactly what she needed. Sadie brought Guillaume to her and whispered in her ear what had happened.

The teacher's face went ashen, but she kept her composure, and grasped tightly to Guillaume's hand. "The good Lord must have sent you and your man," the teacher whispered to Sadie. "I'm make a prayer that you're rewarded with happiness."

If only it were that easy. Sadie shook her head. "Having Guillaume safe is the only reward we need." The way the teacher was hanging on to Guillaume's hand, she was quite certain that she was not going to let go until the end of the day.

Sadie bent down to Guillaume's level. "I will bring you that Roman coin to your school if you'd like."

"Really?" Guillaume asked.

"A promise is a promise," she said, and squeezed his hand good-bye.

"What was the name of the man who climbed out for him?" the teacher said in a low voice so just Sadie could hear the question.

"It was my friend Luc Ocquidant," Sadie said. She felt a flash of pride at being able to say those words.

"I won't go up and thank him now," the teacher said, with wide eyes trying to express something she couldn't say at that moment. "But can you please relay my gratitude to him?"

"Of course."

"He's a hero," said the teacher.

The truth of that settled around Sadie's heart. Luc was a hero and always had been, although he would never see it like that. He would just shake his head and say he'd done what was right, *c'est tout*. Luc's nobility resonated in Sadie's core. Maybe that was what was missing with Frederick, despite all his other qualities. Frederick hadn't risked himself to save the boy. She wondered as she made her way back up to the roof if she would ever be able to forget that fact.

chapter thirty-one

THE STAIRS BACK up to the battlements felt twice as numerous and twice as steep. Her legs wobbled underneath her. She couldn't imagine how Luc must be feeling.

On top, Luc was leaning against the gray stone of the wall he had just climbed over, his hands shoved deep in his pockets. Stella and Frederick were still several feet away, watching Luc like he was a wild animal they weren't sure how to approach.

He did look savage with his hair all sticking up, his face flushed, and his blue eyes blazing. He'd also never looked more magnificent. She knew she should be thinking about how Frederick hadn't been much help besides keeping Stella quiet, but there was only room for thoughts about Luc.

She went right up to him and grasped his hands. "How are you?"

"Sadie," he said on an exhale. He half grimaced, half smiled. "I feel as though I've just run three marathons back to back."

She leaned against the wall beside him, needing to feel him close. "I barely made it up the stairs. I can't even imagine how you must be feeling after being out on the ledge."

"Exhausted," he admitted. "Did the little *charogne* get back to his teacher?"

Sadie nodded. "She'll be keeping a close eye on him. No worries there."

Luc shook his head again. "I can't stop going over it my mind, thinking if just one thing hadn't gone as we planned…" His normally tanned complexion was an odd shade.

Sadie made a decision. "I think we should head back to Savigny."

Frederick must have heard her because he stepped forward then. "You're right." He looked at Luc. "I can't believe you just did that."

Luc met Frederick's face with narrowed eyes and shrugged.

"You risked your life for that boy, and you didn't even know him," Frederick said.

"I couldn't just let him fall."

Frederick said nothing, but his eyebrows drew together as he considered this.

"Do we have to go?" Stella came beside them and grabbed on to Frederick's arm. "I was having a good time before that little boy scared us all to death."

Frederick looked at her. "Surely you must see that Luc and Sadie need to rest now."

She looked at them. "They seem fine to me. Let's finish the visit."

Sadie was amazed once again at her sister's obliviousness. "Frederick's right, Stella. That's enough for today."

"But—"

"Stella." Sadie shook her head at her.

Frederick took Stella's arm in his. "Let's go."

Stella pouted, but she followed, listening to Frederick instead of her sister.

"We'll catch up," Sadie called out. "Take your time."

Frederick and Stella left. Luc's normally tanned complexion had turned ashen. She needed to get him somewhere small and enclosed and safe so he could come back to himself a bit, before they endured the drive home.

"C'mon," Sadie pulled Luc into a little space she remembered—a small hide-out for the archers on the parapet of the chateau that she and Luc had discovered on a Grade Two field trip. It wasn't part of the public visit, which made it perfect. It was enclosed and well tucked away from the roof area, which, now that Stella and Frederick had left, was completely deserted anyway. She highly doubted Guillaume's teacher would be venturing up to the roof with her class, and they seemed to be the only other visitors in the place

She needed to get Luc in there. She pulled him along in her wake, pushed the chain blocking visitors aside, and skirted the wall to the side of the staircase. She found the little side door and opened it. Hopefully pigeons hadn't nested inside.

She looked around to make sure nobody was watching them and pulled Luc in behind her. The tiny space was surrounded by stone on all sides. It had the same feel as their *cabotte*. Maybe that was why her mind had flown to it.

Luc had to bend his head to climb through the door. She didn't remember the ceiling being so low, but then again, they'd both been smaller the last time they'd been in here.

Luc looked around. "Why did you bring me here? I remember this place."

"I just…I just think you need a moment. Or, more accurately, *we* need a moment."

Now they were alone, Sadie needed to hold him. She needed to reassure herself that he hadn't fallen, that he was still with her on this Earth. She knew it was treacherous territory, but surely neither of them would be in the mood to cross any lines after what they'd just been through. The idea of the Universe without him was just… it was just no good at all.

A spark of hope jumped into Luc's eyes.

"Not for that," Sadie tried to explain. "I just need…I need—"

"What?" Luc said softly.

"This." Sadie wrapped her arms around Luc and pushed him up against the stone. He let out a little *oof* sound. "I just have to reassure myself that you're still here."

All the rises and dips of her shape somehow fit against Luc perfectly, like snapping interlocking puzzle pieces together.

He reached up and with a tentative hand, smoothed her curls, which were surely rioting all over her head. "I couldn't have done it without you."

"You would have," she said, certain.

"I'm not so sure. We're a good team."

She drank in the steady beats of his heart like she was parched, each one refilling her soul. When Luc was balancing out there, between life or death, between the solid stone and nothingness, it had hit her over the head like a sledgehammer that without Luc in the world, she would feel as though she'd lost half of herself.

Her hand moved up, not listening to her better judgement, and smoothed out the messy hair at his temples. He hadn't fallen. He was still whole. *Merci Dieu.* She realized he was trembling underneath her touch.

"The adrenaline?" she whispered, gently.

"No," he said, his voice rough.

He shifted slightly and she felt the rigid shape of him. Her stomach swooped, remembering the sight of him outside that parapet. She needed to feel him, all of him, to make herself comprehend that he was truly still with her.

She should step away, but she tightened her grip, unable to let go as if he was still in danger of falling. Or her. She didn't know anything anymore, except that she needed that connection she only had with Luc. She drank in his familiar smell of sunshine and earth and freshly laundered cotton.

"Sadie," Luc said, his voice shaking with desire. God help her, but she loved hearing the effect she had on him. She hated herself for it, but there it was.

Luc slid his hands on either side of her jaw, his fingers molding to the shape of the hard bone underneath her soft skin. He drew her to him. Sadie didn't pull back. She tried to conjure up the image of Frederick, but it was pale and as insubstantial as a ghost compared to the flare in her blood when Luc touched her lips with his.

When their tongues touched, she could feel the need ripple through his body, and her body vibrated with the same urgency. She should step back. She was undoing all the good work she had done in creating a healthier life for herself, but she couldn't help it, not after being faced with the prospect of life without him.

Her hands needed to feel him everywhere. He sighed underneath her touch as she soothed the tight planes of his back and moved down to the waistband of his jeans, undoing the button and the zipper and reaching down.

Just one more time. She needed just one more time.

Luc sucked the air between his teeth with a hiss. "You're going to be the death of me Sadie,"

She responded by running her fingers up and down his silky length. She needed for him to lose himself in her too.

"Sadie," he gasped. "If I don't have you, I'm fairly certain *this* is going to kill me."

"*Moi aussi*," Sadie whispered, "Me too," so low she didn't think he could hear her, but from the way he pushed down her jeans over her hips in one swift moment, she knew he had.

He spun Sadie so the unyielding rock wall was behind her back and Luc was in front of her, everywhere. He lifted her with calloused, weathered winemaker's hands and plunged into her with one definitive movement.

"On my God, Sadie, *mon amour*," he breathed. My love.

Her body welcomed him with relief. Her head hit the wall as she flung it back, overcome with the rightness of him inside of her. He fit perfectly there too. Everywhere. She felt the exhilaration rising up in her almost instantaneously. She wanted to draw this out longer, but the wave was cresting over her already, an unstoppable force.

"Luc," she gasped.

"I'm with you," he said. "Always." She began to convulse around him, beyond words or thoughts of anything but the rightness of them together.

They stayed like that, joined for a long time, until Luc finally eased Sadie down to the ground. He feathered her skin with light kisses as he redressed her with gentle, loving fingers. She couldn't formulate words, and even if she could, her mind was too full of him, and them, to entertain any sort of sense. When they were both dressed again, Luc gathered her in his arms and neither of them said anything.

Sadie drank this moment up. If she left for England, she didn't know when she would get the chance again. *If.*

Finally, she said, "Stella and Frederick will be wondering where we are."

"Let them find us," Luc growled, and his arms tightened around her.

"No," Sadie said. She wasn't sure what she wanted anymore, but she knew she didn't want to have the decision made for her.

"Sadie." Luc said, giving Sadie a final, fierce kiss that felt more like a brand. "We need to talk. I've been trying to get you alone—"

She nodded. "I know. We will."

"When?"

"I just need some time to think."

Luc waved at the wall they had just been against. "I think we just got the answer. This thing between us, that's always been between us…it makes us whole Sadie, don't you see?"

She did, but fear was inexorably transmuting her contentment into a sickening sense of teetering on the edge of a cliff.

"Tonight," she promised. "In the *cabotte*. After dinner."

Luc's muscle jumped in his jaw and then he nodded. "Okay," he said softly. "I'll be there."

When Sadie arrived in the *cabotte*, Luc was already there. He'd stuck a flashlight in one of the stone niches in the wall, which gave the place an eerie glow. He was pacing in circles.

His head snapped around when he heard the door and his face broke out in a smile. "Sadie," he said. "Finally."

"I was held up by Stella," she stammered. "She's decided all of a sudden that she's ready to talk about her Dyslexia now."

"That's good," Luc said. "I'm glad, but I'm not here to talk about Stella."

Yet Stella was all Luc wanted to talk about for years.

Their lovemaking in the castle had stripped off the armor Sadie spent years building around her heart. All that anger she'd pushed down every time Luc gushed on about Stella, or looked at her with googly-eyes, had nowhere to go inside her. She'd suppressed it and denied it so as not to be destroyed by it, but now it was there, pushing against every part of her, demanding to be let out.

He came and gathered her in his arms. *Oh God,* the essential Luc-ness of him…what would she do without that? "I love you Sadie," he whispered in her ear. "I know now I'm never going to stop loving you."

Sadie resisted the urge to melt into him again. "Because Jean's your father?"

Luc frowned down at her. "No, not because of that. I just *know*."

Blinding rage consumed Sadie. She realized now all the suffering she'd stored up within her over the years hadn't gone anywhere. It was still inside her and, whether she liked it or not, it was about to pour out.

She thrust Luc away. "Just like you *knew* you loved Stella since you were seven up until this Christmas?"

Luc held his arms. "No. It's nothing like that at all. With you it's different."

"How can you know Luc?" Sadie snapped, fists on her hips so he couldn't see how her hands were shaking with fury.

"I realize now that the whole thing with Stella was because I was trying to be a different man than Alphonse. I was defining myself using him, when I should have been defining myself by my own heart."

"Yet on Christmas Day you slept with Stella just to make sure? How…how *dare* you come to me saying you love me after that?"

Luc made an incoherent yelp of protest. "Who told you that?"

"Stella. Well…she said as much."

"She was lying." He took Sadie's hands in his, but she tore hers away. "How could you think that?" He shook his head. "But…of course you believed her. Why wouldn't you?"

"You took her to your bedroom. What was I supposed to think?"

Luc raked a hand through his hair. "I was so confused. I needed to know for sure. I only kissed her, and it was…it was all wrong Sadie. There was nothing there. Just a figment of my imagination that had never existed in the first place. I told Stella then and there that there could never be anything between us."

The past reshuffled itself yet again, but the anger rushing through her veins was going nowhere. "Maybe that's true, but between the time you were seven until a few months ago, you chose that figment of your imagination over me." Sadie's voice came out low and throbbing. "Can you imagine how that was for me, when we were in Grade One, and you chose her to be your Queen? We were *best friends,* Luc."

Dammit, she felt the wet of tears on her cheeks and her breathing was jagged. The hurt demanded to be felt, even after all these years.

"I was only seven Sadie," he pleaded. "And traumatized about my father. If I could go back in time and redo it, I would choose you a thousand times over. If you let me be with you, I promise you I will choose you every day, every second for the rest of my life. Just…just *let* me."

"You hurt me Luc," she yelled, her voice hoarse. "You hurt me more than you could ever know. Not just once, but again and again and again. I've kept it from you all these years. I've even kept that pain from myself because I knew it would destroy me if I didn't. I refused to be as pathetic as the world made me feel about being Stella's sister. I could handle the rest of them, but you Luc…when you did it, too…" A ragged sob came from the depths of her battered heart.

"Sadie, I—"

"No, you need to listen. Every time you chose Stella over me, every time you shared your plans to finally date her with me, every time your eyes left mine and then stayed stuck on my sister, even when I was talking to you, you killed a part of me. You bled me by a hundred tiny cuts. If I let you in now and you change your mind again, there would be nothing of me."

Luc stood against the *cabotte* wall, his eyes wide and haunted.

"You made me feel like less of a person, Luc, you made me feel small and unattractive and not special."

Even in the yellow flashlight, Sadie could see Luc flinch. Then, he drew himself and shook his head. "I always knew you were the most special person in my life, from the moment I met you." His voice took on some of Sadie's heat. "I just didn't understand it."

Sadie scoffed. "But you understand it now, because Frederick moved in as competition and you can't stand to be bested." Sadie knew this wasn't entirely fair, but she was beyond caring.

"Don't try that argument on me," Luc said. "I will accept your anger because it's justified, but this thing between us started well before Frederick arrived on the scene. You know that as well as me."

She was in no mood for him to be right. She squeezed her fists so tight her nails dug into her palms. "You hurt me so much Luc," she said. "You have to understand that."

He nodded, grave. "I do, and I swear to you that I'll spend my whole life making up for it, if you just give me the chance."

"It's too dangerous for me Luc."

He gave her a long look, then titled his head. "Remember what you said to Guillaume only this morning?"

Was he seriously going to use her words against her?

"You said that you've learned you can do pretty much anything, even when you're scared. That's one of the millions of reasons why I love you Sadie. You're the bravest person I know."

But she wasn't. Not when it concerned loving Luc. It made her feel more powerless than she'd ever felt in her life.

"The way you reported your professor, even if it meant losing your job," he continued. "The way you accompanied your father when he was dying, the way you figured out a way to continue your work with your dig, even if it was with Frederick," he added sourly.

"I think you've hurt me too much, Luc." She debated telling him about possibly leaving with Frederick for England the next morning, but she just didn't feel she could deal with that too. He would find out soon enough.

"But I had no idea how you felt, Sadie," he said. "How could I have known? If I knew what was in your heart, I never would have hurt you. Ever."

"Oh Luc." she shook her head. "I didn't want to have to tell you what was in my heart. I wanted you to see it on your own."

He bowed his head at this. "I was damaged goods, I know, and

I'm sorry, but have some compassion for the traumatized seven-year-old boy that I was."

"I do," she said. "I just wish I knew a way to undo the past."

"And me," he said, and bit his lip. "Look Sadie." Luc opened his arms, palms out. "When it comes right down to it, you are just going to have to decide to trust me…or at least trust your feelings when we're together. I know it's scary, but rest assured you have the power to hurt me every bit as much as I could hurt you."

Could she, though? She still had a hard time believing that.

She couldn't deny being with Luc felt so viscerally right, like running down the hill with Luc when they were children, equal parts exhilarating and terrifying. But she wasn't that little girl anymore, and Luc wasn't that little boy.

"And what if I can't?" Sadie whispered, her heart aching in her chest.

In the yellow glow of the flashlight, Sadie could make out the hurt in Luc's eyes.

"Then what?" Sadie asked again.

"You're my twin flame, Sadie. We only get one of those in a lifetime."

Sadie turned away, but she heard what Luc said next. "He'll never love you like I do Sadie, and I'll never stop loving you, no matter what you decide. Maybe I've been careless with your heart in the past, but I won't make that mistake again. Ever. I'll show you what fidelity is."

"I need to think," she said. Sadie pushed open the door of the *cabotte* and walked out into the crisp, starry night, Luc's words reverberating through her still.

chapter thirty-two

LUC WAS SO consumed with anger at his past self that there was no hope of getting any sleep. Only now that Sadie finally let down her guard did he finally realize how much he'd wounded her over the years. That intolerable knowledge sat like a *pétanque* ball in his gut, and he didn't think it would ever ease.

The only thing he could do was remain faithful to her, now that it was probably far too late. Maybe he was truly destined to end up like his biological father Jean – remaining single because the love of his life married someone else. Was there any escaping it? One thing he knew for sure was that after being with Sadie, he couldn't settle for anyone else.

At two o'clock in the morning, as he lay staring at the ceiling, reviewing each moment in their shared past in a new, appalling light, his phone rang. Maybe it was her? Instead, Gaspard's voice came down the line.

"Frost," Gaspard croaked. Then—*click*—he hung up.

Luc was out of bed like rocket. If he lost even a small portion of his crop—if those precious buds froze, his family would lose the Domaine. Frost could kill an entire year's crop in a night by freezing the flowering grape buds. It had happened many times before. Even as much as a ten per cent reduction in yield and he would have to declare bankruptcy.

Luc jumped out of bed and threw on clothes, juggling his phone while he yanked on his jeans, and called his fellow winemakers in the village and instructed them to spread the word and to meet by the fountain on the village square.

He needed to assemble supplies and rouse as much of his family as he could to help. Fighting frost was largely determined by the number of bodies helping to make fires and create a smokescreen to protect the delicate buds from the ice and the burning morning sun.

He cursed under his breath. He'd been too upset with himself to check the weather report before going to bed—something he usually never failed to do this time of year.

He roared through the house, yelling to wake his family up. Alphonse appeared at the bottom of the stairs, still blinking with sleep.

"Get all the supplies and begin to truck them to the vineyards, while I meet with the other winemakers to figure out our plan of attack," Luc said.

"Oh, son…" Alphonse's voice took on that lamenting tone that Luc had been hearing too often.

"None of that," Luc snapped. "We all need to get to work. Now!"

Alphonse straightened his spine and nodded briskly. "You can count on me son."

"I know I can Papa," Luc said. Maybe this was exactly what Alphonse needed, something concrete to do.

Luc ran out the front door, leaving it wide open behind him, and ran over to the cottage. If he had to fight this fight, he knew that—no matter what had happened between them—Sadie would want to help. She was not only a damn fine worker and leader, but she also felt like his lucky talisman. *Son amour.* He needed all the luck he could summon.

Luc crept into Sadie's room. As soon as he cracked open the door she sat bolt upright.

"Were you already awake?" Luc whispered to her. "I didn't mean to scare you."

"Yes, I'm awake," she said, sounding so alert that he knew she must not have been sleeping much either. "I haven't decided anything yet. Wait, what time is—"

"I'm not here for that," Luc said, moving closer to the bed. "Gaspard called. There's an early frost. I'm gathering everyone on the village square. Will you help me?"

Sadie flung back her duvet and hopped out of bed, all business, which was slightly undermined by the fact she looked heavenly in her underwear and a T-shirt. If only he could wake up to that every morning.

"Smokescreen?" she asked. She knew enough about winemaking to know that creating the veil of smoke above the vines was the only chance of saving the vineyards.

"Yes." He hesitated for a second, but the need to tell Sadie was overwhelming. "I just need to tell you something, Sadie, so you understand how important this is. Alphonse has sunk the Domaine so deep into debt that if I lose even a portion of this year's yield, we'll lose the Domaine. I'll have no choice but to declare bankruptcy."

She was already up and tugging on jeans and socks. "What?" she gasped. "When did you find out?"

"The day I found out Jean was my father."

"What?! I'm sorry Luc. Why didn't you tell me? No wait, you don't need to answer that."

"Nobody knows right now except Alphonse and me. I've been wanting to tell you for a while, but Alphonse was already so ashamed…I can't believe it. Frost. Of all the crappy luck."

She yanked a sweater over her shoulders. "We're going to save your vineyards Luc," she said. "And the Domaine."

Purée, she was magnificent. "Should I wake up Stella?" he asked as an afterthought.

"No. She wouldn't be much help," Sadie said without hesitation. She pulled on her boots. "Let's go."

Within half an hour they were out in the vineyards, lighting oil-burning heaters contained in metal tubs. The air carried that bite that menaced frost but was now filling up with the acrid smell of smoke.

Sadie, fired by the desire to help Luc, as well as do something concrete besides torturing herself over the decision she needed to make, ran from heater to heater. She lit one after another, coaxing out a flame, then dashed to the next.

She stalked up and down the rows of vineyards, helping or cajoling the fellow villagers that Luc had organized into teams to fan out and ensure that everyone's vineyards were protected.

When they didn't listen, she shamed them into moving faster with the sheer speed and tirelessness of her work. She couldn't light the fires quickly with her work gloves on, they were just too bulky and slowed her down. Her fingers smarted from tiny blisters all over her hands where the flames had licked her skin.

Through her bloodshot eyes, it was impossible to judge whether the smokescreen they'd created was effective in saving the buds on the vines. She saw flashes of Luc through the gusts of smoke, his face smudged with soot, working tirelessly. Alphonse was never far from Luc, laboring like a charging bull. Sadie couldn't even imagine how Luc had felt when he found out Alphonse had all but lost the Domaine. She had suffered, but so had he.

As long as she was around him, nobody else would ever have a chance. Should she just give in to her feelings?

Luc passed her in the vineyard row. He gave her hand a squeeze and that look that was meant just for her. "*Merci ma Sadie*," he whispered, then vanished in the smoke.

She felt as if she was standing on the edge of an abyss. Letting herself fall could be such a relief but could also lead to obliteration. Certainty eluded her and it was driving her half mad.

She remembered what her father had told her, just days before his lung cancer had finally claimed him. Sadie had barely left his hospice room in those last hours, as he drifted in and out of consciousness. Stella had preferred to leave Sadie to it.

The last day, he emerged from unconsciousness—the last time as it turned out. Sadie was gripping on to his hand. She hoped he sensed through the haze of painkillers that he wasn't alone.

His eyelids fluttered, and he smiled at her. "Don't cry my Sadie," he said. "I love you."

"I love you too Dad," she said, trying to blink back her tears but failing.

Then, with a surprising show of force, given that he had physically wasted away, he gripped Sadie's fingers so tight that a ring she was wearing dug into her flesh.

"You must always forge your own path," he said, a shocking lucidity in his eyes. "Never try to follow Stella's. You're worth more than that Sadie."

Should she listen to his advice and go with Frederick? It was a way to create her own path and not follow Stella, but then again, had Stella ever really had Luc in the first place?

The orange tinge of dawn outlined the hills in the distance, then the row upon row of fires they had lit and the blanket of smoke. Doubt flapped its wings in her chest like a bird trapped in a room.

She had to listen to her father's dying words, no matter what sort of alchemy bound her and Luc together. The mere fact that being with him felt so extraordinary stoked her panic tenfold.

The pain took her breath away and she bent over to try and

catch a breath in the acrid air. It was just too much of a risk. All her instincts were telling her to go to Luc, but those were the same instincts that had told her to lose her virginity with Thomas and look how that had ended up. Her instincts with men were not to be trusted.

The movements around her stilled as the early spring sun washed over the vineyards. Once the sun rose, there was no more they could do. Their work would either succeed or fail. The rays of light would be the judge, jury, and possibly the executioner.

Luc walked towards her, a grin on his face. "I think we've done the thing," he said, as he got close and wrapped her in a bear hug. She leaned against him, drinking in the shape of him surrounding her for one last time.

"You were incredible," he said. "When I found myself starting to falter, I would look over at you. You never let up for a second, so neither did I. Don't you see that we are better together, *ma Sadie*?"

Recruiting every ounce of self-denial she could muster, Sadie gently pushed herself back from Luc.

His eyes asked the question.

"I can't be your Sadie Luc," she said. "I can't follow Stella. Ever."

He took a step forward, trying to cross that chasm she had opened between them. "But—"

She held up her hand. "I've made my decision. I'm leaving for England in a few hours with Frederick and Stella."

Luc crossed his arms. "You're still scared."

A wave of fatigue overcame her. Of course, she was scared. She was icy with fear, despite the sweat and heat of the work she'd just done. She didn't know how much energy she had left in her to resist him. "Can you blame me?"

"I blame you for letting your fear dictate your choices."

She didn't answer, just blinked away the tears gathering in her eyes.

"How can you just throw away what we have together, Sadie?"

Luc demanded. "This only comes along once in a lifetime. Look at Jean and my mother. Don't you see?"

"I see that your whole life has changed and you're desperate to hang on to something familiar— me—but I'm not your life raft, Luc. I'm more than that."

"You *are* more Sadie. You're my air, my water, my pulse."

Sadie felt herself weakening again, but she couldn't let herself plunge into that abyss.

"Frederick and I are going to Cambridge," she said. "He's arranged for me to interview for a fellowship position for me. He's a good man."

"But your dig—"

"We'll come back and finish it later, but first…I need time away from you Luc." Her head began to spin.

"You mean time with *him*?" Luc's eyes flashed an unearthly blue. "Do you love him Sadie?"

Sadie averted her eyes from his. She was seconds away from caving. "Frederick and I are compatible in every way that counts. I need to go."

Sadie turned away, but she heard what Luc said next. "I'll be here for you, always. Maybe I've been careless with your heart in the past, but I won't make that mistake again."

Sadie hurried back through the vineyard to the cottage to get ready, even though Luc's words were still reverberated through her.

She shed her jacket and gloves and boots immediately inside the door. She couldn't touch anything until she got in the shower and tried to scrub off the evidence of her night in the vineyards.

"Sadie."

She whipped around. Stella was there on the couch, chicly dressed in one of her many traveling outfits and with a full suitcase at her feet. At least one of them was ready. "Where have you been?"

"There was frost," Sadie said, impatient to get clean and get dressed. Frederick would arrive to pick them up in minutes. "I went with Luc to light fires in the vineyards. Look, I'm exhausted, I have to shower."

"Why didn't you wake me up?" Stella demanded.

Sadie was at a loss for words. Honestly, the thought hadn't even occurred to her that Stella might want to participate. "You've never liked doing that sort of thing in the past," she said. "You know, physical work like that. I always got the impression that you felt it was beneath you."

Stella scowled.

"Am I wrong?" Sadie asked.

"You're just like them," Stella muttered.

"What do you mean? Look, we're going to miss the train if—"

"You make all kinds of assumptions about me without bothering to ask me, or truly get to know me better."

Sadie opened her mouth to protest, but Stella was right. Sadie was making the same mistakes her parents had, and that ultimately led to her sister never learning to read properly. It had been wrong of her parents, and she was doing the exact same thing.

Maybe what her father said to her on his deathbed was wrong too…"I'm sorry Stella. I was wrong not to ask you. I didn't think—"

"No, you never think, do you? You never think of how you fit perfectly in our family. Academic just like Mom and Dad and Max. You guys all liked the same things. Smelly old libraries. Lectures on Greek architecture. Books, books, books. How do you think that made me feel, Sadie? I could barely read. I was reminded every moment of every day that I was the odd one out in our family—the one who didn't belong."

"Stella, I…"

But Stella had stood up and was gesticulating wildly with her arms, letting the hurts of a lifetime of alienation finally pour out. "When I was younger, I always held on to the hope that I was a long-lost child of someone else and that out there was a family that I would actually fit into. I've always felt like an orphan within our family, Sadie. How do you think that feels?"

It had to feel terrible, perhaps just as terrible as it had felt to constantly be compared to a beautiful twin sister. "I'm so sorry. It's just that you have always been so beautiful—"

"That was always our family's excuse, wasn't it? One more thing to set me apart. Do you know how the world looks at beautiful people? Either as someone to be used—to be seen on their arm, or for sex, or to steal their own face from—" Stella's lips clamped shut and she stared down at her feet.

Stella had to be referring to Pablo.

"Nobody ever wanted to hear what I really thought about anything," she continued, after a while. "All they cared about was how I looked. I learned quickly that was my only value, so I made the most of that. Can you blame me?"

Sadie couldn't. Not really. "No, but it wasn't exactly a walk in the park being your sister. Almost every man I've ever liked falls in love with you. How do you think that feels?"

Stella was crying, and she sniffed back tears. "That is not my fault. Guys may fall in love with me, but it never stuck. And the one guy I actually want—"

"Stella, are you in love with Frederick?" Sadie demanded. Better get that out in the open too.

Stella avoided Sadie's eyes. "Maybe," she said. "But it doesn't matter because he has no interest in me. I'm too stupid. He's in love with you."

Was he though? He wasn't ardent like Luc, but then again Luc was French, and Frederick was British—surely that made all the difference, didn't it?

"Even look at Luc!" Stella said. "He seems to have lost interest in me. They all do."

So Luc had been telling her the truth about Christmas Day. Sadie's head was rushing, but the mention of Luc reminded her that she couldn't deal with this right now and get away. "Stella, we need to talk a lot more about this. Both of us, but first I have to get showered and dressed or we're going to miss our train."

Stella waved her away. "Go get ready."

chapter thirty-three

IT HAD STARTED to drizzle by the time Sadie heard Stella open the cottage door for Frederick. Stella said something to him, then he burst into her bedroom where she was sitting on her bed, packed and dressed, but undecided about whether or not she was going to leave. It was not like her to be indecisive, but something told her that this was the most important decision of her life.

More than anything, she wanted a sign that she was making the right choice. She knew she should have faith in her own ability to make a decision about her heart, but a lifetime of blows to her ego left her paralyzed.

Frederick had a grin on his face. "Let's go and get you a fellowship," he said. "And maybe some decent fish and chips."

He was lovely, handsome, and smart, and obsessed with the Gallo-Romans like she was, and apparently rich and aristocratic, according to Stella, though for Sadie those probably landed in the minus rather than the plus columns. Frederick shared her obsession with sedimentation flow rates—surely that meant he was the right choice?

He cleared his throat. "What's wrong?"

She met his eyes. "This thing with Luc…I don't think it's over."

Frederick sat down on the bed and took her hands in his. Again, they felt warm and dependable. "Sadie," he said, his voice grave. "You deserve more than this."

She remained silent.

"It kills me to see a brilliant, beautiful woman like you settling for a man who has loved her sister for most of his life."

She felt the urge to protest, but Frederick was just repeating the same refrain of that bird of panic flapping under her sternum. "If you stay here for Luc, you are selling yourself short Sadie. I hate to see that happen."

Frederick wasn't prone to passionate protestations of his love. He was trying to convince Sadie with logic—with the very same arguments she had used against herself.

"It's just...," she tried to explain. "My heart," she finished lamely.

"Of course you have some residual feelings for him." Frederick stroked her arm, and while it didn't feel exciting, it felt reassuring. "We all have left-over feelings for certain people in our lives."

He sounded like he knew what he was talking about. Who did he have residual feelings for? Was that why he'd been so phlegmatic about her feelings for Luc?"

"But what is your magnificent brain good for," he asked. "If it is not for making the right choices for your future happiness?"

But a future with Luc...it could be the stuff of her wildest dreams...or her worst nightmares.

"Tell me the truth. Could you ever be happy with Luc given his past feelings for Stella?"

Could she? She thought of the feel of Luc's hands on her, pressing hungry kisses against her mouth. It could be everything. A sign. Please Universe, send a sign.

"I don't know," she answered. It was the honest truth. "That's the problem."

"I'm going to tell you a secret that I wasn't going to tell you, maybe ever."

Was he actually a prince or something? He had her attention. "What?"

"The anonymous donor who funded our dig was me."

Sadie gasped. That possibility had never crossed her mind.

"I saw your application and I'd been wanting to work with you, so I made the funding appear anonymously. It was the best investment I've ever made in every sense of the word."

Something about the way he worded it as an investment sat wrong in her gut, but he had believed in her. He had supported her in every possible way. There it was—her sign.

Frederick patted her hand. "You don't have to compromise, Sadie—you have me. Don't settle for a life of *I don't know.*"

Slowly, she nodded. He was right. Her fear about Luc's ability to hurt her was no basis for future happiness. Frederick's concrete presence was. She let Frederick pull her up from the bed and lead her into a different life.

They were only half an hour out of Lille, and the conversation had been desultory on the trip so far. Sadie's heart weighed too heavy as she thought of Luc's reaction when he discovered she'd followed through with her departure.

She couldn't help dwelling on the look in his eye and the feeling of his hand when he squeezed hers as they passed in the vineyards. He saw them as a team, forever and always. Frederick saw her as an investment. Maybe Frederick was merely guilty of an odd choice in words, but it was something that, try as she might, she just couldn't seem to digest.

The weather reflected her emotional state, the light drizzle gaining strength into a steady downpour.

Frederick got back from the café car on the train just then, with a coffee for her and Stella.

"Thank you," Stella said, blinking up at Frederick shyly. She had it bad. Sadie wondered if Stella had ever noticed her looking at Luc that way. It was entirely possible.

Sadie's phone beeped and she checked it, panicked, both hoping and dreading that it was a message from Luc.

"What is it?" Frederick asked.

She should have gotten up to check the message alone, but her screen showed it was not Luc, but Gia. "It's the student that came to me about my advisor and the head of department at Hudson being sexually inappropriate."

Too late, Sadie realized she hadn't told Frederick about that yet.

Frederick squirmed in his seat. "I heard about that through the academic grapevine. How is she?"

Sadie read on and then out of the blue did a fist pump in the air. "They're going to have an inquiry because there have been more complaints from students and those, added to my complaint, gave Hudson no choice but to look into it."

"Wonderful," Frederick said, but he sounded unenthusiastic.

She thought about how Luc had supported her actions unequivocally, and how he would have done the same thing, as he had proven a hundred-fold at the Chateau de la Rochepot. "Can I ask you something?" Sadie said to Frederick.

He leaned forward and cleared his throat. "Certainly."

"If you had been in my position and had a choice between reporting that professor and losing your job, or staying quiet, what would you have done?"

Sadie watched Frederick's profile as he looked out the window with his chin resting on his fist as he pondered her question.

"Well?" she prompted, after a time. *It shouldn't take this long.*

"I'm not saying you did the wrong thing," he said finally. "Not at all, but I would have perhaps seen if there was some other way to go about it."

Sadie's eyebrows snapped together. "How?"

"Maybe not report it directly, but perhaps spread the word around to other professors and students, then maybe you could have created suspicion and kept your spot in the doctoral program. It's not a black and white matter. I don't think anything is when it comes right down to it."

Surely that approach to life was why Frederick hadn't done anything to rescue Guillaume at the chateau. "It's not?"

Frederick chewed on his lip again. "No. I mean, of course that professor was wrong, but to lose your job…I would have to think about that."

But Luc didn't have to think about it.

"I agree with Frederick," said Stella. "It was a bold move to take Sadie, and you lost a lot because of it. You can be a bit impulsive sometimes, like Luc was at the castle."

Sadie sucked in her breath. "Luc saved that boy's life. He didn't hesitate."

"Yes, but he could have been killed," Frederick said. "I don't think he took that into consideration."

"He was well aware of the risk!" Sadie retorted, hotly.

"Why are you defending Luc when you have Frederick?" Stella demanded, her face flushed.

"Because I love Luc," Sadie burst out. Her stomach went all light like she was falling, but oddly enough, it was the same sensation as flying.

Both Frederick and Stella's jaws dropped.

"I love him," Sadie repeated. What a relief to say those words out loud.

Frederick hunched back in his seat and covered his eyes with his hands. "Bloody hell," he groaned.

"Then what are you doing on this train with us?" Stella demanded. "Why aren't you with him?"

"Because I thought he was in love with you for most of my life."

Stella shrugged. "I don't think he was ever really in love with me, to tell you the truth. That night I went to his bedroom at Christmas, I tried to kiss him and he pushed me away. He told me that he'd been mistaken and that things between him and me could never work."

That was almost exactly what Luc had told her. "Why did you make me think he'd thrown himself at you?" Sadie demanded.

"Why do you care?" Frederick snapped, flushed now too. "I paid for our dig!"

"You never asked!" Stella cried out. "Besides, why on earth would you care if he had a schoolboy crush on me? Since when have you defined yourself by me?"

"Always!" Sadie cried.

"Well, I've always defined myself by you, too, and look where it's gotten us." Stella snorted.

Sadie sat heavily back in her seat. Stella was perfectly right. They were both miserable when they compared themselves to each other. Luc had made the same mistake, defining himself by Alphonse when in fact he'd been Jean's son all along. Surely if she could forgive herself, she should be able to forgive him too.

"We are entering the Lille train station." The tinny, disembodied voice of the train conductor came over the speaker with the familiar little dings of the SNCF.

"Let's go," Frederick said. "We need to cross the terminal to get to the Eurostar area."

Why was he pretending like nothing had happened? Sure, the British were stoic, but come on.

When they got down on the platform, Sadie turned to him. "I made a huge mistake, Frederick. I need to go back to Luc."

Frederick looked down at her, then finally sighed. "I know," he said.

"I'm so sorry about the appointment for the fellowship, but—"

He raised his hand and sighed. "I'm disappointed, but if there's one thing I understand, it's the lure of old loves. I'll present your apologies in person and we can reschedule."

"To be honest, I'm not sure Cambridge would suit me anyway."

Frederick cleared his throat. "Well, wherever you decide to go, I still think we make wonderful colleagues."

Sadie clasped his hand. Frederick wasn't for her, but he was undoubtedly a gentleman. "You're absolutely right. Thank you for that and for…well, for everything. What about Stella?"

Frederick turned to her twin. "Will you agree to accompany me Stella?"

Stella gave Sadie the widest, goofiest grin Sadie had seen since they were children. "I'd love that Frederick." She gave Sadie a massive bear hug. "Now, go get him, sister of mine."

Her cell phone had run out of battery because she'd had it in her pocket in the vineyards overnight. She was going crazy. She needed to talk to Luc right away. Would he take her back? Had he meant it when he said he wouldn't stop loving her, even after she'd left him?

On the TGV back down to Dijon, Sadie grew increasingly alarmed by the sheer amount of rain. It was becoming Biblical out there and they hadn't really protected the dig site adequately for this before leaving. It hadn't been in the weather forecast, and their departure had been too rushed and chaotic. The thing was, this much rain could effectively wash out the site and undo all the painstaking organization of their dig.

She was chewing her lip and fretting when a man in an SNCF train uniform tapped her on the shoulder. "*Escusez-moi* Mademoiselle," the man said. "But is your name Sadie Coleman?"

Sadie nodded, confused.

"Somebody is trying to reach you. They managed to get the number for the conductor's phone, which is technically impossible. It must be urgent."

He passed the phone to Sadie who accepted it, her heart beating faster. *Luc?*

"Sadie!" Jean's voice came through the line. "I found out what happened from Stella. You're on your way back to Beaune?"

"*Oui.*"

"Thank God! I need you to know something," Jean said. "Something that Luc would never tell you himself in a million years."

Sadie didn't say anything, so Jean just kept talking. "Did you ever stop to think how Luc convinced Alphonse to allow you to dig on their land?" She could just barely make out his voice over the static.

"Yes. I did wonder about it, but—"

"You didn't wonder enough. Luc didn't tell you, did he?"

"Tell me what?"

"Luc agreed to three extra years of indentured service under Alphonse and wouldn't let anyone tell you. He wanted to protect you from feeling guilty, and he was prepared to give anything so that you could do your dig."

Sadie's heart gave a startling thud. Somehow, this gesture meant light-years more than Frederick's investment. She suspected Frederick had money to spare so, while it was incredibly kind, it was not at all the same kind of sacrifice. She should have trusted Luc all along. Also, she knew if Jean hadn't broken his word, Luc would have never told her like Frederick had.

"Jean, I know— "

"Luc loves you," he cut her off again. "And if you could just forgive him for his past mistakes—which he made as a young, frightened boy whose world was spinning out of control—you will wake up and see it."

"Jean, just let me tell you—"

But the line went dead in her hand.

The train steward looked at her with an arched brow. "Did somebody die?"

"No." She shook her head.

"It can't have been that urgent then," he said, and walked off with the phone.

Sadie was worried about how she was going to get back up to Savigny from the station if there were no taxis, which there often weren't. She needn't have. Jean was waiting for her on the platform, along with Alphonse, of all combinations.

Jean pushed his Citroen to speeds that Sadie would have previously thought were unattainable. Her heart galloped. Where would Luc be at the Domaine? Please let him be there. She couldn't wait one second more.

The constant rain clattered down on the metal roof of the car.

"There's already flooding," Alphonse said to Sadie as they entered Savigny, but she could only nod with her heart in her throat like it was.

"Haven't seen rain like this in years," Jean said as he spun his Citroen into the courtyard of Domaine Ocquidant with a spray of wet gravel.

"Where is he?" Sadie demanded. The rain gushed down, and at the back of her mind, in the tiny part that wasn't focused on finding Luc, she was terrified for the dig.

"I would bet at your dig," Alphonse said. Jean nodded in agreement.

"Does he know I'm coming?"

"No. You need to go up there, Sadie," Jean said.

"Yes. Listen to Jean!" Alphonse cried. "*Allez ma fille*!"

Those two in agreement? Miracles never ceased. Sadie left her bag in the car and dashed up the hill in her best shoes, slipping and sliding in the mud. She was drenched and covered in dirt by the time she got to the dig.

As she exploded through the trees, she caught sight of Luc through the sheets of rain. He was frantically piling stones to secure tarps he must have brought up to protect her work. *He'd been protecting her dig.* What a quiet yet meaningful gesture. It was so him. He'd been telling the truth about loving her, no matter what she decided to do.

Well, she'd decided. Defining her life based on anything but her own heart was reckless. She would no longer distrust her heart, or Luc's. That honest, vulnerable, loving heart.

"Luc," she yelled, over the noise of the loud patter of rain hitting the tarp.

He spun around, and blinked, still on the ground, holding a peg in one hand and another between his teeth. His hair was plastered to his forehead and rain was dripping off his jaw.

"Sadie," he blinked. "I think the dig will be all right. I've been up here since noon; I built a barrier up above that should divert any running water and—"

She fell down on her knees in front of him and grabbed him

for a kiss. Mud squelched under them. "I'm not here for the dig," she said. "But as it is the second most important thing in my life, thank you."

"If it's not for the dig, why aren't you in England?" There was a vulnerable hope in his blue eyes that pierced unmined depths of her soul. "That fellowship. I would never stand in the way of your career. You know that don't you?"

"I do, and I also know that I would never let anyone, even you, *mon amour*, get in the way of my work. I don't want to live in England." She almost had to yell to be heard over the noise of the rain. She could feel the icy trails of water trickle down inside her clothes. "Thanks to this dig, I think I can find another school that would suit me better. I'd rather be here, on the ground, than stuck in some ivory tower."

Luc nodded. "The food in England *is* very bad."

"It has improved over the last decade."

He shook his head. "I don't buy it—mushy peas, boring cheese, and far too many pickles."

She bit back laughter. "We can discuss England's culinary scene more where it's less noisy, but first – the vineyards?"

"They're fine," he said. "We saved them, but Sadie, please will you stop torturing me? I'm dying here. Tell me why you're here."

"I'm here for you." She grinned. "I'm not fighting it anymore. I love you, and I don't think that's going to stop."

"And you're no longer scared?"

"I still am," she admitted, but the bird in her chest seemed to have found a window to escape. "But less. In the meantime, like I recommended to Guillaume, I'm doing it anyway."

"Let's be scared together, *ma Sadie, d'accord*?"

"*D'accord.*"

Luc gathered her to him and kissed her hard, a long bruising kiss, born of disbelief and joy.

"You forgive me?" Luc said.

Sadie kissed him again, the expansion of her heart filling her entire body. "Only if you forgive me. We should make each other work hard to make up for it."

"I can't wait." She felt, rather than saw, Luc smile against her lips. "Let's go somewhere warm and take off these wet clothes so we can start. *Tiens*, here's a novel idea—maybe we can even make it into a bed for the first time?"

A cold trickle of rain slid down Sadie's collar. "That'll be a nice change, given the weather." But before they could move, Luc's hand slid underneath the waistband of her jeans and cupped her bottom, bringing them tighter together.

Sadie didn't want to stop. Ever. "You're humming again." She said as she clutched his biceps under his jacket. How she loved that sound.

"Do you want me to stop?" Luc feathered soft kisses over her eyelids and the ridge of her left cheekbone and then dropped some on her chin.

"Never."

"It's not looking like we're going to make it to a bed this time either," he gasped, a few minutes later with a delicious chuckle in his voice. "You'll be the death of me, Sadie."

"We'll be the death of each other." That's what the French called it anyway—*la petit mort*. Besides, after death came new beginnings, and this one would be with a vulnerable but uncaged heart. One with Luc.

"Here's hoping." Luc's voice was rough with urgency now.

The rain spattered over them, but wasn't that, after all, a blessing of sorts? "When has a bit of dirt ever stopped us?"

"Never," he said, but it came out muffled, as Sadie couldn't wait one second longer to love Luc again.

La fin

the grapevine

Interested in receiving Laura's French recipes, sneak peeks at her new work, as well as exclusive contests and giveaways, insider news, plus countless other goodies? Sign up for Laura's Grapevine newsletter and join our fantastique community. Click here: http: bit.ly/LauraBradburyNewsletter

merci

Love in the Vineyards was written in the weird months of 2020 during the COVID lockdown. In such a time of uncertainty and unease, I needed to escape to a world I knew well—a world of friendship and love in the French vineyards.

Thank you to my wonderful readers who always keep me writing. The best thing I could think of doing for you during these bizarro times was to give you a new heart-warming book to read.

Thank you first of all to my lovely husband Franck. He continues to teach me about love and friendship on the daily and I feel so lucky we have both. I'm also grateful for our daughters Charlotte, Camille, and Clémentine for just being so completely themselves.

A huge merci to Charlotte Buffet who brings so much heart and generosity to her friendship and everything else she does. When I think of Burgundy and smile, a lot of that has to do with her.

Thank you to Nyssa for, you know, saving my life with half of your liver. Three plus years and counting! You remain the Queen of Everything.

To all my PSC family out there, no matter what stage of the journey you are at. I see you and that huge courage of yours, even on your worst days. You are carrying a burden that no one should have to, but you are not carrying it alone.

To my wonderful friend Pam for being a mama for my bigs in Montréal when I can't be there and for being an all-around amazing friend and a bright, glowing light of a person. The world is better with you in it.

To Kathy Chung and Karen Dyer for being such wonderful friends and such integral parts of my writing life. It doesn't feel lonely with you by my side. Same goes for the Surrey International Writers Conference and all the wonderful people there.

Thank you to my wonderful typo hunters Maggie Herbert, Deborah Maddox, and Maureen Gritz.

To Tricia, my assistant—I'm so glad you came into my life. Your work ethic and attention to detail, as well as our overlapping sense of humor has made working with you an absolute joy.

Lastly, thank you to my Grapeviners community (you can join at www.bit.ly/LauraBradburyNewsletter) for helping me with this book at every stage— the cover, the title, the blurb…you are so incredibly awesome and smart. I am honored to do this writing thing with you.

author's note

Just a few notes from *moi* about *Love in the Vineyards.*

First of all, what exactly is a a *cabotte* you ask? Well, I'm just a wee bit obsessed with these small stone huts that dot the Burgundy vineyards. See the stone hut on the cover of Love in the vineyards? Yup. That's a *cabotte.*

I got the idea for *Love in the Vineyards* this October when I was in France for my cookbook *Bisous & Brioche.* As Rebecca, Daisy, Renate and I drove up from Beaune to Villers-la-Faye through the vineyards of Savigny-les-Beaune I pointed out the *cabottes* to them en route.

The vineyards around Savigny-lès-Beaune are particularly blessed with these little gems. Usually they're round, but sometimes they're square or rectangular. Some are well-maintained and some are crumbling down, but they are all fascinating.

When we lived in Burgundy Charlotte and Camille called them "fairy huts" and made up large, elaborate stories in the backseat of our car on the way to and from school in Beaune about the fairies that lived in the *cabottes* and helped the winemakers.

They're still used for the winemakers to store tools or their lunch when tending the vineyards, and they're also extremely handy for protection from Burgundy's sudden hail or fork lightening. Fairies might be a possibility (who knows, really?) and they can also be used for covert trysts like *Love in the Vineyards* because…well…France.

As you've seen, the *cabotte* in *Love in the Vineyards* is a major symbol in the story, and a touchstone for the timelessness of Luc and Sadie's relationship.

About the timing of Luc's pruning in Love in the Vineyards—some may say it's early to prune in December, but climate change is effecting the winemaking cycle in Burgundy just like all over the world. I'm finishing up *Love in the Vineyards* at the end of August, just as the harvest in Burgundy draws to a close. 2020 was the earliest harvest since the mid-1500s. Can you believe that? This unprecedented warmth is pushing everything earlier and the younger winemakers like Luc who are not so caught up by old ways are adapting to this new reality.

The French I use in both *A Vineyard for Two* and *Love in the Vineyards*, as well as my Grape Series of memoirs, is colloquial. While it may not be grammatically correct it's a reflection of how we truly speak in Burgundy, including words of local *patois* such as "*bétion*" (really draw out the 'e' if you want to pronounce this with a true Burgundian accent!).

The Gallo-Roman walls in the forests of Burgundy are real. As a matter of fact, Franck took me to the Gallo-Roman site in the woods outside the village of Arcenant on our third date. A man who enjoyed archeology? I was sold. My sister-in-law Stéphanie did a yoga class for me and three other friends in the middle of the same Gallo-Roman site a few years ago. It was one of the most memorable experiences of my life. We were all alone amongst the rustling trees and ancient stones doing our downward dogs.

If you enjoyed *Love in the Vineyards,* then you will love my bestselling, romantic, and escapist memoirs, the Grape Series.

Turn the page for an excerpt of *My Grape Year*, voted number one in Buzzfeed's "18 Feel-Good Books That Will Make You Believe in Love."

Sneak peek of Chapter One

My Grape Year

AT THE AGE of seventeen in a last-minute twist of fate, Laura Bradbury is sent to Burgundy, France, for a year's exchange. She arrives knowing only a smattering of French and with no idea what to expect in her first foray out of North America. With a head full of dreams and a powerful desire to please, Laura quickly adapts to Burgundian life, learning crucial skills such as the fine art of winetasting and how to savor snails.

However, the charming young men of the region mean Laura soon runs afoul of the rules, particularly the no-dating edict. Romantic afternoons in Dijon, early morning *pain au chocolat* runs, and long walks in the vineyards are wondrous but also present Laura with a conundrum: How can she keep her hosts happy while still managing to follow her heart? Follow along on Laura's journey to *l'amour* in *My Grape Year*.

chapter one

RULES FOR 1990–91 OUTBOUND EXCHANGE STUDENTS— THE FOUR "D"s

1. No Drinking
2. No Drugs
3. No Driving
4. No Dating

By signing this contract, I hereby accept my role as Ursus Youth Ambassador for the 1990–91 exchange year abroad and agree to abide by all four of the "Rules for Exchange Students."

The other outbound exchange students around me were scribbling their signatures on the forms.

No Drinking. I knew I was heading to Europe, Switzerland, if everything went according to plan, and even though I was drawn by the history and beauty and exoticism, I was also hoping to be able to enjoy a nice glass of beer or wine from time to time. I was seventeen and would be graduating from high school in three short months, so I hoped they wouldn't take this rule too seriously in what my grandmother always referred to as "the old country."

No Drugs. I seriously doubted that marijuana was as ubiquitous in Europe as it was on Vancouver Island, Canada, where it self-seeded in many people's back gardens. And since I had no intention of ever trying any other type of drug, this rule wasn't an issue.

No Driving. It would be weird to no longer be able to drive nor enjoy the independence that came with that. Still, like many Canadians, I knew how to drive only an automatic and didn't like traffic very much, so I could live with this rule.

No Dating. This rule bothered me the most. It had just been explained to us that as Ursus Youth Ambassadors we would have to be available and open to all people we encountered during our year abroad. Having an exclusive romantic relationship would interfere with that goal. Also, the Ursus Club hosting us would be responsible for our welfare during our year in its country, and that would be far simpler to ensure when we students remained single. I could see the logic of it all, but my romantic life during my high school years had been seriously disappointing, if not to say practically nonexistent. My heart longed for romance and love.

Still, I felt as if the whole world was out there waiting for me, and I needed to take the step to meet it. If that meant signing this contract, then I would do whatever it took.

I picked up my pen and signed my name.

The men's polyester pants were off-gassing in the stuffy hotel room. The scorched smell of synthetic fabric tickled my nostrils. March was generally a cool month in Victoria, so the hotel staff hosting the annual Ursus District Convention hadn't anticipated the heat wave. The Rotary and Lions clubs, similar community service organizations, had recently begun to welcome female members, which I was sure had lessened the polyester quotient. Ursus, though, stubbornly remained a men-only group, aside from their female International Youth Exchange Ambassadors like me.

A makeshift fan had been unearthed and stuck in the corner of the room, but sweat trickled inside my navy wool blazer, which had already been festooned with at least forty pins. Pins were the currency of the incoming and outgoing exchange students and were traded with the fervor of stocks on Wall Street.

The interview was almost over, thank God. If they liked me, I would get the final confirmation that I would be spending the 1990–1991 academic year as an exchange student in what I hoped would be my first choice of host country, Switzerland. There was only one available spot in Switzerland, and it was contested hotly every year. Belgium, my second choice, was better than nothing. Germany was my third choice, but I knew I definitely didn't want to end up in Germany. I'd never found blond men attractive, and I vastly preferred wine to beer. It was a crime that Italy, France, and Spain weren't options. I could completely envision myself at some Spanish or Italian bar, dancing on the tables after a night fueled by sangria or Prosecco—though I'd apparently signed away my rights to drink either of these.

"I see Switzerland was your first choice, Laura," the head of the committee observed.

Was? Not is?

Every one of the ten or so men around the table had a copy of my application in front of him. "Can you explain your reasons for that?"

I had answered this question so many times in previous interviews that I could do it in my sleep. "One of my main motivations for going on a year abroad is to learn a foreign language," I said. "Switzerland has not one but *three* official languages—French, German, and Italian. I would love to be exposed to more than one language during my year as an Ursus Youth Ambassador." Actually,

I was hell-bent on a year abroad because I sensed this huge, marvelous world waiting for me beyond the mossy shores of my island home, and I vibrated with the need to meet it.

The Ursunian who was chairing the interview cleared his throat. "That is an excellent answer, Miss Bradbury. However, we just received the news that the Switzerland spot was nabbed by another district." The men exchanged shocked looks at this breach of fair play.

What? What about my fantasies of racing up and down the Swiss hills like Maria from *The Sound of Music* and warming myself up with some lovely cheese fondue and wine in a wooden chalet afterward, preferably with an entourage of handsome Swiss men? I knew I would have to deal with my disappointment later; right then wasn't the time. I dug my nails into my palms and smiled brightly. "I'll go to Belgium, then."

"We do have several spots there. I just feel we should let you know, though, that more than half of them are in the Flemish-speaking part of Belgium."

Flemish? I had been so sure I was going to Switzerland that I hadn't even considered the possibility of being sent to Flemish-speaking purgatory.

I flashed another smile. "Of course, I would make the most out of any placement," I said. "However, French is Canada's second official language, and growing up here on the West Coast, I have always regretted the fact that I have never learned to speak it fluently. I hope to go to McGill University in Montreal, so obviously French would be a huge advantage for me."

There was no need to mention that French had actually been my worst subject all through high school, and that I'd had to drop it after Grade 11 because it was torpedoing my GPA. Or that I ran out to the quad after my Grade 11 provincial exam for French and yelled, "Thank God! I will *never* have to speak French again in my life!"

A slighter, bald man piped up. "You may not be aware of this, Miss Bradbury, but there is no way for us to guarantee where you will be placed. We send over the files for the incoming students, and it's up to our Belgian brothers to allocate them as they see fit."

I struggled to maintain my bright-eyed demeanor.

"There's always France, I suppose," mused the head man, as though thinking aloud.

My head snapped in his direction. "I understood there were no exchange spots available in France."

He cleared his throat. "That *was* the case, but there has been a…ah…development."

My heart began to somersault. *France?*

A tall man at the opposite end of the table, who had been picking something fascinating out from under his thumbnail, jerked his head up. "With good reason!" he said, paying attention now. "Every exchange we arranged in France has ended in disaster. The families didn't even bother to come and pick up our students from the airport, or they suddenly decided that they were sick of hosting and locked the child out of the house or left on vacation without them. We couldn't possibly jettison another student into—"

The chair cleared his throat meaningfully. "I have a letter here from the Ursus Club in Beaune, France." He waved the letter, which from what I could see was written in elaborate cursive with a fountain pen. I longed to get a closer look—it possessed a tantalizing whiff of the exotic. "They say that one of their students is being hosted this year by our district, so they would welcome one of our students. Just one student, you see. It would be on a trial basis. They sound sincere."

"Don't believe them," snarled the tall man. "I was president of our club the year our poor student was abandoned at the airport in Paris. He had to take a plane back to Seattle the next day. Try explaining *that* to his parents!"

"We must believe them," the chair insisted. "Ursus spirit

demands we have good faith in our French brothers. Besides, Miss Bradbury here strikes me as a competent sort of person who can deal with extreme situations. I wouldn't even mention the possibility of France to most of our outgoing students."

"I—I..." I stuttered, wondering how I was going to disabuse him of this notion. I couldn't imagine any horror worse than leaving for a year abroad only to have to return to Canada the next day with my tail between my legs. Yet...France! I had always wanted to see Paris and the Eiffel Tower and learn how to drape scarves properly.

"George"—the tall man's voice was stiff with displeasure—"throwing this nice young lady here to the French would be like throwing a lamb to the wolves, and I for one—"

"Neil," the head man said in a quelling tone, "there is an open space for France, and it needs to be filled. Miss Bradbury has explained how urgently she wants to learn French. She is mature and full of positive energy. I have complete confidence in her."

What is the word for "shit" in French? Merde? My mind whirred as I tried to find a way to extract myself from this fix.

But then I thought about red wine. Little cafés. Baguettes. French men were supposed to be very charming, weren't they? In any case, they had to be an improvement on Canadian boys. It could be a disaster, or it could be even better than Switzerland. In any case, I decided, it was definitely better than spending a year learning Flemish.

"I'd be delighted to take that spot in France." I straightened my shoulders.

All the men except Neil nodded approvingly at me as though I had just performed a selfless and heroic act. Darn. Had I?

The chair erased Switzerland and Belgium from my application and wrote "FRANCE" on it in large capital letters. He scrawled something in his notes.

"That settles it, then! You'll be heading to France in August,

Miss Bradbury. I hope you have an excellent year, or shall I say a *bon voyage*?" He chuckled at his own joke.

"Thank you," I said, "or shall I say *merci*?" This got a laugh out of all the men, and they stood up and stretched their polyester-clad legs to indicate that I was dismissed.

I must have missed the sound over the whir of the fan and the muffled scrape of chairs against the carpet, but when I think back to it now, I am convinced there must have been a mighty creak. There had to have been, because at that precise moment my entire life shifted on its axis.

To purchase
My Grape Year
http://bit.ly/2IxCJ7i

about laura

Bestselling author Laura Bradbury published her first book—a heartfelt memoir about her leap away from a prestigious legal career in London to live in a tiny French village with her Burgundian husband in *My Grape Escape*—after being diagnosed with PSC, a rare autoimmune bile duct/liver disease. Since then, Laura has received a lifesaving living donor liver transplant from her friend Nyssa, published many more Grape Series books and the long-anticipated cookbook to accompany her memoirs, entitled *Bisous & Brioche*. She has also written *The Winemakers Trilogy,* romantic novels set in the Burgundy vineyards, and with renewed health, writes with even more passion than ever.

Now living and writing on the West Coast of Canada with a new liver and three Franco-Canuck daughters (collectively known as "the Bevy"), Laura runs three charming vacation rentals in Burgundy with her husband, has an enviable collection of beach glass, and does all she can to support PSC and organ donation awareness and research.

find laura online

The Grapevine Newsletter
http://bit.ly/LauraBradburyNewsletter

Facebook
https://www.facebook.com/AuthorLauraBradbury

Twitter
https://twitter.com/Author_LB

Instagram
https://www.instagram.com/laurabradburywriter/

Pinterest
https://www.pinterest.ca/bradburywriter/

BookBub
https://www.bookbub.com/authors/laura-bradbury

Books by
Laura Bradbury

The Grape Series

My Grape Year: http://mybook.to/MyGrapeYear
My Grape Québec: http://mybook.to/MyGrapeQuebec
My Grape Paris: http://mybook.to/MyGrapeParis
My Grape Wedding: http://mybook.to/MyGrapeWedding
My Grape Escape: http://mybook.to/MyGrapeEscape
My Grape Village: http://mybook.to/MyGrapeVillage
My Grape Cellar: http://mybook.to/MyGrapeCellar

The cookbook based on my Grape Series memoirs that readers have been asking for!

Bisous & Brioche: Classic French Recipes and Family Favorites from a Life in France
by Laura Bradbury and Rebecca Wellman
Bisous & Brioche: mybook.to/bisousandbrioche

The Winemakers Trilogy

A Vineyard for Two: mybook.to/AVineyardforTwo
Love in the Vineyards: mybook.to/loveinthevineyards

Manufactured by Amazon.ca
Bolton, ON

14890104R00203